I0602411

THE TWILIGHT TOWN

THE TWILIGHT TOWN

A DALLAS '63 NOVEL

TERRENCE MCCAULEY

LEVEL
BEST BOOKS

First published by Level Best Books/Historia 2025

Copyright © 2025 by Terrence McCauley

All rights reserved. No part of this publication may be reproduced, stored or transmitted in any form or by any means, electronic, mechanical, photocopying, recording, scanning, or otherwise without written permission from the publisher. It is illegal to copy this book, post it to a website, or distribute it by any other means without permission.

This novel is entirely a work of fiction. The names, characters and incidents portrayed in it are the work of the author's imagination. Any resemblance to actual persons, living or dead, events or localities is entirely coincidental.

Terrence McCauley asserts the moral right to be identified as the author of this work.

Author Photo Credit: Rita McCauley

First edition

ISBN: 978-1-68512-920-0

Cover art by Momir Borocki

This book was professionally typeset on Reedsy.
Find out more at reedsy.com

For Arcenia Ramirez: For all you do

Praise for The Twilight Town

"A hard-boiled what-if that convincingly imagines the dark side of Dallas leading up to the Kennedy assassination—gritty and suspenseful."—Meg Gardiner, author of *Shadowheart*

"Terrence McCauley rocks readers with *The Twilight Town*, a new imagining of a crucial period in American history: the daze before and through the assassination of President JFK in Dallas in '63. McCauley takes a new and crucial approach to fictionalizing history by focusing on the lives of those who worked the streets of Texas and beyond. This novel will blow your mind—and the good news is, it's #1 of a trilogy."—James Grady, creator of *Condor* and 2024 Larry McMurtry-compared author of 2025's coming novel *American Sky*

"Terrence McCauley takes us back to a time and a catastrophic series of events most of us have only viewed through grainy television footage. The Twilight Town puts you on the ground, with descriptions of 1960s Dallas and the players involved in the JFK assassination plot so vivid you can feel the sticky, humid air of conspiracy and the racing heartbeats of the men trying to prevent a disaster from unfolding. McCauley's prose is so eloquent in its economy, each line of punchy dialogue landing with weight, crackling with energy and urgency. The story pulses with the rapid, pounding drumbeats of the best Cold War thrillers. The only time I put this book down was to catch my breath!"—Bruce Borgos, author of *The Bitter Past*

"They tell me this is a novel, but this rocket ride reads like McCauley was an eyewitness to history."—Matthew V. Clemens, co-author of the John Sands series with Max Allan Collins

Chapter One

Dallas, Texas

Friday, February 1, 1963

Detective Dan Wilson cruised into Oak Cliff.

The morning sun blinded him. He flicked down the visor. The sunlight warmed him. So did his prospects for the future.

Bye-bye, Dallas PD. Hello, FBI. I'm about to save your blessed Pipeline.

It was moving day for Hal Farley, but Farley didn't know it yet. He didn't know Wilson. Or that Wilson was about to give him a rare gift. The chance for a new life, whether he liked it or not. Said gift was courtesy of Dallas PD and the FBI. And it would be hand-delivered by Dan Wilson, Criminal Investigations Division (CID), Dallas PD.

Wilson tamped down the anticipation in his gut. He couldn't afford mistakes. Not today.

He checked his watch. Twenty minutes to nine. Hal's place was only five minutes away. He had time to kill. To make sure Hal was alone. Getting there too early would spoil the surprise.

Wilson parked his unmarked Ford Galaxie at the curb. He watched Oak Cliff wake up to begin a new day. There wasn't much to see.

Wilson had patrolled Oak Cliff back when he was in uniform. Nothing had changed in the years since. It had decent blocks and bad blocks, but no good blocks. Third-hand cars parked in front of ugly buildings on ugly streets. Used car lots, second-hand stores, small markets, and dive bars littered the neighborhood.

He watched black nurses—fresh from overnight shifts caring for elderly clients—cluster at bus stops. They waited for rides home to even worse parts of Dallas.

All the large houses in Oak Cliff had been divided into apartments years before. Most tenants were no longer young, but looked older than they were. They were cab drivers and waitresses and bartenders. They worked registers at liquor stores. They pushed brooms on the graveyard shift. They collected betting slips for local bookies on the side.

Smut peddlers like Jack Ruby housed their hustlers there. Their whores and strippers and friends on the lam. They came home around sunrise and never caused trouble. Their land ladies didn't ask questions as long as the rent was on time. Oak Cliff didn't reward curiosity.

No one ever planned on staying in Oak Cliff for long, but few ever got around to leaving. The neighborhood was built atop the ruins of dashed hopes and forgotten dreams.

Wilson's mind drifted as he waited. He got *déjà vu*. He thought of the winding road that had brought him back to this sad place. His ex-partner, JD Tippit.

Wilson and Tippit had patrolled the Oak Cliff sector together. They'd been a good team. They were native Texans. They'd been paratroopers in their respective wars. Tippit was at the Battle of the Bulge. He'd earned a Bronze Star.

Wilson had fought at Munsan-ni in Korea. He'd earned a Bronze Star and Purple Heart.

Tippit was tall and quiet. Wilson resembled the actor Clint Walker and had personality to spare. Tippit's people were farmers. Wilson's daddy was a famous Texas Ranger.

Together, Wilson and Tippit hit Oak Cliff hard. They'd busted heads. They'd made the bad guys bleed. They'd made each other better cops. They'd earned medals. They'd made the department proud.

But Wilson had ambition. He had a college degree. He passed the detective's exam and joined CID. His friendship with Tippit endured years after.

So when Tippit asked for Wilson's help with a delicate problem, Wilson readily agreed. Not out of friendship. Out of self-interest.

Tippit's delicate problem was named Hal Farley. Farley was a rare Oak Cliff resident. He earned good money as a roughneck on the oilfield circuit throughout Texas and the Gulf. He had a young, pretty wife named Molly and two little boys.

Hal had played by the rules. He'd always paid his taxes. He'd never been arrested. Never got a parking ticket. His only offense? He was in somebody's way.

Hal had met Molly as 'Amber Fire' at Ruby's Carousel Club. He'd fallen under her spell. He'd pledged undying love and devotion. He'd promised her a better life. He'd vowed to build that life for her.

Molly had been around. Thirty was right around the corner. She grabbed Hal's glass ring and never looked back.

Jack Ruby gave her a wedding present. The deed to his best stash house in Oak Cliff. *No hard feelings, doll.*

The stripper and the roughneck set up house. They had two sons. It was middle-class bliss until it wasn't.

Middle-class bliss faltered. Hal was away at work for weeks at a time. He was distant at home. He drank beer with his buddies. He came home drunk. He slept late and watched television. He ignored Molly and their boys.

Molly grew tired of Hal's long absences. Of competing with *The Beverly Hillbillies* and *Bonanza* and his bar friends. Molly got bored.

She took a job as a waitress at the Eat Well Diner. To fill the long hours when the boys were in school. It soon became more than that. She got popular fast. New customers flocked to see the friendly raven-haired beauty. She was an attraction again. She'd rediscovered fulfillment.

She'd found something else. JD was one of Molly's old flames from her dancing days. He was the strong, silent type who resembled President Kennedy. She was the neglected, dark-haired beauty with a wholesome vulnerability men liked.

Tippit got careless on duty. He blew off calls. He stretched meal breaks at the diner. He listened to Molly's troubles. He paid attention. He cared.

Their old flame rekindled fast. Proximity and opportunity begat lust. Lust soon begat romance.

Tippit got greedy. He began ignoring his own family. He spent nights and weekends with Molly and her boys.

Their romance begat love or something like it. Their love forced a tough decision: Hal was in the way. Hal had to go.

Wilson had watched their blossoming romance from afar. Not as a friend. As a traitor. As a worker on The Pipeline.

Wilson had called Tippit seemingly out of the blue. He'd invited Tippit for a beer at Austin's. Patsy Cline's 'Faded Love' played on the jukebox. Tippit got drunk. He always ran his mouth when he was loaded. Tippit told his tale of woe. About him and Molly. About sending Hal packing. About Molly begging him not to. Hal was still the father of her boys. She didn't want him hurt. Injured men couldn't work. She had bills to pay.

Wilson had listened. He'd empathized. And just before last call, he offered a simple solution. 'I'll make Hal leave.'

Tippit cried. He couldn't believe his dumb luck.

But there was nothing dumb or lucky about it. Because Wilson was protecting The Pipeline.

The Eat Well Diner, where Molly worked, *was* The Pipeline. The pet project of Bobby Kennedy, the Attorney General of the United States. He'd vowed to wipe out the Mafia. He'd ordered an FBI investigation of mob corruption of America's cities. The conservative democrats of Dallas were a thorn in the Kennedys' side.

The Eat Well Diner was where illegal activity abounded. It was far from the prying eyes of downtown. It was an oilfield of illicit information where crooked cops and criminals colluded. Where deals were struck and promises were made in blood. Where envelopes were left behind in folded newspapers or passed under tables.

The FBI had rented an apartment across from the diner. They'd concealed listening devices among the booths and counters. They took pictures of every customer entering and leaving the place. Their case grew stronger with every cup of coffee poured or slice of pie served.

Captain Will Fritz had caught wind of the investigation early. He'd pulled strings. He'd forced his way in. He pledged loyalty and secrecy to the FBI's mission. He privately sought to limit damage to Dallas PD. He'd needed someone for the grunt work. A man he could trust.

Dan Wilson was perfect. Fritz and Wilson's father were old friends. Wilson was Fritz's godson. Wilson knew Dallas. He knew the department. Police work was in his blood. He'd worked intelligence during the war. He worked CID now. CID was Dallas PD's FBI. CID gave him range of movement. To ask questions without drawing attention. *Them boys are always digging into something.*

Wilson saw the upside. The potential for career growth. His father had been a Texas Ranger. Wilson wanted to surpass him. To be a fed.

Betraying his department should've been a hard decision. It wasn't. They thought he'd coasted on his daddy's name.

Wilson had expected to do spy stuff. The feds stuck him transcribing tapes and analyzing photographs instead. He was a secretary with a badge. A joke.

Molly didn't know she was vital to The Pipeline. She drew bugs to the fed web. She kept crooked customers coming back. The tawdry Tippit-Molly-Hal triangle had threatened the steady flow of information. The feds saw complications ahead.

Again, Wilson saw the upside. He would show the feds his worth. He'd bounce Hal and protect The Pipeline.

Wilson's agreement to bounce Hal for Tippit had one condition. JD had to stay away until Hal to leave. Tippit had agreed. No questions asked.

Wilson checked his watch again. Fifteen minutes to nine. He'd covered a lot of mental ground in five minutes. He smiled. *Fifteen minutes to a new life for Hal. For me. Next stop, Washington.*

His police radio crackled. A dispatcher said, "*All units, all units. Ten-Fifty-Seven in progress at East Ninth and Patton in Oak Cliff. Officer needs assistance. All units respond and proceed with caution.*"

Wilson punched the steering wheel. All hopes of impending glory evaporated.

A 'ten-fifty-seven' was Dallas PD radio code for 'shots fired.' The Farley home was on Ninth and Patton. The officer in distress had to be Tippit.

Every available cop in Dallas would descend on the area in minutes. Wilson had to get there first. To salvage his opportunity. To save his own ass.

Wilson threw the Galaxies in gear and floored it. The V-8 engine roared. The prowler flew along Ninth.

He gripped the wheel with his left. He snatched the mic off the cradle with his right. "Victor-David-Seven in route to Ninth Street."

He tossed the mic aside. *Goddamn Tippit.*

* * *

Wilson skidded to a halt in front of the Farley place. Tippit was crouched behind his cruiser at the curb, his service pistol drawn.

Wilson stopped crooked. He blocked traffic in both directions.

Combat training kicked in. He pulled his Magnum from his shoulder rig. He stayed low as he ran to Tippit at a crouch.

He checked the street as he moved. Old women and welfare cases peered out from behind faded curtains and half-open doors.

The Farley home was a rundown one-story bungalow. Peeling paint. Buckling slats. Crooked shutters. Sun scorched lawn. Hal had let more than his marriage go to seed.

Wilson stopped next to Tippit. "You're not supposed to be here."

Tippit chanced a quick look over the hood. "I came by to make sure Molly and the boys weren't around. Next thing I know, Hal started shooting at me. It's like he knew I was coming."

Shit. Farley wasn't supposed to know about moving day. Wilson and Tippit had picked their time carefully. When Molly was at the diner and the kids were in school. Something had gone wrong. "Is he alone?"

"I don't know." Tippit looked around the front of his unit. "Garage door's closed. But if he's hurt Molly or the boys, I'll—."

They heard approaching sirens in the distance. Help was only a few minutes out. An eternity for Molly and her boys if they were inside. A sad end to his FBI dreams, too.

Wilson told Tippit, "Get on the radio. Have dispatch call the diner. See if Molly showed up this morning."

A shriek rose from inside the house. A woman's shriek. Molly's shriek. *Shit.*

Wilson broke cover first. He bolted up the cracked concrete path to the front door. Tippit followed despite a bum knee.

Academy training kicked in. Tippit took the left side of the door. Wilson took the right.

Wilson tried the doorknob. *Locked.* He was about to kick it in.

Tippit produced a key. He wasn't just sleeping with Hal's wife and stealing his family. He had a key to the poor bastard's house.

Tippit unlocked the door. Wilson pushed it open. His .357 led the way. Tippit moved in close.

Wilson's eyes watered. His throat burned. He gagged into his sleeve.

The stench was undeniable. *Gasoline.*

Wilson blinked his eyes clear. He squinted through the vapors. The house resembled rage itself. Stuffing from slashed cushions covered everything like dirty snow. Cigarette butts overflowed from ashtrays. Dents in the plaster walls from Hal's fists. Bowling trophies knocked from the fireplace mantle, one jutting out of the busted screen of the television tube. Broken table lamps and stomped toys everywhere. Crushed cans of Lone Star, too.

A patrol car screeched out front and killed its siren.

Farley shouted from somewhere deep in the house. Wilson couldn't make out the words. He heard Molly scream.

Tippit moved past him.

Wilson grabbed him. "He tried killing you once. Get out front and make the others stay back."

Tippit shook loose. "This is my fight, not yours."

Wilson grabbed him again. "It's your fight, but my mess." He shoved

Tippit toward the door. "Get the fire department over here. This place could go up any second. And leave the door open. Air this place out."

Tippit cursed, then went outside.

Wilson wiped his eyes on his sleeve. He stifled another cough and moved into the kitchen. Roaches scuttled over unwashed dishes piled in the sink. Shards of broken plates littered the yellowed linoleum floor. Cabinet doors were kicked in.

Smears of blood on the countertops turned Wilson's blood cold.

The shard of a broken plate cracked beneath his boot heel.

Hal Farley yelled, "Somebody out there?"

Wilson rasped from the fumes. "Dan Wilson, Dallas PD. We got a report of shots fired in the area. Everyone okay in there?"

"Never been better. We're all one big happy family in here, ain't we, honey?"

Molly sobbed.

Wilson moved into the hall. Hostage training kicked in. He kept Hal talking. "That you doing all that shooting just now?"

"Sure was." There was pride in his voice. "Found a rat sneaking around. Happened to have a badge pinned on him, but it was still a rat. Did I get him?"

Two bedrooms on the left. Bloody handprints streaked the wall. Another bloody handprint on a sliding glass door to a side yard. A low picket fence just beyond.

"No, but you came mighty close." The carpet was spongy under his boots. Gasoline had soaked through to the padding. "Guess you must've taken him for a prowler."

Farley said, "I knew who I was aiming at."

"Cop or no cop, I ain't letting that bastard steal what's mine."

Gas cans on the carpet outside the second bedroom. *The crazy bastard doused the whole house.*

"No one's looking to steal anything from you, Hal. I'm just here to talk." Wilson checked the first bedroom. A pair of bunk beds. Pennants tacked on the walls. A closet door open. Empty. He dropped to a knee. He looked under the bed. Just toy cars and dirty clothes. *Damn.*

Wilson stood. He moved toward the second bedroom. Gasoline had soaked through the knee of his pants, burning his skin.

Farley said, "How'd you know my name?"

Wilson winced. *Me and my big mouth.* "Guess the officer outside told me."

"Tippit." Farley said it like a curse. "That bastard's got no right to take my family from me. And not you or every damned cop in this city can make me give them up, either. I'd sooner see them dead than end up with the likes of him."

"No one wants that, Hal." Wilson moved to the second bedroom. More gouges in the wall. Family pictures ripped down. Glass from shattered frames sank beneath his boots into the sodden carpet. Pictures of picnics and ballgames and swimming in a lake. Memories now soaked in gasoline and stained with blood. "I promise no one else will step one foot in this house without your say-so. This is still your home. A man's home's his castle, ain't it?"

"You're damned right it is. And before you ask, I ain't coming out until you send Tippit in here."

Wilson got closer. The gasoline almost overwhelmed him. "Let's you and me talk about that."

"Talk?" Farley's laugh was jagged. "You don't want me talking, hoss. You wouldn't like what I have to say."

More units pulled up outside. Car doors slammed. A command officer had to be on the scene by now. Wilson had to move fast. Someone might order something stupid for the right reasons.

Wilson stopped outside the main bedroom. "You can say whatever you want, Hal." *Let him think he's still in control.* "This is your house, remember?"

Farley giggled. "Ya'll don't think I know what really goes on down at that diner? My wife hears all sorts of things while she's serving you bastards. She told me everything last night when I finally got it out of her. Hell, I've got half a mind to pick up the phone and call one of them reporters down at the paper. They'd be mighty interested in what I have to say."

Wilson heard the boys whimpering. They were a little older than his own kids. "Go ahead and call them. I won't stop you."

Farley got quiet. "I ripped the phone out of the wall last night when I caught her calling her boyfriend. And don't offer to bring me another. You just want to worm your way in here to get my gun off me, so I'll save you the trouble."

A .38 pistol sailed out of the bedroom. It crashed through the sliding glass door.

Wilson saw Patrolman Harry Denton duck. He was kneeling beside an overgrown box tree in the yard. He was loading an Enfield rifle with a scope on it.

He wasn't there to save Molly and her boys. He'd been sent to keep things under control.

Hal yelled, "That gun's empty, but my lighter's full. One spark and we all go up." Another giggle. "Almost fitting, ain't it? Since oil keeps a roof over our heads, I figured I ought to use it to bring it down."

Wilson tried waving Denton off.

Denton raised the Enfield to his shoulder. He sighted his scope. He'd seen Farley toss his pistol. He didn't know about the gasoline. Or didn't care.

Wilson had to block Denton's shot. He could still bring everyone out alive. "I'm right outside your bedroom, Hal. I'm gonna keep my pistol at my side while I lean against the doorframe. I'm gonna do it nice and slow. You and me can quit shouting and talk face-to-face."

"Stay the hell out of here, you bastard!"

Wilson started praying. Praying Hal didn't burn him alive. Praying that Denton didn't shoot.

He slowly came around and leaned against the doorframe.

The bedroom reeked of gasoline and fear. Thin blue curtains cast everything in a pale light. A shattered mirror on the dresser. Broken reflections of the Farley family on the floor between the bed and the wall.

Hal's thick forearm around Molly's slender neck. Two frightened boys against her breast.

Farley's Zippo lighter opened, his thumb on the flint wheel, his hair matted with sweat.

He smiled as he squinted up at Wilson, his eyes red from tears and rage. "Pleased to meet you."

Wilson gripped the Magnum at his side. Molly's ruined mascara. Bruises around her eyes. Red lipstick smeared across her swollen mouth. Dried blood from her broken nose stained her face. It stained the top of the brown waitress uniform. She hadn't changed since yesterday's shift.

Wilson would've shot the son of a bitch. But Molly was in the way.

Farley pulled her closer. She pulled her sons with her. "Ain't she just the prettiest little thing you ever saw? She's got a drop of Mexican blood in her. Gives her that exotic look I fell in love with."

Wilson said, "Take it easy, Hal."

But Farley didn't hear him. "I helped her with her makeup this morning. Figured if she wanted to act like a whore, the least she could do is look like one."

Wilson said, "This is between you and Molly and me. Let the boys go, and I'll get you that phone you wanted. You can call any newspaper you like. Anyone you want. You've got my word on that."

Farley's red eyes flared. "Why? So everyone can laugh at me? Like my neighbors laughed at me when Tippit was playing catch with my boys in my yard? When his car was parked in my driveway? When they knew what they were doing on this very bed!"

The boys whimpered. Their mother still too close for a headshot.

Hal's thumb came off the flint wheel. *He's going to light it.*

"Don't!" Wilson moved into the room. "You said you know about what goes on in that diner. I know it, too. I'll get you that phone so you can tell the world everything. The payoffs, the crooked cops, all of it. You can pull down the whole department if you want. Let the boys go and take me instead."

Farley's lower lip trembled. His rage faltered. His voice cracked. Streaks of sweat ran down his face like dirty tears. "You know?" His expression softened. "How the hell could you know all that?"

"I do." Wilson felt him weaken. Someone had finally heard him. "Let the boys go and we'll show everyone just how right you are. Just you and me. I give you my word."

Farley lowered the lighter. "You believe me, don't -"

A rifle shot. Breaking glass.

Farley's head snapped back.

Molly screamed. She fell on top of her boys.

Wilson watched Farley sag to his right. The top of his head a pulpy mess. The wall behind him covered in gore.

His eyes locked with Wilson's. *You gave me your word.*

Wilson came around the bed. He kicked the Zippo clear. He pulled Molly to her feet. Her boys moved with her. He brought them out as Denton knocked the remaining glass from the sliding door.

Wilson bundled them into the yard. A wall of patrolmen enveloped them. Tippit wrapped an arm around Molly's shoulders. She collapsed against him. The boys clung to Tippit's legs as he took them to the street.

Wilson watched them leave. Cops rushed past him. Tippit led Molly and her children to a patrol car. She got inside. She pulled the door shut in his face.

Wilson hung his head. *I had him. He was giving up. Wasn't he?*

Chapter Two

Harry Denton hadn't killed a man in years. Not in the line of duty, anyway.

Shooting a loudmouthed bastard like Farley felt good. It felt right. It protected the diner. It protected what happened there. Captain Eastbrook would be pleased. Denton had just saved him the trouble of finding a new place to do business.

Patrolmen gathered around Denton. They patted his back. They shook his shoulders. They messed up his hair. He felt like he'd scored a winning touchdown.

They marveled at his marksmanship. They praised him. Razzed him. They spoke all at once. Some phrases stuck out.

"Damn, fellas. Look at all that blood."

"You scalped that fella good, Harry. If I didn't know better, I'd think you was some kind of Injun instead of an honest to God white man."

"And here I was, thinking Hal's head was empty this whole time."

"It sure is empty now."

Denton loved the attention. The admiration and adulation from his comrades in arms. Good and loyal white men, every last one of them. Men who knew policing was about more than the written law. That certain people had to be kept in their place. Woman beaters and gossipers and race traitors didn't deserve to live.

These men were all customers at the Eat Well Diner. They were Eastbrook men. They were 'Eastbrook's Posse'. They profited from the business the captain conducted there. The captain always took care of his boys. He rewarded loyalty.

Another patrolman joined in. "Served that son of a bitch right if you ask me. Had it coming for what he done to poor Molly."

Denton figured a dash of humility couldn't hurt. "Hope you boys'll remember that when Homicide asks for your statements."

He knew he could count on them. They'd swear the shooting was justified even if they hadn't seen it. Perjury was a lawyer's word. Blue stuck with blue. Right was right.

They wanted to stay on Eastbrook's good side. Denton was an Eastbrook man to his core. Always had been. Always would be.

Denton turned away from the gore of the bedroom. He rested the butt of his Enfield on his hip. "I could've nailed him sooner if that idiot Wilson wasn't in the way. Damned fool blocked my shot."

"Who cares about that candy ass anyway?" another uniform said. "He ain't half the cop you are. All he's got is his daddy's name."

"You done the Lord's work today, Harry. Ain't no denying that. I'm sure Molly will be eternally grateful."

Someone jostled Denton. "I hope she's *real* grateful, if you know what I mean. You done her a favor. She's single now, thanks to you."

The boys laughed. Gallows humor kept them sane.

But Denton didn't laugh. The joke wasn't funny. He was a white man of pure stock. Molly had Mexican blood in her veins. She was impure. He wouldn't give her kind the time of day.

Denton saw a blur of movement. He saw his friends knocked aside. A heavy blow lifted him off his feet. The back of his head slammed against the wall. His Enfield clattered to the floor.

Dan Wilson's forearm pinned him to the wall. It was like an iron bar across his windpipe.

Denton squirmed. He couldn't breathe.

The others tried pulling Wilson away. But Wilson was a big man. He stayed in shape. The more they pulled, the harder he pressed.

"I had him, you goddamned shit heel." His spittle hit Denton's face. "He was giving up! You didn't have to shoot!"

14

Denton couldn't breathe. He couldn't break Wilson's grip. His strength began to ebb.

Wilson's face grew redder. Denton felt his hate.

"I know why you did it, you son of a bitch." He pressed harder. He pushed Denton further up the wall. "I know why you did it, and I'll see you swing for it!"

Denton's vision doubled. Tripled. His arms burned. Everything was getting muffled. His brain was robbed of oxygen.

He heard someone say, "That's enough, Dan. Let him go."

Denton had heard that voice before. It wasn't Captain Eastbrook. He'd sent Denton to handle this. He tried to place the voice. His brain was too foggy.

His vision blurred. He saw Captain Fritz swim into view. He saw him next to Wilson.

"Damn it, boy. I said, let him go."

Wilson eased up. Denton slid down the wall. He gasped.

Wilson threw him aside. Denton's face hit the carpet. Gasoline stung his face. His eyes. Gulps of toxic air burned his lungs.

The uniforms grabbed him. They hauled him to his feet. They crowded him toward the door.

Denton wobbled. He shook his vision straight. He got a second wind. He saw Wilson glaring at him.

Denton's pride gave him strength. He tried lunging for Wilson. The boys held him back. They kept pushing him toward the street.

Wilson grinned.

The boys walled Denton off. They shoved him outside.

The air stung his face. It stung from gasoline and embarrassment. Wilson had ruined his moment. His deserved glory.

The boys stayed around him. They patted his back. They told him to breathe slow and deep.

Denton hacked. He gasped for clean air. His throat ached. His pride smoldered.

Wait until the captain hears about this. He'll make Wilson pay. And so will I.

* * *

Wilson rested his head against the wall. A dull ache settled behind Wilson's eyes. It happened whenever he lost control. It had been that way since Korea. He prayed it would stop. He prayed hard.

Fritz told a uniform, "Secure that rifle and give it over here. I'll be needing it for the inquiry."

The uniform handed it to him. Fritz sent him on his way. "And make sure no one else comes in here except my detectives. This is a crime scene, not a circus."

Fritz told Wilson, "Let's go into the yard. This place can still go up like a tinderbox."

The captain ordered the yard cleared. He shut the gate behind the last man. No one questioned orders from Fritz. Ever.

Wilson's boot kicked something. Denton's spent shell casing. Wilson picked it up and pocketed it.

Fritz checked the rifle's chamber. He ejected the magazine. "Enfield .303. Not department issue. Too fine a weapon for a man like Denton to own. Wonder where he got it."

Wilson blinked his eyes clear. The fresh air dulled his headache some.

Fritz continued examining the Enfield. "You better now?"

"Yeah."

"Good." Fritz pushed his gray Stetson back on his head. All of his Homicide-Robbery detectives wore one. It set them apart. "Your daddy told me you had that temper of yours in check. Never knew him to be wrong about such a thing before."

Fritz and Duke Wilson had battled fugitives and moonshiners in the thirties. Fritz for Dallas PD. Duke for the Texas Rangers. They'd tracked Bonnie and Clyde. They'd made headlines. Thirty years later, they still spoke by phone at least once a day.

Wilson said, "Guess my temper's a work in progress."

"Most things worthwhile are." Fritz peered through the broken glass door. He looked inside the bedroom. At Hal Farley's ruined corpse.

Fritz lowered his voice. "You told the feds you'd get Farley to leave quietly. This look quiet to you?"

"I didn't have the chance. Tippit got here first, and Hal shot at him, not that it matters. Something set Hal off, but don't ask me what. He beat the hell out of Molly, and she told him everything."

Fritz ran his thumb over his brow. He did it when he heard bad news. "It's still Tippit's fault. That boy's pecker put us in a hell of a fix. And him with a wife and brood of his own waiting for him at home. Someone should've gelded him years ago."

"He's usually late for everything. He picked a hell of a day to be early."

Fritz nodded toward the house. "Why'd you bust in there?"

"Molly screamed, and we moved in together. We didn't know about the gasoline until we were inside."

"You should've retreated and waited until more units got here."

"She didn't have that kind of time." His Army pride kicked in. "Rangers don't retreat."

"But smart cops do. Good cops follow procedure."

"Procedure." It was almost funny. "I didn't see anything about saving a fed surveillance investigation in the manual."

Fritz grew still. "It's in the same section about not beating up a fellow officer. Guess you forgot."

"Denton deserved it."

"That's a discussion for another time."

Wilson pointed at the box tree. "He was kneeling right there when Farley tossed his gun. He didn't know about the gas, but he knew he was unarmed. He killed him to keep him quiet. And we both know who ordered it."

Fritz glared up at him. "I said that's a discussion for another time. You and me better figure out how to make this mess right. Not for Denton or Molly or even them boys, but for ourselves. I warned you not to promise the feds anything, but you did it anyway. They'll be mighty sore about this. The quicker we put it to bed, the better for everyone."

Wilson knew Fritz was right. He usually was. And this wasn't the time or place to talk about it. "Tell me what to do, and I'll do it."

Fritz thought it over. Wilson knew the captain had spent his life protecting the department. He was a cop's cop. An honest cop. A legend whose status had won him friends in many circles. Friends who'd tipped him off about the FBI corruption investigation.

Fritz ran his hand over his mouth. His plan began to gel. "I'll take charge of the investigation. I'll put it to bed, quick and quiet. The papers will run with it for a day or two, but it'll be a distant memory in a week."

Fritz said, "Get back to the office and type up your report. Say you were in the area on official business, meeting up with an informant. No one questions you CID boys anyway. That'll explain why you were the first on the scene. Say you heard the Farley woman scream and rushed in to investigate. Once inside, you smelled gasoline but set your own safety aside and tried to talk Farley out. Then say Denton shot the suspect in the interest of saving your life."

That was too much, even for Fritz. "I won't justify what that son of a bitch did. Farley was ready to give up. I saw it in his eyes."

Fritz quieted him with a glare. "Farley's dead. How and why he got that way doesn't matter. Clearing Denton makes this go away quietly and quickly. If your report to that effect isn't on my desk when I get back this afternoon, I won't be happy." He thrust the Enfield and magazine against Wilson's chest. "Take them back to headquarters. Sign them into evidence. I want a clear chain of custody for the investigation."

Wilson didn't argue.

And Fritz wasn't done. "Go straight home after that. Someone from Operations will come by to review your side of things for the investigation." He lowered his voice again. "And don't go near the apartment. Eastbrook might have someone watching you. Stay home, lie low, and I'll call if anything else happens. That's all."

"There's more." Wilson braced for Fritz's temper. "Farley said he got Molly to tell him about what happened at the diner. She knows more than we thought. She told him everything."

"Christ." Fritz whisked off his Stetson. "Did Denton hear that?"

"I don't know. But Hal was ready to burn everyone down. I told him I knew about the diner. That I'd help him tell the press about it if he let the boys go."

Fritz froze. "Did Denton hear *that?*"

"I don't think so. Molly did, but she might not have understood me."

Fritz wiped at the side of his face. The gears of his mind running hot. He pulled his Stetson back on. "I'll interview her personally. Privately. I'll make sure anything you said doesn't make it into her official statement. If it comes up, I'll tell her you were saying anything that might save her and the boys."

Wilson was concerned about more than that. "She knows things. She might've told other people. She might've told Tippit. That means—"

"I'll handle it," Fritz said. "Forget about what I said about going straight home. You should pay our friend a visit on your way home. He'll want to hear this from you."

Wilson got going. "I'll handle it."

"Handle it better than you handled this."

Wilson let it go. Fritz had earned the last word.

* * *

Tippit leaned against his patrol car. He smoked a Chesterfield as Molly wept in the back seat. She held her boys close. She wouldn't open the door. She wouldn't let the ambulance doc near her.

He understood why. She was a widow because of him. She'd been beaten because of him. Her boys had gone through hell because of him. Their lives ruined because of him.

Because their mother had gotten lonely. Bored. Human.

Tippit exhaled. He sent a long trail of smoke toward the sky. *I should've killed Farley himself. Made it look like a suicide.*

He saw the door of the picket fence open. Dan Wilson stepped out. He was lugging Denton's Enfield rifle.

Had Wilson been a customer at the diner, Molly never would've noticed Tippit. Wilson had Hollywood looks. He looked like Clint Walker. Women

19

dug his dark hair. His square jaw. His blue eyes. How he made off-the-rack suits look custom-cut. The decorated war hero with a college degree.

But Wilson didn't care what women thought. He only had eyes for his Connie May, his Junior League wife. Their two perfect kids. Their big house in Highland Park. Her daddy's trust fund to lean on if needed. His father's name to open doors.

Tippit should've hated him. He admired him instead. They'd worked Oak Cliff together. Wilson was tougher than he looked.

Wilson wasn't just tough. He had a gift. He had a knack with people. With witnesses and skels alike. He could talk folks into doing what he wanted.

He would've gotten Hal to leave without a scratch. He would've made Hal think he'd done him a favor. Hal would've been grateful.

But Wilson never had that chance. Something had set Hal off. Someone had put Hal wise. Someone had caused Hal to beat Molly to a pulp. They'd gotten Hal killed.

They'd ruined Tippit's future. Tippit had to know who. He had to make someone pay.

Tippit watched Harry Denton and his bunch turn their backs as Wilson walked by. They were all Eastbrook men. Birchers and Minutemen. Some were even Klan.

Wilson didn't notice. He didn't care. He'd never tried to fit in. He didn't have to. He was Duke Wilson's son. He was a detective. A war hero. Their approval wasn't required. Another reason why Tippit liked him. Why he trusted him.

Tippit watched him pop the trunk of his unmarked Galaxie. Watched him place Denton's Enfield inside and shut the lid.

Tippit caught his eye as Wilson got behind the wheel. Tippit touched the brim of his cap.

Wilson drove away. He didn't return the gesture.

Chapter Three

Early afternoon in The Carousel Club. 1312 ½ Commerce Street. The cracked jewel in Jack Ruby's tarnished crown of vice.

Ruby thought the '½' gave the place class and allure. Wilson knew better. The place was a dump.

Wilson hated the club. Hated being there during the day. But he had one final report to make before going home. His toughest of the day.

Wilson killed time. He chain-smoked Luckies. He sipped J&B. He watched Jack Crawford play with Ruby's dachshunds. He watched him dodge between tables. The three mutts yipped. They nipped at his heels.

Ruby called the dogs his 'children'. He expected everyone to treat them as such. Failure to do so invoked his rage. Ruby wasn't called 'Sparky' for nothing.

Larry Crawford was one of Ruby's many flunkies. He ran errands in exchange for cigarettes, beer, and a cot in the back room. He joined Ruby at the Eat Well Diner. He occasionally picked up envelopes on Ruby's behalf.

The Pipeline feds had pulled Crawford's record. He wasn't like Ruby's usual drifters. He'd been a bad boy in California. A small-time hitter for the dregs of the Cohen mob. His cases never made it to trial. Witnesses either disappeared or died. He was valuable to someone.

Crawford didn't look dangerous. He was in his twenties, slight and balding, with several teeth missing. A nervous tic made him blink constantly. If Wilson looked at him for too long, he found himself blinking, too. The dumb bastard's affliction was contagious.

Wilson heard Crawford baby-talk the dachshunds. He teased them with a biscuit. Two mutts yipped. A third took a dump on the stage.

Wilson looked down at his scotch. *Welcome to The Carousel Club, folks. Elegance personified.*

With all the lights on, as they were now, the strip joint looked like a hangover. The stage background was draped in cheap tinsel. The drum set was crooked. Stale cigarette smoke mingled with cheap perfume and whiskey sour mix. Echoes of bawdy laughter lingered with gaudy music from the night before. The ghosts of debauchery lasted long after last call.

Wealthy businessmen packed the joint each night. Each hoped to win the affections of Ruby's exotic dancers. The girls sashayed and grinded. The men whistled and howled. They patted empty seats at their table in anxious expectation. A dancer might join them if they flashed enough cash. For a little extra money, they tried to act interested until their shift was over. An endless carousel of frustration where no one ever got what they wanted. In that respect, the club was well named.

The place was closed during the day, but Ruby had a soft spot for cops. He let detectives drink whenever they wanted, usually on the house. Some detectives met him at the diner. They did favors for Ruby and Ruby did favors for them. Favors that—just like his club—didn't look good in the stark light of day.

Wilson sipped his scotch. The warmth dulled his simmering headache.

The Pipeline feds were fascinated with Ruby. Jack Ruby, *nee* Jacob Rubenstein of Chicago, Illinois. Pimp. Drug pusher. Blackmailer. Gun runner. Bag man for the mob. Glad-hander extraordinaire. The feds couldn't understand how a Jewish hoodlum from Chicago could thrive in Dallas.

But Wilson knew how. He knew Dallas.

Ruby was a huckster. Southerners were suckers for good schtick. Some shilled for Jesus. Some sold oil. Some burned crosses. Ruby shilled sex.

Step right up, folks. Your illicit Eden is just a short flight of stairs away. Come hear aging vaudevillians tell tired jokes that tickle your funny bone. Hear our lousy band play loud. Sip cheap champagne while our strip joint Salomes do the dance of the seven veils, Dallas style. All of it compliments of your host, Jack

Ruby.

The bureau didn't get the joke. They didn't understand that Dallas wasn't like New York or Chicago or LA. Dallas might be in Texas, but Texas wasn't in Dallas. It was different here. A twilight town. A big city with a down-home sensibility. Where underworld and overworld overlapped. Where cops were cozy with criminals. Where oil men mixed with pool hall grifters and moochers mingled with millionaires. Where ministers blessed hate at Klan meetings.

But there was an order to things here. Unwritten laws were sacred. White stayed with white. Black stayed with black. Brown stayed with brown. Catholics were tolerated but held in quiet contempt.

Lines in Dallas were often blurred, but always there. They ran deep. Forgetting that brought consequences.

The hypocrisy was thick enough to choke a horse, but Wilson swallowed it whole. He played the game, too. He was betraying Dallas PD to save it. A logic all his own.

Wilson got the joke. He'd been in on it his whole life. But after the Farley killing, he felt like a punchline.

Wilson sipped his J&B. Memories from the house flashed. The empty gas can. Molly's ruined face. Her bloody uniform. The whimpering kids. Denton's shot. Farley's eyes locked with his own. *You gave me your word!*

Wilson took a deeper swallow. The scotch burned. *I watched Death claim your soul.*

He didn't know Ruby was there until he rapped Wilson's shoulder with a newspaper.

"Hey ya, kid. How's it going? How's every little thing?" Ruby never waited for an answer. Concern was part of his patter. "Say, why the long face, soldier? You look like you've been through the wars. Korea, wasn't it? But that was ages ago. What troubles you now?"

Wilson sipped more scotch. He'd drink the fat man's booze, but didn't owe him shit. "It's been a day, Jack. It's been a day."

"I can tell. Why, a blind man could see that. Know what I mean?" Ruby's eyes never stopped moving. His squat, round body bore too much flab. He wore gray fedoras like the tough guys of his Chicago youth. He had three strands of hair on his head, but always smelled like hair tonic and Old Spice.

"You look like you need a drink, tiger." Ruby snapped his fingers at Zeke. "Get this man another of whatever he's having. Make it a double." Fiscal responsibility quickly intruded on his generosity. "Say, what are you having anyway? Nothing top shelf, I hope."

"J & B on the rocks."

"That's fine. Just fine." Ruby snapped his fingers at Zeke again. "You heard the man. Get him a J & B. Put it on the house. Nothing's ever too good for my boys in blue. Know what I mean?"

Zeke refilled his glass.

Ruby never let a quiet moment sit. "Say, you hear about that thing over in Oak Cliff this morning? A couple of friends of mine were mixed up in that business. A nice girl who works in the diner near my apartment got herself in trouble. Heard her husband got a snootful and flipped his wig. Can you believe that?"

Wilson knew how Ruby had heard about it. Harry Denton and Ruby were close. He was married to one of Jack's strippers. "I know. I was there."

"No kidding?" Ruby wiped at his mouth. "Bad business if you ask me. Molly's a nice girl, too. Used to work for me, you know. She doesn't deserve getting slapped around like that. Know what I mean?"

Wilson took a drag. "No one deserves that."

"Don't let it get you down, kid. It's all part of life's rich pageant. These kinds of things happen now and then. You know how it is. These guys come in from the rigs, all worked up. Money in their pocket. Nerves shot. Take it out on the wife and kids. Molly's young. She'll get over it in no time. Know what I mean?"

Wilson drowned the memory in another sip of scotch. "Let's hope."

Ruby laughed at himself. "Listen to me. Standing here telling a big shot detective like you how the world works. Say, how's everything up at CID? Still split your bullpen with the Homicide guys."

"Always have and always will unless someone redecorates the place."

Ruby said, "I've been meaning to swing by there to visit you boys, but you know how it is. This place and all my other businesses run me ragged, I tell you. Just ragged. Been burning the candle at both ends like they say."

Ruby's rambling made Wilson's headache worse. He tossed him a compliment to shut him up. "Hard work agrees with you, Jack. You've dropped a couple of pounds since last I saw you."

"You really think so? No kidding?" Ruby tried to tuck his thumbs between his gut and his pants. He couldn't. "Maybe you're right. I've been feeling a bit lighter lately."

The dogs yipped and growled. Ruby's head snapped toward the stage. Crawford was picking up turds with a cloth napkin.

Ruby yelled to his lackey, "You be good to my kids, you crumb, or I'll box your ears for you."

Crawford wadded up the napkin. "They're fine. Just playful."

"It's your hide if they ain't." Ruby gave Wilson another rap on the shoulder on his way out the door. "Well, I'm off, fellas. Places to go. People to see. You know how it is. Always good talking to you, Danny Boy. Anything you need, just let me know. Keep an eye on the place for me, Zeke. I'll be back later."

Ruby kept talking as he rumbled down the stairs and out into the street. Wilson bet the son of a bitch talked in his sleep.

Wilson drained the last of his scotch. He pulled the fresh one toward him. Crawford cooed the dachshunds. *There's a good puppy. Who's my good girl?*

Zeke looked at Crawford. "If you put two behind his ear right now, you'd be doing him a favor."

Wilson swirled the scotch closer. "I wouldn't waste the bullets."

Zeke dumped out Wilson's ashtray. He wiped it clean with a bar towel and slid it back to him. "Sounds like you've had quite a day."

Wilson checked Crawford's reflection in the mirror behind the bar. He was gently scolding the dachshund who'd desecrated the sacred stage. "As bad as it was, my day was better than his."

"Which one were you? Crawford or the dachshund?"

Wilson sipped his scotch. "I was the stage."

Zeke flipped his towel to the clean side. He began wiping the bar.

25

"Anything you want to report, detective?"

"I was waiting until Ruby left to tell you." Wilson toasted him with his drink. "For a Fed, you're a good bartender."

Zeke had been the first bureau man sent to Dallas. Part of Bobby Kennedy's fight against mob corruption. Zeke's cover was a professional skel. He'd spent weeks knocking around Ruby's dives. Playing small-time hustler. Listening to the tall tales of cops after work. Identifying potential Dallas PD targets. Cops led to politicians, who led to businessmen friends. He pandered bureau-approved girls who plied their trade in bureau-wired hotel rooms.

The FBI files grew. The bureau was pleased.

Zeke's reputation grew. Ruby took notice. He liked Zeke's style. He made him the head bartender at The Carousel Club.

Zeke had been Wilson's bureau handler ever since. When Zeke wasn't working the club, he was manning The Pipeline.

Zeke eyed Crawford as he wiped the bar. "Talk fast while that idiot is distracted."

Wilson took another sip. The scotch burn dulled the damage from the gas fumes. It made bad news easier to deliver. "The Farley thing went south. Hal's dead."

Zeke stopped in mid-wipe. "You said you had that situation handled. You said it wouldn't hurt The Pipeline."

Wilson watched Crawford's reflection. He gave him a stripped-down rundown. "Farley shot at Tippit and held his family hostage. Doused the place in gasoline and threatened to burn everyone alive. I almost got Farley to leave, but someone shot him before that happened."

Zeke wiped the bar down hard. "I knew Tippit would louse up the works. He never should've called it in."

Wilson got defensive. "The whole neighborhood heard the shots. If he hadn't called it in, a civilian would have. Besides, it was a bust long before he showed up. Farley tormented Molly for hours. Got her to admit her affair with Tippit." He flicked his ash into the ashtray. "Got her to tell him about the diner. About who eats there and why. He even threatened to go to the papers."

Zeke stopped wiping. "Did he?"

"No, but something set him off. I don't know what."

Zeke resumed wiping. "Who cares? He's dead. And I've got to explain your screw up to Washington."

"You're not asking the right questions." Wilson took a drag. "Ask me who killed Farley."

Zeke didn't give him the satisfaction of asking.

Wilson told him anyway. "Harry Denton killed him."

Zeke recognized the name from the files. From the tapes Wilson had transcribed. "Was he on duty?"

"Nope. He showed up and shot Farley from the yard. Used his own Enfield rifle to do it." Wilson thumbed his forehead. "Hit him right here."

Zeke began wiping down the bottles in the well. "And Denton's one of Eastbrook's men. Interesting."

Captain William R. Eastbrook. The head of Dallas PD's Personnel Office was Zeke's white whale. The department's resident magician. He made evidence match a crime. He made guns appear or disappear in a dead perp's hand. He made witnesses change their statements with a wave of his pen. He controlled the favors Ruby doled out. For a price, of course. Every favor had a price in Dallas.

The Eat Well Diner was their domain. The Eat Well Diner was the FBI's Pipeline.

Zeke saw Eastbrook as the brick that would make the Dallas PD's blue wall crumble. Fritz and Wilson hoped to make the wall fall away from the department.

Zeke continued cleaning bottles. "You think Eastbrook had Denton shoot Hal to keep him quiet."

"It's a theory." Wilson took his scotch. "A strong one you can tell Washington. And you can tell them Fritz is running the investigation. The whole thing will be forgotten in a week. The Pipeline is secure."

Zeke checked a bottle of bourbon. "And we can use this to squeeze Denton when the time comes. Get him to give up Eastbrook and the rest."

Zeke was living in dreamland. Most cops in Dallas owed Eastbrook and Ruby. They got loans. They got abortions for their mistresses. They sold them junk for their addictions. They made sure the right men got promoted. They sowed favors like mustard seeds and harvested them when needed.

The price for their generosity? Your soul. The owners? Not Ruby or Eastbrook. The Campisi Brothers and Carlos Marcello in New Orleans held the deed. And once they had you, they had you for life.

Zeke tossed his towel on his shoulder. He snagged the J & B. He topped off Wilson's drink. "Stay away from the apartment until Fritz's investigation is over."

"Hope the boys don't miss me too much."

Zeke ignored the sarcasm. "You're still on the hook for transcribing the tapes. I'll have today's batch dropped off at your house tonight. Tomorrow, we'll go back to using the dead drop."

The dead drop was the shelves of the Classics section of the Oak Cliff library. Texans didn't care for dead languages.

Zeke said, "I understand The Director enjoys reading your transcriptions. You wouldn't want to disappoint him twice in one day."

Wilson doubted Hoover even knew he was alive. She stirred the ice in his refreshed drink. "Enough about my day, darling. What's new on your end? Got anything I can bring back to my bosses? They're calling me a hero for the Farley thing. Tell me something that'll make me look even better."

Zeke took a half-empty bottle of gin from the top shelf. He filled it with swill from the drink well. "The river of information flows uphill around here, Danny Boy, and you're on the wrong end of the Nile. You're in the doghouse after this Farley business. You'll have to earn your way out of it."

Wilson shrugged. *It was worth a try.*

The street door creaked open downstairs. Zeke's head jerked around. "Somebody meeting you here?"

"Nope." Wilson sipped his scotch.

Wilson checked the mirror. Crawford was scolding a dachshund. It had lifted a leg beside the bandstand.

Wilson watched a scrawny kid trudge up the stairs. He could've been

Crawford's twin. His sparse hair uncombed. His weak chin bore a week's worth of stubble. A faded work shirt half tucked in. He looked like Wilson felt.

Zeke slipped back to street-speak. "Get out of here. We ain't open yet."

"Jack around?" The kid looked about twenty-five. "He told me to meet him here."

Zeke gestured toward the stage. "He's over there on doggie duty."

Wilson watched a puddle spread beneath the bandstand. Crawford trotted off to get another napkin.

"Not Larry," the kid said. "Jack Ruby."

Zeke went back to checking the liquor bottles. "You just missed him. Come back later, but not like that. Tuck in your shirt. This here's a respectable joint."

The kid ducked his head. He went back downstairs like he'd been sent to bed without supper.

Wilson watched him leave. "Who's that mope?"

Zeke refilled an empty bottle of rum. "Who knows? Name's Lee or Harry. Something like that. Another one of Jack's charity cases. I don't know what Ruby sees in bums like that."

"The same thing he sees in all of us." Wilson ground his cigarette into the ashtray. "Potential. Lots and lots of potential."

Chapter Four

Denton looked up from the rifle butt. The chatter was spoiling his concentration.

Eastbrook had ordered the Posse to meet at the firing range. They were there to conduct business. Not to swill beer and waste time. The Farley investigation was ongoing. Denton hadn't been cleared yet.

Denton remained in the prone position. He was itching to shoot. "Will one of you drunks throw the damned bottle already?"

Reserve Officer Kenny Croy chucked an empty beer bottle down range.

Denton waited. He didn't squeeze the trigger. His father had taught him to never rush a shot. The army had taught him precision and patience.

The bottle tumbled six inches off the ground. Denton squeezed. The bottle shattered.

The others cheered.

Detective Jerry Sill of the Personnel Department whistled. "I reckon you could thread a needle with that thing if you had a scope on it."

His Enfield had a scope. He hoped he got the rifle back soon. It would mean the Farley investigation was over.

Denton told Croy. "Get ready to throw another."

Croy was pouting from the earlier insult. "Shit, Harry. After this morning, I'd have thought you'd had your fill of shooting for one day."

The others roared. They slapped their knees. Dead civilians were always good for a cheap laugh.

But Denton didn't laugh. "Don't think so much, Kenny. You ain't good at it." He worked the bolt. He ejected the spent round. "Throw!"

"Hold on a minute," Sill said. "Old Man Sikes won't be happy about cleaning up all that busted glass. You know how cranky he gets about messes."

Denton didn't care. "That old leatherneck was born miserable." He told Croy, "Throw it."

Croy threw the bottle too hard and too high. Denton barely hit it before it struck the back wall of the range.

"Make sure the next one's lower, stupid."

Gus Rhodes from Homicide took a swig of beer. "You ought to listen to Jerry." Rhodes worked for Fritz, but had been an Eastbrook man for years. "You'd be better off emptying them bottles instead of shooting them, Harry. You ain't had a single sip since we got here. Have a snort. Let off some steam."

"When I drink, I drink. When I shoot, I shoot." Denton worked the bolt. He ejected the spent casing. The sound of brass hitting concrete was music to him. "This is my way of relaxing."

The boys laughed. *Harry never changes.*

Croy was still pouting. "I don't know why you're so cross. You said the captain took it easy on you."

Denton hated repeating himself. It was like reliving his indignity twice. "I said I *thought* Eastbrook would clear me. It's not the same thing, you ignorant bastard."

His pride had been gnawing at Denton all day. He was only in this mess because some stupid half-breed couldn't keep her mouth shut.

Molly had always been a chatterbox. Always saying more than she should. Gossiping about what she saw and heard at the diner. Eastbrook had warned her several times. She just simpered, apologized, and went back to gossiping. The girl couldn't help herself.

So when Molly told another waitress she was throwing out Hal for Tippit, Eastbrook took an interest. Tippit was a cop. The diner was Eastbrook's territory. He wanted Molly to learn a lesson.

Eastbrook had ordered Denton to warn Hal. To watch the house after. To see what happened next. To see how Tippit handled Hal.

No one expected Hal to go bat shit crazy.

Denton hadn't planned to kill Hal, but he didn't regret it. He'd banged up Molly pretty good. She must've spilled her guts. Denton killed him to protect Eastbrook. The operation. He expected Eastbrook to protect him now.

But Eastbrook had shown no mercy during questioning. He'd made it look good for the other brass in the room.

Denton's pride was hurt. "They treated me like a damned rookie in there, boys. Like some lousy reserve officer, no better than Croy here. We're supposed to be special."

Sergeant 'Cal' Calvin took a long pull on his beer. "That's just your pride talking." He'd been with Eastbrook the longest. "Shooting a civilian means a mountain of paperwork. In triplicate, no less. Even he has to follow the rules sometimes."

Rules didn't apply to Eastbrook men. Crossing one always cost something. Dan Wilson had laid hands on him. He should have to pay for that. "We should be out there kicking Wilson's head in, not sitting around here."

"Now you're just talking crazy." Calvin let out a loud beer belch. "You wouldn't last three seconds against Wilson. I don't care for him, but that boy's a bull. Hell, ten of us couldn't pry him off you."

Memory of the humiliation burned through Denton's gut.

Sill said, "Look on the bright side, Harry. As bad as you got it, Tippit had it worse. I heard Fritz raked that boy over the coals. Serves him right for letting things with Molly get out of hand." He sat back with his beer. He pontificated. "Don't get me wrong, boys. Molly's a fine-looking woman. Nice little gal, too, but I wouldn't ruin my for her."

Denton set his rifle aside. He got to his feet. Sill was drunk. Too drunk to realize he'd just committed a grave offense. Against nature. Against God Almighty and the natural order of things. "You telling me you go in for that sort, Jerry?"

Sill set his beer on the table. "What sort? The pretty kind? With lots of dark hair and a fine figure? A nice smile and pleasant disposition?" He slammed the table like he was a judge. "Guilty as charged!" He thrust out his hands like he was ready to be cuffed. "Lock me up and throw away the key, officer. I plead guilty."

The others howled. They slapped knees. *Jerry was a gas with a few in him.*

Denton spoke over them. "Molly ain't white, Jerry."

The laughter died away. They'd forgotten that.

Denton hadn't. "She's got Mexican blood in her, which is plain enough for any sensible white man to see. Fraternizing with her kind is wrong. Mixing the blood ain't right."

The others grew quiet. They didn't look at Sill. They didn't look at Denton. They looked everywhere else. The joke a distant memory.

Sill got up slow. "Hell, Harry. I didn't say I'd marry the girl, just that I can see why Tippit..."

Denton took a step forward. "I heard what you said. I know what it meant. That kind of talk is dangerous talk. It can get out of hand right quick if we let it pass. Loose talk got Hal Farley killed today."

Calvin got up. He moved between them. "Simmer down, Harry. Jerry didn't mean nothing by it. Just fellas talking is all."

Denton knew better. "Not that kind of talk."

Calvin took a beer from the bucket of ice. He slapped off the cap on the edge of the table. He handed it out to Denton. "You're wound way too tight. Drink this down and you'll feel better right quick. Doctor's orders."

They all turned when a man said, "You heard the man. Drink up, boys. This here's a celebration."

Captain William Eastbrook was toting a jug under each arm. His brother's homemade moonshine.

He was forty-five years old and clean-shaven. He sported a gray Stetson. His double-breasted suit coat was unbuttoned. His tie still done up like he was on his way to work. Denton had never seen him ruffled. He exuded calm in all things. There hadn't been a problem invented that he couldn't fix.

Eastbrook set the moonshine on the table. He sneered down at the bucket of beer. "I taught you boys better than to celebrate with that piss."

Jerry Sill pulled the cork from the moonshine jug. He didn't drink. He waited for Eastbrook's approval. "Didn't know we had anything to celebrate yet, boss. We've been too busy consoling young Harry here. The boy still smarting on account of that chunk you took out of his ass this afternoon."

The others laughed.

Eastbrook smiled but his eyes didn't. He placed his hands on his hips. He looked at Denton. "That so, Harry?"

Denton stammered. Complaining about Eastbrook was one thing. Talking to him was another.

Eastbrook said, "That was just some play acting, is all. Had to make it look good for the others. Couldn't let them think I was favoring one of my boys. You understand, don't you?" It was a statement, not a question.

Denton's resentment disappeared. He felt stupid for saying it. Even thinking it. "Guess I was a touch mouthy."

Eastbrook looked at the others. "The Incident Committee voted thirty minutes ago. The shooting was justified. Chief Curry will sign off on our decision first thing in the morning."

The men cheered again. Sill took a swig. He passed the jug to Calvin. They all gave Denton hearty pats on the back. Even Sill.

Eastbrook threw his arm around Denton. He moved them away from the others.

Denton's chest got tight. He hoped Eastbrook wouldn't punish him.

Eastbrook took a fatherly tone. "I know I was rough on you today, but that's just part of the game, Harry. I've never left one of my men in the cold yet, have I?"

Denton knew that. "Guess that thing with Wilson threw me for a loop."

Eastbrook said. "He actually did you a favor. His report said the shooting was justified. It was why you got cleared so quickly."

Denton hadn't expected that. "Wonder why?"

"Who cares? We'll get him in our own way and in our own time." He slid an envelope from his inside pocket. He slipped it to Denton. "That's something from your Uncle Jack. Call it appreciation for a job well done."

Denton tucked it under his shirt. "Feels like he was grateful."

"We both are." He clapped Denton on the shoulder. "You're one of my best, Harry. Never forget that. I promise I never will."

Some of Denton's pride returned. He couldn't speak.

Eastbrook tapped the envelope under Denton's shirt. "Spend some of that on Kay, but put the rest away for a rainy day. That day might come sooner than you think."

"Sounds like trouble's coming our way."

Eastbrook looked around the shooting range. "The savages are closing in on all sides, Harry. We must be ready to do what's necessary when the time comes. I know I can count on you to be ready."

How could I ever have doubted this man? "Of course, boss."

Eastbrook winked. "Good. I don't have details yet, but I'll tell you when I can."

The door to the range flew open. Sikes, the owner, marched toward them. His hair regulation short. His head scarlet with anger. "Glad you're here, Will. Your boys have been making a mess. I expect you to rein them in."

"That so?" Eastbrook made a show of looking over his men. "What've they been getting up to?"

"Loud, foul-mouthed drunken nonsense for starters," Sikes said. "And shooting up bottles, which is against regulations." He pointed a crooked finger up at a sign that read: 'PAPER TARGETS ONLY ON RANGE.'

Sikes continued. "If you don't put a stop to it, I'm gonna have to throw them out on their ears."

Eastbrook smiled at the threat. "Hell, they're just having a little fun at the end of a long day. Trying to cheer up Harry here until I showed up. If you let them stay, I promise they'll clean up. They'll leave the place better than they found it. Might even leave behind a jug of my brother's moonshine for the trouble. Show there's no hard feelings."

Sikes stood his ground. "Rules are rules, Will. They broke them. Now they have to pay."

Eastbrook set his hands on his hips. He appeared to think it over.

Denton knew that look. The captain was getting annoyed.

"You've got a point. Rules are rules. Just like the law's the law." He nodded toward the shop. "I hit the head when I got here just now. Too much coffee today. And you'd be surprised what I found just sitting there on the sink."

He produced a small manila envelope from his pocket. He opened it. He let Sikes see the white powder inside. "I believe there's a good chance this might be cocaine."

Sikes's mouth became a thin line. "Don't you dare."

"Take it easy." Eastbrook closed the envelope. He slid it into his shirt pocket. "I'm sure you knew nothing about it. And I'll bet my bottom dollar the narcotics boys will agree with me. After they finish their investigation, of course." He sighed. "Never can tell how long an investigation like that might take. Could be a week. Could be a month. Could be longer. I could turn a blind eye, of course, but like you said, rules are rules."

Sikes balled his fists at his side. "You've always been one grade-A son of a bitch, Will."

Eastbrook leaned toward him. He wasn't smiling now. "Don't you forget it." He touched the brim of his Stetson. "You have yourself a good night. And thank you for your hospitality and understanding."

Denton watched the range owner go back inside. He hated seeing a brave man humbled. But this wasn't World War Two. And Dallas was a long way from the Pacific. The captain wasn't like the Japanese. He didn't lose.

Eastbrook gave the cocaine to Denton. "For Kay. I know she's got a taste for the stuff."

Denton didn't remember telling Eastbrook about her habit. Eastbrook just knew things like that.

Eastbrook faced his men and threw open his arms. They stood and applauded their leader.

He bowed. "Say, what the hell kind of Texans are you boys? A party ain't hardly a party unless you're shooting something."

He pulled his service revolver. He fired at the paper targets down range. The others joined in. They missed more than they struck, but fired anyway. Bullets pinged the walls. Paper targets shredded.

Denton didn't join in. He found the open jug. He took a healthy pull. He'd done enough shooting for one day.

He'd hold his fire for when it counted.

Chapter Five

Wilson cursed when he saw Duke's truck parked in front of his house. Fritz must've called him. Told him about Farley and Denton.

Wilson pulled into his driveway and killed the engine. He wasn't in the mood for one of his father's lectures about life and law enforcement.

Wilson got out. He slung his suit coat over his shoulder. He walked up the winding brick path to his front door.

He found Duke sitting on the stairs of the porch. His father hadn't changed much in retirement. He resembled the man whose picture had always been in the newspaper.

He was sixty, tall, and lanky. His jawline was strong. His eyes were deep-set. Only his family knew his hair had turned gray. He rarely took off his faded black hat.

Wilson sat on the step below his father. "Mama with you?"

"She is, but this ain't a social call." Duke's voice was as smooth as the bottle of Crown Royal between his boots. He'd only brought out one glass. "I'd offer you a drink, but it smells like you've already had your share. You'd better watch your drinking, son. Nasty habits like that can ruin a man's reputation."

Wilson folded his coat. He placed it next to him. "Fritz called you."

"He did. I figured you needed an ear to bend. Smells like I was right."

Wilson rubbed his temples. *I'm not drunk enough for this.* "I had to report to the feds before I came home. Zeke works at The Carousel Club."

"I know where he works." Fritz had asked Duke's permission before

37

inviting Wilson to join the Pipeline. "Just like I know a man can always find an excuse to drink if he looks hard enough. Hal Farley ain't an excuse to debase yourself. That man needed killing." Duke looked at his son. "Fritz also told me you assaulted a fellow officer today."

Fritz had told Duke a lot. "Denton killed Farley to protect Eastbrook and the diner. He deserved to get knocked on his ass."

"I warned you that working for the feds ain't easy." Duke stretched his long legs. His rheumatism acted up in damp weather. Rain was in the forecast. "You can't crawl through a sewer without smelling like shit. Denton's a rat. He runs with a lot of the other rats you're trying to put behind bars. He's popular and he's protected by Eastbrook. You're neither of those things. That temper of yours risked your entire operation, and for what? A man who deserved killing anyway?"

Duke picked up the glass from between his boots. "You can't fix what ain't broken and Dallas ain't broken. It was born crooked. That's why no one's ever tried to change it before."

Duke drank. He lowered his voice. "You're in a hell of a position, Danny. The Pipeline business ain't official business. The department doesn't know about it. They'd hate you if they ever find out. The feds are using you and won't protect you. If something happens to you, they'll just get someone else. The second you forget that, you're in a world of trouble. So's your family."

Wilson bristled. "I'm only doing this because of my family. To give them a better life."

"Horseshit." Duke set his glass on the step. "You could quit tomorrow and live off Connie's inheritance for the rest of your lives. You're doing this because you like being a cop. You're helping the feds because you think it'll help your career. I'm not blaming you for it. Hell, I encouraged you to do it. But stop thinking there's any right or wrong in any of this. You'll drive yourself crazy if you do. You'll make a mistake that could get you hurt or worse. If you can't do that, then walk away from it now."

Wilson looked up at his father. "Rangers don't quit."

"Then keep your head on straight and your eyes open. And the next time something's eating at you, call me day or night." He pointed at the stairs. "Leave your bad day out here where it belongs. You'll upset your wife and your mother."

Wilson didn't like the lecture. But the words struck home. "Mama know why you're here?"

"God, no." Duke poured himself more Crown Royal. "I told her I wanted to talk to you about something. Told her she didn't have to come, but she insisted. You'd think after forty years, I'd know better than to try to talk that woman out of anything. Her and Connie have been talking up a storm since we got here. All that chatter gives me a headache. Fetch me when dinner's on the table."

Wilson grinned as he stepped inside. Some things change, but Duke Wilson never did. *Something to be grateful for.*

* * *

"Daddy!"

Brad and Sue Ann had been in front of the television but ran to greet him. Brad was seven. He looked like Wilson at that age. Sue Ann was almost five. She had her mother's fair features.

Wilson knelt and drew them to him. He remembered the terror of the Farley boys. He held them closer than usual.

"Pick us up," Brad pleaded. "Grandpa wouldn't do it. His back was hurting."

Wilson exaggerated a grunt as he slowly lifted his children. "You two are getting heavy. Mommy's going to have to put you on bread and water."

Connie came out of the kitchen smiling. Even her plain blue dress and frilly pink apron were fashionable. Her pageboy cut was from the beauty parlor. Her blonde hair was courtesy of her Norwegian lineage.

"There you are." Her expression said more than she did. She always kept it light in front of their children. "Duke told us you'd be coming home early."

She popped on her tiptoes to kiss him. She used her thumbs to wipe away tears he didn't know were there.

39

Brad reached out for his mother. He used her to climb down and run back to the television. "Those men are yelling on TV again, Daddy. Come look. They're funny."

Sue wrapped her arms around her father's neck as he looked at the television. He expected to see a cartoon cat chasing a mouse. But it was Reverend Billy Hargis standing beside General Edwin Walker. Walker was a firebrand of Dallas's far-right community. The want-to-be governor had finished sixth against John Connally in the Democratic primary last year.

Walker banged his fist on a podium. Crowds applauded and cheered. Someone held up a sign: UN OUT OF USA. USA OUT OF UN. Another sign read: THE UN = UNAMERICAN.

Before Wilson could tell Brad to change the channel, Sue nuzzled his neck.

Connie squeezed her husband's hand. "How was your day?"

"Over now."

Sue picked up her head. She looked at her father. "Why are you sad, Daddy? Aren't you happy to see us?"

He forced a smile. Kids were the best lie detectors on earth. "How could anyone be sad around you, honey?"

"You sure look sad." She tapped his shoulder. Her way of asking to be put down. "I know. I'll go find Missy. She'll cheer you up!"

Missy was the tabby kitten they'd found crying in the back yard that weekend. She'd been hiding since Suzie had brought it into the house. It only came out when the kids were in school or asleep. Neither parent had the heart to tell their children.

Connie took both of her husband's hands in her own. "Jack Revill called. He told me what happened this morning."

Revill was Wilson's boss at CID. Duke's admonition was still fresh in his mind. *Leave your troubles outside.* "Looks like you'll have me around here for the next few days. Hope you won't mind."

"You and me?" She slowly slid her hands around his middle. "All alone in this great big house? While the kids are at school? What could we possibly do with all that free time?"

Wilson was amazed how she always managed to smell good, even when cooking. "Is that any way for a Junior League girl to act?"

She rested her chin on his chest. "You'd be surprised what a girl can learn in Junior League."

Wilson smiled. His first real smile of a long, ugly day. "Keep that up, and Brad just might get that baby brother he's been asking for."

She slapped his backside. "Go get yourself cleaned up. Your mother's in the kitchen helping me with a roast. It'll be ready soon."

But Wilson kept holding her. She felt soft and warm and good after a day of misery.

The phone rang. Their children shouted that each would get it. Connie hushed them as she went to the table in the hallway to answer it. When it stopped in the middle of the second ring, Wilson knew why.

His mother popped out of the kitchen. She held the receiver out to him. "It's for you, Danny. Fella says he works with you."

Tessie Wilson pecked her son on the cheek, then went back to the kitchen.

Connie herded the children back into the living room to watch the loud man on television.

Wilson stretched the phone cord to a relatively quiet spot to talk. "Wilson here."

"Figured you and me oughta talk sooner rather than later." It was Tippit. "Got some things I'd like to square between us."

Sweat broke out across Wilson's back. *Had Molly told him about what he'd said to Farley?* "Bad idea. We should wait until the investigation is settled."

Tippit laughed. "You're getting old on me, Danny Boy. Since when have you been such a stickler for the rules? Besides, the investigation's over. Eastbrook already cleared Denton."

"That was fast."

"Your report helped close it quick. You'll be back at your desk by tomorrow afternoon, so meeting me tonight won't be a problem."

Wilson saw a package on the table next to the phone. The diner tapes and photographs from that day. Zeke would be expecting his transcripts at the dead drop first thing in the morning. But they could wait. "Where and when?"

"I'm working security at Austin's tonight. Swing by at seven-thirty. Consider it a favor."

"I already did one favor for you today. Look where it got me."

"From what I hear," Tippit said, "it just might get you another medal. I ain't promising that much, but it'll still be interesting."

The line went dead.

Wilson went into the kitchen to hang up the phone. His mother was hauling a simmering roast from the oven. He tried to help her, but she shooed him away.

"For heaven's sake. I'm not so old that I can't take a roast from an oven. Is your father still brooding outside?"

"He told me to get him when supper's ready."

"Oliver!" Tessie Wilson had descended from a long line of Texas hog callers. Her voice could cut through the bulkhead of a carrier. She'd never cottoned to her husband's 'Duke' mystique. She only used his given name. "Oliver! Get in here. Your dinner's getting cold."

Tessie's voice returned to normal as she spoke to her son. "And get that wife of yours in here, too. Here I am, slaving away over a hot stove while her children are starving."

Wilson made a tactful retreat into the dining room. Connie was already setting the table. "I don't know what she's rushing for. That roast had at least ten more minutes left. She knows I don't like my meat undercooked."

Wilson figured that was why her mother had done it. He kept it to himself. The two women had a healthy rivalry. Tessie hadn't approved of any of her daughters-in-law.

Connie kept setting the table. "Who was that on the phone just now?"

"JD. He's working over at Austin's tonight. Wants me to swing by to see him. It won't take long."

She stopped setting the table. "Is that a good idea?" Her eyes flicked toward the living room. She lowered her voice for the children's sake. "After what happened today?"

"That's why he called. To tell me we're in the clear."

She never pried about his work. She only knew his job was dangerous and important.

"That's awfully fast, isn't it?"

Too fast. "Guess it was an open and shut case."

She went back to placing plates on the table. "I haven't seen JD and Marie in ages. You should invite them to come over for dinner tomorrow night. We could…" She snapped her fingers as she remembered something. "Shoot. That won't work. We already have a dinner party tomorrow night."

It ranked among the worst news he'd heard that day. "Another one?"

"Hush," Connie scolded. "I'll have you know it's at the de Mohrenschildt residence." She curtsied. "Very fancy if you please. Mrs. de Mohrenschildt is helping my Junior League committee with our Russian émigré charity. She's been very generous with her time."

"Doesn't mean I have to be generous with mine."

"Don't be such a pill." Connie stuck her tongue out at him. "You always complain about these things and wind up having a wonderful time. And you won't be the only husband there. And don't go telling me you have to work late because you just told me that you didn't. Besides, there's liable to be some Russian folks there, too. It would do you good to meet new people."

Wilson had already met enough Russians—or at least their Kalashnikov rifles—in Korea. "I'll get the kids cleaned up for dinner. Another one of Mama's hog calls will deafen me."

He went into the living room. He told the children to go wash their hands.

As they ran out, he saw Reverend Hargis on the television, his arms outstretched in prayer. General Walker tore up a poster bearing the U.N. seal. The crowd went wild.

He flicked off the set. *Enough of the real world for one day.*

The bottom of the chair cover next to the television rustled. Missy stuck her head out. The orange ball looked up at Wilson. She yawned.

"You and me both, sister."

Chapter Six

The neon sign of Austin's Barbeque glowed high above the intersection of Hampton and Illinois.

It was a warm Friday night for February. Business was good. Wilson parked in a spot at the edge of the lot. He got out and looked for Tippit.

Inside, families ate beef sandwiches, hamburgers, and fries while slurping down Dr. Pepper. Every booth had a mini jukebox that made Austin decent coin. After the Campisi Brothers got their cut, of course. The Boys owned every jukebox in Dallas, even the minis.

"He's So Fine" played over the parking lot speakers. Carhops brought meals to car-bound customers. Kids cried in back seats. Patient parents abided. Lone men in cars ogled the young girls.

Packs of teens huddled near cars. They exchanged giggles and long looks. Groups slowly inched toward each other before melding. *The ancient mating dance continues.*

He spotted Tippit prowling the back row of cars. He was looking for underage kids sneaking beers and overzealous rocking. His bobbing flashlight made him easy to spot. That was the point. He was paid to keep the fun to a dull roar. To keep young libidos in check. Too many pregnant teens were bad for business.

Tippit spotted Wilson. He started walking toward him.

Wilson lit a Lucky and roamed. The wind caught the odor of meat and cooking grease from the roof vent. It made him nauseous. The pot roast sat like a brick in his stomach. He needed an Alka-Seltzer and sleep. Not a parking lot with a legion of horny kids.

During the day, Austin's was a different place. It was Oak Cliff's unofficial city hall. A favorite hangout for politicians and notables. The owner was a John Birch man. He let the society hold meetings there a few times a month. So did the Minutemen.

A month prior, Wilson had pitched Zeke on bugging the place. Opening a second Pipeline made sense. Two locales would yield more black gold. It could lead to independent collaboration of information and new leads.

Zeke had turned him down flat. He cited budget and manpower concerns. *The feds have no imagination.*

Wilson was half done with his smoke when Tippit fell in beside him. He lit a cigarette. The sight of the Zippo flashed Wilson back to the Farley's house. Hal thumbing the wheel of his lighter. The gasoline fumes burning his throat. *Stop that.*

Tippit pocketed his lighter. "I was starting to think you wouldn't show."

"My parents were over for dinner. They took their time finishing up." He cradled his stomach. He didn't want to think about food.

Tippit knew the Wilson Family dynamic. "Duke pin your ears back for belting Denton?"

"A bit. The lecture was worth it. Denton deserved it."

"That's part of why I wanted to see you." Tippit watched a young blonde carhop make a delivery to a family in a beat-up Ford. Despite what had happened with Molly, he was still a hound. "Denton's been making noise. He was talking about making you pay for slugging him."

Wilson wasn't worried. "I'm easy to find." The smell of burgers from the Ford made him belch. "Don't tell me you brought me here because of that little shit."

Tippit shifted his weight. He was always fidgeting or moving or whistling. He never looked anyone in the eye. Not even perps. His size had saved him from getting a rep of being weak on the street. The war had done a number on him. On a lot of combat vets like him.

Tippit said, "You stuck your neck out for me, and it caused you a heap of trouble. I'm grateful."

Wilson started to get angry again. "I'd told you to stay away from that house."

Tippit toed some gravel. "Guess I wasn't thinking. I never think straight when it comes to Molly."

"The understatement of the century. How'd it go with the brass?"

"Rough." Tippit shrugged. "Read me the riot act, but I wasn't in on the shooting, so they glossed over it. My sergeant called me earlier. Said we're in the clear. So is Denton. Curry's supposed to sign off on it tomorrow."

Wilson wasn't surprised. Denton was one of Eastbrook's boys. Eastbrook always took care of his own. "Denton's in the clear. You're not. You don't have his connections."

"We all are," Tippit said. "Your report saw to that."

Wilson flicked his ash. He hated writing anything that saved Harry Denton. "Don't remind me."

Tippit took another drag. "Fritz's homicide case is still open. You've always been close with him. Think he'll wrap it up quick?"

Wilson knew he would. But he needed answers more than Tippit needed assurances. "Guess that'll depend on what Molly told him."

Tippit kicked more gravel. "I was at the hospital when Fritz interviewed her. She's in a bad way. When she wasn't screaming, she was babbling nonsense. Fritz took down her statement and got her to sign it. After what Hal did to her, I was surprised she could even speak."

It was the first good news Wilson had heard all day. He hoped her memory didn't improve with time. If it did, it could be written off as hysteria. "She spending the night in the hospital?"

"Parkland." Tippit touched his face. "The docs say she's got a couple of cracked bones around here. The kids are staying with her sister until she's better. She can't take them back to the house, though. I heard the fire department tore up the floors on account of the gasoline."

Wilson didn't care about the house. "Sounds like Molly doesn't remember much. Guess that's a blessing."

"I'm gonna swing by the hospital after this. Badge my way past the nurse. Make sure she's doing okay." Tippit plucked tobacco leaves from his tongue.

"I've got the time. Marie kicked me out."

"Can you blame her? You're lucky she didn't take a shot at you herself."

"I ain't mad at her," Tippit said. "I'm mad at whoever told her. Used to be that a cop kept his mouth shut about such things. Guess one of the guys must've told his wife, who called Marie."

Wilson knew cops were the biggest gossips in the world. The tapes from The Eat Well Diner had proved that. "If you need a place to stay, the couch in my den is yours. Brad and Sue would love to see their Uncle JD again."

"Nah, I'll be fine." Tippit flicked his ash. "I still can't believe my old partner's got himself a den. You sure married up when you got Connie."

"Being an oilman's daughter has its privileges." Wilson dropped his cigarette. He ground it under his boot. "Good thing I didn't know she had all that money until after I proposed to her. That girl knows how to keep a secret."

"Money's good to have, not that I'd know." Tippit flicked away his smoke, James Dean style. "I'll be stuck driving a beat for the rest of my life after this."

Wilson caught that. Tippit had never been the ambitious type. "I thought you liked patrol."

Another shrug. "I like it well enough, but pay's lousy, and I've got bills. And bills are all I'll have if Marie kicks me out. She'll get half of what little I have, and the pie is small enough as it is."

Wilson had an idea. An idea that might help both of them. "Have you talked to Eastbrook? He might be open to moving you off the street after today."

Tippit tapped out another smoke from his pack and lit it. "Even if he liked me, there's no way around those department tests. I've always been lousy at tests." He tapped his temple with his thumb. "This thing hasn't worked too good since I got home."

"Maybe you should take another run at him in the next day or so. Maybe he can find you something off the books." He wasn't betraying any Pipeline knowledge. Eastbrook's resourcefulness was an open secret within the department.

And having a pair of eyes on Eastbrook's side businesses could make Wilson's time Zeke's doghouse that much shorter. "Want me to talk to him for you?"

Tippit looked over the parking lot. "Don't burn a favor on my account. Besides, he saves the best gigs for his boys like Denton. I'm not part of his club."

Wilson and Tippit turned when they heard shouting from one of the cars. A blue Rambler station wagon. Two men in the front seat. Both slim, around thirty. The driver was pale. The passenger was darker with thick rimmed glasses. He spoke a lot with his hands.

He expected Tippit to go check it out. But Tippit stayed put.

Wilson asked, "Shouldn't you break that up?"

"No need. That car's special."

"Sounds like a lover's quarrel. I didn't think Austin encouraged that kind of thing."

"He doesn't." Tippit took a drag. He let the smoke trail out slow. "They're not queer. The driver's a friend of Ruby's."

Wilson knew Tippit had worked for Ruby in the past. "What kind of friend?"

"Who knows? Jack's screwy that way. He didn't give me details. He just slips me a ten spot each week to keep an eye on him. Tell how often he comes here and who with."

The Rambler became more civil, but remained animated. Wilson thought he heard Spanish, but couldn't make it out.

Ruby's interest in the driver was curious. "How often does he come here?"

"A couple of nights a week. Always with another guy but never the same guy twice. Most of them look Mexican, but who knows these days? Made a point of telling me all about his pretty Russian wife one night, not that I gave a shit. I never liked foreign women much."

Wilson grinned. "That's because the domestic variety keep you plenty busy."

Tippit kicked at the gravel again. "Knock it off."

Wilson kept eyeing the Rambler. "This mystery man got a name?"

"Said his name's Lee something-or-other."

Lee. The name rang bells. Zeke had called the kid who'd wandered into The Carousel Club that afternoon 'Lee'.

Wilson took a closer look at the driver. He resembled Carousel Lee. Same thin build and similar haircut. But Rambler Lee was older. Closer to thirty. Rambler Lee was taller, too. He sat too high to be the same kid from the club.

Ruby knew two men named 'Lee'. Men who looked similar. Ruby had Tippit keeping tabs on Rambler Lee. *Why?* Another question popped: *Why so animated, boys?* "You get a last name on the driver?"

"No. We just got to talking for a few minutes one night. It's not like we went for beers or anything. Why? You know him?"

Wilson didn't, but soon would. It was like Hoover and Kennedy. Anything Ruby wanted to know was worth knowing for The Pipeline. Make his time in Zeke's doghouse that much shorter. "Forget it. Just my detective brain working."

He changed the subject. He didn't want Tippit remembering his interest. "You mean about what you said just now? About looking for a better spot for yourself in the department?"

Tippit took another deep drag. "I'm moonlighting here and a couple of other places, but I'm still behind the eight ball. If you hear of anything paying, and I mean anything, let me know."

Zeke wouldn't want him on The Pipeline. Tippit didn't have the brains or the experience. But his desperation could make him useful. It could get Wilson closer to his office in Washington, D.C.

Wilson started heading back to his car. "Promise to keep your nose clean, and I'll put in a good word for you with Eastbrook. He owes me a favor for making Denton look good in my report."

"Sure. And maybe Denton will be your new best buddy now."

"That'll be the day."

Wilson glanced at the Rambler on his way back to the car. The two men were back to quiet conversation.

Wilson memorized the license plate. He'd look it up as soon as he was allowed back at the office.

Maybe the driver's name really was 'Lee'. It would be a hell of a coincidence. And there weren't too many coincidences in Dallas.

Chapter Seven

Saturday, February 2, 1963

Connie was out shopping and running errands. Wilson was transcribing Zeke's tapes in his den. He felt something tugging on his shoe.

He rolled back and looked down. Missy was gnawing on one of his shoelaces. He moved his foot. The kitten pounced. She renewed her attack in earnest.

Wilson didn't have the heart to move her. He went back to transcribing the tapes.

He always ran through the entire package once before transcribing. He looked for inconsistencies and details in the photos. It took more time, but it was his way.

Ruby was Pal-Around-Jack at his club. He was Mr. Ruby at the diner. He ate while Helen Markham—Eastbrook's pet waitress—gossiped with the regulars. Ruby's friends—Barbara Davis and her sister-in-law Charlie sat one booth over. The Farley Family's troubles from earlier that morning were big news.

Wilson heard two of Ruby's strippers walk in. Joyce MacDonald (stage name 'Joy Dale') and Kay Coleman (stage name 'Kathy Kay'). Kay wasn't just one of Ruby's show girls. She was also Harry Denton's girlfriend. *Interesting.*

Wilson listened. Kay talked up her beau's heroics at the Farley house. "Did you hear about what happened with Molly? My Harry was there. He

51

told me all about it."

Ruby cut her off. "I don't need you or anyone else telling me about what went on at Oak Cliff. I already got the straight dope from the horse's mouth."

Kay's tone was sharp. "Quit talking over me. My Harry called me as soon as it was over. He told me everything."

"Oh, yeah?" Ruby wouldn't be outdone. "Well, your Harry called *me* before he called *you*." Wilson could see him punctuating each word with a jab of his fork. "The real hero is over at my club right now drinking his troubles away. And he sure as hell ain't Harry Denton."

A quiet male voice said, "No kidding? I think I saw him."

Wilson could recognize the voices of all the patrons. This was a new voice. He flipped through the photos. To match a face to the voice.

Kay said, "Oh yeah? And who's this big hero of yours?"

"Dan Wilson, that's who." There was pride in Ruby's voice. "A real straight shooter, too. Guess it served him well when he went up against Hal."

Ruby laughed. No one else did. Ruby was his own biggest fan. "And while Harry was nice and safe outside, Dan was risking life and limb to save Molly and those kids. He's a bona fide war hero, Dan is. He's got the medals to prove it, too. A whole mess of them from Korea. That kid's the real deal. Harry's just a lot of hot air."

Wilson closed his eyes. Ruby was prouder of his medals than he was.

"Not according to my Harry," Kay argued. "He said Wilson got in the way. Kept him from shooting Hal sooner."

"Harry does what he's told," Ruby said. "Always has. But Wilson don't need anyone to tell him what to do."

Wilson heard Joy MacDonald say, "You two are talking about killing a man like he was an animal. It turns my stomach. Think of Molly. She and the boys must've been scared out of their minds. Have some compassion for Christ's sake."

"Compassion's for saints, *shiksa*," Ruby said. "And in case you haven't noticed, I don't qualify for sainthood. Know what I mean?"

The women's voices faded into the background. The mic picked up Ruby speaking to the other man at his table. "You and me gotta talk, kid. Not here, but back at my place after. Got some big changes coming up, and I need you."

"Sure, Jack." The voice wasn't just quiet. It was young. "Whatever you need."

Wilson flipped through the surveillance photos. He saw pics of Kay and Joy sauntering into the diner.

The picture after that caught Wilson's eye. He stopped the tape. He grabbed a magnifying glass. He took a closer look at the image. Ruby's back was to the window. A stranger sat across from him.

Wilson checked the surveillance log. Ruby and Crawford at Ruby's regular booth.

Wilson flipped the photo to the back. One of Zeke's agents had scrawled: **Ruby and Crawford. 14:30.**

The time didn't fit. It couldn't be Crawford. He was still wiping up dog piss at The Carousel Club at 14:30.

Wilson looked at the stranger. He looked closer. The resemblance was strong. But the feds had it wrong. The man with Ruby wasn't Crawford. He had front teeth. He looked healthier.

Wilson squinted. He recognized him. The same kid who'd come to the club looking for Ruby.

Carousel Lee.

Wilson set the magnifier aside. Three men in Ruby's orbit. Crawford. Carousel Lee. Rambler Lee. Three men who resembled each other. *Curiouser and curiouser.*

Wilson slid his scratch pad over. He wrote that down.

Wilson tapped his pencil on the notepad. The resemblances were too close. They weren't a coincidence. *What are you up to, Jack? Who's Lee to you?*

Wilson's desk phone began to ring.

Missy had grown bored with his laces. She dug into his ankle. He scooped up the kitten and placed her on the desk. He answered the phone.

It was Eastbrook. "Be in my office at three o'clock. It's about the Denton business."

Not Farley. Denton. Eastbrook's purview was strictly DPD personnel. *Technically.* "I'll be there."

"Don't be late. I hate lateness in an officer."

The line went dead. Wilson hung up.

The clock on his desk said noon. He could finish transcribing the tapes, place them at the library dead drop for Zeke, and get to the office by two.

More than enough time to look up the Rambler's plate number. Check Ruby's file for Known Associates named 'Lee'.

Missy dug out a pencil from beneath some papers. She flicked it off the desk. She jumped down in pursuit.

"It's going to be one of those days, isn't it, sister?"

* * *

Criminal Investigations shared a bullpen with some of the boys from Homicide squad.

Detective Jim Leavelle was entertaining some uniforms. He was reenacting a jump shot when Wilson walked in.

"Look who's here?" Leavelle boomed. "Our conquering hero. The Pride of Texas."

The uniforms were from Denton's clique. Kenny Croy and other Eastbrook men. Memories were still fresh from yesterday. They didn't laugh.

Wilson took off his suit jacket. He draped it on the back of his chair. "Knock it off."

"Don't take my word for it." Leavelle held up a copy of the Dallas Morning News. The headline blared:

COP STOPS MASSACRE IN OAK CLIFF
DPD Detective Saves Family From Inferno

Wilson had seen it at the Oak Cliff Library. He'd seen it at a couple of newsstands on the drive into the office. He hadn't stopped to get a copy. He was sure Connie had bought several for her scrapbook.

Leavelle said, "Hope you'll put in a good word for me with the mayor at the medal ceremony, Danny Boy. Hell, you might even get yourself invited to the White House to meet Kennedy."

"That bastard," Croy said. "I'd spit in his eye over what he's done to this country."

The others grumbled their support.

Tracking politics was part of Wilson's job. He'd never cared much for politics or politicians. "The whole thing will be forgotten by Monday."

Leavelle read from the article. "Says here that 'Detective Dan Wilson, setting aside his own personal safety, charged into the gasoline-soaked home to rescue the frightened family.'" He tossed the paper on the desk. "Sounds like some gen-u-ine hero stuff to me. Why, with your looks, you'll wind up on television before it's all said and done." He smiled at the uniforms. "Mark it down, boys. Wilson's bound for *Gunsmoke*. Give Marshal Dillon a run for his money."

"Bullshit," Croy laughed. "I was there, and that ain't what happened. Not by a long shot. *Gunsmoke* my ass. What that reporter wrote is straight out of *The Twilight Zone* if you ask me."

Leavelle was enjoying himself. He asked Wilson, "You gonna let Reserve Officer Croy get away with saying that?"

Wilson took a pack of Luckies from the top drawer of his desk. "Nobody cares about what Croy thinks. Including Mrs. Croy."

The men chuckled. Croy gave him the finger. Leavelle resumed acting out his basketball story.

Wilson checked his watch. It was just before two. An hour before his meeting with Eastbrook. *Plenty of time for some homework.*

He shook a cigarette from the pack. He slipped it behind his ear. He dug his notebook from his coat pocket. He went around the corner. He opened the vehicle registry book. He found Rambler Lee's plate.

It was registered to Michael R. Blaine of Fort Worth, Texas.

Wilson didn't recognize the name. He wrote it down.

He took the pad into the CID file room. All of Dallas's dirty laundry was kept under lock and key there. People and groups who had or could pose threats. Notable citizens. Criminals. Politicians. Political committee members. Foreign nationals. Exchange students. Their Known Associates (KAs). Any pertinent information provided by the feds.

CID tracked them all. CID guarded them closely. Not even Chief Curry had a key to the room or the cabinets. Only CID men had one.

Wilson unlocked the 'B' cabinet. He found the **BLAINE, MICHAEL R.** file. He pulled it and began to read.

Surveillance photos confirmed Wilson's suspicions. Rambler Lee was Michael Ralph Blaine. Thirty-five years old, five-ten, and about one hundred and forty pounds. A taller, healthier version of Carousel Lee. The two men could be taken for brothers. Wilson wrote it down in his notebook.

The file said Blaine was fluent in Spanish. He was proficient in Russian. He was married to Ruth Blaine (*nee* Hyde) of New York City. They had two sons together.

Blaine was an engineer with Bell Helicopter. Wilson knew the company from Korea. He'd ridden in Bell H-13s on several enemy observation flights. Men owed those helicopters their lives. The Bell 47 had rescued wounded from the battlefield.

Wilson checked the file. Blaine had a 'pink sheet'. CID jargon for subjects with ties to known leftist organizations. Right-wingers had 'blue sheets'.

Wilson started reading. Blaine was lifelong pinko. He bordered on Red. He belonged to The American Civil Liberties Union. He had affiliations with every leftist group on every college campus in the Dallas-Fort Worth area. He'd been photographed at Red rallies and events. His name was on mimeographed sign-in sheets. *Michael got around.*

Wilson kept reading. A list of events Blaine had either attended or spoken at. It had been updated the previous month. He was quoted in a college newspaper. Blaine supported Castro but denounced his Communism.

Wilson flipped to the back. An FBI profile. It verified Blaine's lineage. He came from a long line of old money. His family owned an island in Massachusetts. His family went back to the Mayflower days.

Wilson wrote it down. Blue bloods rarely turned pink, much less Red. The proletariat didn't respect pedigree.

Working for Bell Helicopter didn't fit Blaine's leftist bent. Why would a leftist work for a defense contractor? His job required security clearance. Leftists had a tough time obtaining such clearance.

Wilson checked the file. Comrade Blaine had sailed through the process. No objections. No exceptions.

Wilson wrote that down, too. *Had family connections greased the wheels?*

Wilson knew every important extremist in Dallas. Birchers. Communists. Minutemen. Reds. Klan. ACLU. Names cross-pollinated CID lists.

But Wilson had never heard of Blaine before. Not in any report he'd seen or compiled. Not in any briefing he'd attended or prepared. His file was substantial. Someone had been watching him.

Wilson checked the log. He checked for the CID case officer who'd opened the file.

Nothing. Not a single Dallas PD report had been signed by a supervisor, either. Only the copies of reports from outside agencies bore names.

Wilson rechecked. Maybe it had been misplaced. He couldn't find it.

Wilson stopped. Every file in that room could be traced back to an originating officer. But not Blaine's. Someone had been updating his file. They'd kept it accessible. They'd kept it anonymous. *Why wasn't it official?*

Wilson wrote fast. Questions multiplied.

No Dallas PD case officer. Why? Why was the file in the cabinet? Why was a lefty helicopter engineer arguing with a Latin man in Austin's parking lot? How could a known Red get security clearance?

A deeper question emerged. *Why was a helicopter engineer friends with Jack Ruby?*

Wilson checked Blaine's Known Associates. It read like a roll call of every leftist in Dallas. He recognized them all. But not a single 'Lee' in the bunch. No Jack Ruby, either.

Ruby had told Tippit that Blaine was 'Lee'. Blaine had gone out of his way to confirm it. He'd even lied about having a Russian wife. Ruth was an all-American gal. *Why? What made Carousel Lee worth the effort?*

Wilson heard the racket from the bullpen grow louder. He put the file back. He relocked the cabinet. He went outside and down the hall.

He saw Jack Ruby standing on a box in the middle of the floor. A crowd of uniforms and detectives gathered to watch the spectacle.

Ruby's access to headquarters had always bothered Wilson. Bothered him long before The Pipeline started. The gangster came and went with ease. He had too many friends in the department.

"Gather 'round, fellas." Ruby sounded like a carnival barker. "Come feast your eyes on my next big invention. I call it 'The Twister'. It'll make the pounds just melt right off you. Get a load of how it works."

Wilson ducked back into the file room. Ruby had them distracted. No one would notice he was gone.

Wilson unlocked the 'R' cabinet. Ruby's file was easy to spot. It was dog-eared from use. It was thicker than a bible. New entries were added weekly. No specific information from The Pipeline, of course, but some stray details intermingled.

Wilson knew Ruby's file by heart. He flipped to the KAs. He looked for 'Lee'.

The list of associates ran for ten double-columned sheets. It read like an Old Testament genealogy and the Litany of the Saints combined. Ruby was linked to most of the important people in Dallas. Bankers. Oil men. Captains of various industries. Business executives. Politicians. Cops. Criminals. They all visited The Carousel Club or one of his other dives.

No Michael Blaine. No variation thereof.

A recent entry stood out. **Oswald, Lee H.**

Wilson scribbled the name down. He replaced the Ruby file. He hit the 'O' drawer. Outside, cops cackled at Ruby's schtick. *See that fat man go!*

He found Oswald's file. It was new but already substantial. It had been started by a CID cop who'd retired a month ago.

Oswald's Selective Service photo. The same man he'd seen at the club. The resemblance to Blaine was striking.

Wilson jotted down specifics. Oswald was twenty-four, five-nine, and weighed one-fifty. He'd been born in New Orleans. He'd moved around as a kid. He'd spent time in Manhattan. He'd been a truant. He'd enlisted in the Marines early. He'd become a radar operator. He'd been stationed in Japan. His unit had tracked U-2 spy planes over Asia.

He'd gotten out of the corps early. A hardship discharge back in '59. He didn't go home. He promptly defected to the Soviet Union.

Wilson re-read that part. *Why haven't I heard of this kid before?*

Wilson stayed with the file. Moscow wanted to ship Oswald back. He'd tried suicide. He'd cut his wrists. They gave him a job in a radio factory in Minsk.

Wilson had analyzed intercepted Russian intelligence reports in Korea. He had a sense of how the KGB thought. They'd seen Oswald as a curiosity. They stuck him under a glass jar. They watched what he did.

Oswald married Marina in '61. She was related to a KGB official. Blaine had told Tippit his Russian wife was pretty. Her passport photo proved it.

The Oswalds re-defected back to the U.S. last year. They had a daughter. They were currently living in Dallas. Oswald worked for Jaggars-Chiles-Stovall.

Wilson stopped. His finger hovered over the page. JCS developed photos from the U-2 spy planes. It required security clearance. It had been granted. No exceptions.

Wilson re-read that part. The FBI didn't let defectors waltz back into the country. Not ex-servicemen with KGB brides and babies in tow. Oswald's security clearance should've been DOA. But it wasn't. Just like Blaine.

Wilson wrote down 'Why?'. He underlined it twice.

Oswald and Blaine. Kindred souls. Lefties who worked for big companies with big defense contracts. Both had security clearances they shouldn't have received. Both were linked by one man. Jack Ruby.

Wilson flipped to Oswald's 'pink sheet.' He swam in the same waters as Blaine. They knew a lot of the same people.

But Blaine wasn't listed. Neither was Ruby. By now, he didn't expect them to be.

The 'blue sheet' caught Wilson's attention. Oswald had right-wing ties, too. He'd been seen at Alpha 66 meetings. His KAs read like a roster of the group.

That didn't fit. Alpha 66 was rabidly anti-communist and anti-Castro. It didn't jibe with Oswald's lefty politics. Wilson wrote it down. *What are you up to, Lee?*

Wilson remembered the time. He checked his watch. Time flew in rabbit holes. It had flown now. His meeting with Eastbrook was in ten minutes.

He packed up the file. He locked the cabinet. He'd read more later.

The Ruby-Blaine-Oswald trifecta felt wrong. Intentional. It had purpose. *Who's protecting Blaine at Dallas PD? Why is Blaine pretending to be Oswald? Why the link to Ruby? Why is a somebody playing a nobody?*

A greater question loomed. *What makes Oswald worth the effort?*

Wilson went back outside. The group watching Ruby demonstrate his gizmo had tripled. They clapped like kids at a circus.

Ruby waved at Wilson as he wiggled his hips on the contraption. "Get over here, Danny. Buy one of these for the missus. The pounds practically melt right off. Know what I mean?"

Wilson excused himself past the cops on his way back to his desk. "What are you doing here, Jack? Shouldn't you be at the club?"

"Aw, Zeke can handle that stuff." Ruby's head was slick with sweat. His shirt was soaked through. "Get a load of this thing. I'll even throw in a policeman's discount."

The cops laughed at Ruby's gyrations. *Dig that fat man's sweaty swivel!*

Leavelle dropped his head into his hands. "Jesus, Jack. Get out of here. Some of us have work to do."

But Ruby kept twisting. Kept schvitzing. "Quit it with the negative stuff, Jimmy. I've been doing it for a couple of days now, and it's already knocked a couple of inches off the old waistline. Just ask Danny here. He said as much yesterday. Tell him, Danny."

Wilson wasn't worried about the public reference to his time in the club. Ruby spoke in broad generalities. 'Yesterday' could've been a month ago in Ruby-speak.

Wilson said, "Jack LaLanne's got nothing on you, Jack."

"You said it, brother." Ruby's tongue stuck out of the side of his mouth as he continued twisting. "Why should you *goyim* get all that fitness money? Know what I mean?"

Wilson saw Croy and Denton standing by his desk. Denton was in street clothes. Croy did a poor job of looking mean.

Some of the cops turned from Ruby. They watched the possible confrontation. Word of the Farley house fight had spread. Fat Jack was good for laughs, but this could be fun.

Leavelle's chair squeaked as he turned. "You boys play nice, now. I heard about that business from yesterday. This ain't the time nor place for such nonsense. I won't have it."

Denton raised his chin at Wilson. "Captain Eastbrook sent me. Says he wants to see you PDQ."

Wilson looked Denton up and down. The kid was playing tough for his pals. The act fell short. Wilson was half a head taller. He had thirty pounds more muscle on him. "Thanks. I'll tell him you told me."

Wilson tried to move between Denton and Croy. Denton didn't move. "He wants us to shake hands right here and now. Show everyone there's no hard feelings. Says bad blood is bad for morale."

Wilson slid his pad into his back pocket. "Let's not and say we did."

"Fine by me," Denton said. "But I'll be happy to accept some gratitude from you. Gratitude for saving your life yesterday."

Wilson moved around him. "That'll be the day."

Denton rocked up on his toes. "That's how the captain sees it. That's how the department sees it, too. There's talk I might be in line for a medal."

Wilson felt the other cops watching them. Even Jack had given up his gizmo. Everyone looked on. They wanted a show.

Wilson wouldn't give it to them. He pulled on his coat. "Give it up, Harry. My girl's kitten has more fight than you."

Denton moved. Croy eased him back. "Not now. Not here. There's a time and place for everything, and this ain't it."

Wilson got going. "Your buddy's smarter than he looks. And if you ever feel like biting instead of barking, give me a call. But I won't hold my breath."

Wilson shot his cuffs. He walked away.

Denton yelled after him, "You think you're above it all, don't you? That nothing and nobody can touch you. You'd best mind your enemies, boy. The man you piss off today just might be pissing on you tomorrow."

Wilson kept walking. He heard Ruby say, "Jesus, fellas. Never a dull moment around here, is there?"

Wilson flexed his knuckles until they cracked. *One asshole down. One to go.*

Chapter Eight

Eastbrook hadn't acknowledged Wilson. He'd kept reading paperwork since the secretary brought him into the office.

The old sit-and-stew tactic. Wilson had worked for a major back in Korea who played the same game. It was meant to assert dominance over subordinates. A vintage maneuver from the martinet manual.

Captain William R. Eastbrook's office was a glorified broom closet. It had a view of a brick wall across the alley. Metal filing cabinets added to the claustrophobic mood. The cracked plaster walls were beige. They were barren of framed photos or awards. They bore only faded smears where roaches and flies had met their deaths.

It smelled of stale air and molding paper. It was clear Eastbrook had been overzealous with the Old Spice that morning.

The desk bore no knick-knacks. No pictures of family or friends. Just a couple of ashtrays overflowing with cigarette butts.

Piles of files were stacked like sandbags along the edge of the scuffed desk. They'd remained the same height for years. It was rumored that Davey Crockett's application for the Alamo was among them, waiting for Eastbrook's approval. Men speculated if they were just for show. A bureaucratic ruin passed down from one generation to the next.

The office wasn't meant to impress or comfort. Details and drudgery dwelled here. Benefit claims and civilian complaints against cops and misconduct investigations. Bad news. Personnel was the dustbin of Dallas PD. But it gave Eastbrook access. It gave him reach. Influence. Personnel saw and knew all.

Wilson wouldn't give Eastbrook the satisfaction of looking bored. He didn't allow his mind to drift. He blocked thoughts of The Pipeline. He blocked the dirt he'd just read in the file room. He kept his mind blank and sharp. Eastbrook was a crafty bastard. He deserved Wilson's full attention.

He allowed himself to think of Zeke. His misguided view of Eastbrook as a paragon of police corruption. To Wilson, Eastbrook was crooked because it was his job to be crooked. To fix things for the good of the department. If he didn't do it, someone else would. His vices were virtues in Dallas.

If Eastbrook keeled over tonight, another hack would be in his place by breakfast tomorrow. Even Eastbrook's Posse would forget him after his funeral. Any tears Denton shed would be for himself. Cemeteries were full of indispensable men.

Wilson remembered the cigarette he'd tucked behind his ear. He popped it in his mouth and was about to light it.

Eastbrook said, "No smoking in here while the door is closed, detective."

Wilson eyed the full ashtrays. He didn't argue. He slid the cigarette back behind his ear.

Eastbrook spoke without looking up from the file. "You know why I called you here?"

Wilson nodded. The less said, the better. Some thought he had a tape recorder hidden someplace. Eastbrook thought he was slick. *If he only knew.*

"I'll take that as a yes." Eastbrook closed the file and tossed it on his desk. "The internal investigation into the Farley shooting has been officially concluded. Officer Denton has been cleared of any wrongdoing."

"Harry must be relieved. He's always been a nervous boy."

Eastbrook ignored the remark. "The department has ruled that Hal Farley's death was the result of Officer Denton's duty to prevent any further harm from coming to you or that family."

Wilson kept his expression blank. "Glad it's behind us."

Eastbrook said, "The investigation was concluded quickly due, in large part, to your written report to Lieutenant Revill and Captain Fritz. It answered a lot of outstanding questions, but not all." He placed his elbows on his armrests. He tented his fingers under his chin. "However, some

64

questions remain. About you."

Wilson kept his hands on his lap. He wouldn't cross his legs. He didn't want to look defensive. "What questions, sir?"

"We'll get to that," Eastbrook said. "I'm sure you're happy to have played an important part in clearing a good officer's name."

"Thrilled beyond words. But it'll take a lot more than one report to clear Denton's name."

Eastbrook tapped his tented fingers together. "That's your opinion."

"It is."

"Do you disagree with the department's findings?" Eastbrook prodded. "Of my findings and those of Captain Fritz? Of the other senior officers on the committee?"

"My remark was about Denton in general. It wasn't about a specific event. I was only there when it happened. You had the benefit of reading reports."

Eastbrook's right eyebrow arched. He let the jab slide. "Now would be a good time to discuss our findings about your conduct at the Farley house."

There it is. Eastbrook dangled the lure. Wilson took a nibble, but didn't bite. "Everything I saw was included in my report."

"Not everything. It didn't justify your complete lack of judgment and total disregard for both the hostages, not to mention your fellow officers, when you barged into that home."

Wilson glided past the bait. "My justification is all there in my report, sir."

Eastbrook went on. "You ignored department procedure. You refused to wait for backup. You tried to resolve the situation on your own. You're lucky no one got killed."

"Someone got killed, sir. Hal Farley."

Eastbrook's left eye twitched. "You know damned well what I mean."

Wilson stuck to the facts. "An armed lunatic had just shot at an officer. I entered the house to save the family and found it doused in gasoline. There wasn't time to go outside and hope for the best."

"What was good for Tippit wasn't good for you? Or was he too scared to stay with you?"

"He followed my order." It sounded like a criticism, so he added, "I needed him to handle the cops arriving on the scene. If men started charging into the house, Farley might've panicked."

"That's one way to look at it." Eastbrook folded his tented fingers. He cupped one hand over the other. "Another way is that you were using the situation to make a name for yourself. To become a hero. Like your father."

You're not fit to shine Duke's boots. "As I said, my reasons are clearly stated in my report, sir."

Eastbrook picked up a copy of the Dallas Morning Herald. He showed Wilson the headline. "You may not have your father's record, but you seem to have his knack for getting press coverage. Must be a family trait."

Eastbrook was pulling every lever he could. Duke's wisdom echoed. *You don't have the luxury of emotions.* "That's your opinion, sir."

Eastbrook dumped the newspaper in the wastebasket beside his desk. "And unlike your opinion, detective, mine counts. Your actions were reckless and thoughtless."

Wilson's temper strained. "Is that your opinion or the opinion of the review board?"

Eastbrook's eyes narrowed. "Mine. There are other questions, too. About how you arrived on the scene so quickly."

"The same could be asked about Denton."

"Asked and answered. I'm asking you."

"It's all in my report, sir. I was working."

Eastbrook lowered his hands. "You don't pass Oak Cliff on your way to the office. Highland Park is on the other side of the city. Not that I'd know." A small smile. "Not all of us had the good fortune of marrying into money like you."

Wilson would fight Zeke for the honor of slapping the cuffs on Eastbrook when the time came. For now, Duke's wisdom creaked, but held. "I was running down a lead for an ongoing investigation when the call came over the radio."

"What lead? What investigation?"

Wilson shook his head. Eastbrook had just made his first mistake. "CID investigations are confidential. Telling you would violate department policy.

We wouldn't want that. You being such a stickler for policy and all."

Eastbrook's slow smile was far from friendly. "Well, would you look at that? Finally, something we can agree on." He leaned forward. He folded his hands on his desk. All corn pone and cornbread. A bit of down-home in his voice. "Sounds like you understand that some questions are best left unanswered. Some inconsistencies are best left alone. Reasons and correlations and such. No telling where they might lead once the shovel breaks the soil. No telling who they might hurt."

Even with all the dirt The Pipeline had dredged up on him, Eastbrook was craftier than Wilson thought. He didn't want Denton's actions questioned. He didn't want questions about Denton's motives for shooting Farley.

Wilson responded with silence.

"I'll take that as an agreement." Eastbrook sat back. Like Sunday dinner was over, and Ma was serving up some coffee and pie. "Now that we've got that out of the way, there's the question of your assault on Officer Denton to consider. You conveniently left that out of your report."

"Assault?" Wilson's eyes narrowed. "If I'd assaulted him, he'd be in traction right now."

"You threw him against a wall," Eastbrook said. "Set to choking him despite the best efforts of several men to separate you. They said you were in a rage. Completely out of control."

"Men." Wilson sneered. "Your men."

"Uniformed officers who took the same oath you took. To uphold the law." Eastbrook wagged a finger at him. "You've been warned about your temper before. A temper I might say you're on the verge of displaying now."

Wilson forced his mind blank again. "My disagreement with Officer Denton was after the incident. My report only covered the incident itself."

Eastbrook said, "Count yourself lucky that Denton isn't pressing charges. He had plenty of witnesses willing to testify on his behalf if he had."

Wilson didn't doubt it. "Lucky me."

Eastbrook opened his hands. "Harry isn't pressing charges because he's a good officer. He's what my daddy would've called a good white man who thinks the right way. The kind of officer you could've been had you taken the trouble to try." A slight rise of the shoulders. "But you're still relatively young. Maybe you can change. Can you change, Danny? Do you want to change?"

Wilson stayed flat. "Going along to get along has never been my style, sir."

Eastbrook laughed. "Don't act like you've pulled yourself up by your bootstraps, son. If it wasn't for your daddy, you'd still be working patrol with Tippit."

Wilson choked down his anger. *You don't have the luxury of emotions.* "You're entitled to your opinion, sir."

Eastbrook raised his chin at him. Denton had done the same back in the bullpen. A shared trait of the Eastbrook's Posse. Like the white Stetsons worn by Fritz's detectives. "Something you'd like to add, detective?"

Wilson focused on a blank piece of wall above Eastbrook's head. "Not a thing, sir."

"Good. Now, there's been some loose talk going around that you might be up for some kind of medal because of this Farley business. Your attack on Denton has made that impossible. We can't reward such behavior. Bad for morale. I'm sure you understand."

Wilson couldn't pass up a dig. "I've already got my share of medals at home." He knew Eastbrook didn't. "But I'll take a favor instead."

Eastbrook threw his head back. He laughed. "You've got some pair of balls on you, boy. You're in no position to ask me for a single goddamned thing."

Wilson said, "My report helped you close the Farley shooting quick. It helped clear Denton. So yeah, you owe me. But the favor's not for me. It's for Tippit."

Eastbrook went still. "What about him?"

"You spouted off about a lot of things just now, but never mentioned Tippit's involvement with Molly Farley. Must be one of those tough questions we were talking about."

Eastbrook grew curt. "It wasn't germane to this investigation."

"Marie's thrown JD out, and he's hard up for money. I helped you clear Denton. Help Tippit, and we're even. More overtime or something off the books somewhere."

The captain drummed his fingers on his desk. "What makes you think I can do anything for him outside the department?"

Wilson grinned. He stood and buttoned his suit coat. "Like a wise man once told me, 'some questions are best left unanswered.'"

* * *

Wilson left Eastbrook's office. He wasn't surprised to find Lieutenant Jack Revill waiting in the hallway. His boss was flipping through a file like he didn't have a care in the world.

To anyone watching, they looked like they'd bumped into each other. But Revill never did anything by accident.

"Well?" Revill fell in next to Wilson as he walked. He was around Wilson's age. His mind was as sharp as he dressed. Some said he was too slick for his own good. He backed up his style with substance. There was talk he might become Chief of Police someday. "How'd it go?"

"The Farley investigation's over. They cleared Denton."

"I already knew that." As a lieutenant from CID, Revill had a knack for finding out information early. "I'm more concerned about you."

"Denton's not pressing charges against me." The mere possibility galled him. "Eastbrook said I assaulted him. Imagine that."

"He's the head of Personnel. He gets to call it whatever he wants." Revill was an expert at navigating the stormy seas of Dallas PD bureaucracy. "I saw Croy and Denton baiting you at your desk earlier. You could've knocked both of them on their asses. I'm glad you didn't. It would've meant a lot of paperwork for yours truly."

Wilson wanted to forget about it. "It wasn't easy."

But Revill was already on to the next topic. "Say, what are you doing Monday morning? I've got a big meeting first thing with the mayor's office. I was kind of hoping you could join me."

It was vintage Revill style. He didn't give direct orders. He only made requests. Like the men under his command were doing him a favor. He always made a point of thanking them after. It was a nice touch. Make a man feel like he'd gone above and beyond what was asked of him, and one day, he would. "I'll make sure I'm available. Who's it with?"

Revill lowered his voice. "General Walker and Reverend Hargis. How do you like that?"

Wilson didn't like it. He didn't have to. "They've been all over the news lately. What's it about?"

"The mayor's office didn't tell me, but I hear they're planning on holding a couple of rallies here in Dallas." Revill heard gossip, but didn't spread it. He only repeated what he knew. "The mayor wants us to work with them. To keep an eye on things and have our ears to the ground for any trouble. Make sure no one gets too carried away on either side. You'd be a big help in making sure it all goes as smooth as silk."

Zeke would be glad to hear the news. Hoover would be pleased by the intel. Walker and Hargis hated the Kennedys. Just like J. Edgar. "Just let me know the time and I'll be there."

"Meeting's at nine, so it'd be great if you could be there by eight-thirty." Revill acted as if he had just remembered something. "I almost forgot. Are you and Connie still going to that shin dig at the de Mohrenschildt place tonight?"

Wilson had forgotten he'd told Revill about it the previous week. But Revill never forgot anything.

"Unfortunately. Some kind of benefit for Russian refugees. Connie's been looking forward to it."

"I don't blame her," Revill said. "I hear the de Mohrenschildts really know how to throw a good party."

"You should go in my place."

"Connie would kill both of us. But it might be a good idea if you paid attention to everyone who's there. De Mohrenschildt runs with an interesting crowd. Knowing who his friends are could come in handy later."

Wilson had the CID drill down cold. "I'll write up a full report and have it on your desk in the morning."

"Nah, Monday's soon enough." Revill rarely flat-out asked his men for anything. He led them in a certain direction. He let them think it was their idea. "And don't forget to have a great time. You're a celebrity now. I read it in the papers."

They passed the traffic department. They saw Ruby still doing his thing for a whole new crowd. He'd sweated through his shirt again. Cops and detectives laughed.

"Get a load of that clown," Revill said. "Hard to think he's a convicted felon."

But Wilson had seen through Ruby's act long ago. Long before The Pipeline had opened up. Seeing things as they were had never been Wilson's problem. Living with them was.

"No. It isn't hard at all."

Chapter Nine

Wilson drove to the de Mohrenschildts' house. Connie clutched the casserole on her lap as Wilson stopped for a red light.

"Careful, Dan. Don't forget about my casserole."

He couldn't have forgotten it if he'd tried. It made their house smell awful. "These people are supposed to be rich. Why do we have to bring food?"

"Because it's a potluck dinner for poor Russian emigres." She adjusted the baking dish on her lap. "Everyone has to bring something to contribute."

Émigré is a society word for pauper. Just like 'pipeline' is Fed-speak for eavesdropping.

Wilson rolled down his window to let in more air. Connie was normally an excellent cook. This promised to be one of her rare misses. "It smells like something Missy threw up."

Connie slapped her husband's shoulder. "What a horrible thing to say. It's a new dish I'm trying out. It's called Baked Shrimp Surprise."

"The only surprise will be if anyone eats it. Why didn't you make something people like? Another roast or a cake?"

"Because we had roast last night, and Kim said she's bringing rabbit stew. I thought this would be a good time to try the new seafood dish I created."

Wilson waited for the light to turn green. "Smells like—."

She shot him a scolding look usually reserved for the children. "Behave, Daniel Wilson."

"Don't know why you're trying to impress a bunch of Russians. They aren't so particular about their meals on the other side of the Iron Curtain."

"Listen to him," Connie scoffed. "One tiny little mention in the papers and he turns into a snob." She angled the rearview mirror to check her makeup. "Helping people in need is the Christian thing to do. These people are refugees. We should make them feel welcome here in their new home."

The light turned green. Wilson eased on the gas. "One whiff of that stuff and they'll be on the next thing flying back to Mother Russia. You could've brought some of those sandwiches you make for your garden club."

"Tea sandwiches? At a dinner party?" The very idea of it was an affront to her. "Haven't I taught you anything after all these years?"

He enjoyed teasing her. She took entertaining seriously. "At least I wouldn't smell like a fishing trawler all night."

She checked her reflection in the rearview mirror. "That's the aroma of the sea, dear heart, and it pales in comparison to how you'll smell on the drive back home. I never complain about you smelling of bourbon and cigar smoke, do I?"

Wilson smiled. "That's the aroma of men, dear heart." He hoped de Mohrenschildt was a good host. He was down to a half a pack of cigarettes.

Connie moved the mirror back to where it belonged. "What's with you anyhow? You've been cranky since you got back from the office. I'd have thought that headline would've cheered you up. It's not every day that you get to read about yourself in the papers."

The novelty of seeing the Wilson name in print had worn off long ago. He'd grown up reading newspaper clippings of Duke's exploits. How he'd hunted Bonnie and Clyde. How he'd brought in Pa Marsh alone and shot Checo Diaz dead.

Wilson had seen his own name in papers, too. From when he'd made it into Texas A&M, then graduated paratrooper school, and later for his medals at Munsan-ni.

He'd been proud of those articles. Today's was different. "A man died for that article, honey. A man who shouldn't have died. Let's leave it at that."

She took her left hand from steadying the casserole. She stroked the back of his head. "I didn't mean it like that. I wasn't thinking."

He took her hand and kissed it. "I just hate losing someone for no reason, even a criminal. Even when they deserve it. Especially when they deserve it."

"That's why I married you," she said. "You know how to keep all the bad men and all the bad things they do where they belong. And if that article was only half right, you were very brave for what you did yesterday."

Wilson didn't agree but loved her for thinking so. "It'll pale in comparison to what we're facing tonight." He glanced at the Shrimp Surprise. "Every cat in the neighborhood will be on us the second we step out of the car."

Connie returned both hands to her prized casserole. "Cats, I can handle. It's those bitches at the party I'm worried about."

His wife rarely cursed. "Since when do Junior League girls talk like that?"

"Stop being modest. You know how the girls love to fall all over you, especially Kim."

Wilson enjoyed her jealousy. "It'd be tough to fend her off. She's got me beat by fifty pounds."

Her delicate laugh drove away any thoughts of Farley, Ruby, Oswald, and Blaine. "She's gained a few pounds since you saw her last." She giggled. "Oh, Dan. Now you've done it. I won't be able to look at that woman the rest of the night without thinking about that."

Wilson was glad he'd made someone happy besides Captain Eastbrook.

* * *

The street in front of the de Mohrenschildt home was lined with cars. Wilson let Connie and her casserole out at the walkway. He drove on. He looked for a place to park.

He parked in a spot at the curb a block and a half away.

He locked the Galaxie. He caught a flare out of the corner of his eye. He looked at the line of cars parked across the street. A thin trail of cigarette smoke drifted out the driver-side window. A black-over-white Impala. The driver was in shadow. Wilson looked for the license plate. It was parked too close to the car in front of it.

A Dallas PD detective would've recognized him. He would've flashed his lights in acknowledgement. So would one of Zeke's men. They knew he was attending the dinner.

This was someone else. A charity dinner for Russians was bound to attract attention from any number of agencies. He'd include the Impala's description in his report to Revill and Zeke. He was glad he had his .38 Special holstered in his left boot, just in case.

The inside of the de Mohrenschildt house was as crowded as he'd expected. Men and women tried talking over each other. His heart sank when he saw wine glasses and champagne flutes. Not a glass of scotch or bourbon in sight. A disappointing start to the evening. And he was barely over the threshold.

Connie was talking to a woman Wilson recognized. He'd met Mrs. Jeanne de Mohrenschildt at another one of Connie's Junior League functions. Her husband told people she was his second wife. But Wilson had read de Mohrenschildt's file. She was his fourth. He wondered if she knew that.

Connie beckoned to Wilson to join them. He cut through the thick throng of partygoers.

Connie said, "Jeanne, you remember my husband, Dan."

"Who could forget the brave and famous husband, Dan?" Her heavy Russian accent had acquired a slight Dallas lilt. "I would have remembered him even if I hadn't read about him in the paper this morning. It's hard for a woman to forget such a handsome man."

Compliments always made Wilson uneasy. "Glad to see such a fine turnout for such a good cause."

A tall man, graying at the temples and wearing a crisp blue suit, extended his hand. "Allow me to join my wife in welcoming you both to our home."

Wilson shook his host's hand. George Sergius de Mohrenschildt was a suave customer. He was Russian-born and tall. Worldly and urbane. Cultured and courteous, whether he was attending a black-tie gala or a backyard barbeque. He carried himself like an important man because he was. Though not for the reasons most people thought.

Wilson had reread de Mohrenschildt's file that afternoon. There was no pink sheet in it. Only deep blue. He was a White Russian. A tsarist who hated what the Communists had done to his native country. He'd worked for the OSS during the war. He'd worked for the CIA afterwards.

He'd made a name for himself as a geologist. He had ties to every oil company in town. The Agency had use for such men.

Connie and Jeanne left the two men alone to make small talk.

Wilson hated small talk. "Quite a home you've got here." All the mirrors and paintings had gilt edges. The chandeliers sparkled. Packed bookshelves sported treasures from his troubled homeland.

De Mohrenschildt looked surprised. "Surely this isn't your first time here."

"Afraid so. My wife does most of the socializing for the family."

De Mohrenschildt smiled. "I suppose the life of a CID man isn't his own."

That detail hadn't appeared in the article. And Connie never talked about his work. "How'd you know I work CID?"

De Mohrenschildt dismissed it with a shrug. "I don't remember. Someone must've told me. You know Dallas is just a small town at heart. Everyone talks about everyone here." He looked toward the entryway. "Ah, more guests arriving. I don't know where we'll fit them all. Please excuse me. The bar is over in the corner. The barman will be happy to make you anything you wish."

His host glided away. *A tactful retreat.*

Wilson looked over the crowd. He placed familiar faces. He noticed notable attendees.

Members of Dallas's Russian community chatted with Junior League couples. He recognized others from de Mohrenschildt's CID files. Oil executives and attorneys and a couple of congressmen. Someone from Mayor Cabell's office was entertaining a small cluster of women.

One man stood out. A young man alone by the patio door next to the bar. Awkward. His face red from shaving. Either a dull razor or cheap shaving cream. He looked comfortable in the loud room. A thin sheen of sweat on his brow. On his upper lip.

It was Carousel Lee. The real Lee Oswald. A nobody who knew somebody.

Wilson moved toward him. To strike up a casual conversation while waiting for his drink.

But Oswald ducked outside.

Wilson skipped the drink. He followed Oswald.

A string of outdoor lights had been strung from the house and fences to a wooden pagoda in the middle of the manicured yard.

Oswald froze when he saw Wilson step outside.

Wilson shut the door and rubbed his ears. "You had the right idea. I could hardly hear myself think in there."

Oswald dropped into an iron lawn chair. "Everyone shouting to be heard and saying nothing. A great big waste of time if you ask me. So...phony."

Wilson's interrogation training kicked in. *Keep him talking. Establish rapport.* "Sounds like you got dragged to this thing, too. Your wife Russian or Junior League?"

"Russia," Oswald said. "I met her while I was working in Minsk. We even got married and had a baby there."

Wilson remembered that from his file. He played naïve. "Never been to Russia myself. Always wondered what it would be like to visit."

"They're just as screwed up as we are." Oswald frowned. "That's the trouble with people. They take hold of a good notion and ruin it."

That didn't jibe with his file. Commies didn't criticize Mother Russia. "Sounds like you just saved me a long flight for nothing. You two live around here?"

"Not far." Lee looked around the large fenced-in yard. "It's not as nice as this place, but one house is as good as another. It's what you make of it that counts."

Wilson shook a Lucky from the pack. He held it out to him. "Want one?"

"I don't smoke. Don't drink, either. Makes me dizzy. I like to keep my wits about me."

"You're better off." Wilson took the cigarette and lit it. He pocketed the pack and the lighter. He extended his hand. "My name's Dan, by the way. Dan Wilson. Nice to meet you."

Oswald rose from his chair. His handshake was weak. He avoided eye contact. "Lee." He sank back in his chair. "You sound like a local. No offense."

"None taken." Wilson leaned against the pagoda. Nonthreatening. *Keep it nice and friendly.* "I've lived here my whole life except for when I was in the service. I was a paratrooper in Korea. A bit before your time."

"I was overseas, too." Oswald got comfortable. "Radar operator near Tokyo. Marines, not Navy. I didn't see any action, which was just fine with me." Oswald glanced at him. "I'll bet you were an officer."

Wilson grinned. "That obvious, huh?"

Oswald shrugged. "Officers just carry themselves different. I was a private." He quickly added, "But I was a crew chief with a training detachment before I mustered out. Hardship leave. My ma got sick and needed me."

He mentioned the hardship discharge, not the defection. Wilson tried a compliment. "Hope she's okay now. A good Marine always knows his duty, whether at home or abroad."

"I guess." Oswald grew quiet. "Did you like being overseas? Did you like the army?"

Repeat a phrase the subject used whenever possible. "Sometimes I did. Sometimes I didn't. It's like you said. A place is what you make of it."

Oswald thought it over. "I never fit in with the rest of the fellas." He looked at the house. "Kinda like it was in there just now. After a while, I guess I just stopped trying."

Oswald's file included evaluations. He had loner tendencies. Wilson played to them. "Same here. I can put it over well enough when I have to, but fitting in isn't my style. Never has been."

"Guess that makes us two loners." Oswald folded his hands between his legs. *He's engaged. Opening up.* "You know, you're the first fella I've met who didn't ask why I was in Russia inside of a minute flat."

Wilson took a casual drag. "Figured it was none of my business." He dredged up some Marx he'd read during his intel training before Korea. "A man is more than his job."

Oswald enjoyed the reference. "Well said." He looked at Wilson closer now. "Are you famous? I feel like I've seen you somewhere before."

The newspaper hadn't included his picture in the article. *Does he remember me from The Carousel Club?* "I get that a lot. My wife tells folks I look like Clint Walker. The guy from 'Cheyenne'. I don't see it myself."

Oswald snapped his fingers. "That's who you look like. I love that show. Not as tall as him, but you've got that same sort of look."

Exercise humility whenever possible. "Nothing I can do about it. Some guys look like Clint Walker. Some look like Elmer Fudd." He tossed a thumb over his right shoulder. "Come to think of it, I saw a gal in there who kinda looks like ol' Elmer."

Lee snorted. "I saw her too. Poor gal." He frowned again. "Life's a lot easier when you're handsome."

Wilson played to Oswald's philosophical bent. "Life's hard for everyone, no matter how they look."

Oswald didn't just hear the words. He absorbed them. Let them sink in. He wasn't the dullard Wilson had suspected. "Now, you sound like a philosopher. I'm in the photography business. What line of work are you in?"

Wilson played shy. "I was hoping you wouldn't ask." He flicked his ash. "I'm a detective. Dallas PD. But don't tell anyone. It'll spoil the party. People act different when they know a cop is around."

Oswald's expression soured. "I've had a few run-ins with cops. I hate them. No offense."

"None taken." Wilson worked the relatability angle. "If it makes you feel any better, I hate a few of them, too. The feeling's mutual. Guess it goes back to not fitting in. It's not easy having a father who's a famous lawman."

Oswald perked up.

Wilson went on. "Duke Wilson, Texas Ranger. Helped hunt Bonnie and Clyde clear across Texas. Got his name in the paper a bunch of times. His picture, too."

Oswald looked impressed. "I liked watching cop shows on TV growing up. 'I Led Three Lives' was my favorite. Guess that sounds silly to a cop."

Wilson remembered the show. It was about a fed who'd infiltrated the Communist underground. "I liked that one, too. Saw it when I got back home from the war. They managed to get a few things right. Guess that's why it was so popular."

Oswald dimmed again. "Sorry for just blurting that out in the middle of your story. I do that sometimes. Things come to me and I say them without thinking. Drives Marina crazy."

His mind is all over the place. "No sense in letting a good thought go to waste."

Oswald got quiet. "Bet it was tough growing up with a famous father. At least you had one. Mine died when I was a baby."

Another chance to bond. "Duke was a mighty tough act to follow. I've never really been able to get out from under his shadow. It's not his fault. It's just the way it is."

Oswald's shoulders sagged a bit. "His first name really Duke?"

"Oliver." Wilson forced a laugh. "Not exactly the kind of name you'd pick for a big Texas lawman, is it? He got it on account of..."

Oswald's eyes widened. He bolted upright.

Wilson caught it. "What's wrong?"

"I *do* know you." He looked around for a gate in the fence. "From yesterday at—"

Oswald went rigid. He remembered.

Wilson stayed calm. *Why not say The Carousel Club?* "Maybe you saw my name in the paper this morning."

Oswald's mouth twitched. He blinked. He got up. The bond broken. He started back toward the house. "I need to go check on my wife."

Wilson didn't try to stop him. "Sounds like you need a friend. A friend who can help when that confusion sets in. Life's tough for everyone. It's even tougher without friends."

Oswald stopped halfway to the door. He didn't turn around. His hands flexed and unflexed at his sides. "I have to go now."

Wilson took a business card from his sports coat. It had a number for the Yellow Rose Answering Service. If someone found it, they couldn't trace it back to Wilson.

"I can be a friend to you, Lee." Wilson placed the card in Oswald's hand. "Call me day or night. Not as a cop. As a friend you can talk to."

He expected Oswald to drop the card. To tear it up.

He slid it in his back pocket and rushed inside.

Wilson let him leave. A harder sell would scare him. It might draw attention from anyone watching them now.

He finished his cigarette. He ground it out in the ashtray on a lawn table. He lit another. He sat in Oswald's chair. He took a deep drag. He gave Oswald time to blend into the party.

The kid was wound tight. He'd left a lot of questions in his wake.

Why so afraid to admit you saw me in the club? What kind of trouble are you in?

Maybe Oswald didn't have many friends. But someone thought he was useful. Someone had him scared. Maybe that's why he'd kept Wilson's card.

Wilson took his time. He finished his smoke. He ground it into the ashtray. *Why so scared, Lee?*

Chapter Ten

Wilson rejoined the party.

He went to the bar. He got a J&B on the rocks and eyed the crowd. There wasn't a square foot of vacant space. He was the only one not in a conversation.

Connie was talking to Kim and other Junior Leaguers. They were near a side table lined with appetizers. None of them looked appetizing.

He looked to the opposite end of the house. He saw Oswald and de Mohrenschildt huddled by the staircase. Lee looked down at his shoes. George tried looking casual. His body language said different. His eyes were angry. He took Oswald's arm. He practically pushed him up the stairs.

Wilson sipped his scotch. *Sorry, Lee. Guess we hit a nerve.*

Someone touched his arm. "Detective Wilson?"

It was Michael Blaine. Rambler Lee.

He looked different than he had at Austin's. He was clean-shaven and smiling. "I wanted to introduce myself. I'm Mike Blaine. I read about you in the newspaper this morning. It's not every day I get to meet a celebrity."

They shook hands. *What are you up to?* "I'm no celebrity. I was just doing my job. And call me Dan."

"Only if you call me Mike." He was drinking something clear on the rocks. A slice of lime, too. It could've been gin, vodka, or soda water. "I admire a man who puts himself in harm's way for others."

"Just part of the job." Wilson looked him over. He could've passed for Oswald's older brother. Larry Crawford, too. "I wish it had ended better."

Blaine sipped his drink. "I don't know how you do it. Making life-and-death decisions in a split second. I can't help but feel sorry for that man's poor widow and children. Will they be provided for, now that he's…well, no longer with us?"

"I don't know," Wilson admitted. "I don't know if she has money or family. You a friend of the de Mohrenschildts?"

Blaine swallowed. "More like acquaintances, really. Why do you ask?"

Why the evasion? "You're here, so you're obviously charitable people. Might be nice if someone called her. To see if she and the boys need anything."

"I'll mention it to my wife," Blaine said. "She's always up for helping worthy causes. I believe I read that Farley worked on oil rigs all over the Gulf. Did I get that part right?"

"He was a welder, I think."

"A tragedy," Blaine frowned. "The stress of his job must've gotten to the poor man. Made him crack. Should serve as a reminder to us all. It's a shame the way our society grinds working men under its boot. I'm surprised this kind of thing doesn't happen more often, especially among the poorer classes."

Wilson remembered Blaine's pink sheet in the file. But his speech felt forced. "I wouldn't know. I steer clear of politics."

"Is that so? I'd think a CID detective would need to follow politics and political groups. As part of your official duties, I mean."

Wilson grinned. De Mohrenschildt had mentioned CID, too. "I'm an equal opportunity cop. If you break the law, I lock you up. Doesn't matter if you're a Republican or a Democrat." He tossed a rock into Blaine's pond. To see where the ripples went. "Or a Red, for that matter."

Blaine was good. He didn't react. "So many crazies running around Dallas these days. Extremists, I mean. Pro-Castro Cubans, anti-Castro Cubans. Pro-Kennedy men, anti-Kennedy men. Pro-segregationists, anti-segregationists. And that awful General Walker spouting hate every time I turn on a radio or television." He forced a laugh. "You boys must have your hands full keeping track of them all."

Blaine's affable act was wearing thin. Wilson tossed another rock. "How'd you know I worked CID?"

Blaine grew thoughtful. "I guess I must've read it in the article this morning."

"The article I read didn't mention my squad. It just said I was a detective. George mentioned it earlier when I got here."

"De Mohrenschildt?" Blaine rubbed his nose. "Maybe I heard it from him. You're the talk of the party, you know." He forced another laugh. He tapped his own temple. "That's how my mind works. I can hardly do my own taxes every year, but all these odd bits of information get stuck in the old brainpan."

Wilson went along with the act. "I'm the same way. In my line of work, you find out all sorts of things about all sorts of people."

"I suppose you do." Blaine's smile dimmed. "Though I'll admit that this Farley business has been troubling me all day. It's a shame when a man loses perspective. How he can get caught up in his work that he forgets what grounds him. It's always the family that ultimately suffers."

Wilson sipped his scotch. *He's working up to something.*

Blaine sighed. "Life is so complicated these days. It's not like it was when we were kids. Men came back from the war. They busied themselves with building a life. A family. Today's man has lost that clarity. That sense of what's really important. He forgets why he's working so hard in the first place." He added, "For his wife and children, of course. Why, if a man loses sight of that, he loses everything worthwhile. Nothing's more important than keeping our families safe. Certainly not a job, no matter how important we think it is. Wouldn't you agree?"

There it is. A subtle threat.

Blaine liked playing games. Wilson joined in. "Letting off some steam now and then is the best medicine." He held up his scotch. "This stuff helps."

"I wouldn't know," Blaine demurred. "I'm a Quaker. I don't drink or smoke."

"There's lots of other ways to relax. Some guys go bowling. Some go dancing or play cards with the boys. Me? I like barbeque joints."

Blaine's fake smile disappeared.

Wilson kept going. "Sometimes Connie and me load the kids in the car and head on over to Austin's. We love their burgers and ribs. Ever been?"

Blaine sipped his drink. "Can't say that I have."

Wilson acted friendly. "A buddy of mine works security over there on weekends. I stop by to see him sometimes. The food's pretty good. Attracts folks from all walks of life."

Blaine's eyes wandered. "I stay away from barbecue. Sour stomach."

Wilson wasn't ready to let him off the hook. "Their milkshakes are practically a meal. We all ought to go sometime." *Twist the knife.* "I bet Ruth and Lynn and little Christopher would have a ball."

Blaine's eyes narrowed. He hadn't mentioned the names of his wife and children. "We prefer our meals at home. Now, if you'll excuse me, my wife has been trying to get my attention."

Wilson snatched Blaine's belt. He held him in place. Held him close. "You look downright scared. We were just talking about family outings. Weren't we?"

Blaine's mouth was a thin line. No hint of the affable husband. He was Rambler Lee now. "Don't discount fear, detective. A reasonable amount of it can be healthy. Don't you think?"

Wilson let him go. He'd made his point. And Blaine had made his.

Blaine slipped into the crowd.

Wilson remained. He swirled his scotch around the ice in his glass. He drained it and asked the bartender for another. *Everyone liked games until they started losing.*

He looked for Blaine or his wife. Neither was anywhere in sight. He toasted Blaine in absentia.

Point taken, you little shit. But score one for me, too.

* * *

Harry Denton watched the alley.

Ruby threw Stiger against the wall. "What did I tell you?" He buried a right hook in Stiger's gut. "What did I tell you about selling junk in my club without my say-so?"

Stiger puked. Ruby jumped back. *The fat man could hit.*

Stiger groaned. He wiped at his mouth. "I had to do it. I'm in trouble."

"Trouble?" Ruby looked at Denton. "Did you hear what this crumb said? He thought he was in trouble then. Wait 'til he sees how much trouble he's in now. For treating me like a jerk. And in my own joint, no less."

Denton wished Ruby would keep it down. The line to get into the club was growing. Someone might hear. They might see. Blood was bad for business.

Ruby kicked Stiger in the kidney. The dealer's knees buckled. Ruby propped him up. He didn't let him fall. "What did I tell you would happen if I ever caught you selling shit again?"

Stiger groaned. "I've had a bad streak with the ponies."

Ruby kneed Stiger in the balls. This time, he let him drop.

Ruby fixed his jacket. He straightened his tie. He started pacing. A matador ready to deliver the killing blow. "How much did you sell tonight? If you lie, I'll kick your lousy teeth in."

But Stiger was too busy cradling his sore crotch to speak.

Ruby threw up his hands. "Can you believe this shit? This crumb peddles coke in my club and now I can't get a straight answer out of him."

Denton kept watching the alley. Watching for stray citizens. There was no reasoning with Ruby when he was like this. He'd been popping Preludin like aspirin for days. The drug made his pupils as big as saucers. The drug made his nerves raw. Every face became a target.

Ruby kicked Stiger in the gut. He dragged him away from the wall. He tore at his pockets. He shredded Stiger's jacket and pants.

Pocket change spilled onto the alley floor. So did a comb. A pack of gum. Three vials of powder. A wad of cash. A wallet. A switchblade.

Ruby ripped Stiger's sports coat up the back.

Ruby looked like he'd discovered King Solomon's Mines. He looked at Denton. "You seeing what I'm seeing? Our boy here is packing."

Denton saw a .38 was tucked in the back of Stiger's pants. Ruby had a strict no guns rule. Even the wise guys obliged. Cops were the exception.

Ruby liked cops. Trusted them. He owned most of them.

Denton tried to confiscate the pistol.

Ruby snatched it first. "What's this, you crumb?" He stood over Stiger. "You brought a piece into my club?"

Stiger kept moaning. "My nuts!"

"Were you gonna shoot somebody?" Ruby didn't wait for an answer. "You gonna shoot me?" He aimed the .38 down at Stiger. "How about I shoot you instead?"

Denton slapped his hand over the hammer. He pulled the gun free. "There's people around. Someone will hear."

Denton backed away. He opened the cylinder. He pocketed the shells before Jack changed his mind.

Ruby snatched Stiger by the shoulders. He hauled him to his feet. The dealer fell against the wall.

Ruby crowded him. He stuck his finger in Stiger's face. "This time, I taught you a lesson. Next time? There won't be a next time. Know what I mean?"

"I know." Stiger cradled his loins. "It won't happen again. I swear."

Ruby kicked him in the ass. He picked up Stiger's wallet. He threw it down the alley. "The rest stays with me. Clear outta here before I change my mind."

Stiger hobbled up the alley. He stooped to snatch his wallet without stopping. His ruined jacket billowed behind him.

Ruby sniffed. He tucked in his shirt. He watched Stiger flee. "I sure taught him a thing or two, didn't I? The crumb."

Denton thumbed sweat from his brow. He hated working for Ruby. Eastbrook had insisted. He liked the added influence it gave him. He liked the information Denton fed him. Ruby had a big mouth. He spouted off more than Old Faithful. Denton heard things that Eastbrook hadn't told him. Denton heard things Eastbrook didn't know. Sometimes he passed it along.

Sometimes, Denton played both ends against each other. Denton liked the influence it gave *him*.

"You've got to quit taking that shit, Jack. It turns you into an animal."

"What shit?" Ruby sneered. "The pills? They keep me sharp. Keep my troubles at bay?"

Denton got interested. "What troubles?"

Ruby chuckled. "Pick one." He pulled out his comb. He raked it across his three strands. "Your prick boss has me under the gun. Says his hillbilly friends need more toys ASAP."

Denton knew the 'hillbillies'. Eastbrook was tight with the Birchers, and the Minutemen and the anti-Castro groups. He worked with Ruby to supply them with weapons and ammo.

Denton had made deliveries to training camps in Louisiana. He didn't know what they were training for. But he knew the camps were on land owned by Carlos Marcello. The Little Man liked having Cuban mercenaries at his disposal. They strengthened his grip on the Gulf and Miami.

Denton kept Ruby talking. "That's kinda sudden. You just made a delivery last month."

Ruby pocketed his comb. "Your boss is pushing for another delivery now. Pushing hard. Says something big is happening. That we can't risk having so much ordinance in city limits. He wasn't exactly in a talkative mood when he told me. You know how he is."

Denton knew the captain was a careful man. He never rushed his operations. *Why the sudden change, boss?*

Denton wanted to find out. To make himself useful. Ruby and Eastbrook liked useful men. "I've got some time off coming to me. Need me to make the trip?"

Ruby pulled a handkerchief and patted his brow dry. "Your boss had me get a couple of flunkies to make the run instead. If the cops pick them up, they won't be missed. They won't talk, either."

Denton let it drop. Asking more questions might put Ruby wise. He liked listening to the fat man talk. He always learned something. *What has you scared, cap?*

Ruby pocketed Stiger's cash and coke. He walked up the steel stairs to the stage door. "We oughtta do this kind of thing more often, you and me. It was fun."

Denton opened the stage door for Ruby. He was glad the band was playing loud. He wouldn't have to hear Ruby talk anymore.

Chapter Eleven

Sunday, February 3, 1963

Wilson drove to the parking lot of the Cliff Temple Baptist Church. The lot was only half full. Some of the faithful had slept in.

Wilson parked next to Zeke's sedan. Wilson faced east. Zeke faced west. Wilson put the Galaxie in park. He killed the engine.

Zeke said, "You'd better have a damned good reason for calling this face-to-face. The Club closed late. I haven't been to bed yet. I hate meeting in the open like this."

"Relax. It's Sunday, remember? The library's closed." An organ playing 'Rock of Ages' drifted out from the church. "They'll be in there a while. No one will see us. This is too important to wait. Did you have anyone watching the de Mohrenschildt party last night?"

"Besides you? No. You know I don't have the manpower for that. Why?"

Wilson said, "I spotted a car when I got there, but they were gone when I left. I couldn't get a plate number. He was too close to the car in front of him. I can't be sure, but he felt like a pro."

"It was a Russian event. Could've been anyone." Zeke eyed a car speeding along Tenth. "I'll ask around. This better not be why I'm here."

Wilson handed over a carbon copy of his report for Revill about the dinner. "That's my full account of what happened and who I saw last night. Everything's there except my wife's recipe for Baked Shrimp Surprise."

"I hate seafood anyway." Zeke placed it on the passenger seat without reading it. "This is what the dead-drop is for. It could've waited until the library opens on Monday."

"Take it easy." He enjoyed dragging this out. Torturing Zeke made up for his snarky comments and sneers. "De Mohrenschildt couldn't have squeezed another couple in there if he'd had a shoehorn and a bucket of grease. Junior Leaguers, rich American Russians, poor Russian Russians."

"No kidding? Russians at a Russian charity event." Zeke drummed the wheel. "I'm getting bored."

Wilson made it interesting. "I ran into an old buddy of yours. The kid who'd stopped by the club while I was there on Friday. Lee."

Zeke stopped drumming. "Ruby's new playmate?"

"The very same."

"Swanky company for a bum like him. I'm mildly interested. Tell me more."

Wilson skipped the details. He blurred facts for the sake of brevity. "I chatted him up. Just two bored husbands who'd gotten dragged along by our wives. Found out his full name is Lee Oswald. His wife's from Russia, which explains why he was there. We shot the shit for a while. Had a good rapport going, but the mood soured when he recognized me. From the club on Friday."

Zeke waited for more. "And?"

"You should've seen his face when he placed me. The poor bastard was absolutely terrified. He fumbled some half-assed excuse about checking on his wife. Took off inside like a scared rabbit."

Wilson didn't tell him he'd given Oswald his card. Zeke didn't need to know everything. Not until Wilson saw how it played out.

But Zeke still didn't understand. "He panicked at recognizing you from the club?"

"I wondered the same thing. But when I went back inside, I saw George de Mohrenschildt giving Lee hell."

Zeke's interest ticked up a notch. "What were they saying?"

"They were on the other side of the house, but it wasn't a friendly conversation. George corralled him upstairs like he was being sent to bed without his supper. I didn't see Oswald for the rest of the night. Not even after George returned to the party."

"The bum and the playboy." Zeke resumed drumming his fingers on the steering wheel. "A tale of two cities. What about Oswald's wife?"

"Name's Marina. Connie happened to talk with her for a bit. Said she seemed nice. If she was worried about where Lee was, she hid it well. My wife's pretty good about picking up signs like that."

"Sounds like I have the wrong Wilson on the payroll."

Wilson gave him the finger. He remembered they were in a church parking lot. A Baptist church, no less. Duke would've belted him.

Zeke asked, "What did you make of Oswald?"

"Smarter than he looks, but not as smart as he thinks. Feels like a lost soul."

"Sounds like he needs a pal," Zeke said. "A pal who treats him better than de Mohrenschildt. And he's linked to Ruby. Try winning Oswald over. Another pair of eyes on Ruby could help The Pipeline."

Zeke had a one-track mind. *Pipeline Uber Alles.* "I'll try to bump into him in a couple of days. I can't make it obvious. I don't want to spook him again."

Zeke chewed over what Wilson had told him. "De Mohrenschildt's interest in Oswald is curious. I'll ask what Washington makes of it. See what Dallas PD has on Oswald. I want a copy of everything." Zeke yawned. "Can I go home now?"

Wilson played a hunch. "After Oswald ran off, one of those blue-blood intellectual types cornered me. Name's Michael Blaine. Know him?"

Zeke thought. "Sounds familiar, but I can't place it."

Wilson could tell when Zeke hedged. He wasn't hedging now. The name meant nothing to him. "Probably just another drunk at a dinner party. But I think his name will come up again."

"Keep me posted." Zeke turned the key in the ignition. "You put in a good night's work, Danny Boy. Keep this up and you might find a way out of that doghouse in a couple of years."

"Woof, woof." *Asshole.*

Zeke pulled away. He drove off.

Wilson hung back. He lit a cigarette. He watched the street. He made sure Zeke wasn't followed. That no one had been watching them.

The car on de Mohrenschildt's street had spooked him. The driver hadn't acknowledged him. Cops always gave other cops the high sign. Feds, too. Someone watching a house full of Russians made sense. The car didn't feel right.

Michael Blaine's threat lingered. It felt awkward. Rushed. He'd known Wilson was CID. So had de Mohrenschildt. They'd done their homework on him. They'd wanted him to know they'd done it. De Mohrenschildt and Blaine and Ruby and Oswald. An interesting square.

De Mohrenschildt, the old spy. Spies never truly retired. Blaine's and Oswald's security clearances loomed. *Had George helped?*

Wilson kept smoking. Tobacco gave him clarity. Blaine's threat plus Oswald's panic equaled de Mohrenschildt's influence. *They're working for George? How does Ruby fit in?*

Wilson didn't know. It was time to find out.

The cigarette singed Wilson's fingers. He'd lost track of time in thought. He flicked the butt out the window.

Wilson started up the engine. He couldn't leave a dead butt behind. In the parking lot of a Baptist church. Some things still deserved reverence.

He stepped outside. He picked up the butt. He tossed it into the street.

He caught the outlines of two men parked at the corner. A brown Mercury Comet. The windows cracked open. The windshield slightly foggy. No exhaust from the engine. Both men in front. Both perfectly still.

The car from last night had been a black-over-white Impala. This was someone else.

Wilson got back behind the wheel. He pulled out of the parking lot. He angled like he was turning left on Tenth.

Exhaust fumes from the back of the Comet. They were going to follow him.

Wilson cut the wheel to the right. He hit the gas. He sped toward the Comet.

Tires squealed. The Merc darted away from the curb. It sped down Zang.

Wilson took the turn hard. He careened onto the boulevard. Traffic was light. Pedestrians few. Most were in church. *Praise Jesus.*

The fleeing coupe was faster than it looked. It flew along the straightaway. It shimmied from the speed.

Wilson's Galaxie didn't have lights or sirens. Its big V-8 engine hummed. He closed on the Merc fast.

He reached for the radio mic to call in the plate. But the Merc didn't have one. *They'd thought this through.*

The Comet reached Jefferson Boulevard. Wilson closed in. He braced to ram it.

The Comet broke left. It skidded across three lanes on Jefferson. It sped east.

Horns blared. Brakes squealed. Curses flew. The Comet laced through crosstown traffic.

Wilson's Galaxie couldn't make the tight turn in time. He figured they were headed for the freeway. He knew a shortcut.

He leaned on his horn. He steered hard left. The Galaxie fishtailed onto 12th. Horns blared. Brakes squealed. More curses flew.

Wilson's tires bumped the curb. He fought the wheel but kept control. The Comet was more agile. Wilson's Ford was faster.

He looked left when he reached Beckley. The Comet blurred eastbound on Jefferson. They were running for the freeway entrance on Storey Street. *Just like I thought.*

Wilson kept his foot on the gas. He leaned on the horn as he blew through the next intersection. The next blocks were residential. No traffic or pedestrians. Wilson floored it. He overtook them. He'd block them at the freeway entrance.

Wilson swerved onto Storey. He slammed on the brakes. He blocked the street to the freeway entrance. There were too many cars parked on the narrow street for a clean U-turn.

He pulled his Magnum. He remained in the car. He exceeded the mandatory firing range time each month. He'd put six rounds into the driver before the Comet got close. The parked cars would absorb the aftermath.

The Comet screeched off Jefferson on two wheels. It sped up. It hurtled toward his position.

Wilson aimed at the driver.

The Comet jumped the curb. It drove on the sidewalk. It sped between a fence and utility pole. The driver and passenger both hunched forward. Coat collars up. Their hats pulled low. Their eyes hidden by sunglasses.

The passenger-side mirror was sheared off by the fence. The Comet bounced onto the street. It sped toward the freeway entrance.

Wilson pulled a three-point turn. He drove onto the freeway. Traffic flow was heavy. No Comet.

Wilson drove one-handed. He kept the Magnum out. He threaded through traffic. He watched for any sign of them. For buckling lanes or brake lights. Any proof of the fleeing coupe.

But all he saw was a steady stream of cars coasting along. Typical Dallas Sunday morning traffic. They'd probably slipped off at the first exit.

But they hadn't gotten away clean. They'd lost a mirror back on Storey. A mirror that was bound to have usable prints.

Wilson took the next exit. He drove back to find it.

They knew he was on to them now. They would be more careful next time.

And so would he.

Chapter Twelve

Monday, February 4, 1963

Dallas City Hall

Wilson checked his watch. Five minutes until Mayor Cabell's meeting with General Walker and Reverend Hargis. Cabell would be on time. He was a stickler for punctuality. Just like Eastbrook.

The cold water in the City Hall bathrooms was always lukewarm. He splashed some on his face anyway. He hadn't slept all night.

The car chase had frayed his nerves. He wondered how the Comet had found him. Had they followed Zeke? Had they tailed Wilson from home?

Wilson cashed in some favors with Carl Day of the Crime Scene Unit. He gave him the Comet's sideview mirror. Day disappointed. No usable prints anywhere. Just smudges.

Wilson should've told Zeke The Pipeline was at risk. He didn't. The feds might get spooked. They might shut down The Pipeline. The evidence against Ruby and Eastbrook was weak. The Farley incident had put Wilson in Zeke's doghouse. Wilson needed the feds engaged. He needed to be in the FBI's good graces. He needed a win.

He went home to fortify his house. He locked every window. He checked every door lock. He made repairs where needed. He stashed his twelve-gauge on top of the refrigerator. He hid an Ithaca pump in the grandfather clock near the front door. He hid another one behind the headboard in his bedroom.

After the kids were in bed, he told Connie why. He told her to watch for an Impala or a Comet following her or the kids. He told her about the weapons he'd stashed around the house.

He gave her his old .38 for her handbag. She didn't complain. She didn't ask questions. She'd opened the cylinder. She made sure it was loaded. *God, how I love that woman.*

Wilson heard chairs moving across the hall. He heard voices raised in greeting. Mayor Cabell had arrived.

Wilson dried his face with a towel. He straightened his coat and tie. He and Revill had a plan. Chief Curry had approved it.

Wilson would join the meeting after the mayor sat down. Wilson would remain standing. To throw off the balance of the room. To study Walker and Hargis. Study those with them. Watch their reactions.

He walked into the conference room as everyone sat down. Jack Revill, Chief Curry, Mayor Cabell, and his staff were on the left. General Walker, Reverend Hargis, and their men on the right. Wilson stood by the door.

The general was broad-shouldered and imposing even in civilian clothes. He looked like a leader.

Reverend Hargis was short, fleshy and round. He brimmed with biblical bluster. "Bless you all for agreeing to meet with us today. These are perilous times indeed for those of us who care about..."

Wilson tuned out the preacher's empty praise. He watched General Walker instead. He'd briefed Walker once in Korea. The general had his own section in Wilson's weekly extremist reports for Revill and Curry. He knew Walker's CID file cold.

Walker had long been a vocal anti-Communist. He'd denounced the Soviets while commanding soldiers stationed in Germany. He'd given his men John Birch Society tracts. He told his men how to vote back home.

The Kennedy administration was furious. It was post-Bay of Pigs. It was post-Cuban Missile Crisis. JFK sought world peace through appeasement, not antagonism. Walker got booted during the 'Kennedy Cleanse' that cleared out the intelligence and military leadership. Eisenhower's men were gone. Even the heads of the CIA were sent packing.

But Walker remained a favorite son of the South. Dixie hated Kennedys and Commies. He became a vocal segregationist. He'd led the student revolt at the University of Mississippi. People got killed. Cops got injured. Bobby Kennedy arrested Walker for sedition. He'd locked him in a psychiatric ward for evaluation. The charges didn't stick. Walker's Kennedy hatred grew.

Reverend Hargis stopped spouting platitudes. He gave the floor to General Walker.

Walker asked Wilson, "Who are you and why are you standing?"

Wilson had an excuse ready. "I'm Detective Dan Wilson, CID. I prefer to stand, sir. My back's been bothering me. Guess I jumped out of one too many planes in Korea."

The general pondered the name. "Captain Dan Wilson? Paratrooper?"

He hadn't expected Walker to remember. *Or had he done his homework?* "Great memory, sir. Nice to see you again."

Walker spoke to the aide on his left. "He was on Colonel Bowen's staff. Cited for bravery at Munsan-ni." He looked at Wilson. "Good to have you with us, son."

Revill hid a smile. *Mission accomplished.*

Hargis intoned, "We'll need battalions of strong Christian soldiers for the many battles to come."

One of the general's aides eyeballed Wilson. He looked at him longer than the others. Wilson recognized him from Walker's KAs. Tommie Schneider from California. He saw the bulge under Schneider's coat. Wilson would ask him about it later.

Mayor Cabell laid on the southern hospitality thick. "General, I speak for every man in this room when I say I was appalled by the way the Kennedys treated you in Mississippi last year. I'd expect such a thing in the Soviet Union, not here at home."

General Walker folded his hands. "The Brothers have smeared many good men, Mayor Cabell. Driving your brother from the CIA was inexcusable and uncalled for. Charlie's a patriot who deserved better."

Wilson knew Charles Cabell had been pushed out during the Kennedy Cleanse.

Hargis swaggered in his seat. "History has taught us that evil triumphs when good men do nothing. The time has come for us to repel the heathen horde. To take the offensive."

The mayor sat back. He glanced at the men on his right and left. He made sure they were listening. "How can we help, reverend?"

But Wilson sensed he already knew.

Hargis said, "By helping us launch an ambitious national campaign that, with God's help, will light a fire under every good man and woman in this country. A clarion call to rouse them to action. To throw off the yoke of socialism before the Kennedy cabal can set it on our shoulders."

Walker gestured to the man on his right. "Bob Carter has prepared some particulars for your review."

Carter took a stack of papers from his briefcase. He slid them across the table to Cabell. The mayor split the pile. He didn't keep one for himself.

He already knows what's in it.

Carter began. "On February 24th, General Walker and Reverend Hargis will announce a series of rallies in twenty-nine cities from Florida to California. These rallies are meant to whip up support for our pro-American cause. To like-minded individuals who want to restore freedom and liberty not only to this country but to the world over. And we'd like to announce it right here in Dallas."

"That only gives us two weeks to prepare." Chief Curry paged through Carter's document. "Where in Dallas?"

Carter said, "We have some ideas, but would welcome any suggestions."

Revill handed the document to Wilson without reading it. "Why Dallas?"

"Because the general lives here," Carter explained. "He has many friends here. And, quite frankly, we won't get the same level of press coverage anywhere else in the state. We're counting on the strong anti-Kennedy sentiment here to bolster our national campaign."

Revill said, "The general and the reverend are polarizing figures. They have a lot of supporters here, but a lot of detractors, too."

Hargis frowned. "Damned Communists." The tremble in his voice was pitch-perfect. "Freedom of speech is a God given right in this country. It's enshrined in the Constitution."

Revill said, "We saw what happened in Mississippi, General. You play rough. Two people got killed."

"Godless trash," Hargis said.

"Cops got hurt, too," Revill added. "They're not trash."

Chief Curry leaned forward. "Lieutenant Revill has a point. We can't allow the same chaos of Mississippi to happen here. Not from you. Not from those who oppose you."

General Walker took an agreeable tone. "That's why we've come here today. To ask for your help in ensuring a spirited, yet peaceful announcement. To ask Lieutenant Revill and his men to prevent the subversive elements in this city from instigating trouble. For any reason."

Wilson flipped through the document. It was long on rhetoric. It was short on specifics.

Revill looked at Wilson. *Speak up any time, Danny.*

Wilson held up the report. "Why are you calling the tour 'Operation Midnight Ride'?"

Carter said, "After Paul Revere's famous midnight ride to warn Boston that the British were coming. Can't get more patriotic than Paul Revere."

Wilson heard Carter's accent. "You're not from around here, are you?"

"I'm from Connecticut." Carter tried a smile. "I hope no one here will hold that against me."

A polite round of laughter.

Wilson said, "Connecticut's a long way from Dallas. Down here, a midnight ride's got certain implications. Klan implications. That'll draw hotheads from both sides."

Mayor Cabell cleared his throat. "We won't have to worry about that sort of thing happening here. Thanks to Chief Curry, we have the finest police force in the country. I'm confident Lieutenant Revill and his men will stop any troublemakers long before the announcement. The people of Dallas are good, law-abiding folk. Passionate and patriotic, not like that rabble up in Mississippi. There won't be a lick of trouble. We'll see to that."

The mayor made more assurances. The event would take place. Both sides pledged cooperation. The reverend blessed the assembly. The meeting ended fast. Both sides stood. They shook hands across the table.

Tommy Schneider left first.

Wilson followed him into the hall. "Not so fast."

Schneider kept walking. "I've got to bring around the general's car."

"Not until I see that gun."

Schneider stopped. He turned around.

Wilson took a step closer. "I won't ask again."

Schneider opened his jacket. An automatic was holstered under his left arm.

"Colt .45 Commander," Wilson said. "Fancy."

"It gets the job done." Schneider let go of his jacket. "The general gets lots of threats. If anyone shoots at us, we shoot back." He gestured at Wilson's jacket. "What are you packing?"

"Pray you never have to find out. Give me your wallet."

Schneider patted his pockets. "Guess I left it in the car. Or maybe it's on my dresser. I was in a hurry this morning."

Wilson said, "Failure to produce valid identification to a police officer is a sign of indigence. Give me your wallet or I'll run you in on a vagrancy charge. The general won't like bailing you out for being stupid."

Schneider dug out his billfold. He handed it over.

Wilson flipped it open. A California driver's license. A concealed carry permit signed by Chief Curry himself. A VA card confirmed Schneider's honorable discharge from the army the previous year.

"Schneider." Wilson prodded him. "Guess that makes you a Kraut."

"Makes me an American patriot. Says so right there on my VA card."

Wilson tossed him the wallet. "We meet before? You were looking at me like you knew me."

Schneider shrugged it off. "The general said you'd served in Korea. I was trying to see if I recognized you. I didn't."

"I know what you mean." Wilson played a hunch. "You look like a fella I saw this weekend."

"Wasn't me." Schneider pointed to Carter's document. "I spent all weekend at my typewriter putting that together. A lot of us did. The general's got lots of men willing to help him fight Communism."

Bob Carter came into the hall. He eased between them with a smile. "Now you've gone and done it, Dan. Tommy's on his soapbox now. He'll be singing 'Onward Christian Soldiers' the whole way back to the office."

Carter aimed his smile at Wilson. "I'm looking forward to working with you on this. The general was mighty impressed with you, and he doesn't impress easy."

Wilson kept watching Schneider. "We might be working closer than some would like."

Mayor Cabell led Reverend Hargis and General Walker from the conference room. The others filed out behind their respective masters.

Hargis said, "Together with you, Mayor Cabell, we'll don the full armor of God, and the breastplate of righteousness will protect us."

General Walker stopped in front of Wilson. "I was hoping to see you before I left. Still keep in touch with Frank Bowen? I wonder what he's up to these days."

Wilson felt himself stand straighter. Like he was back in uniform. "I understand he's set to retire next year, sir."

"He's a good man, and so are you. I'll rest easier knowing you're on the case, Wilson. We'll need men of your caliber in the fight ahead. I know I can count on your support when the time comes."

The mayor, the general, the reverend, and their staffers walked down the hall together.

Chief Curry and Revill stood in the doorway of the conference room.

"This is a first," Revill said to Chief Curry. "I've never seen Danny star-struck before."

"I half expected him to snap off a salute," Curry kidded. "Hell, I barely get him to call me 'sir' these days."

Wilson felt himself blush. He'd been out of the army almost ten years.

But a general was a general. "An old reflex, I guess."

"Who'd have thought it?" Curry clapped Wilson on the shoulder. "Dan's human after all." He told Revill, "You'll be running this Walker business for the department. I want to know every detail, no matter how trivial. Security. Intelligence. Have your boys hit the street hard. Turn every nutcase and crackpot upside down. See if any guns fall out. Walker's got the mayor's ear now. I need to be informed. We'll decide what we share with them. Dallas PD isn't his private goon squad."

Curry went back to his office.

Wilson told Revill, "How the hell does he expect us to build intelligence and create a security plan and raid gun nuts at the same time?"

"Because we're CID." Revill smiled. "We perform miracles. I'll worry about the other stuff. I need you to build files on Walker's men. Carter, Schneider, and the rest. And while you're at it, include any man or group who support or oppose him. We'll submit reports to Curry until he's drowning in paper. When he cries 'uncle', we'll go back to the fun stuff like busting gun runners."

But there was nothing fun about Walker or Hargis. "I've got a bad feeling about them, Jack."

"You've got a bad feeling about everyone. That's why you're so good at this."

Revill went back to his office. Wilson went to a payphone in the lobby. He called his service for messages.

The operator ran through messages from various informants. One stood out. "A man named Lee called. He wouldn't leave a last name."

Wilson pulled out his notebook. "What's the message?"

"He wants to meet for lunch at noon today. Across from where he works. Said you'd know the address."

Wilson checked his watch. It was only ten o'clock. Plenty of time to hit the files before having lunch with a new friend.

Chapter Thirteen

Wilson crossed his legs. He lit a cigarette. He waited for Oswald to start talking. To explain why they were meeting.

Wilson didn't rush him. His interrogation training kicked in again. *Let the subject talk at his own pace.*

He let his cigarette smoke drift between them. He scanned the park. It was warm for a February afternoon. A hint of the brief spring before the furnace of another Dallas summer.

Office workers strolled by on their lunch break. He looked for anyone lingering. For cars idling on the street. Memories of the Impala and Comet lingered.

No one paid undue attention. Not even the pigeons.

Oswald fretted with an apple. His brown paper lunch bag was on the bench beside him. He'd devolved since Saturday night. The stubble on both sides of his face was uneven. He was pale. His eyes sunken and bloodshot. His fingernails gnawed down to the quick.

De Mohrenschildt must've put him through the ringer. *Is that why you wanted to meet?*

Oswald blurted out, "Did you really rescue that lady and her boys like it said in the paper?"

Wilson flicked his ash. *Feign indifference to assert dominance over the suspect.* "More or less."

"That was a pretty brave thing to do. Guess I was right about you. When we first met at the party, I mean." He turned the apple over. "I guess I shouldn't have run away like that. I've felt bad about it ever since."

"No need to apologize," Wilson said. "Something upset you. I didn't ask because it was none of my business. That's why I gave you my card. Figured you'd call if you wanted to talk about it. And since I'm here, it sounds like you do."

Oswald looked down at his worn shoes. "You recognized me from Jack's club, didn't you?"

"Not at first," Wilson lied. "But I remembered later. Can't blame you. It's not exactly the most reputable place in town."

Oswald crossed his legs at the ankles. "Why were you there?"

Wilson told him most of the truth. "Ruby lets cops drink at his dives for free whenever we want. You read about what happened that morning. I stopped in for a few belts to calm me down." *Maintain rapport through mutual vulnerability.* "I'm not proud to admit that. Even cops get rattled sometimes."

"Jack likes cops," Oswald said. "Does favors for them all the time. They do favors for him, too." A forced laugh. "For a minute there, I had the crazy idea he'd sent you to keep an eye on me."

Now, we're getting somewhere. "Why would Ruby want to keep an eye on you?"

Oswald played with his apple. He shrugged.

Wilson tried a different angle. "You ever hear Jack call me a friend? Ever see me with him?"

"I only heard him talk about you that day at lunch," Oswald said. "But I don't know all of Jack's friends."

Wilson put a finer point on it. "We're not friends. I drink his booze because it's free. I was at the club because it was closed and quiet. I didn't want anyone seeing me drinking during the day. I didn't want them asking me about what had happened in Oak Cliff." He finished it off with a declaration. "I've never needed Ruby's help, and I never will. I'll never do a favor for him, either."

"Never is a long time."

"Not long enough when it comes to men like Ruby. I think you understand why."

Oswald futzed with his apple. He looked at his shoes again.

Wilson had to get him talking. "How'd you meet up with Ruby anyway? You don't drink, you don't smoke, and you don't chase girls."

Oswald rubbed his palms on his pants. "I don't think I should tell you that."

Hesitation means the truth is close. "But you want to tell me. That's why you called. Something's bothering you. Something that scares you a little."

Oswald looked away.

Wilson leaned in. "Anything you tell me stays between you, me, and the pigeons." He flicked an ash at one of the fat birds waddling by. "They won't talk, and neither will I. Right now, I'm Dan Wilson, the citizen, not Dan Wilson, the cop."

"A cop is always a cop."

Wilson brushed it aside with a smile. "A cop sitting on a park bench, talking to a friend on his lunch break. A friend who might be able to help if you let me."

Oswald turned the apple. The pot was starting to bubble. "Do you remember what I told you at the party? About my favorite TV show when I was a kid?"

Wilson remembered. "The spy show. What about it?"

Oswald kept turning the apple. "Did you ever watch something and wonder what it would be like to do it in real life?"

Wilson played along. "Sure. Everyone has. Who wouldn't want to be like John Wayne? Get the bad guy, get the girl, and ride off into the sunset happily ever after."

Oswald stopped turning his apple. "What if someone gave you the chance to be John Wayne?"

Wilson sat back. *Where is this headed?* "I'd have a lot of questions."

Oswald bit his lip. "Somebody gave me the chance to be a hero once. Back when I was a kid in New Orleans." A jagged laugh. He looked away. "Man, I really shouldn't be telling you this."

Wilson watched him wade into the Rubicon. *Be patient.*

Oswald looked at the sky. "I knew people like the ones in that TV show.

106

They did the same thing, but for real. One day, they asked me to help them."

Wilson's hopes sagged. He'd come for dirt on Ruby. On maybe de Mohrenschildt and Blaine. He didn't need cloak-and-dagger mumbo jumbo. "They were spies? Who hunted Communists?"

Oswald nodded.

Wilson took a drag. *He'll be talking about decoder rings next.*

Oswald saw his disappointment. "I can prove it. I know Dallas PD has a file on me. I'll bet you read it, haven't you?"

Wilson didn't want him making a scene. "I've read it. I know you defected to Russia, but—"

"Defected." Another forced laugh. "I didn't defect. They sent me there. Told me I'd help like I'd helped in New Orleans. Said I'd come home a hero. They lied to me. They just cut me off without a friend in the world."

Oswald kept talking. He kept proving his case. He told him what he'd done and why.

Wilson tuned him out. He didn't care. It might even be true. He'd heard crazier stories. The Chinese tried mind control experiments on American POWs during the war.

Maybe Oswald had been sent to spy on Russia. So what? It might explain how he'd gotten...

Wilson's mind seized up.

Memories of the dinner party returned. Bits from the CID files congealed.

Wilson cut him off without realizing it. "But you had friends. Friends here in Dallas. Friends who got you a job."

Wilson looked at the building behind Oswald. At the Jaggars-Chiles-Stovall Building. Oswald's building.

Oswald watched Wilson answer his own question. Oswald hung his head.

It came together fast. "George De Mohrenschildt got you the job at JSC. He got your security clearance restored."

Oswald turned the apple. "I didn't say that."

He didn't have to. "Why did he help you?"

Oswald turned the apple faster. "We know some of the same people from New Orleans. The people I told you about earlier. Who I helped when I was a kid."

Wilson grew still. Questions multiplied. Everything about Saturday night made sense. Oswald's sudden fear. De Mohrenschildt's anger at Oswald. Blaine's subtle threat. "He could've gotten you a job anywhere. Why JSC?"

Oswald swallowed hard. "It was similar to my posting in Korea. I develop pictures taken over Cuba. Security's tight, so I can't get him copies of the photos. But I tell him coordinates and dates. Stuff like that. Sometimes I draw it out from memory."

Wilson dropped his cigarette. De Mohrenschildt had quite a racket going. The Pipeline could be a leaky faucet compared to this. "Why does he want to know?"

Oswald shrugged. "He has his reasons, I guess. He doesn't tell me much."

Wilson thought fast. De Mohrenschildt was Agency-adjacent. He could've worked his contacts for Cuban information. He didn't have to. He had his own source at JSC. He had Oswald.

An old question reemerged. *Why Oswald? Why not a fresh face? Why not pick someone who could've sailed through the clearance process?*

Oswald's spy fantasy became reality. Oswald was perfect. He was a trusted hand. He'd worked for him in New Orleans.

Oswald. De Mohrenschildt. Blaine. One link outstanding. "Where does Ruby fit in?"

Oswald moaned. He tried to leave again.

Wilson grabbed his arm. He kept him on the bench. Oswald's apple rolled free. "That's why you ran away at the party. You were afraid I'd put you and Ruby together. De Mohrenschildt yelled at you because you were talking to me. Something made them afraid. It wasn't just about me, was it? It wasn't because I'm a cop. They're worried about something, aren't they?" He took a calculated leap. "Something's about to happen, isn't it?"

Oswald whimpered. He looked for his apple.

Wilson kept him on the bench. "Tell me so I can help you."

Oswald shut his eyes. "They want me to make a delivery to New Orleans on Friday night."

Finally. "What kind of delivery?"

108

Oswald relented. "Guns. Ammunition. Equipment. Stuff like that. A whole truckload of it. I'm supposed to bring it to some kind of training camp outside Lake Pontchartrain. I've brought guns here a couple of times. He wants Larry Crawford to go with me."

Wilson let him go.

That made sense. That fit.

Ruby was a gun runner from way back. His CID file proved it. The Boys had him running guns to Cuba pre-revolution. The Boys had him running guns to their liberation camps pre-Bay of Pigs.

Oswald couldn't know that. He couldn't make that up. Too many pieces fit. Pieces he didn't know about.

De Mohrenschildt's interest in Cuba fit. Oswald was his eyes on the spy plane photos. Ruby ran guns to stateside refugee camps. A second Cuban invasion beckoned.

The purpose of the camps didn't matter. The invasion angle didn't matter.

But Lake Pontchartrain mattered. Lake Pontchartrain was in Louisiana. Ruby's guns were in Dallas. The transportation and distribution of firearms across state lines violated federal laws. It carried major federal jail time.

Wilson's mouth watered. Busts like that made careers. *It could make mine.*

De Mohrenschildt was the cherry on top. He was an old CIA hand. Hoover lived for dirt on rival agencies. It gave him leverage. With leverage like this, Hoover could turn Mount Fuji into stones.

Zeke could keep his doghouse. Wilson was about to own the property.

Oswald bordered on tears. "Don't you understand? I've never seen Mr. de Mohrenschildt like this before. He never yells at me. Something about this shipment has him scared. Now I'm scared, too. I've got a wife and family. I can't go to jail. I can't stop thinking of what could happen to them if I get caught."

Wilson almost pitied him. Marina was young and pretty. Even with a kid in tow, she wouldn't be alone long.

But to Wilson, Oswald was Prince Charming. He had to keep Oswald safe. Keep him productive.

Sink the hook deep. "Do what I say and you'll never see the inside of a cell.

That's a promise."

Oswald found his apple under the bench. He picked it up. "You can't promise that."

"I just did." *Keep it simple. Too many details will scare him off.* "Have you told anyone about this? Marina? A friend?"

"Nobody." Oswald wiped the apple on his pants. "A guy named Mike Blaine might know. Mr. de Mohrenschildt tells him everything."

Bagging Blaine would be Wilson's personal trifecta. "From now on, I need you to check in with me twice a day every day. When you're at work. When you get home. Even on the drive to Louisiana. Use that same number you used today. Reverse the charges if you have to. If you're safe, tell the operator you want me to call you back. If you're in trouble, give her your number and location. Tell her you're meeting Duke there. That'll be our emergency signal. Leave that message and I'll come running."

"Duke," Oswald repeated. "From our talk at the party. But if I'm in Louisiana, how can you help me all the way from Dallas?"

"Ruby's not the only one with friends everywhere," Wilson said. "Call any time you're feeling scared or think you're in trouble. I'll come get you. Got that?"

"Yeah. But Friday's a long way off. Maybe something will change between now and then."

"Tell me if it does. We'll figure something out."

Oswald checked his watch. "Say, I've got to get back to work. My break's almost up. I don't want to get in trouble with my boss." He picked up his lunch bag and stood. "Guess I've got bigger things to worry about than my boss, don't I?"

"You don't have anything to worry about anymore. I'm on your side. I'll take care of you."

"Like you took care of that lady and her kids in Oak Cliff."

Oswald walked away. He rubbed the apple on the sleeve of his shirt. He jaywalked across the street. A taxi almost flattened him.

Wilson sighed. *Upon this rock...*

He lit another cigarette. He sat back on the bench. He drew the smoke in deep.

Possibilities abounded. Reality set in.

Zeke would never buy it. He'd laugh at Oswald's file. The kid was a headcase. A defector. A bum. The Ruby angle was far-fetched. The de Mohrenschildt angle was pure fiction. Zeke would be beyond skeptical.

But files never told the whole story. Zeke hadn't felt Oswald's fear.

Oswald was mixed up in something. But anything short of firm evidence wouldn't convince Zeke. Or Washington.

Oswald was right about something. Friday was still four long days away. A lot could happen between now and then.

Oswald needed a babysitter.

Fortunately, the best man for the job owed Wilson a big favor.

Chapter Fourteen

Tippit pulled into The Rebel Drive-In on East Ledbetter. He parked his prowler next to Wilson's Galaxie.

Wilson had hooked his boot heel on the bumper of the Ford. He watched traffic and smoked. Ray-Bans rounded out his elegant vibe.

The small pile of dead butts on the asphalt proved Wilson had been early. They meant he was nervous. Wilson only chained Luckies when he was nervous. It must be something big. Dan Wilson wasn't the worrying kind.

Tippit radioed dispatch that he was on a break. He got out.

"You remember to code out with dispatch?" Wilson asked. "You forget sometimes."

Tippit fished out a Chesterfield from his pack. "I didn't forget." He pulled out his Zippo. He remembered Wilson's reaction at Austin's. "You gonna get the vapors again if I use this? I can grab some matches."

Cars along Ledbetter reflected on Wilson's lenses. "I didn't know you saw that."

"I'm a cop." Tippit lit his cigarette. "A trained observer." He pocketed the Zippo. "How'd it go with Eastbrook?"

Wilson shrugged. "I still have my badge. Tossed in a good word for you while I was at it."

"I figured." Tippit kicked some gravel. "Haven't heard from him yet. He'd have called by now if he had something for me."

"Eastbrook's always been a deliberate boy. Give him time. I made helping you worth his while. But you might want to grab a shower before you see him. You smell worse than you look."

Tippit didn't doubt it. "The water pressure at the station is lousy. I'm sleeping on a cot in the locker room. Plays hell with my bum knee." A housewife had stabbed him with an icepick on a domestic call back in '56. He'd gotten a medal and a permanent limp for his trouble. "Damned cold weather makes it worse. I can't wait for summer."

"That makes one of us." Wilson flicked away his cigarette and lit another. "Things still raw at home?"

"I don't know. Marie won't let me in the house."

"Give her time," Wilson said. "She'll get over it. She always has before. If not for you, then for the kids."

Tippit knew this time was different. No one had gotten killed during his other dalliances. He exhaled a long stream of smoke through his nose. "Molly ain't talking to me either. The hospital said she got out this morning. I know, I know. Give her time. Everybody gets all the time they need except me. My life is just one big goddamned game of Patience."

Wilson flicked his ash. "Need a hug?"

"Up yours."

Wilson grinned. "You had your fun. Everybody pays the piper eventually."

"Thanks, reverend, but Sunday was yesterday. And you didn't call me here for a lecture on clean living."

Wilson kept eyeing traffic. "Still looking for a job?"

Tippit hated giving in to desperation. Their frank talk at Austin's had been a rare exception. A moment of weakness not to be repeated. He'd seen too many men ruin themselves in self-pity. Wallowing wasn't his style. "Depends on the job. I've already got two."

"How'd you like to make the same money for half the work?"

"I'd like it fine. Who do I have to kill?" He was only half-joking.

"Nobody. It's a babysitting gig."

"Hubba, hubba, hubba." Tippit got interested. "Who's the baby? Hope she's pretty. I'm partial to brunettes."

"He has a face like a ferret and is poorer than a church mouse. But he could be important someday."

Tippit knew Wilson didn't exaggerate. "Why?"

"I'm not sure yet. I need you on him when you're off duty. Tell me where he goes and who he meets. He's no night owl, so you can knock off once he's home, but there might be exceptions. It's simple."

"If it's so simple, why are you nervous?"

Wilson watched traffic. "Who said I'm nervous?"

"You did. You're chaining like a death row con. You're eyeballing the road like a junkie sweats a dealer. Tell me I'm wrong."

Wilson blew smoke from the corner of his mouth. "You make a good detective for a patrolman."

Tippit finished his cigarette. He ground it under his boot. "Who's the mark?"

Wilson slipped his hands into his pockets. "Lee Oswald."

Tippit recognized the name. "That square from Austin's? Why him?"

"I got curious after the argument at Austin's. My reasons don't matter. I looked up the Rambler's plate. It's registered to Michael Blaine. That's who you know from Austin's. He's just pretending to be Oswald."

Tippit hated complications. "That means Ruby knows Blaine ain't really Oswald."

"That's true."

"That means Blaine is friends with Jack Ruby."

"That's also true. Ruby's also friends with the real Lee Oswald."

Tippit almost got dizzy. "Then why's that asshole from Austin's pretending to be Oswald?"

"I don't know. That's why I need you to follow him. Like I said, it could turn out to be nothing. It could be important."

Tippit hated complications. He hated the idea of crossing Ruby even more.

Tippit fished out another cigarette and lit it. "This isn't an official investigation, is it?"

Wilson shook his head. "It could become one with your help. If it does, you'll come along for the ride."

"Yeah. We'll share the same trunk to a swamp somewhere."

Wilson frowned. "Now it's you who's getting vapors."

"You're damned right I am." Tippit half inhaled his cigarette. "Ruby works for Marcello. Do you know what happened to the last guy who crossed Marcello? He got fed to his pigs. Feet first."

"That was a mob thing. We're cops. Ruby's got half a dozen open investigations on him right now."

"Official investigations," Tippit said. "By friends of his. This ain't official."

Wilson took off his Ray-Bans. He squeezed the bridge of his nose.

Tippit saw the strain. *He hasn't thought this through. He hasn't had time. He's reacting, not thinking.*

Wilson slid his sunglasses back on. "Tail Oswald. Take notes. Where he goes. Who he sees. That's it. I've got a copy of his file in my car. If it becomes an official case, I can keep your name out of it if you want. The money's good and so is my word."

Tippit had never doubted Wilson's word. "Who's paying?"

Wilson watched cars on Ledbetter. Silence was its own answer.

Tippit tossed his cigarette. He owed Wilson. Owed him for Farley. For a lot of other things. "Give me the file."

Wilson whooped. He got behind the wheel. He handed Tippit Oswald's file.

"His pictures and relevant addresses are on the first page. I'm especially interested in whoever he meets. Ruby or Blaine in particular."

Tippit tucked the file under his arm. He'd read it later. "I'll start tailing him tonight. You'll have my report in the morning. I'll leave it in my locker. The combination is still the same."

Wilson turned the ignition key. "Hand-written notes are fine." The engine came alive. "You never could type worth a damn anyway."

Tippit leaned on the passenger door. "Tell me you know this is dangerous. Tell me you know we could get clipped."

"I don't know that." Wilson smiled. "Neither do you."

Tippit stood back. He watched Wilson drive off. A thin cloud of dust rose in its wake.

Tippit opened the file. Oswald's photo was clipped to the inside cover.

Dig those beady eyes. Check that weak chin. This boy was a bounced

115

check. The bottom of the barrel.

This boy looked cursed. Secrets swirled around him. A thin black cat on thin black ice. He'd pull everyone down with him if he fell. He had that look about him.

Tippit got back in his prowler. He still had a few minutes left on his break. He perused the rest of the file. He drew conclusions. Tippit's conclusions came up aces.

Wilson wanted Oswald protected. Oswald was impersonated by Blaine. Blaine was somehow tied to Ruby.

Tippit skipped the confusion. He didn't care about reasons. He cared about intent. He cared about one thing: Oswald was valuable.

Tippit would find out how much.

He tossed the file on the passenger seat. He grabbed the mic. He coded into dispatch and started the engine.

Officer Tippit was back on the job. And he finally had something to trade.

* * *

Wilson drove north on Highway 75. He had an errand to run. A question to answer.

He checked his mirrors for tails. He varied speeds and switched lanes. He looked for cars maintaining pace and distance.

He moved into the right-hand lane. He let traffic flow around him. No drivers looked at him. He kept checking anyway.

Questions fired as he drove. Facts and suspicions jumbled. Brief pictures formed before breaking apart.

Tippit and Duke had taught Wilson how to be a cop. Revill had taught him how to be a detective. *Organization closes cases. Organization puts bad guys behind bars.*

Wilson organized his mind as he drove. Oswald was at the eye of his brainstorm. He'd spun a strange tale. Spies and mobsters. Spy planes and spy photos. Guns and training camps. It added up to a quasi-military operation.

116

Wilson pegged those around Oswald. De Mohrenschildt was the brains. Blaine was his assistant. Ruby was the smuggler. Their operation was paramilitary. Their objective was Cuba. Wilson didn't care.

De Mohrenschildt needed guns delivered to the camps pronto. Ruby scrambled to comply. Why the rush?

Two possibilities. Something had changed at the camp. Or had something changed in Dallas?

Wilson bet it all on Dallas. Coincidences were as rare as the truth. And truth depended on one's perspective. What was happening in Dallas? General Walker's Midnight Ride Tour announcement.

The math worked. The present predicted the future. This week, CID identifies threats to Walker. Next week, Dallas PD investigates those threats. They hit the street hard. Cops kick over cages. Cops cast wide nets. Sea roaches scuttle. Bottom-feeders get snagged and dragged up. Uniforms find three types of street fauna: zealots, wannabe revolutionaries, and skels.

Zealots were smart. They kept their mouths shut. They waited for their lawyers. They'd be released with a warning.

Wannabes regurgitated pablum. *Viva Fidel! UN out of US!* They called arresting officers fascist pigs. They never knew shit. They were out by dinner time.

Skels were different. There was gold in the gutters of Dallas. Shiny nuggets of information mined by an army of the unseen. Whores, hustlers, grifters and drifters could be a detective's best friend. They traded up to get out. To get back to the streets. To their next score. To get well. Information about a truckload of guns would buy a skel's freedom quick.

Ruby needed those guns out of Dallas. De Mohrenschildt needed those guns at the camps.

The reason led only one place. The next exit on the highway.

Turtle Creek was the quiet, leafy section of North Dallas. It had stately homes on winding roads. Patrol Division considered it a dead assignment.

Wilson stopped outside 4011 Turtle Creek Boulevard. Three flags billowed in the front yard. Old Glory. The Lone Star Flag of Texas. And the Stars and Bars of the Confederacy.

Several signs dotted the lawn. GET U.S. <u>OUT</u> OF THE U.N. and KENNEDY = COMMUNISM.

Wilson braked at the curb. He didn't put it in park. He might need to get away fast.

He took his binoculars from the glove box. He worked the dial until the house was in focus.

He counted five cars in the driveway. Only two were familiar.

The black-on-white Chevy Impala from outside de Mohrenschildt's house. And the Mercury Comet from yesterday. The passenger side mirror was still missing.

Wilson lowered the binoculars. He took his pad. He wrote down the plate numbers. He underlined the Impala and Comet plates. He didn't know who owned them, but he knew who they worked for.

Wilson saw movement at the house. The front door opened. Bob Carter stepped outside. Tommy Schneider, too.

Wilson hit the gas. He checked his rearview as he rounded the corner. Carter and Schneider were in the street. They hadn't seen his plate.

Walker's men had been watching de Mohrenschildt's party. Walker's men had been following Wilson. Walker was tied to de Mohrenschildt and Ruby. Maybe even to the camps and the guns.

Wilson drove back to the office. Walker was playing a game. And it had just gotten more even.

Chapter Fifteen

Harry Denton hated bowling. He hated The Bronco Bowl. The place gave him an itch.

Seventy-eight lanes of middle-class mediocrity. Sticky floors and squeaky shoes. Beer bellies in bowling leagues. Rolling balls at a bunch of stupid pins. The stench of cheap cigars, fried food, and foot powder gagged him. The ceaseless clattering of pins, the cheering and jeering of strikes made and missed grated his nerves. *Give me the Carousel Club any time.*

Ruby was easy to spot. He was shilling his weight loss gizmo for a church bowling team. They watched him shuck and schvitz at the same time.

"Feast your eyes, boys," Ruby shouted as he twisted. "Why sit around like a bump on a log when you can move? Don't wait to lose weight! All you have to do is twist."

Ruby saw Denton. He waved him over. "There's one of my best customers right now. One of Dallas's finest. He's got three Twisters at home and just look at him. Dig that narrow waistline. Marvel at those muscles. Get that gleam in his eye and the pep in his step. I'm telling you, this thing is nothing short of a miracle. A flat-out miracle. Praise the Lord!"

The Baptist bowler howled.

Denton hated attention. He told Ruby, "Someone's waiting to see you. Let's go. Time's wasting."

Ruby climbed off his contraption with a flourish. He gave the churchmen a parting word. "Looks like I've gotta see a man about a horse, but I'll be back to take your orders. Go ahead and climb aboard. Give it a twist. You're gonna love it."

The bowlers gathered around the device. None of them touched it. They shook their heads and looked at Jack. *What a character!*

Ruby scooped up his hat and coat. Denton walked him out of the bowling alley.

Ruby shrugged into his coat. "You should've given me a couple of more minutes. I had them hooked." He plopped his hat on. "I might've lost a couple of sales in there. That how I make my living. Know what I mean?"

Denton kept him moving. Ruby didn't know people laughed at him, not with him. "The captain's waiting."

"You're a killjoy, you know that?" Ruby shrugged into his coat. He plopped his hat on his head. "A real killjoy."

Eastbrook's unmarked Galaxie was parked in the alley. A busted streetlight assured privacy.

Eastbrook had already rolled down the back seat window.

Jack doffed his hat. He scraped the ground with it. "Pardon my appearance, your eminence, but you caught me in the middle of a demonstration."

Denton leaned against the trunk. He kept an eye out for bystanders and the curious.

Eastbrook remained inside. "Been trying to reach you all day, Jack. You been avoiding my calls?"

"Never." Ruby pulled a handkerchief. He patted his brow. "Just been busy on account of Friday. I had a lot of calls to make." Ruby kept patting his brow. "Walker's announcement's loused everything up. The truck ain't even half full, and I'm doing three weeks of work in four days."

Eastbrook said, "Bannister paid for a full shipment. He'll raise hell if he don't get it. I don't want that."

Ruby laughed. "Don't worry your pretty little head about it."

Eastbrook snatched Ruby's tie. He yanked it down hard. Ruby's chin snapped off the roof. He stumbled.

Eastbrook threw the car door open. It knocked Ruby against the wall.

Eastbrook leapt out. He drew his revolver. He grabbed Ruby's collar.

Denton watched for civilians.

Eastbrook pressed his .38 under Ruby's chin. "Who do you think you're talking to, you Jew bastard. I could plug you right now and call it a suicide. No one would even bat an eye." He shook Ruby by the neck. "I'll worry my pretty little head over any goddamned thing I please."

Ruby's eyes were wide. "You're right. I'm sorry. Don't hurt me."

"You're goddamned right you're sorry." Eastbrook twisted Ruby's collar. "When I ask questions, you answer. When I call, you pick up the phone. *Sabe?*"

"I *sabe*. Lay off me, will you? I just got this suit back from the cleaners."

Eastbrook pressed the gun barrel into Ruby's cheek. "Tell me how you're fixing to fill that truck. Explain why it ain't already heading to Louisiana."

Ruby turned his head. He spat blood and sweat into the alley. "Because we aren't ready. This rush order threw everything off. A shipment from Argentina's arriving in Houston tonight."

Denton watched the parking lot. The captain wouldn't like that.

Eastbrook shook Ruby. "You were supposed to go through our man in Mexico."

"He's tapped out," Ruby whined. "I had to get creative. This shipment was heading to New York. I got Carlos to make some calls. We're getting it instead. Getting it wholesale, too."

Denton watched a Studebaker pull into the lot. It was parked on the far side. A bowling team stumbled out like it was a clown car. Their shirts had 'Murray's Garage' across the back.

Denton whispered to Eastbrook. "Civilians."

Eastbrook didn't care. "What time's the shipment getting to Houston?"

"After midnight," Ruby said. "The port's backed up, and there's a line to dock. I can't say when they'll unload. That's the truth. You can check."

Eastbrook jerked Ruby's collar. "Call my office tomorrow at eight sharp with an update. God help you if you don't."

"Anything you say. Now get off me, please. I've got sales to make in there."

Denton looked away. Ruby was a piece of work.

Eastbrook holstered his pistol. He didn't let Ruby go. "You know an Officer Tippit?"

"Sure. Helped him get a job once upon a time. What about him?"

"Find him something off the books. Parking cars, bouncing at one of your dives. I don't care what it is as long as it pays. If he doesn't take it, that's on him, but make the offer."

Eastbrook let him go. He went back in the car.

Ruby looked to Denton for sympathy. Denton closed Eastbrook's door. He got back behind the wheel. Eastbrook didn't like waiting.

Denton backed out of the alley. His headlights lit up Ruby. The fat man straightened his tie. His suit was dirty. He picked up his hat. He fixed the crease in the brim.

Denton drove away. He adjusted the rearview mirror.

He watched Eastbrook check his suit for stains. "Can you believe the balls on that fat bastard? Talking to me like I was one of his whores." The captain remembered himself. "Sorry, Harry. I didn't mean Kay. You know that."

Denton didn't think he had, but appreciated the gesture.

Eastbrook wiped his hands on a handkerchief. "I need you to stick particularly close to Ruby until he gets these guns to Bannister."

Denton stroked Eastbrook's ego. "He won't cross you again anytime soon. You sure taught him a lesson tonight. He'll mind his words from now on."

"Familiarity breeds contempt." Eastbrook wiped his hands on the handkerchief. "But he was right about Walker. That goddamned announcement of his caused us a world of trouble. We need those guns out of here before Revill's Boy Scouts hit the streets on Monday. Everything hinges on that. Everything."

Denton knew the captain. He was susceptible to talking after delivering an ass-kicking. "Why not just keep them in Houston until after the announcement? Or until you've got a full load?"

Eastbrook pocketed his handkerchief. "Because waiting is too risky, and Bannister needs them now. And Walker's people won't call off his announcement."

Denton stopped at a red light. He had to ask. "These guns have anything to do with what you said at the shooting range? About me being ready?"

Eastbrook looked out the window. "If it does, I'll tell you."

Chapter Sixteen

Thursday, February 7, 1963

T he Federal Arms. The Hotel Hoover. The apartment across from The Eat Well Diner had many nicknames.

Wilson was transcribing tapes from that morning. Special Agent Frank Marsh was at the window. He took pictures of customers coming and going.

Marsh asked his partner, "You ever work with a brave and distinguished hero like Dan Wilson before?"

Special Agent Dale Smith yawned. "Can't say that I have." He thumbed through the late edition of *The Dallas Morning News*. "It's kind of like working with Audie Murphy. One day, I'll tell my grandkids that I worked with the bravest shit-heel cop in Dallas, Texas. Might have it etched on my gravestone."

"That'll never happen." Wilson kept typing. "You'd have to get laid to have a kid."

Marsh snapped a picture. "Wilson has a point."

Smith gave them both the finger.

Wilson took a break. He flexed his hands. He cracked his knuckles. His fingers ached from typing.

Compiling General Walker's threat assessment reports was a full-time job. A full time pain in the ass, too. Walker had as many enemies as allies. Keeping them straight meant endless typing and collating.

Revill and Curry redacted DPD sources and methods from the final product. Bob Carey complained. Carey wanted sources and methods. Revill threatened to withhold the reports. Curry relented.

The general filled Wilson's days. The Pipeline dominated his nights. Fritz had been right. The Farley shooting had been forgotten by Monday. The Pipeline kept flowing. Transcripts and photo analysis continued.

Oswald had been easy. He checked in twice a day like clockwork. Tippit said he was boring. Wilson was glad. Boring was good.

Tomorrow was Oswald's big trip to the Big Easy. Oswald's day of reckoning.

Wilson hadn't told Zeke about the guns. About Oswald's trip. About the possible Walker-de Mohrenschildt-Ruby triangle.

Wilson had to be careful. He was still in Zeke's doghouse. One more mistake would bury him. Oswald was untested. He might be lying. He might be wrong. Zeke only wanted solid evidence. Wilson would have it after tomorrow.

Wilson had kept Zeke entertained. He'd fed Zeke dirt on Walker's City Hall meeting. The upcoming announcement. Hoover craved anti-Kennedy sentiment. Zeke said the report made the old man's week.

Wilson leaned back in the chair. He stretched. He pondered other worries.

He'd traced the license plates from Walker's house. Suspicions were confirmed. Bob Carter owned the black-on-white Impala from de Mohrenschildt's party on Saturday. Tommy Schneider owned the Mercury Comet that Wilson had chased on Sunday.

Carey's Impala confirmed the general's interest in de Mohrenschildt. Schneider's Comet confirmed the general's interest in Wilson.

Questions lingered. Ruby had known about Walker's tour announcement since last Friday. He'd told Oswald they'd move de Mohrenschildt's guns. *Why watch de Mohrenschildt's house? An abundance of caution? Or something deeper?*

Wilson sipped cold coffee. He focused on the transcriptions. Ruby and an unidentified male at eleven-thirty that morning. The day's surveillance photos were still drying in the bathroom. He'd look for the stranger's picture later.

Wilson hit PLAY. He increased the volume.

RUBY: (utensils scraping on plate) Would you believe it? The short-order cook here is better than any of my guys. I should hire him to work at one of my clubs, but then the food here would be lousy. Know what I mean?

MALE #1: I've got some news that won't spoil your appetite. We've selected a replacement for our mutual friend.

RUBY: (chewing) I've got lots of friends. Which one?

MALE #1: Don't be dense. How many mutual friends do we have? I'm talking about the replacement of our traveling friend.

Wilson made notes. The stranger pronounced his words. No twang. He wasn't a local. *Who are you?* Wilson turned up the volume.

RUBY: Him? That snob ain't no friend of mine. I don't care who you pick as long as he doesn't louse up the works. Our other friends wouldn't like that.

MALE #1: (Pause.) What happened to your lip? It's swollen.

Wilson made a note to check the photo. *Who hit Ruby?*

RUBY: Cut myself shaving. Tell me who's replacing Fancy Pants. Don't keep me in suspense. Gives me agita.

MALE #1: His assistant.

RUBY: That drip? He's worse than the other guy.

MALE #1: He's the only sane choice. He knows all the players. He knows how things are done. He knows what's at stake.

Wilson hit STOP. He wrote fast. *Who's leaving? Who's taking over? What is he taking over? Who's Ruby talking to?*

Wilson wished the photos were dry. He hit PLAY.

MALE #1: Like I said, we anticipate a smooth transition on all fronts.

RUBY: Some new blood might be what you need right now. My friends aren't too happy. You soldier boys have become a royal pain in our collective. *tuchas.*

Wilson didn't have to write down 'soldier'. He'd remember it. He turned the volume way up.

MALE #1: You've been compensated for the inconvenience.

RUBY: Inconvenience is nothing. It's part of the job. But rushing is different. Rushing is bad. It leads to mistakes."

MALE #1: You're paid not to make mistakes.

RUBY: (laughing) Everyone makes mistakes. That's why they're called mistakes. Shit happens. A truck might break down. One of my guys could get pinched in a random roadblock. That'd be bad for everyone. For you, worst of all.

Wilson hit STOP.

They're talking about Oswald's gun shipment.

Wilson hit PLAY.

MALE #1: The schedule change was unavoidable. You've had time to make other plans. Are there any hiccups about Friday?

RUBY: Hiccups? (Belch.) You *goyim* prick. I don't get hiccups. I cause them. I've got two good boys on it.

Sweat broke across Wilson's back.

MALE #1: The usual two?

RUBY: Different guys. (Belch.) I like to switch things around now and then. Keeps them from getting curious and comfortable. Say, what's the long puss for? I thought you guys hated patterns.

MALE #1: We hate change even more. Altering the schedule was unavoidable. We want men we can trust making this run. Who are they?

RUBY: (utensils drop. Pounding on the table.) What do you want? Names? Their draft cards? Get a load of Mr. Secrets over here wanting specifics all of a sudden.

MALE #1: Calm down. You're drawing attention.

RUBY: I always talk like this. Ask anybody. They start looking at me funny if I *don't* yell at least once a meal.

Background chatter continued. The regulars were used to Ruby's outbursts. Wilson kept listening.

MALE #1: I don't need names. Just tell me how you found them. We're too close now to be careless.

RUBY: They're good boys. They won't screw it up.

MALE #1: You're not the only one here who answers to someone.

126

RUBY: Fine, fine. And here I was thinking you California boys were supposed to be all laid back and calm. You know. 'Surfing Safari' and all that jazz? Beach Boys my aching ass.

MALE #1: Jack...

RUBY: Yeah, yeah. I know. Cool your heels. One of them's been in the game for years. He's made a few runs before. Don't take my word for it. Ask Fancy Pants. He'll vouch for him.

Wilson hit STOP. They were talking about Oswald.

'Fancy Pants' was de Mohrenschildt. That means de Mohrenschildt is leaving Dallas. *Why?*

Wilson hit PLAY.

MALE #1: I think I know who you mean. He's acceptable. And the other?

RUBY: Knocks around my clubs. Does whatever I tell him. Treats my kids like they're his own. He's solid. He's from California, too, but not as buttoned down as you. He's more of a salt-of-the-earth type. Know what I mean?

Wilson hit STOP. *Score another one for Oswald.* He'd said Crawford would be making the run with him. Crawford was from California, just like Male #1.

Male #1 was from California. He was a soldier. He was linked to Walker. He sounded like Schneider. The surveillance photos would confirm it.

Wilson hit PLAY.

RUBY: (Belch). Again with the agita. Every time we talk, my gut acts up. And I was doing good with my diet, too. Losing weight. Feeling great. My clothes were getting big on me. Then you come along and I fall apart. Goddamned *tsuris.* That's what you are.

MALE #1: Maybe more time on that Twister contraption will help.

RUBY: (laughs) You heard about that, huh? Jesus, you guys...

MALE #1: We hear everything, Jack.

RUBY: Yeah, well, fitness advice from a scarecrow like you is another thing I don't need. Say, you want some pie? They've got the best Key Lime Pie this side of the Keys.

MALE #1: Tempting, but I'm needed back at the office. Let me know how things go this weekend. Talk Sunday evening?

RUBY: Yeah, yeah. Sure. Now get out of here before you ruin my dessert. (Fingers snap) Hey, Helen. How about a cup of coffee and a slice of pie? And don't be skimpy this time.

Wilson hit STOP. He tossed off the headphones. He rolled away from the desk. He asked the agents, "Which one of you caught the unidentified male talking to Ruby this morning?"

"That was me." Marsh snapped another picture. "I was covering for Smith while he was in the john. He spent half the morning in there. I told him to cut back on the coffee, but he never listens."

Smith didn't look up from the funny pages. "No one listens to you."

Wilson had no time for banter. "You get pictures?"

"Going in and coming out," Marsh said. "Didn't look familiar. Didn't get a good shot of him walking in, but the one of him leaving might have his face."

Wilson asked Smith, "Think the pics are dry?"

"Should be. I'll check in a minute."

Wilson went to the bathroom. That day's surveillance pictures were drying on clotheslines Smith had rigged up over the tub. A red bulb the only light.

Smith had a system. He developed photos in the exact order they'd been taken. He matched them to surveillance log entries.

Wilson remembered the log. Ruby's conversation with MALE #1 had been at 11:30 AM.

Wilson looked at the late morning shots. He saw Ruby entering the diner. A white male in a fedora and raincoat followed. The collar of his coat up.

They took a booth. The stranger kept his hat on. Kept his collar up. Kept his back to the window.

Wilson skipped to the later pictures, of the stranger leaving the diner. Wilson pulled it off the clothesline. He studied it beneath the red light.

The man had kept his head down, his face obscured. *Shit.*

Smith called to him from outside. "Find anything?"

Wilson brought the photo with him. He looked at it under normal light.

128

The stranger's face was hidden. But he recognized the hat. The overcoat. The driver he'd chased in Oak Cliff on Sunday morning.

Ruby had called the man a soldier. Ruby had said the man was from California. Ruby said the soldier from California had ties to General Walker.

Wilson knew it had to be Tommy Schneider. He had to prove it.

Wilson handed the photo to Smith. "Can you blow this up? I want a better look at his face."

Smith forgot about his newspaper. He took the loupe hanging from his neck. He set the photo on the table. He moved the loupe over the image. "He's wrapped up like 'The Invisible Man'. He didn't want to be photographed. I'll send the whole set to Washington. See if they can draw up a composite." He looked up from the loupe. "Might take a couple of days, though."

"I'll take it whenever you get it." He showed the picture to Marsh at the window. "Did you get any snaps of him getting in his car?"

Marsh glanced at it. "Nope. He didn't park in the lot or on the street. He walked here from the north. Left in that direction. Stayed hunched over the whole time. I saw him in the diner. He moved like he could take care of himself. He's a crafty one, isn't he?"

Wilson handed the photo back to Smith. "Yeah, but we're craftier."

* * *

Connie smoked an L&M. She watched her husband finish his breaded chicken. She enjoyed a smoke with her evening coffee.

"You look tired, but good," she said. "How are things at work?"

"Better." These late dinners were their quiet time together. "You still watching for anyone following you?"

"Like a hawk. Haven't seen a soul."

Wilson changed the subject. "I saw Jack Revill today. He sends his regards."

"He's a charmer, that one." Connie smiled as she tapped her ash in the ashtray. Everyone liked Jack. "Have you seen JD this week?"

"Marie kicked him out. He's been sleeping at the precinct. Showering

129

there, too."

"I can't say that I blame her," Connie said. "But I hate the idea of him sleeping on a cot in that drafty old precinct. We can make room for him here. The kids would love to see him."

"I offered, but you know him. Stoic to a fault."

"Except where curvy brunettes are concerned."

Wilson smiled. "Makes me glad you're a blonde." He felt a tug on his shoe. He looked beneath the table. Missy was gnawing on his shoelace. She looked up and licked her chops, then resumed her attack.

"This cat has an obsession with my shoes."

"She's just playful," Connie said, "Poor thing spends half the day hiding. Though she's started coming into the hall to watch the kids and I eat dinner. That's progress."

"Cook up your Shrimp Surprise. That'll bring her running."

"Your daughter hates shrimp, remember?" Connie remembered something. She quickly patted his hand. "That reminds me. No more dinner parties at the de Mohrenschildt's."

Wilson stopped chewing. "Why not?"

"They've put their house on the market. Kim told me when I dropped off the kids this morning. I drove by their place after I picked up the kids. Saw the realtor sign for myself."

Wilson remembered the tapes. Ruby and the stranger at the diner. De Mohrenschildt wasn't long for Dallas.

Connie frowned at his reaction. "Don't look so disappointed. You had a miserable time at their party, not that I can blame you. All those poor Russian girls are old before their time. And the meringue on Mrs. Holland's Baked Alaska was bitter. The Jell-O was tasteless. I still can't understand how anyone could ruin Jell-O."

Wilson didn't care about desserts. "Any idea on where they're going?"

"The de Mohrenschildts?" Connie thought about it. "Somewhere south. Tahiti maybe? Or is it Haiti? Which one's closer?"

Wilson wiped his mouth on his napkin. "Haiti."

"That's it. Serves me right for being bad at geography."

Wilson set his napkin on the table. Haiti was near Cuba.

Oswald had told him about the camps. About a second invasion of Cuba. Of de Mohrenschildt's interest in Cuba.

Son of a bitch. Everything Oswald had told him fit. It was independently verified.

Connie squeezed his hand. "Is the chicken okay? Maybe I left it out too long."

"It's fine." He quickly took her hand in his. "Kim tell you how she found out about the de Mohrenschildts?"

Connie said, "One of the girls on the refugee committee told her. I don't know which one. Why? Did I say something wrong? You look awful."

"It's nothing." Wilson faked a smile for her sake. "Guess the memory of your Shrimp Surprise still haunts me."

She tapped him on the nose. "Brat." She got up to clear the plates. "Hope you've left room for some Jell-O. And not the flavorless kind, either. I still don't know how that woman managed to ruin Jell-O. The directions are right there on the box."

Wilson decided his bad news about the weekend could wait. New Orleans beckoned.

Chapter Seventeen

Friday, February 8, 1963

Eastbound on Highway 190.

Wilson trailed Oswald's truck from ten cars back. The truck was white and easy to spot. Traffic was steady. New Orleans was still seven hours away.

Tippit's Studebaker Lark handled like a pig. The alignment was shot. The tires were balder than Yul Brynner. The engine strained to maintain speed. Wilson hoped it didn't fall apart before Lake Pontchartrain. Or at Lake Pontchartrain. Or on their way back.

He checked the mirrors. Same story all week. Nobody there.

Tippit rode shotgun. Cartons of Luckies and Chesterfields sat between them.

Tippit lit a Chesterfield. "Are we there yet?"

Wilson watched the road. "It wasn't funny the first five times you said it. Still isn't."

Tippit flexed his aching knee. "Thanks for driving. This thing's been aching something awful."

Wilson was glad Tippit agreed to join him. He didn't know what they'd find at Lake Pontchartrain. Bum knee aside, JD was good in a fight. "Grab some sleep. I'll wake you when it's your turn to drive."

Tippit stretched and yawned. "You said this camp is near Lake Pontchartrain."

"Yeah." Wilson watched the highway.

"Lots of militia out that way," Tippit said. "Klan. Minutemen, too."

Wilson didn't care. He had to confirm the camp existed. Its use wasn't important. "Hope you packed heavy."

"Heavy enough." Tippit patted his camp shirt above his right hip. "Got Mabel right here and my 870 in the trunk. Brought a couple of boxes of rounds for each in case things get interesting."

'Mabel' was his Colt .45 automatic. The Remington 870 pump was Tippit's favorite shotgun. Tippit kept them both under lock and key at home. "Marie let you get them?"

Tippit soured. "I snuck in last night after she and the kids fell asleep. I was in and out before they knew I was there."

Wilson wished he hadn't asked. "Sorry."

Tippit looked out at the blurring scenery. "You really think Ruby's got Oswald running guns to New Orleans?"

Wilson didn't think. He knew. He couldn't tell JD how he knew. He couldn't risk The Pipeline. "I wouldn't be following him if I didn't."

Tippit took another drag. "The kid's a drip. Eats his lunch alone in the park. Gnaws apples. Looks at squirrels, but not girls. Never has a beers after work. Heads home to the family every night."

"Most people do." Wilson grinned. "Present company excluded, of course."

"Up yours." Tippit gave him both middle fingers. "Ruby hiring Oswald to make this run doesn't add up. Oswald's a snooze, and the other guy's a freak. What's his name again?"

"Crawford. Larry Crawford."

"Bastard blinks all the time. Like he's sending Morse code or something. Makes me anxious."

"We don't have to look at him. We just have to follow him."

Tippit flicked his cigarette out the window. "Never known you to take a snitch's word as gospel. Not without corroboration."

Wilson acted like he hadn't heard him. He hoped he'd let it go.

Tippit shook loose another Chesterfield and lit it. "Now might be a good time for you to tell me you're working for the feds."

Wilson swerved over the line. A car in the left lane hit the horn. Wilson stayed in his lane.

Tippit took a drag. "At least you didn't deny it." He sounded resigned, not angry. "Ask me how I know."

Wilson thought fast. "JD, I—"

Tippit said, "It started that night at Austin's. You didn't look up that plate because the argument caught your attention. You looked up the plate because Lee's name caught your attention. Because you'd heard it as part of another investigation. Just not a CID investigation."

Wilson's gut tightened. *Shit.*

Tippit kept talking. "That story about needing more proof to open an investigation? That sealed it for me. Revill would let you CID boys run down any hunches you have. I'll bet he doesn't even know we're here, does he?"

Wilson's gut went from tight to squeezed.

"I didn't think so." Tippit went on. "Because if Revill knew, you would've signed out weapons from the armory. That's why you brought your own guns instead. That's why we're using my car to trail Oswald instead of your Galaxie. Eastbrook checks the mileage on all DPD cars. You don't want him seeing the odometer jump after a Louisiana round trip."

Wilson thought about pulling over. *Triple shit.*

Tippit was on a roll. "Don't get me started on the other questions I've got. Like why a Dallas detective is following guns out of city limits and across state lines. With no state police or federal boys to back us up."

Wilson had to salvage this. "JD…"

Tippit held up one finger. "You'd never take a sixteen-hour round trip on a snitch's word. He held up a second finger. "That means you know there are guns in that truck." He held up a third finger. "You're paying me out of your own pocket, and you brought your own guns along. That means all this is unofficial." He held up a fourth finger. "You could be working for one of Ruby's competitors, but you're too damned honest to be crooked." He held up a fifth finger. "You hate the state police, so that leaves the feds."

Wilson's mouth went dry. He hadn't been as careful as he'd thought.

Tippit watched him through his smoke. "I don't blame you for holding out on me, but don't lie to me. I don't deserve that."

Oswald's delivery truck had a twelve-car lead. Wilson had lost pace. "You tell anyone else about this?"

Tippit blew smoke. "Don't be a dope."

Wilson couldn't admit it. He'd risk The Pipeline if he did. He couldn't deny it. He'd lose Tippit's trust when he might need it most.

Wilson split the difference. *Admit to something to protect everything.*

"I'm not working for the feds," Wilson lied. "Not yet. Oswald's name came up in a related CID investigation of Ruby. But this goes way beyond Ruby. I'm talking about his job at JCS."

"Oswald a spy?" Tippit laughed until he coughed.

"He's running guns for Ruby," Wilson said. "Selling secrets is a lot easier."

"Then feed him to the feds and get a pat on the head."

Wilson framed it so Tippit would understand. "Not until I know I have something. If I can spin Oswald's straw into gold, it might lead to a spot with the feds. That could be good for both of us."

Tippit took a drag. "Not in a million years. Not even before that Molly stuff. I'm a beat cop with a bum knee who barely made it out of high school."

Wilson tried to lighten the mood. "Maybe not the FBI, but I could get you something else. Maybe a ranger in Angelina National Forest. You could watch squirrels like your buddy Oswald."

Tippit tossed his cigarette out the window. "That's as close to the truth as you'll get, ain't it?"

Wilson didn't risk another lie. He watched Oswald's truck. He tried to maintain a steady distance.

"Serves me right for asking a direct question." Tippit slid down in the seat. He shut his eyes. "Quit gabbing and let me get some sleep. You talk too much."

Wilson was more than happy to oblige.

* * *

Tippit shoved Wilson awake. "Wake up. Show's starting."

Wilson didn't know the time. The sky was pre-dawn bright.

The taillights from Oswald's delivery truck flared up ahead. It turned left off the roadway.

Tippit killed his headlights. He made the same turn. The dirt road was uneven. He watched Oswald's taillights bob up and down.

Reeds and brush scraped the sides. Divots and tree roots rattled the Studebaker. Wilson thought they'd cracked an axle. But Tippit's car kept rolling through the overgrowth.

Wilson saw Oswald's truck stop fifty yards ahead. Its headlights lit up a six-foot-high barbed wire fence. They revealed a ten-foot-high gate.

Tippit eased on the brake. He killed the engine. They'd moved the shotguns from the trunk to the back seat when they'd switched positions.

Wilson took his binoculars from the glove box. He slipped the strap over his head. He and Tippit got out together. They left the doors open.

Tippit retrieved the shotguns from the back seat. Wilson focused his binoculars on Oswald's truck. The gate was still closed.

Tippit handed Wilson his shotgun. Wilson took point. He stuck to the cleared portion of the dirt path. It was still dark enough to conceal them on the road.

Wilson crouched behind the thick trunk of a rotted willow tree. Oswald's truck was thirty yards ahead. Tippit stopped. He kept watch.

Wilson saw Oswald at the fence. He looked up the dirt road toward the camp. Crawford smoked a cigarette.

Wilson heard the familiar whine of a jeep rattling in the darkness. He gestured for Tippit to get down.

Circular headlights bobbed from the other side of the gate.

Sweat broke out across Wilson's back. Not just from the Louisiana humidity. He peered through the binoculars. The jeep's brakes squealed to a stop. He watched as four men stepped out. Wilson studied each closely. He didn't have a camera. He'd need to describe them in detail later.

The man opening the padlock would be hard to forget. He was five-six and decked out in Foreign Legion fatigues. Tufts of orange hair stuck out from under a maroon beret. His eyebrows looked like they'd been drawn with a black marker.

Oswald helped the clown push the gate open. The other three approached Crawford and the truck.

The leader was square-faced. His graying hair was swept back. His army surplus fatigues bore no insignias. His pants were tucked into his boots. A .45 holstered on his hip.

The other two also wore army surplus. They had dark complexions. Wilson took them for Cuban. Their AK-47s were Russian.

More sweat streaked down Wilson's back. Oswald had been right.

Oswald and Crawford led the four newcomers to the rear of the truck.

The square man's voice carried on the night wind. "Have any trouble finding the place?"

Crawford said, "We're here, ain't we?"

Oswald flinched.

The square man said something to the Cubans. They opened the tailgate. They climbed inside.

The square man asked Crawford, "Think you could find this place again? Find it without Lee helping you?"

"Probably." Crawford was sassy. A far cry from the meek mouse who'd tended to Ruby's mutts. "It ain't an easy place to find."

The square man pinned Crawford's head against the truck. The square man drew his sidearm. He jammed it against Crawford's cheek.

Oswald shied away.

The clown shouted, "Guy! What are you doing? He's with us."

Wilson heard that. The square man was 'Guy.'

Guy kept Crawford pinned. He pressed the .45 against Crawford's cheek. "You want to live? Forget this place. Forget what you delivered and when. Forget everything you see here. Don't defy me. You'll be a short time talking and a long time dying. Understand?"

"Yes, sir." Wilson saw Crawford's pants leg began to darken. The moron had pissed himself. "I know how to keep my mouth shut."

Guy pushed Crawford toward Oswald. Guy told the Cubans, "Make sure it's all there, boys.

Oswald attended to Crawford, but didn't get too close.

The clown pulled Guy aside. "Was that necessary? He pissed himself, for Chrissake."

Guy holstered his sidearm. "Got the message, didn't he? Certitude is important, David. You know that."

The clown had a name. David.

David folded his arms. "You can't show up and start slapping my people around. This is my camp, not yours."

Wilson grinned. One name down. *Guy Bannister.* He'd check the files when they got back to Dallas.

Wilson watched Bannister grow still. "You only run this camp because we let you run it. Keep running your mouth, and that'll change."

The Cubans climbed down from the truck. One said something to Bannister before shutting the tailgate.

Bannister followed the Cubans back to the jeep. "Let's get this show rolling. Lee, you and your buddy ride with me. The air will do you both some good. Ferrie and the others will take care of the gate and drive the truck. We'll get you two a meal. Maybe some dry britches before you head back."

Wilson had the clown's full name, too. *David Ferrie.*

Oswald and Crawford joined Bannister in the jeep.

Wilson watched Ferrie walk beside the truck as it rolled through the gate.

Ferrie stopped as he pulled the gate closed. He looked into the darkness. In Wilson's direction. Like he'd sensed something.

Wilson hadn't moved. Neither had Tippit.

Ferrie's painted eyebrows rose as he locked the gate. He jumped on the running board of the truck. The truck moved back to camp.

Wilson waited until the truck's taillights disappeared behind a bend in the road.

Tippit followed Wilson as they got back to the Studebaker.

Wilson got behind the wheel. "How much did you see and hear?"

"I saw those AK-47s. Don't see too many of those back home."

Wilson hadn't seen one since Korea. He started up the engine. "Get in. I'm driving back."

Tippit got in the passenger side. "Ain't we stopping off to grab some shuteye? We've been driving for eight hours straight."

Wilson tossed him the shotgun. "Sleep in the back seat. I need to get my head around some things."

Wilson threw the Studebaker in reverse. They backed out the pocked dirt road. He repeated 'David Ferrie' and 'Guy Bannister' in his mind. He couldn't forget those names.

Wilson checked his watch. They'd make it back to Dallas around mid-afternoon. Connie and the kids weren't expecting him back until Sunday. Plenty of time to read Bannister and Ferrie's CID files.

Wilson avoided most of the divots as he backed up to the main road. He headed back toward Dallas.

Damn you, Lee. You told the truth.

Chapter Eighteen

Saturday, February 9, 1963

Captain Fritz's den smelled of old books and leather. Of whiskey and conversation.

A small desk lamp cast the captain in an uneasy light. His glasses off and his eyes closed, he resembled a tired Buddha as he absorbed Wilson's report. He'd missed attending the new Kirk Douglas film with his family for this. He loved Kirk Douglas movies.

He'd hated what Wilson told him. Tippit. Oswald. De Mohrenschildt. Blaine. The general. The reverend. Bannister. Ferrie. Guns. Camps. Cuba.

When his godson stopped talking, Fritz opened his eyes. "That all of it?"

"Yeah." Wilson sipped some of Fritz's bourbon. The burn soothed his dry throat. It dulled his growing headache.

After New Orleans, Wilson had hit the CID file room. He'd dug into Guy Bannister's file. He'd dug into David Ferrie's file. They offered disturbing clarity. They offered perspective. Disturbing possibilities.

Wilson needed a cigarette. But Mrs. Fritz forbade smoking in her house. "What do you make of it, Uncle Billy?"

"Where to begin?" Fritz cleaned his glasses with his tie. "Involving Tippit was a mistake. He saw Bannister and Ferrie. He heard what they said." Fritz put on his glasses.

"I needed someone to watch Oswald," Wilson said. "He was my only choice."

"He's a desperate man, and his judgment is lousy. If he breathes a word of this to Ruby, we're finished."

"Tippit wouldn't do that."

"Smart people get awfully stupid when money's involved. And Tippit's not a smart man."

Wilson knew Tippit. "He's too afraid of Ruby to say anything. And I'm taking care of JD on the financial end."

"I wish he was our only concern." Fritz frowned deeply. "You should've told me about the rest of it sooner. About Oswald and the rest of it. You've got poor Connie carrying a pistol, for God's sake."

The bourbon dulled the sting of Fritz's rebuke. "I was trying to keep it contained until I had proof."

Fritz squinted at him. "You left your wife and children alone to follow a gun shipment to New Orleans. What if you'd been killed? What if you'd broken your leg watching the camp? No one would've known where you were or why you were there. We might never have found you. Did you even consider that?"

Wilson focused on the positive. "It was worth the risk. I had to know Oswald was telling the truth. Now we have another set of eyes on Ruby's organization and beyond. Our own eyes besides The Pipeline. Zeke only cares about Ruby and Eastbrook. But if we reveal this camp to the FBI at exactly the right time, we can make the feds back off Dallas PD."

"It won't be that simple." Fritz held up one of the files Wilson had brought. "I know Guy Bannister. Your daddy knows him, too. He was Hoover's best Red hunter after the war. Ran the FBI's Chicago Field Office, then worked for New Orleans PD after he retired." He tossed the file on his desk. "Big drinker, too. Surprised he ain't dead by now."

Fritz picked up another file. He read the tab. "David Ferrie. I don't know him."

Wilson gave him broad strokes. "A pilot for Eastern Airlines until he got busted for moral deviance back in '61. Flies for the CIA from time to time. Mostly to the Caribbean and Central America, which fits our Cuba angle. Been working on and off for Bannister for years."

Fritz took off his glasses. He rubbed his eyes. "Quite a cast of characters. Bannister the Fed. Ferrie the Fairy. Oswald the Stooge. De Mohrenschildt the Spy. Ruby the Pimp. Add a couple of dancing girls and we'd have a vaudeville act. And all of it ties back to New Orleans. The heat drives men mad."

Wilson added another fact from the file. "Oswald was in Ferrie's Civil Air Patrol unit in New Orleans. I think Ferrie introduced Oswald to Bannister."

Fritz popped on his glasses. He leaned back in his chair. "You're an old Army man. You worked intelligence. What do you make of this mess? Be candid."

Wilson gave him the condensed version. "Ruby and de Mohrenschildt are running guns from Dallas to Ferrie and Bannister's training camp in New Orleans. I don't care why. I only care that we can use it to make ourselves well in the bargain."

"Still dreaming of a corner office in Washington, aren't you?" Fritz didn't wait for an answer. He ran his fingers along the edge of his desk. "If that's the case, take my advice. Forget this business entirely."

Wilson blinked. "What business?"

"This." Fritz waved a hand over the files. "The camp, the guns, Bannister, Ferrie, Oswald. All the other characters. Forget it entirely. It's a federal matter. It's beyond our purview. If you want to help the department and yourself, limit your efforts to The Pipeline."

Wilson set his glass down. "You can't mean that. Not after all we know."

"Knowledge isn't just about information, Danny. It's about wisdom. Everyone you've mentioned tonight is possibly connected to the FBI or the CIA. I know for a fact that Bannister has always had Hoover's ear. What if Hoover knows about Bannister's camp? What if the CIA runs it? What if it's part of another Cuban invasion? They won't pat you on the head for finding it. They won't reward you for being clever. They'll crucify both of us. They'll destroy your career. We'll lose any influence over The Pipeline. The department will be in more peril than ever."

Wilson's head spun. His eyes swam. It wasn't from the bourbon.

Fritz had flattened him. The old man's fear wrecked his hard work. His plans.

Wilson's disappointment in Fritz ran soul deep. Knowledge is about more than information and wisdom. Knowledge is also about the courage to use it. Like Hoover used it. Information as leverage. Security. The future.

Old men didn't care about the future. They wanted peace. To become lotus eaters and pray for fate's benevolence.

Fritz read Wilson's expression. "I know this ain't what you wanted to hear, son. The truth is never easy. Go home to that pretty little wife waiting for you in that beautiful home and tuck your perfect children to bed. And when you wake up in the morning, you'll see I'm right."

Fritz took the files in both hands. He handed them to Wilson. "Being right about something ain't enough. It's a bitter pill to swallow, but good medicine."

Wilson took the files. He set them on his lap. Words failed him.

Fritz went to the bar. He retrieved the bourbon. "Cheer up. Zeke said Hoover loved your Walker dirt. That'll earn us some points with Washington."

His uncle's homespun platitudes added insult to injury. Wilson didn't want to win points. He wanted to be the one who doled out the points.

Wilson realized he was no different than Oswald. Oswald was Wilson's informant. Wilson was Fritz's informant. A useful tool for Fritz's aims. The protection of Dallas PD. Of Fritz's legacy within it. Wilson's dreams be damned.

Fritz filled Wilson's glass. He set the decanter on the blotter. He clinked his glass with Wilson's. "Here's to clarity. There's nothing in the world like it."

"To clarity." Wilson drank. *I'm worse than Oswald. I'm in this alone.*

Chapter Nineteen

Sunday, February 10, 1963

Wilson's late-night call had killed Tippit's sleep. His order was clear. *Get to the butcher shop. Wait for Oswald and Crawford to return from New Orleans. See where they go.*

Tippit didn't complain. He needed the money. He'd been dozing in his Studebaker when

Oswald and Crawford returned after dawn. They left the delivery truck at the butcher shop. They'd hopped into Ruby's Oldsmobile. They went to Ruby's apartment. Tippit had followed at a respectable distance.

He'd parked half a block away. Two-Twenty-Three South Ewing was three floors of middle-class mediocrity. Ruby played house with an aging dress salesman named George Senator. Ruby's dancers had nothing to fear from their Uncle Jack.

Tippit flicked his ash out the window. He flexed his aching knee. He'd been parked for over an hour. No sign of anyone in or out since.

He bet George had cooked up a nice breakfast. Steak and eggs and all the trimmings. Tippit had fought a roach for a stale doughnut from the break room. His stomach growled. He fed it with cold coffee.

Tippit watched. He waited. An idle mind was the devil's workshop. Old memories filtered through. Tippit had passed Molly's house while following Crawford and Oswald to Ruby's. The windows and doors were boarded over. Shreds of carpet and flooring littered the overgrown lawn. No sign of Molly or the boys. No sign of life. Only dark memories of death and destruction. Of what he'd lost. Molly had disappeared.

Maria had begun to thaw a bit. She hadn't hung up when he'd called after New Orleans. She'd even let the kids come to the phone.

He tried to forget New Orleans. He'd seen behind a curtain he shouldn't have known was there. He'd heard things best left unheard. The bayous of The Big Easy were a long way from The Big D. Let Wilson figure it out.

Tippit saw Ruby strut down the stone steps of his apartment building. He whistled like he didn't have a care in the world.

Tippit expected him to go right. To where Crawford had parked his Oldsmobile.

Ruby went left. Toward Tippit's Studebaker.

Tippit slid low. His aching knee complained.

Ruby opened the passenger door. He sat beside Tippit.

"Hey, kid." He grunted as he pulled the door shut. "Fancy meeting you here. Figured you'd be in church, what with this being Sunday and all."

Tippit knew Ruby's temper. The fat man was stronger and faster than he looked. Tippit could take him on the street. The close confines of the car made it even money.

Tippit had left his .45 in his locker. He had a .38 stashed in his right boot. Ruby would see if he went for it. "What are you doing, Jack?"

Ruby laughed. "I live here, dummy. What are *you* doing here?"

Ruby produced a small pocketknife. He started cleaning his fingernails. "Relax. You ain't in trouble. I ain't even sore at you. I'm just curious."

Tippit worked out an escape plan. *Open the door. Fall into the road. Pull the .38 and fire.* "Curious about what?"

"About why you were tailing my friends." He held up a finger. "And don't lie."

Shit. "I didn't know I was easy to spot."

Ruby grinned. "Crawford's an old wheel man from way back. He notices things like that. Force of habit." He took a closer look at a hangnail on his thumb. "I'm still waiting for your answer. I'm an impatient man."

Tippit went for the .38 in his boot.

Ruby grabbed his wrist. He locked Tippit's arm in place. The short blade of his pocketknife pressed under Tippit's right eye.

Tippit froze.

Ruby stank of hot sauce and peppers. "You followed Crawford to New Orleans. You came back early to see where he went." Ruby's grip grew tighter. "Lie to me again, and I'll shove this through your eye. I'll take your gun and make it look like a suicide. Who are you working for? The feds?"

Ruby had Tippit off balance. He couldn't go for the knife. "I'm not working for anyone."

Ruby answered his own question. "The feds wouldn't use you. They only like smart boys. College boys like your old partner Wilson." Ruby got used to that idea. "He helped you with Hal Farley."

Tippit swallowed again. "How'd you know about that?"

Ruby lowered his blade. His grip on Tippit held. "Answer my question. Who are you working for?"

Tippit tried to limit the damage. "I don't know anything about New Orleans. Wilson asked me to wait for Crawford to show up at the butcher shop and follow him afterward."

Ruby's grip tightened. "Why?"

"He didn't say why, and I didn't ask. I owe him for Farley, just like you said. I followed them here, then you showed up. That's all."

Ruby pulled Tippit's wrist up. He placed it on the steering wheel. "Both hands up there where I can see them."

Tippit did it.

Ruby moved the pocketknife to his left hand. "Wilson investigating me?"

"Never. He didn't say where Crawford was going. I didn't know myself until I followed him here."

Ruby examined the fingernails of his right hand. "What'll you tell Wilson?"

Tippit kept his hands on the wheel. "You tell me."

Ruby stopped with his fingernails. "You gettin' smart with me?"

"Smart enough to not cross you. I don't know why Wilson wanted Crawford followed. I don't care. You do. Tell me what to tell him, and it's done."

Ruby grunted. He went back to his fingernails. "How did Wilson know where to find Crawford?"

"He didn't say. He knew I'd seen Crawford around."

Ruby kept cleaning his nails. "And the guy who was with Crawford?"

Tippit hoped he was a good actor. "Never saw him before."

"Rats," Ruby huffed. "This city's full of rats. Can't hardly spit without hitting one." He closed the pocketknife. "What does Wilson want you doing next?"

Tippit didn't have to lie. "Tail Crawford home, I guess. He didn't give a lot of instructions." He made it sound more innocent. "It sounded like he hadn't thought it through. Like it was last minute."

"Don't worry about Crawford." Ruby held up the pocketknife. "You and me square? You going for that gun in your boot again?"

"If we're square, I won't have to."

Ruby pocketed the knife. He tossed car keys in Tippit's lap. "Crawford's got the rest of the day off. You're gonna drive me around. Maybe we'll figure out what you'll tell Wilson later. Know what I mean?"

Tippit picked up the keys to the Oldsmobile. He saw the .38 Colt Cobra in Ruby's lap. He'd wanted Tippit to see it.

"From here on in, I own you, cowboy. You don't work for Wilson. You don't work for Eastbrook. You're mine. You do what I say. You'll make a lot of money. You tell Wilson whatever I want you to tell him. You'll make even more money."

Tippit didn't doubt it.

Ruby pocketed the piece as he got out. "Leave this pile of junk here. Maybe you'll get lucky and someone'll steal it. We'll take my car instead. After all, a man like me has an image to protect. Know what I mean?"

Tippit got out of his Studebaker and locked it. He moved the gun from his boot to his pocket. Just in case.

* * *

Harry Denton nursed his beer while the band set up. Ruby was over two hours late. Probably on the nod while the pills wore off. The fat bastard popped them like candy. He wouldn't lose weight the old-fashioned way. Jack always took the shortcut.

Zeke the bartender made for lousy company. He took pride in being a drip when Ruby wasn't around. "You want another? That one's warm."

Denton was bored. He tried to get a rise out of him. "Maybe I like warm beer."

Zeke moved on. "Suit yourself."

"What the hell's that supposed to mean?"

Zeke kept wiping. "It means suit yourself."

Denton resented contempt from bartenders. "You don't like me, do you?"

Zeke kept wiping. "I don't get paid to like people. I get paid to pour drinks and chat up customers. *Paying* customers. I don't get paid to let two-bit pipsqueaks with badges pick fights with me. You want a fight? Slug a stumblebum in an alley. Just get off my back."

Zeke tossed his rag under the bar. He went backstage.

Denton thought about following him. He remembered Kay was back there getting ready. They'd been fighting all weekend. He hoped the rouge covered the bruise on her cheek. She'd gotten mouthy lately. Just like everyone in his life.

Eastbrook had been different since the Farley killing. Secretive. Edgy. Talking around things instead of stating them plain. Cautious to the point of paranoia.

Eastbrook had gone too far with Ruby. Joe Campisi called the day after. Told him to stop by when he had time. Denton drove him to Campisi's Egyptian Lounge that night. Eastbrook went in tall. He came out pale. Denton didn't say a word.

Eastbrook had been on edge all weekend. New Orleans weighed heavy. The camp needed those guns. Everyone needed those guns out of Dallas before Revill's men got busy.

Eastbrook had called Ruby all day. Ruby hadn't picked up the phone. Ruby hadn't returned Eastbrook's calls. Ruby thumbed his nose. Ruby's silence said '*Fuck You*'.

Eastbrook sent Denton to look for him.

Denton sipped some warm beer. He pondered a change. Moving away from Eastbrook, but closer to Ruby. Share Dallas PD business sans Eastbrook's permission. Build good will with The Boys.

He checked his watch again. The Jew prick was almost three hours late. Making a good Christian wait wasn't right. There should be a law. Maybe one day there would be.

Denton heard the door open downstairs. He heard Ruby say, "Take them cases upstairs. Zeke will tell you where he wants them."

Denton saw the cases of Cutty Sark coming up the stairs first. He thought Crawford was lugging them. But it was JD Tippit.

Tippit didn't belong. He wasn't a Posse man. He was less than a nobody. He was Dan Wilson's pal.

Tippit laid the cases of scotch on the bar. "Zeke around?"

Denton wanted answers. "What are you doing here?"

Tippit looked past him. He looked around the bar. He was about to go backstage.

Denton grabbed his arm.

Tippit backhanded him across the mouth.

Denton stumbled. He knocked over two stools. He grabbed the bar rail. His leg almost buckled.

The boys in the band stifled giggles.

Denton heard Ruby yelling. "What the hell is wrong with you?" He looked at the beer. "Are you tight?"

Denton felt his lip. His fingers came away bloody. "You're not answering calls. You've been warned about that."

Ruby steered Denton toward the door. "Tell him it went off fine. Everyone's happy." He pushed him toward the stairs. "Get going. I don't want you here. It's too hard on the furniture."

Denton didn't like being dismissed. He didn't like that Tippit was allowed to stay.

Denton took his time going downstairs.

He heard Ruby complain as he picked up stools. "I've gotta do everything

149

around here. Straighten up. Haul booze. Keep fellas in line. It ain't right, I tell you. Know what I mean?"

The band said they did. In unison.

Denton punched the door. He hit the street.

I know what you mean, Jack. More than you wish I did.

Chapter Twenty

Two Weeks Later—February 24, 1963

Walker's big day. The Midnight Ride Tour announcement.

Wilson watched cops struggle with protesters. They struggled to keep the entrance to the Municipal Auditorium clear. Pro-Kennedy people on the left. Pro-Walker people on the right. Cops with nightsticks in the middle.

Dueling chants rose. Signs on the left had three variations:

HARGIS, WALKER GO HOME!

HARGIS + WALKER = HATE!

DALLAS IS JFK COUNTRY!

The signs on the right also had three variations:

UN OUT OF U.S.A.!

KENNEDY IS A KOMMIE!

DOWN WITH KOMRADE KENNEDY!

One sign had JFK wearing a Russian fur hat. The picture was ridiculous. Everyone knew Kennedy hated hats. They ruined his hair.

Dueling chants grew louder. Wilson maxed the volume on his hand radio. No reports of incidents elsewhere. Ticketed attendees entered via side entrances. Some reporters were inside. Most were at the entrance with Wilson. This was where the action was.

Wilson hadn't slept in weeks. He'd interviewed every extremist brought in for questioning. Commies, Birchers and Minutemen. Campus radicals.

Anti-Castro types. Self-described Patriots and Reds. Every loudmouth with a political gripe.

Each interview had required a threat assessment report. Every report reviewed daily by Jack Revill and Chief Curry.

Nightly fed duties continued. The Pipeline had slowed to a trickle. Ruby ate elsewhere after New Orleans. The correlation was clear. There are no coincidences in Dallas.

Zeke got scared. Washington wanted results. Zeke wanted to bug Ruby's apartment. He wanted to bug Ruby's Olds. Bugging Austin's Barbecue was now a consideration.

Wilson's Walker announcement intel had kept Zeke afloat with Washington. Hoover enjoyed sharing bad news with the brothers in the Oval Office.

His disappointment with Fritz was short-lived. Wilson used the Walker announcement as cover. He'd launched his own investigation. He began compiling his own private dirt pile. He amassed information on key players. Ruby. Blaine. De Mohrenschildt. Walker. Bannister. Eastbrook. Known Associates both in Dallas and beyond.

He tracked hate tracts from hate organizations. He mapped out correlations and relationships. Common friends and enemies. Trips made. Events attended. Speeches made. Memberships listed. Articles written. Associates known and associates suspected.

He built cases. He worked each player like a perp. His dirt pile grew fast. He remembered Revill's lessons. Organization leads to convictions.

He worked past midnight. He got up before dawn. Sleep was elusive. So was the purpose of the Lake Pontchartrain camp. Oswald's belief in a second Cuban invasion lingered. Wilson kept digging. Belief wasn't enough to get him to Washington.

Wilson's diligence paid off elsewhere. He'd linked General Walker and Guy Bannister to right-wing hate groups across the country. Anti-Kennedy, anti-Commie, and pro-segregation rhetoric was white hot hate.

The scope was daunting. The volume of material became crushing. Wilson violated a sacred rule. He blurred the line between his personal and private worlds. Connie's cousin was the president of a bank downtown. Wilson asked for vault space. Cousin Bob gave him three large safe deposit boxes. An oil baron's widow had once kept her jewelry collection there.

Wilson hoped perseverance and patience would pay off soon.

Oswald had been his only bright spot. The kid checked in like clockwork twice a day. They met in his car twice a week. No new gun runs scheduled.

Tippit began dogging Oswald surveillance. He made excuses. He'd stopped returning calls. He'd pulled away since New Orleans. Since he'd followed Crawford and Oswald to Ruby's place.

Wilson got suspicious. He had a theory. He cruised Ruby's hot spots. He saw Tippit working the door. He watched Tippit eyeballing brunettes. Ruby had put him on the payroll. Maybe Eastbrook had come through. The timing was a coincidence. Dallas didn't do coincidences. He'd corner JD for details soon.

Wilson heard someone rapping the glass wall behind him. Jack Revill beckoned him inside.

Wilson pushed through the door. He could still hear the crowd out in the lobby.

Revill held up his radio. "I've been calling you on the radio for five minutes."

Wilson hid his embarrassment. "Guess I couldn't hear it over the crowd."

"They're about to get a whole lot louder. Hargis and Walker are coming through the main entrance."

Wilson had put the entrance plan together. He had uniforms securing the stage entrance for their arrival. "We're not set up for that. The stage door is safer."

"They don't care," Revill said. "They don't want to look like they're sneaking into their own announcement. They want pictures of them walking through the middle of the protesters. Said it'll be good for their tour. The mayor told the chief to approve it."

Wilson didn't waste time complaining. "How far out are they?"

"A minute if we're lucky. You and I will escort them up the center aisle to the stage. Stay sharp."

Wilson followed Revill back outside. Two black limousines turned onto the long driveway to the auditorium. Dueling chants became shrills of support and protest.

Wilson and Revill waded into the narrow corridor of uniforms, keeping the entrance clear. Harry Denton used his nightstick to push back anti-Walker men. Ken Croy shoved anti-Kennedy men back.

Wilson saw an elderly black woman in the anti-Walker crowd. She clutched a bible and mouthed prayers. An oasis of peace among the chaos.

Wilson yelled in Denton's ear. "Watch the old lady on your left. Bring her inside if there's trouble."

"I don't take orders from you." Denton drove his nightstick into a protester's chest. "The old bitch should've stayed home. Get out of here and let the real cops do their job."

Wilson went to pull the old lady inside as the limos pulled up. Both sides surged toward the middle. Wilson lost the woman in the crowd. Revill pulled him toward the curb.

The back door of the first limo opened. Tommy Schneider and another Walker aide got out. They helped Reverend Hargis emerge. The fleshy clergyman threw up his hands and waved. Supporters cheered. Detractors jeered.

GOD BLESS HARGIS!

GOD BLESS JFK!

The anti-Walker side swelled. Uniforms held them back. Wilson got knocked aside. He almost lost his footing.

A protester spat at him. A glob caught Wilson in the eye.

Wilson throat-punched him. The protester gagged and sagged. Protesters bent to help him.

Wilson used his bulk. He helped the uniforms restore the line. They cleared a jagged path for Hargis.

The reverend bestowed blessings. The first limo pulled away. The second limo pulled up. Bob Carey and four Walker men spilled out of the car. The general emerged. He doffed his Stetson. His supporters cheered. The Kennedy crowd hurled insults.

A tomato struck the limo. Walker's aides closed around him. A second tomato splattered on the ground between the lines of cops.

Revill pulled Hargis toward the auditorium entrance. Wilson shouldered aside Carey. He pulled Walker toward the entrance.

Wilson saw a blur of fire streak overhead. A bottle shattered. Flames spread over the top of the limo.

Wilson grabbed Walker's arm and neck. He steered him toward the auditorium.

Uniforms on either side buckled. Protesters surged forward. They surged away from the flames. Both sides merged. Chaos ensued.

Wilson covered Walker. He kept him moving.

The human wave swelled. Cops lost ground fast. They fought for control. Nightsticks cracked skulls. They slammed stomachs. They broke ribs. They busted kneecaps.

People screamed as they fell. They hit the ground bleeding.

Wilson shielded Walker. Wilson absorbed punches to the back and shoulders. He pulled free from people grabbing his coat.

A blow to the base of his skull rocked him. He stayed upright. There was no room to fall down. He pulled the general through the knot of humanity.

A protester leapt out and blocked their path. Wilson headbutted him and threw him aside.

Wilson shoved Walker into the auditorium.

Wilson stumbled into the lobby. A uniform and Revill grabbed him. The uniform was Chief Curry.

Wilson shook his head clear. The lobby tilted.

Revill propped him up. "You hurt?"

Wilson's bravado kicked in. "I'm fine." His voice sounded hollow to him.

He looked outside. Cops were lost among the protesters. Uniforms locked the glass doors. The locks strained. Glass creaked. Protesters howled Walker's name.

Revill told a uniform, "I want every available man right here. If those windows break, we can't hold them back."

Chief Curry told Walker and Hargis. "I think we ought to delay your program until we—"

"Nonsense." Reverend Hargis lifted his fleshy chin to straighten his tie. "The good Lord above sent his angels to protect us from the godless rabble. He will continue with our program."

Walker raised his Stetson toward the main aisle. "Kindly lead the way, reverend."

The two men entered the auditorium. They began their procession up the main aisle.

The crowd erupted. Thunderous applause. Stomping feet. Clapping hands. Cheers.

Carey and Schneider and other aides followed. They made straight their boss's path.

Wilson and Revill brought up the rear. The cacophony of sound echoed. Wilson weaved. The auditorium pitched sideways. His stomach lurched. Bile rose in his mouth.

The faithful roared. Uniforms closed in as darkness swallowed him whole.

* * *

Tippit badged the nurse at the station. She told him Wilson's room number.

Tippit hadn't brought flowers. The latest edition of the newspaper would have to do.

Tippit knew they'd kept Wilson overnight. He must've been hurt bad. Wilson hated hospitals. He hoped Wilson was in no shape to grill him. There was too much Tippit couldn't share.

Tippit found Wilson's private room. He was propped up in bed. Awake. His head heavily bandaged.

Wilson groaned when Tippit walked in. "The Prodigal Partner. As I live and breathe."

Tippit dragged a chair to the bed and sat. "How's the head?"

"I've got a concussion. They think my skull has a hairline fracture. Nurses won't let me sleep. I told them I'm fine. This happened to me a few times in Korea. They don't know what they're talking about."

"And look how that turned out." Tippit dug out a cigarette. "Connie home with the kids?"

Wilson watched him light it. "Yeah. She'll be back after she gets them off to school in the morning. Doc says I ought to be out around noon."

Tippit pocketed his lighter. "You'll be lucky to be out by dinner." He tossed the newspaper on Wilson's chest. "I'll tell Connie to bring something to powder your nose. You're famous again."

Wilson glanced at the headline.

HERO COP SAVES GENERAL
Dozens Injured at Walker Rally Riot

Tippit tapped the photo beneath the headline. Wilson, shielding Walker as he headbutted a protester. Wilson scowling. The protester, reeling in pain.

Tippit smiled. "I kinda like that shot. Makes you look meaner than hell."

Wilson set the paper aside. "A lot of people got hurt last night."

"I heard." Tippit sat back. "An old colored woman caught the worst of it. Name's Mrs. Ford. She got trampled in the riot. They're treating her downstairs now."

Wilson blinked. "I saw her. I tried to reach her, but…" His voice trailed off.

Tippit said, "One son is a preacher. And get this. Her other son's a cop. Works out of South Dallas."

"I tried to get her inside." Wilson's jaw clenched. He clutched the bed sheets. "But then the limos pulled up, and I lost her when the crowd broke. The papers ought to be writing about her, not me."

Tippit tried to lighten the mood. "Cheer up. She'll sue the city and get a nice settlement."

Wilson grew still. "You've been quiet lately."

Tippit blew smoke. "Life's been busy. I'm driving for Ruby these days."

"I know." Wilson pushed himself further up on the pillow. "That used to be Harry Denton's gig. How'd you get it?"

Tippit shrugged. "Maybe he pissed off Eastbrook. Maybe Ruby didn't like Eastbrook spying on him."

"Or maybe you traded up." A vein bulged in Wilson's neck. "Maybe you traded me."

Tippit looked at his boots. He never could lie worth a damn. "It ain't like that."

"Eastbrook wouldn't lose a direct line to Ruby." Wilson pushed himself higher in bed. "What did you give Ruby, JD?"

Tippit smoked. Stalling was pointless. He had nothing to be ashamed of. "Crawford spotted me tailing him and Oswald from the butcher's shop to Ruby's apartment. Ruby confronted me. I had to tell him something, so I said you had me following Crawford."

Wilson pounded the mattress. "And you didn't tell me."

"Relax. He asked me why you wanted Crawford followed. I told him it was nothing. That it was probably just some CID bullshit. He believed me. I kept Oswald and New Orleans out of it."

Wilson punched the bed again. He winced. His head reminded him it was injured. "There's no way he bought a bullshit story like that. You gave him something."

Tippit flicked his ash. "We'd both be in a ditch if I had. I said Crawford's name came up as part of your Walker intel sweep. He bought it."

Wilson lifted his bandaged head. *He's impressed. Score one for dumb ol' JD.*

Tippit had saved the best for last. "I've been driving Jack around most nights since. He runs with an interesting crowd. Rubs elbows with a lot of Dallas PD brass besides Eastbrook."

"Who?"

"Can't tell you that. My ass, my rules, Danny Boy. If we're gonna keep talking shop, some things have to change."

Wilson's eyes flared. He hit the brakes on his mouth. He gritted his teeth. He looked at the ceiling and shut his eyes. He chose his words carefully. "What kinds of changes?"

Tippit had thought long and hard about it. "You work your side of the street. I work mine. I tell you what I hear about New Orleans or other things. In exchange, I feed Jack info you want him to know."

He expected Wilson to argue. He expected him to buck. He was used to being out front. Running even might not sit well.

But Wilson would remember. They'd used each other. Tippit had used him for Farley. Wilson had used Tippit for Oswald and New Orleans. The scales were balanced. In balance, there was trust. *You have dirt on me. I have dirt on you. Let's not bury each other.*

Tippit could help Ruby and Wilson while helping himself. *If that idiot Denton could do it, so can I.*

Wilson picked up the newspaper. He re-read the front page. "You really fold your Crawford tail into my Walker intel?"

"I had a good teacher." Tippit ground out his cigarette in the ashtray on the table. "Don't worry. You're still the smartest guy in the room. Help me maintain this Ruby angle. Tell me what you want him to know."

Wilson finished reading the article. He motioned to the phone on the side table. "Hand it over. I've got an important phone call to make." He started to dial. "And pay attention. I want Jack to hear every word."

Chapter Twenty-One

Monday, February 25, 1963

Harry Denton had backed into Eastbrook's driveway. He wanted to watch the sunrise. Purple bands slowly gave way to red. The sun an angry ball behind thick clouds.

Denton felt particularly good that morning. He'd belted Wilson good during the Walker riot. Sent him to the hospital. He would've hit him again if the crowd hadn't collapsed. Self-preservation took precedence.

Eastbrook had ordered him to drive him to work that morning. *Maybe my luck is changing.* Denton had been iced out since killing Farley. He'd lost his side gig driving Ruby. Eastbrook had been distant since New Orleans. Maybe the Walker event changed things.

Denton missed the access. The action. A new assignment would give him renewed relevance.

He started the car when Eastbrook came outside. The captain flung a newspaper on the backseat and climbed in. "Headquarters. On the double."

Denton drove. The captain wasn't a morning person. "Everything okay, boss?"

"Hardly," Eastbrook grumbled. "I've been on the phone all night. Walker's announcement turned into a goddamned circus. What happened?"

Denton summarized the violence. The chaos. The Molotov cocktails. Even the old black bitch who'd gotten herself trampled. It served her right for protesting good men like Walker and Hargis.

160

Denton had found her bible later. He'd dumped it in the trash. The given word was wasted on her kind anyway. Salvation wasn't meant for them. It said so in the very book she'd clung to.

Eastbrook wasn't interested. "Who tagged Wilson? Was it you?"

Denton grinned in the rearview mirror. "Got away with it, too."

"You should've hit him harder." He flung the newspaper at him. "Wilson's in the paper again. They're calling him a hero. That he sacrificed himself to save Walker last night."

Denton almost punched the steering wheel. Wilson was like a goddamned cockroach. "That's not how it happened, boss."

"That's how the papers wrote it. That's all that matters. Last night's violence has the mayor clutching his pearls. He told the chief to start an extremist task force. Revill's running it, but three guess who's spearheading it."

Denton only needed one. "Wilson."

Eastbrook pounded his armrest. "Walker's announcement gave Revill and Wilson an excuse to stir up all kinds of shit. I told Walker to do it in Houston or New Orleans, but the stubborn bastard wouldn't listen to me. Carter told me to handle it. Now, they're off on their goddamned crusade and I'm stuck cleaning up their mess."

Denton saw an opening. A way to repledge his allegiance to the captain. "Just tell me what needs doing and it's done, boss."

Eastbrook gathered up his Stetson. He checked the folds. "You still on the outs with Ruby?"

Denton phrased it carefully. *I'm no good to him if I'm useless.* "Not on the outs, but Tippit drives for him most days."

"Ruby did that to spite me for that beating I threw him. No matter. I'll put you on something more important."

Denton perked up. His luck had changed after all.

Eastbrook said, "You're working with Bob Carter until further notice. Tell me everything he shares about Walker. You'll help him keep an eye on Wilson for all of us. Do whatever he wants. Spare me the details unless it's urgent."

Denton tried to control himself. Eastbrook had just handed him a blank check. It was the major assignment he'd been waiting for. Hoping for. "Thank you, sir. I won't let you down."

"Just don't get too carried away," Eastbrook cautioned. "Revill is crafty, and Wilson is almost as bad. If we can hobble him, this ridiculous task force of his will dry up and blow away."

Denton saw the traffic light turning yellow. He hit the gas.

Humiliating Wilson would be fun.

* * *

Wilson had wanted to walk out of the hospital. Regulations dictated a wheelchair.

Connie held his hand as a Negro orderly wheeled him out of the hospital.

His headache was there, but manageable. His vision was almost normal. The doc said the buzzing in his ears was temporary.

Connie had a full day of rest planned. "We're going to get you home and straight to bed. You're going to rest like the doctor said. You'll get plenty of sleep."

Wilson didn't need sleep. He needed to get back to work. "Yes, dear."

"Don't 'yes dear' me, Daniel Wilson. You've got a cracked skull and a concussion. You need time to regain your strength."

"You forgot the tetanus shot they gave me for the scratches."

The orderly wheeled him around the corner. Wilson had a clear view down the main corridor of the hospital.

A uniform kept a gaggle of reporters and photographers away from the entrance. They wanted a shot of the hero cop walking out on his own two feet.

Walker grabbed the wheels. "I'm not going out that way."

The orderly stopped. "I've got to take you to the curb, Mr. Wilson. Regulations."

Connie was annoyed. "Don't be so bashful. You deserve some attention after what you've been through."

Wilson wanted attention. But not that kind of attention. The picture of him headbutting a scumbag was good. A shot of him in sweatpants and a head bandage wasn't.

He told the orderly, "There's a curb at the side entrance to the parking lot. You can let me out there. Regulations and all."

Connie was more than annoyed. "This is all so silly."

"But necessary." He had something to do before he left. He told Connie, "Go out there and talk to them. Tell them you've got to run home to get a couple of things before they let me go. Drive away, then come back to the side entrance in half an hour."

"But you've got everything you need. Why should I lie?"

"It's not a lie when you tell it to the press." He took her hand and kissed it. "Please, honey. I don't want them seeing me like this."

She reluctantly agreed. She opened her purse and pulled out a compact. She checked her look in the mirror. It was a waste of time. She was always beautiful.

She looked down at him. She flashed her best Junior League smile. "Am I ready for my close-up, Mr. DeMille?"

He kissed her hand again. "You were born ready."

She kissed his cheek and told the orderly, "Keep an eye on him. Don't let him get into trouble while I'm gone. I'll be back in thirty minutes sharp."

Wilson watched her toss her head as she walked down the hall. She walked straight and tall. She pushed through the doors. Flashes popped. Reporters crowded. She glided through them. The boys loved her. She'd make great copy.

The orderly smiled. "If you don't mind me saying so, your wife is quite a woman, Mr. Wilson."

"You don't know the half of it." He dug into his pocket. He handed the orderly a note and a five-spot. "After you leave me at the curb, take this to Carl Ford. He's with his mother. She was brought in here the same night I was."

The orderly took the note and the money. "I'll hand it to him personally. Poor woman's in a bad way."

163

He wheeled Wilson down a hallway through the side door of the hospital.

* * *

Wilson stood against the hospital and waited. He was dying for a cigarette. He'd forgotten to ask Connie for his Luckies. It served him right for being cunning.

The doc told him to wear the head bandage for a few more days. Wilson trashed it as soon as the orderly went back inside. Connie would be furious. But he couldn't look like an invalid. He had too much to do.

He'd struck while the iron was hot. He'd used his newfound celebrity to his advantage. He'd talked Revill into talking Mayor Cabell and Chief Curry into forming the Extremist Task Force. He'd had them put him in charge.

The announcement would be made tomorrow. The papers would love it. **Hero Cop Takes on Hate.** Cabell would look responsive. Curry would look like he cared. Revill would take the credit.

And Wilson would add to his dirt pile on department time. He'd work angles and amass information. He'd blend Oswald's dirt into the task force.

The brass would have questions about scope, staff, and targets. Wilson would give them broad strokes. Official targets would be Walker, Hargis, Carter, and Schneider. His off-book targets were still De Mohrenschildt, Bannister, and Blaine.

He'd have to broaden his public scope. Black militants, the NAACP, and anti-segregationists for balance. Window dressing for his files.

Tippit as an ad hoc member. Oswald as prime resource. He hoped the kid hadn't wandered off in the past few days. He needed him close. Engaged.

The Pipeline would move to the background. He'd feed Zeke what suited Wilson's purposes. He'd use FBI resources for his own leverage. *Look out, Hoover. Here I come.*

Wilson saw a black man exit the side entrance. He was holding the note the orderly had given him. "Detective Wilson?"

Wilson extended his hand. "Call me Dan."

"Carl." They shook hands. Carl Ford's grip was firm. He had a farmer's lean build and a street cop's eyes. His file said he was in his mid-twenties. He could've passed for a teenager. Versatility played a role in his plans.

Wilson noticed a square outline on Carl's shirt pocket. "You smoke?"

"Kools. Want one? They're menthol."

Wilson almost drooled. "I don't care if it's shoe leather."

Carl shook one out for him and lit it. Wilson drew the menthol deep into his lungs. He held it before letting it out slow.

Wilson realized Carl was watching him. "Sorry. Long night."

Carl lit his own cigarette. "Same here."

Wilson said, "I was sorry to hear about your mother. How's she doing?"

Carl's right eye twitched. "Busted right shoulder. Busted right hip. Fractured right ankle." The words choked him. "She didn't deserve that. Not for just standing there and praying."

"I saw her at the front of the crowd. I tried to bring her inside before things turned to shit. I wish it had."

"It wouldn't have worked," Carl said. "She's little but strong. She never would've stepped foot in an auditorium full of people who hated her." Carl watched the wind take their smoke. "Mind if I ask you a question?"

"Sure." He had a good idea what it would be.

"What happened? We had enough cops. How did it break so ugly?"

Wilson had to be careful. Ford had an excellent service record, but his mother had been injured. He may be looking to bust heads. And not necessarily civilian heads, either. But he had to give him something. "This stays between us, but I don't think it was an accident. They didn't just throw Molotov cocktails on a whim. Some folks went there to cause trouble."

Carl flicked his ash. "Heard it was the Kennedy side who threw them."

"They might've come from that direction, but they weren't from Kennedy's side. That's why I wanted to meet you. Thought maybe you'd want to find out who did this."

"White people don't care about what happens to us. No offense."

"None taken. But it doesn't have to be that way."

Carl laughed, but there was no humor in it. "You can stow that 'We Shall Overcome' shit. Nothing's ever gonna change because too many folks on

165

both sides like things just the way they are."

"We're not folks," Wilson reminded him. "We're cops. You and me took the same oath. And if no one's going to look out for us, we'll have to look out for ourselves."

Carl looked away. "So that's what this is. I knew you were building up to something when I got your note. White folks always have a reason for showing kindness. What is it? You afraid we'll sue the city?"

"Go ahead and sue. Put me down as a witness for your side. But I was talking about something different. I'm talking about other ways you can get even."

Carl looked him up and down. "You're giving me an opportunity? White folks love that word. A carrot you people dangle just to keep folks moving."

"I'm talking about revenge."

Carl didn't laugh this time. "On who?"

"The men who hurt your mother. The men who planned it. The men protecting them. The men who benefited from this."

"White men." Carl squinted through the cigarette smoke. "Revenge is expensive for men like me. It's liable to get me strung up from the nearest tree." He gestured at his groin. "I came into this world whole, and I aim to leave it the same way. I'm not getting killed over some white man's pipe dream."

"This is different. I'm different. And I've got a plan. I want you to be part of it."

Carl licked his fingers and crushed the cigarette tip. He put it back in the pack. He'd smoke the rest later. "The hell you say."

"You've read the papers. Last night's riot woke up a lot of people. The mayor wants Chief Curry to start an Extremist Task Force. I'm running it. If you want in, there's a spot for you."

"You've gotta be shitting me. A colored beat cop out of South Dallas? Half of Dallas PD is Klan. They'd never stand for it."

Wilson took a drag. "I'm a hero, remember? The brass'll go for whatever I tell them." He finished his cigarette. He ground it under his hospital slipper. "Nobody wants a repeat of what happened last night. It makes the city look bad. They'll want to make a show of rooting out the bad seeds. Nail a couple of hides on Cabell's wall. It'll make him look like he cares. You and me will have the knife and the nails."

"How many will we get?"

"Not many before they stop us," Wilson admitted, "but more than we have now. I figure six months max before they mothball it. But we could do a lot of good in six months. Kick in some doors. Shine some light. It won't take away your mama's pain, but we can inflict some of our own if we do it right. If we do it together."

Carl looked interested. He didn't look sold.

Wilson said, "Take a few days to think about it. Chances like this don't come around often."

"Especially for a colored cop."

"For any cop. The brass and the news boys like me. Let's use it for some good." Wilson put a finer point on it. "You've got a choice. You can sit around here and worry about your mother. Or you can hurt the men who hurt her."

Carl's brown eyes narrowed. Wilson's words had struck bone.

Carl said, "Let's say I come work for you. I stick my neck out. What happens when the brass calls it off? You'll go back to your cushy CID gig. I'll be back on the street with nothing to show for it. My friends will think I'm uppity. And every cracker with a badge will be gunning for my ass. I'll be found in an alley in a week."

"We won't let that happen."

Carl grinned. A weary grin. *Another empty promise from a white man.* "No one's got that much juice."

Wilson was glad to disappoint him. "I hear they've got your mom in the colored ward. Have her on a bed with fifty moaners and head cases."

Carl looked insulted. "It's all we can afford."

"I spoke to the head of the hospital. I had her moved to my old room upstairs. An orderly is bringing her there now."

Carl squared up. "Don't bullshit me like that."

"I don't bullshit." He held out his hand. "Come work for me and I'll prove that to you. Every day."

Carl looked at Wilson's hand. Wilson didn't know if he'd shake on it. But he was glad when he did.

Chapter Twenty-Two

Monday, April 1, 1963

"Nothing!" Zeke threw his paper cup at the trash bin. It missed. Coffee sloshed.

Dale Smith cursed. Frank Marsh jumped. Coffee hit their pant legs.

Zeke didn't care. "Not a single shred of new information in a month. You've generated absolutely nothing. Washington is not happy with your lack of progress, gentlemen. The director is bitterly disappointed."

Wilson had been expecting the outburst. The Pipeline had run bone dry. Ruby and Eastbrook had pulled up stakes. The transcripts were mostly neighborhood gossip and low-level crime.

Marsh snagged a napkin. He dabbed at the coffee on his pant leg. "It's nobody's fault, Zeke. We can't make the crooks go in there and implicate themselves."

Smith said, "We can only record what we see and hear. I haven't seen a source yet that didn't dry up eventually."

Zeke fumed. "But why did *this one* dry up overnight? We had a steady flow of information out of that dump. Then one day, zilch. Everything came to a screeching halt, and I'm the one with tire tracks across his back."

Wilson knew why. New Orleans had clogged The Pipeline. Ruby had gotten wise. He knew Crawford had been compromised. He circled the wagons. He took his evil doings elsewhere. So did Eastbrook. Ruby held

169

meetings on the street while he walked. Booth mics gave them only dregs now.

Wilson didn't care. His own investigations thrived. Carl Ford had become his right hand. He'd built Extremist Task Force files. They steered clear of the Dallas machine. Politicians and civic leaders were catalogued, but deemed not threatening. Wilson and Carl focused on unaffiliated oddballs. Police brass was pleased.

Wilson trusted Carl with his dirt pile. He tracked Bannister and Walker leads. He tracked hate group literature and meetings. Tippit and Oswald delivered steady streams of sweet crude on Ruby, Eastbrook and friends. Wilson's dirt pile grew. He'd gotten Connie's cousin to give him two more vault boxes at his bank.

The lynch pin remained elusive. Walker and Hargis and Bannister weren't working alone. Someone was orchestrating their actions. When Wilson found that man, he'd have the leverage he needed. He'd pry his way into the FBI. Into Washington.

Zeke turned his anger on Wilson. "And what about you? You used to be full of big ideas."

"I still am."

"You're too busy with your goddamned task force. Getting your name in the paper." He shook a finger at him. "You'll never get to Washington with that kind of attitude."

Wilson enjoyed Zeke's panic. "You get copies of every report I write." It was a lie. He fed Zeke sludge. The real dirt went into his files. "Yelling at us won't do any good. The Pipeline could've dried up for any number of reasons. Maybe one of the waitresses spotted our wire. Maybe someone saw one of us coming in and out of here once too often."

Zeke threw up his hands. "Excuses."

Wilson tossed Zeke an old bone he'd already coughed up. "I suggested we tap Austin's a couple of months ago. Maybe we should consider it."

"Austin's." Zeke spat it out like a curse. "Locals bitching about local bullshit. Washington doesn't want to hear Rotarians bragging about banging each other's wives. They want results." He pointed down at the diner. "Ruby and

Eastbrook haven't found Jesus. They're doing business elsewhere. I want to know where, and I want to know fast."

Marsh set his camera down on the desk. "You work The Carousel Club. You hear all sorts of things. Why don't you tell us where to go next?"

Smith added, "I don't hear you coming up with any leads."

Zeke reddened. "Insolence. Insubordination. A mutiny. That's what this is."

Wilson enjoyed watching Zeke unravel. "Let's bug Ruby's office and apartment. See what we pick up."

"Or his car," Smith said. "The quality will be lousy, but we might get something."

"Pointless." Zeke rubbed his hands over his face. "Jack hasn't been spending much time at the club lately. Something's changed. I just can't put my finger on what."

Wilson knew why. But Zeke didn't need to know. *Let the arrogant prick twist in the wind.*

Marsh piped up. "We've got enough to charge Ruby and Eastbrook right now. I say we cut our losses and bring them in."

Wilson didn't want that. Not yet. He needed the proximity that an active federal investigation gave him. He didn't want the bureau to forget him. Out of sight, out of mind.

Zeke dismissed Marsh's idea. "We've got dozens of individual infractions with minimal jail time. Washington wants something big. A landmark case."

Wilson doubted Washington cared that much. *Zeke* wanted a landmark case. Wilson decided it was time to make The Pipeline work for him.

"I might have an idea, but it's just an idea."

Zeke threw up his hands again. "I'm waiting!"

Here we go. "My old partner Tippit's been doing odd jobs for Ruby. Drives him here and there every once in a while."

Marsh and Smith traded glances. Marsh said, "That guy from the Farley thing a while back."

Zeke shushed him. "Tippit's been hanging around the club lately. He's taken Denton's place. Denton wasn't happy about it."

171

Wilson primed the bait. "JD's also strapped for cash. Maybe I can get him to rat on Ruby if we make it worth his while. I can tell him it's part of my task force work. Maybe promise to take care of him after."

Zeke started pacing. He was warming to the idea. "Did Eastbrook get Tippit the job with Ruby?"

"I don't know," Wilson lied, "but it doesn't matter. For the right amount of money, Tippit might go for it. And the promise of a better job later for cooperation now wouldn't hurt." *Help Tippit. Help me. Combine operations and resources.*

Zeke kept pacing. "We can get him to work for nothing." He hated asking Washington for a penny over budget. "The threat of prison is a powerful motivator."

Wilson appealed to Zeke's ambition. "Nabbing a crooked beat cop won't grab headlines. Ratting on Ruby could get Tippit killed. He might flip for the right reasons." He tossed in a shrug for good measure. "Let me make a run at him. It's not like we've got anything to lose."

Zeke stopped pacing. "The last time you told me you could control Tippit led to disaster."

"That was love," Wilson said. "This is business."

Zeke resumed pacing. He licked his lips. He needed a win. He needed something for Washington. He didn't want to leave Dallas empty-handed.

He stopped at the window. He looked down at the diner. "Do it."

Wilson tried not to gloat. He avoided looking at Marsh and Smith.

You all work for me now.

* * *

Wilson and Carl had taken precautions. Headquarters was too dangerous to discuss details. The walls had eyes and ears. The rank and file were watchful. So were his fellow detectives. They clocked all of Wilson's meetings. They eyed his desk with interest. Friends of theirs might get swept up in Wilson's dragnet.

Carl had secured an off-site meeting place. His brother's congregation owned an old Baptist church in South Dallas. The neighborhood was off the Dallas PD map. No Klansman worth his Aryan blood went near that part of town. They'd stick out if they did. Privacy was assured.

Wilson and Carl discussed task force business there. They debriefed Oswald there.

But that night, Oswald found no solace in the place of worship. He fidgeted in the first pew. Wilson hadn't seen him this worked up since de Mohrenschildt's party.

Carl sat next to him. "What's wrong, Lee?" He'd built a rapport with Oswald fast. Oswald trusted him. A black cop didn't run with the far-right crowd. "I've never seen you like this."

Oswald pulled at a thread on his shirt. "I told you everything would fall apart, and now it has."

Wilson watched Carl keep him grounded. "What's falling apart?"

Oswald looked at his stubby fingernails. "Marina's having a baby."

Wilson didn't see the problem. Oswald enjoyed being a father. "Congratulations. That's great news."

"Except it isn't." Oswald pouted. "I got fired from JCS today."

Wilson hadn't expected that. Oswald hadn't mentioned work trouble in past debriefings. "They tell you why?"

Oswald scratched at his arm. "They said I was disruptive. That I didn't get along with anyone. But that's not why they did it. Mr. Blaine said they didn't need me working there anymore. 'Priorities have changed'. His exact words." Oswald ran a shaking hand over his hair. "They want me to move back to New Orleans at the end of the month."

Wilson noted how Michael Blaine had become Mr. Blaine after de Mohrenschildt left Dallas. "Who's they? Blaine and who else?"

"My New Orleans friends." Oswald never named them. He never said Guy Bannister or David Ferrie. "They want me to help them with their Commie work. To stir the pot and cause trouble. Make the Reds look bad."

Oswald looked at Carl. "I liked my job. I like Dallas. I don't want to go back to New Orleans. I want to stay here."

Wilson recognized Blaine and Bannister's tactic. Upend an informant's life. Isolate him. Limit his options to assure compliance. It was a classic cop strategy.

Bannister wanted Oswald in New Orleans for a reason. He was about to make a move. *But what move?*

Wilson needed more. "Why not bring you to New Orleans now? Why wait?"

"I don't know," Oswald whined, "and Mr. Blaine won't tell me. Mr. de Mohrenschildt would've told me. He always looked out for me." He rubbed his hands on his pants. "Mr. Blaine wants me to start hawking pamphlets downtown this week."

Carl took over. "What kind of pamphlets?"

"Pro-commie stuff. Anti-Walker stuff. Some pro-NAACP stuff, too, which I don't mind as much. He says it'll help keep the fires hot when Walker comes home after his tour. Give him something to rail against. It'll bait the Reds and make folks hate the Commies even more. But I'm the one who'll get arrested and beaten up, not them."

Oswald sagged. Resigned to his fate. "It's all for the greater cause, I guess, but I don't like it. I can't go to jail. I need a job. My family needs me."

Wilson pitied the poor bastard. *This is your job, Lee. You're the straw man. The punching bag. The lightning rod. You'll get battered and bloodied while Blaine and Bannister keep their hands clean.*

Carl had a suggestion. "Tell Blaine you won't do it."

"I don't have any choice," Oswald moaned. "Mrs. Blaine's charity is helping us with the bills. He'll cut us off if I refuse. He raked his fingers through his hair. "I'm getting squeezed from every direction, and I don't like it."

Oswald looked up at Wilson. Tears flowed. "Can you help me? You promised you would."

Wilson had to keep him calm. "Give me a few days to see what I can do." He'd get Connie's friends to help. He'd throw in some money of his own if he had to. He was still paying Tippit, but he'd find more somewhere. "In the meantime, you've got to keep being smart, Lee. Keep checking in with me twice a day. That's more important now than ever. Do whatever Blaine asks.

When you check in with me, tell the operator where you're handing out literature. Either Carl or I will keep an eye on you. And if you get arrested, keep your mouth shut and call me. Not Marina, not Blaine, not a lawyer. Just me. One of us will get you out."

"But I don't want to have to call anyone," Oswald cried. "I just want a job."

Carl nudged him out of it. "You've got a job. A full-time one. To protect yourself and your family."

Wilson couldn't let Bannister win. He couldn't let Oswald feel isolated. "We'll meet right here two times a week until further notice. Keep your ears open. Tell me everything Blaine says and does. Tell me anything you about going to New Orleans. Even the slightest detail might help. Do that and I can keep you safe."

"That's what I've been doing." Oswald dropped his head into his hands. "I tell you everything, and all I get is a pep talk. A pat on the head."

"You're not doing this for me," Wilson reminded him. "You're doing this to help yourself and your family. You haven't needed my help before, but now, you do. And you'll get it." Wilson had fifty bucks on him. He handed it to Oswald. "That's a promise."

Oswald looked at the cash before he took it. He sank deeper into his own despair.

Wilson beckoned for Carl to follow him. They stopped in the narrow hallway next to the pulpit.

Carl said, "That is one terrified white man. I think he's ready to crack."

Wilson knew Bannister wanted him to crack. To turn to him as his only way out. "Take him home. Tell him we'll meet back here the day after tomorrow. Forget about the task force. You'll need to keep an eye on him. Reinforce that he can trust us. If he thinks he's alone, he might do something desperate."

"I'll watch him hawking pamphlets," Carl said. "See if he's got someone else minding him."

Wilson liked it. Making Carl part of the task force had been one of the few high points of the past few weeks.

They looked out at Oswald. He looked small and alone in the front pew of the church. "We've got to protect him, Carl. He's our only link to Blaine and the others. He doesn't deserve to be treated like this."

Carl went to get Oswald on his feet. "Neither do we."

Chapter Twenty-Three

Wilson checked his mirrors on the drive home. Traffic was light. No obvious tails. It gave him time to think.

Things were going well. Better than well. Consolidation was at hand and ahead of schedule.

Tippit's select intel on Ruby would keep The Pipeline open. Wilson could get him to share more than he had. Money from Zeke would help. Immunity from prosecution would seal the deal.

Oswald's New Orleans move was an unexpected boon. It would expand Wilson's reach. It would give him more dirt on Bannister and Walker. They wanted Oswald in The Big Easy by month's end. *Why the rush, boys?*

The Extremist Task Force had already paid dividends. Carl had tracked Walker's Midnight Ride tour. The general and the reverend had earned some decent coin for the cause. The links between Bannister and Walker had become undeniable. In a few more weeks, Wilson might discover their boss. He just needed more time.

New Orleans played at the edges of his mind. The Lake Pontchartrain camp teased him. Its relevance eluded him. So did its purpose. *Was that why Bannister was recalling Oswald? Was Bannister using Oswald to help stir anti-Red sentiment? Was a second Cuban invasion imminent?*

Wilson had Carl check property ownership. It was murky. Locals ignored their calls. They stalled written requests. NOPD was further right than Dallas PD. Pushing harder would raise questions Wilson couldn't answer. He didn't have the authority. *Yet.*

Wilson reached his neighborhood. He took a right off the main road.

His task force work had made him cautious. He never went straight home anymore. He cruised the block first. He looked for things that didn't belong. Strange cars. Pedestrians. Unfamiliar faces. Anything out of place. Walker's crowd had lots of tricks. So did their friends on Dallas PD.

He took a wide left onto his street. He rolled slow. He scanned everything.

A Pontiac Tempest sedan was parked at the curb in front of the Campbell place. The Campbells were a retired couple. Rich Campbell drove a Cadillac. So did his kids. The Tempest wasn't his style.

Wilson rolled by. The driver's window was down. No sign of the driver. Highland Park was a safe neighborhood, but locals always rolled up their windows. No point in tempting fate.

The neighbors' dogs were barking as Wilson pulled into his driveway. Highland Park was a quiet neighborhood. Dogs never barked for long. A stranger's scent on the night wind had set them off.

Wilson locked his Galaxie and went inside the house. The kids had been in bed for hours. Connie had fallen asleep on the couch. The local news was on TV. She woke when she heard the front door close.

"There you are." She smiled and stretched as she stood to greet him. "I was wondering how long you'd be. You didn't call."

Wilson laid his finger on her lips. He took her by the hand and led her upstairs.

She giggled. "Not yet, honey. I have supper on the stove."

He brought her into their darkened bedroom. He stood back from the window. He pointed down at the Tempest. It was still in front of the Campbell place. A passing car's headlights revealed the outline of a man in the driver's seat.

Connie saw it. She went ramrod straight. She navigated the dark room. She took her purse from the headboard. She got her .38.

Wilson took his old .22 from the closet. He handed it to her.

"Lock yourself in the kids' bedroom. Don't move until I come back."

She whispered, "You're not going anywhere. Call the precinct. Have them send a car to check it out."

But Wilson couldn't call the precinct. The Tempest driver could be anyone.

A Walker man. An Eastbrook man. The precinct could blow it off. *Teenagers necking. A pining boyfriend. Nothing to worry about.*

This was his family. His home. His responsibility. A line had been crossed. Someone had to pay for crossing it.

"I'll be right back."

He kissed her cheek and walked her toward the kids' bedroom. He stood in the hall until he heard the bedroom door lock.

Wilson ran downstairs. He went to the kitchen phone. He dialed the only man he knew would die for his family.

Duke Wilson answered on the fourth ring. His voice was heavy with sleep. "Whoever's calling at this ungodly hour, it better be good."

Wilson said, "I need you at the house. Connie and the kids are in trouble."

"On my way."

Wilson hung up. His parents lived twenty minutes away. Duke would make it in ten. And he'd come ready to kill.

Wilson pulled his Magnum. He moved to the back door. He parted the curtain and checked outside. Lights from neighboring houses showed it was clear.

He felt something brush his boot. Missy was crouched beside the door. Her front low. Her back up. She was ready to run outside with him.

He nudged her aside with his boot. "You stay here and watch the house."

She scratched at the door as he pulled it closed behind him.

* * *

Wilson cut through his neighbor's yard. His Magnum led the way. Dogs still barking.

His combat training kicked in. Wilson moved low and fast. The Lominos' backyard was first, then the Hollands'. He hopped a low brick wall into the Campbells' yard.

The Tempest was still parked in front of the alley between the Campbell and Nolan homes. He'd come out directly behind it.

Wilson crept through the gap in the shrubbery between the two properties.

He raised his Magnum as he reached the sidewalk.

He aimed at the driver's head and closed in from behind.

The driver saw him too late. He slowly raised his hands. "Don't shoot. I ain't going for my gun."

One flinch and he catches three behind the ear.

Wilson kept the pistol steady as he moved to the driver's side. There was just enough light to identify the bastard at the wheel.

Tommy Schneider. General Walker's driver.

Wilson thumbed back the hammer. "With two fingers of your left hand, pull that Colt and toss it in the backseat."

"Why?" Schneider grinned. "So you can shoot me?"

"I'll shoot you if you don't."

Schneider slowly reached into his jacket and complied. He dumped the .45 over his shoulder. He pinched the lapels of his coat and held them open. "I'm unarmed."

Wilson opened the back door and got in. He saw a camera on the front seat. They'd get to that later. "Drive."

Schneider grinned at him in the rearview mirror. "You sure about that, captain? You just got home. You should spend time with that pretty wife of yours. That task force has been keeping you mighty busy."

Wilson picked up the Colt. He clipped him with it on the back of the head. He set the pistol beside him on the seat. "Shut up and drive."

Schneider shook off the blow. He turned the key and pulled away from the curb. "I've sure got to hand it to you, cap. There ain't a speck of rust on you. Getting the jump on me like that? Popping out of the dark like you did. You old plane jumpers sure have quite the bag of tricks."

Wilson sat back. He kept himself and the Magnum out of Schneider's reach. "Take a left at the corner. Keep going until I tell you otherwise."

Schneider made the left. "Whatever you say, captain." He laughed. "I'll bet you just about burst your buttons when the general called you 'captain' that day at City Hall. Sounds a whole lot better than 'detective', now don't it?"

Wilson resisted the urge to belt him again. "I'm surprised you're not on the tour. Guess only the smart guys got to go."

"The general needed me here. Someone had to stay back and keep track of all that skullduggery you've been up to. That task force of yours is rankling a lot of important people something awful."

Wilson checked the back window. Schneider might not be alone. No one was following. "Keep going until you reach Seventy-Five, then take it south. Don't speed. And if you slam on the brakes, I'll blow your fucking head off."

"Such language," Schneider scolded. "That's conduct unbecoming an officer. The general will be mighty disappointed when I tell him. And that's on top of all the big news I've got for him." He glanced back at Wilson. "About your friend Oswald, of course. Working him was a nice touch. I'll admit we didn't see that coming."

"Seventy-Five south," Wilson repeated. "Keep it under forty."

Schneider obeyed. "Yes, sir. You sure had us fooled. We knew someone was whispering in your ear. My money was on Ruby doing all the talking. That kike's mouth always has been too big for his own good. The way he runs his mouth, I figured he'd said too much to the wrong fella. We thought he might've cut some kind of deal for himself with you boys. To save his own skin and all. Know what I mean?"

Wilson ignored the Ruby reference. "Maybe he did."

"Nah. Tonight confirmed otherwise. I told the general not to trust him. Ruby, I mean. But the general has a mind of his own. He said Ruby's guns were good and at a fair price. He said Ruby served a purpose. But don't worry. We'll put him in his place when the time comes. Oswald, too." He winked in the rearview mirror. "I won't leave you out. I'm gonna see look forward to taking care of you personally." Schneider beamed as he watched the road. "Yes, sir. That will be one fine and glorious day."

"Banners and drums," Wilson said. "Pomp and circumstance."

"That's the idea."

Wilson checked the speedometer. Schneider kept it at thirty-five. "Was it Walker's idea to watch my house? To scare an innocent woman and her children?"

"We didn't scare no women and children." Schneider coasted onto Seventy-Five. "Not even yours. I just took some pictures of your house with your car in the driveway. Figured they might serve as something of a warning to you. Get you to make your task force ease off some. To quit nosing around where you don't belong. To see reason."

"Too bad for you I'm not reasonable."

Schneider laughed. He kept the Tempest between the lines. "Aw, don't sell yourself short, Captain. Every man's reasonable when he has to be. You're no exception. Remember what they taught us back in basic training. Apply the right pressure in the right place? Everyone cracks eventually. And if the general understands anything, it's how to apply enough pressure."

Schneider liked to talk. Wilson led him to say something useful. "You tell anyone about seeing Oswald with me?"

"Haven't had the chance," Schneider admitted. "I've been too busy following you around for the past couple of days. You're a tough man to tail, but I got the knack eventually. When I followed you to that colored church, I didn't know what to expect. But seeing Oswald get off that bus tonight? Hell, that was better than Christmas morning. That boy stuck out like a fungus on an eggplant."

He looked at Wilson in the rearview. "I've got to hand it to you, captain. I ain't been that surprised in quite a while. Guess that colored boy you hired put that one together. We'll take our time teaching him a lesson when the time comes."

Wilson ignored the threat. Schneider hadn't told anyone about Oswald. That was good. "The night's young. Anything can happen in Dallas."

"That a threat?" Schneider grinned. "Come on, captain. Didn't you learn anything in the army? A threat's no good unless you can carry it out. A straight shooter like you won't do a damned thing to me."

Wilson watched the Dallas skyline draw closer. "That so?"

"Damned right it is. Oh, I don't doubt you want to take a swing at me. Rough me up some, but that's just your pride gnawing at you. Come the morning, you'll see things in a better light. A thoughtful man such as yourself. An educated man. A planner. You wouldn't have made captain if you weren't. I've seen how you operate. That big brain of yours is always cooking. You'll see reason before long."

Wilson watched the road. The exit was coming up.

Schneider went on. "As for me? Why, I'm just a foot soldier. Always have been. A cog in the wheel, just like you."

"Now look at who's selling himself short."

"Just speaking the honest truth," Schneider said. "Hurting me will get you nothing. There are a dozen guys who'd be willing to take my place. Hell, maybe even hundreds once the general wraps up his tour."

Wilson said, "Take the next left."

Schneider obeyed. "Give it up, captain. You made your play. You tried to spook me, but it ain't working. It won't work on the general, either. You think all of this is just about him? You know better than that. This is way bigger than him. Way bigger than all of us combined, especially you and me." He snapped his fingers. Like he'd remembered something. "Say, you want to know what happens next?"

"I already know. You're taking the next left."

Schneider took the turn slow. "I'm gonna tell Carter and the general everything I saw tonight. And when the general gets word of it, you're gonna get a phone call. He's gonna ask to see you. I'd give you his address, but you've probably already got it somewhere in your files and such. He'll sit you down and lay things out for you. Man to man. Nice and simple like. He's got a knack for talking to people. Yes, sir. The two of you will sit down and hash out some kind of an agreement. You'll tell him what it'll take for you to leave him and his friends alone. Don't be afraid to be greedy. Shoot for the moon and you just might hit it. Money. A promotion. All of the above. Just ask. You'll find him a mighty generous man."

They were in the city now. "Take a right on Ervay."

Again, Schneider complied. "Say, I know this area. That's real funny, Captain. I didn't take you for that kind of man." Another laugh. "Guess you never really know a fella 'til you know him. Let me guess. You're gonna buy me a drink. Just be warned. I ain't a cheap date. I like the good stuff."

"Keep driving."

Schneider sighed. "Yes, sir. I can see it now. You'll back off on the general and his friends and forget all you know about them. Focus on something important, like locking up Reds. That's where the real threat is anyway."

Schneider gestured at the passing buildings. "Just look at this place. You know the mongrels who fraternize around here. Abominations to God and nature. The same kind of folks who want to bring us down. To put good white men like ourselves in chains."

Wilson saw a spot just past Marilla. "Park at the curb up there and kill the engine. Leave the keys in the ignition."

Schneider did as he was told. He slid into the spot and turned off the car. "Now, I ain't telling you it's gonna be easy. I'm sure a principled man such as yourself is bound to have a few sleepless nights over it. But it's like I told you before. That'll just be your pride talking. You'll get over it when you realize it's the right thing to do."

Schneider adjusted the rearview. He looked back at Wilson. "You'll do it because you don't have a choice. Because deep down you know nothing you say or do will make a damned bit of difference. You can't stop what's coming, Captain. Ain't nobody alive who can stop us. You had the right idea earlier. About drums beating and banners flying. You could be right up front with the rest of us. And despite it all, I for one would be proud to stand with you. After we get a few things straight between us, of course."

He turned in his seat. He looked at Wilson. "Now, how about we quit playing games? Let me drive you back home to that pretty little wife of yours." He looked around at the dark buildings lining the street. That grin again. "Unless you've got something else on your mind."

Wilson let him see him tuck the Magnum in his shoulder rig. "You really meant what you said? About you boys never stopping."

The shit-eating grin went wide. "I surely did."

Wilson picked up Schneider's .45. "That's what I thought."

Wilson shot him in the right temple. Gore splashed the windshield. Blood went everywhere. Schneider's head snapped left. His body slumped portside.

Wilson's cop training kicked in. He sat still. He waited. He let the cordite burn his nose. He watched the street. He listened.

Most criminals got caught running away from a crime. To put distance between themselves and their deed.

Wilson knew there was no reason to hurry. Because this was 'Swish Street'. The pink part of Dallas, where the feminine set met like-minded men in quiet bars off the street. Where residents kept their shades drawn and their heads down. Hustlers saw nothing and didn't want to be seen. Curiosity was costly here. That's why Wilson picked it.

Dallas PD avoided the area. Queer crimes were tedious. Violence there was common, but charges were rare. Most victims had wives and kids at home.

Wilson remained still. He listened. The street was quiet. No reaction to the shot. No lights had come on. No heads out windows. No sirens approaching.

Time to move. Wilson reached over the seat. He took Schneider's camera. He got out of the car. He tucked Schneider's .45 in his belt. He'd ditch it later. He held the camera low and walked toward The Adolphus Hotel. *Slow and steady. Blend in. Nothing to see here.*

He entered the hotel via the back entrance off Main. He strolled through the lobby like any other guest. He avoided eye contact with the desk clerk. He passed the lobby bar. A piano played a Doris Day tune. Martini drinkers swooned.

Wilson went out the front door on Commerce. He snagged a cab on the line. The driver might've remembered him if he got in from the street. By coming out the front door, he was just another tourist out for a night on the town.

He had the driver take him to Oak Lawn and Rawlins. It was a block away from where he wanted to go.

He tried not to remember he'd just murdered a man. And his night wasn't over yet.

* * *

Tippit liked working the front door of The Vegas Club. The scenery was tough to beat.

He watched a two-bit skel squire a tall blonde in a short red dress to a Cadillac. She eyed Tippit as they glided past. Tippit eyed back. He'd look for her later after the pipsqueak's meter ran out.

He spotted something in a doorway across the street. A new shadow that didn't belong.

He didn't react at first. He watched it closely. He saw it was Dan Wilson. Something was wrong. Wilson wasn't a night owl.

Tippit told one of the guys he was taking a break. No one asked questions. Being Ruby's driver came with privileges. No one complained when he disappeared for a while. They didn't ask questions. They figured he was handling something for the boss. Sometimes he was.

Tippit had parked his Studebaker in a lot around the corner. Wilson was already waiting when he got there. His shirt and suit had dark splotches. His hair, too.

Questions could wait.

Tippit unlocked the car. Wilson climbed in. He set a camera next to him on the seat.

Tippit got behind the wheel and started the engine. "Where are we going?"

"Back to my place. I can't risk a taxi driver remembering where I live."

Tippit put the Studebaker in gear. He pulled out of the lot. His mind raced. Wilson's house was ten minutes away. Tippit could make it there and back to the club in twenty. He'd been away from the door much longer than that.

Tippit pushed the rearview mirror toward Wilson. "Your lipstick got smudged."

Wilson looked at his reflection. At the blood on his cheek. On his collar. In his hair. "Shit."

Tippit kept driving. He had preliminary questions. "How'd you get here?"

"Taxi." Wilson lowered the mirror. He saw the streaks of blood on his suit. "If he saw me like this, he'll remember me."

Tippit stayed calm. "Where'd he pick you up?"

"At the Adolphus."

"The driver won't remember you. Besides, it's not that noticeable." He pointed at the glove box. "I've got some cocktail napkins from the club in there." He entertained young ladies in the Studebaker. The napkins came in handy. "A little spit might make the blood less obvious."

Wilson snagged a napkin. He scrubbed at the blood on his face. The napkin pilled and frayed. The blood smeared. Wilson rubbed anyway. "It's not coming off."

"Blood never does. Whose is it?"

"A nobody." Wilson tossed the napkin out the window. He took another and rubbed at the smear.

"Had to be somebody. Ghosts don't bleed."

The blood smear turned tannish. "Nobody who matters."

Tippit took Turtle Creek Drive north to Highland Park. A quiet stretch that time of night. Lightly patrolled by Dallas PD. Wilson wouldn't clear a random traffic stop. Their badges would only inspire more questions. Wilson looked like hell and smelled of death.

"You hit?"

"No, and that's enough questions. It's better if you don't know the details."

Tippit drove. "I'm already an accessory after the fact, Danny Boy. That means I get to know a few things. My ass, my rules, remember. Did you use a drop piece or your Magnum?"

Wilson worked on the blood in his hair. "His .45. I've still got it."

"Good. Clear it and use one of those napkins to wipe your prints. Leave it there on the floor. I'll break it down and scatter the pieces near the club later."

Wilson ejected the magazine. He cleared the chamber. He wiped down the piece with a cocktail napkin. He set it between his feet in the wheel well.

Tippit minded his speed. No cops so far. "Any witnesses?"

"Nobody." Wilson noticed his hands. "Christ, there's blood all over my fingers."

"Keep spitting and wiping. You just have to make it into the house without a neighbor seeing you. Connie's probably already asleep."

Wilson kept working on the blood. "Connie already knows. She saw the bastard parked in front of our house tonight."

This keeps getting worse. "She and the kids okay?"

"I called Duke to come watch them." Wilson tossed napkins out the window and grabbed more. "This task force has kicked over a lot of rocks. You'd be surprised what's crawling out."

Tippit wasn't surprised. Wilson was the most dedicated man he'd ever known. "Is it worth what it's doing to your family? You've got guys sitting around in front of your house. You just killed one of them. You think this is just gonna stop? The closer you get, the worse it'll get."

Wilson stopped working on a blood smear near his left thumb. "I've got something to tell you. You're going to listen, then you're going to do exactly what I say."

Tippit didn't like the tone. "I'm already aiding and abetting a murderer after the fact. How bad could it be?"

Wilson threw the napkin out the window. "The feds are moving on Ruby. You're in the crosshairs. You'll be indicted if you don't cooperate. I'll get them to give you money. You're going to take it."

Tippit wasn't angry. Wilson had been up to something since before New Orleans. He hadn't blindly stumbled upon Oswald. The kid was part of a larger investigation. Wilson wasn't hoping to be a walk-on player for the feds. He'd been working with them all along.

Tippit wasn't angry, just concerned. "When are they moving on him?"

"Soon." Wilson resumed wiping at the blood. "I said you'd flip on Ruby if you got immunity and money. They approved my idea. Just tell us where Ruby goes, who he sees and what he does from here on in."

Now Tippit *was* angry. "You signed me up to stop a bullet."

"Not with this crew. These feds are solid."

"I'm not worried about Ruby. I'm worried about the Campisis and Marcello. They've got lots of feds on the payroll. If they find out, I'm dead."

"They won't find out," Wilson said. "Besides, it's too late to back out. I took the liberty of accepting on your behalf. Told them it was your idea. I hinted that you'd been working for me for a while. They liked that. Made you look like a hero to them."

"It'll look great on my tombstone. Who's 'them'?"

"You'll never meet them. It's better that way."

Wilson's house was close. "Better for everyone or just you?"

Wilson pointed down at the gun between his feet. "We've always trusted each other. If we can't trust each other now, we're both dead."

Chapter Twenty-Four

Wednesday, April 10, 1963

Revill flipped through Wilson's weekly Extremist Task Force report. He was thorough. He always read every word. "You haven't updated the section on the Schneider shooting since last week. What's the latest? Who did Fritz put on that case again?"

"Jim Leavelle." Wilson needed the case to slip from relevance. "Sounds like a typical Swish Street slay. Schneider picked up the wrong guy and got himself killed."

Revill said, "Not much of a mugging. Schneider still had his wallet on him."

Wilson wished he'd taken Schneider's wallet, too. "I just know what I've overheard Leavelle say out in the bullpen. I'll ask him for an update."

Revill tossed his glasses on the desk. "Tell him to wrap it up quick. Walker's raising hell. He swears up and down that Schneider had no reason to be on Swish Street. Says Schneider was a good old-fashioned, red-blooded American boy."

Wilson had read Walker's letters. "Lots of good old-fashioned, red-blooded American boys on Swish Street. Guess that's the appeal."

"All part of life's rich pageant." Revill squinted as he read the rest of the report. "Walker told Curry that Reds might've done in Schneider. To get back at him. You haven't come across any Red factions in Dallas, have you?"

"Just the usual campus stuff. This problem is pink, not red."

"Agreed." Revill closed the report. He placed it on his desk beside his glasses. "I'll admit that I had some high hopes when I put you in charge of this task force. You've exceeded my expectations. The chief and the mayor are pleased. The intelligence you've gathered has been nothing short of extraordinary. And Carl Ford was an inspiring hire. He's uncovered a lot about the radical Negro element in Dallas."

"Carl's a good officer who'd make a fine detective." Wilson took out his Luckies. He shook one loose. "You've buttered me up enough, Jack. I can hear a train coming and it's heading straight for me." He used the lighter on Revill's desk to light his cigarette. "Let's get it over with."

"There's no train." Revill shrugged. "Okay, maybe a train *horn*, but the train's still a long ways off. Hell, the train hasn't even left the station yet. Nor will it, depending on how this conversation goes."

Wilson took a drag. *Christ.*

Revill eased into the bad news. "It's just that some folks are starting to wonder if maybe it's time for the task force to lay off a little. Not hit it so hard."

Wilson pocketed his cigarettes. "Folks like General Walker."

"Walker. The mayor. The chief. The NAACP folks, too. You've shined a light on their ties to Red organizations, too. You've done a great job of offending everyone, which was what we'd hoped for."

Wilson smoked. He waited for the qualifier.

"But," Revill added, "the Walker riot was a long time ago. People have already started to forget. They want to move on. Digging around like this just keeps the wound open. Causes it to fester."

"It's been festering for years. I'm trying to keep it from turning gangrene."

"And you have. But the mayor's friends are getting nervous. He answers to people too, you know. It's not like ending the task force will cost you anything. You'll be in a great position. Your work has impressed a lot of people. The right kind of people who can help you move up in the department. You're not just Duke Wilson's boy anymore."

I was never just Duke Wilson's boy.

Revill continued. "You're seen as your own man now. After the Farley and

191

Walker incidents, there's talk about possibly promoting you. The mayor and the chief like the idea."

Wilson called it what it was. "A payoff."

"A way of you getting a squad of your own. And sooner than you think. I know you're fond of Carl. Maybe you'll be in a position to help him."

Wilson flicked his ash in the tray on the desk. They thought shutting down the task force would stop him. They didn't know about his dirt pile. About the evidence he'd stashed in a bank vault across town. "How long before you shut me down?"

"We're not there yet. This is Jack and Dan talking now. Think of it as some unofficial advice. Think about your future. Know enough to quit when you're ahead. Take your chips off the table and enjoy your winnings."

"Gambling analogies?" Wilson shifted in his chair. "Jesus, Jack. Come on."

Revill surrendered. "Okay, so I'm not a philosopher or an orator. But you know I'm right. Start thinking of ways you can gradually scale down your operations with…"

There were two black phones on Revill's desk. One only rang when it was important. It rang now.

Revill answered it on the first ring. "Yes, chief."

Revill's expression told all. Wilson was on his feet before Revill hung up.

Revill said, "Grab your coat. Someone just tried to kill General Walker."

* * *

The street in front of Walker's home was choked with cars. Dallas PD prowlers had boxed in civilian cars. Lights flashed. Police radios chattered.

A uniform waved Wilson in. He parked the Galaxie and followed Revill up to Walker's house. The general in the front yard. He was talking to a gaggle of reporters. Shutterbugs snapped pictures of the animated general outside his stately home.

"Just look at me!" Walker shook dust from his hair and shirt. "I survive war and almost get killed in my own den. I've been warning you people that the Communists will be the death of this country. Now you see just how ruthless they can be. But I won't stop. If anything, I'm more emboldened than ever."

Revill and Wilson went into the house. Lieutenant E.L. 'Elmo' Cunningham was in the hallway. He was interviewing Walker's aide Bob Carter. Elmo worked the Forgery squad. He answered other calls when necessary.

Elmo wrote down Carter's answers. But you weren't here when it happened?"

"No." Carter would've failed an inspection. His hair hadn't been combed. His shirt tails were out. His sweater was crooked. "I was at home when the general called me. I came over as soon as I could."

Detective Ira Van Cleave was in Walker's office. He caught Wilson's eye. He beckoned him to look at something.

Van Cleave pointed at a window sash with a gouge in it. "The bullet cut through there before ending up in the wall over here. Walker said he was at his desk doing his taxes when it happened. Said he thought it was just some kids lighting firecrackers until he saw the bullet hole."

Wilson went to the window. He saw the gash from the bullet. A church parking lot was behind the house. A wooden picket fence divided the two properties. A floodlight illuminated all.

Wilson traced the path from the window to the bullet hole in the wall. The round was still embedded in the plaster. "Firecrackers in April? He knows what a rifle sounds like."

"Don't shoot the messenger," Van Cleave said. "I just wrote down what the general told me. Said he didn't know it was a shot until some of the debris landed on him."

Wilson looked at a credenza. It was against the wall below the bullet hole. A thin coating of plaster dust was smeared on the wood. *Like it had been scooped up. Or pinched.*

"You touch anything since you got here?"

Van Cleave looked insulted. "Are you nuts? I can't even dig the round out of the wall until the photographer takes pictures of the crime scene."

Wilson looked down at the general's desk. A folder with 'Taxes' handwritten on the tab was among other papers and correspondence. Among, not on top. *He was doing his taxes, got shot at, then put away the file?*

"Anyone canvassing the area?"

Van Cleave said, "Cunningham's handling that side of things."

Wilson looked out into the hall. Cunningham and Revill were still interviewing Carter. Cunningham wrote down every word on his notepad.

Wilson went outside. He walked to the fence line. Three uniforms were using flashlights to search the ground for spent shells. Wilson called out to them, "Find anything?"

They shook their heads. They kept looking.

A boy of about fourteen was standing at a gap in the fence. "Hey, mister. You a cop?"

Wilson said, "That's what it says on my badge. Get to bed. It's a school night."

"Can't sleep." The kid looked around Walker's yard. He looked at the house. "I'm a witness, you know? I saw it happen."

Wilson knew kids made lousy witnesses. They were highly suggestible. They were prone to exaggeration. He'd probably seen a masked man on a white horse named Silver.

Wilson pulled out his pad and pen anyway. "Okay, mister. What's your name?"

"Kirk Coleman, and I'm fourteen years old. Hey, did anyone ever tell you that you look like Clint Walker?"

"You're the first. What do you think you saw?"

"My uncle and me were putting up shelves in my room when I heard this loud bang come from right over there." He pointed to the church parking lot. The same direction from where Van Cleave thought the shot had come. "I ran out on the back porch and saw them over the fence. Saw them plain as day."

Wilson stopped writing. The kid was specific. "Them? How many?"

The kid held up two fingers. "Two men and two cars. One of them had bushy hair. He had tan pants. The same color as his Ford. He had a sports shirt. Was skinny and had a long nose. He drove off in a tan Ford that way." Kirk pointed out toward Turtle Creek Boulevard. "He took his time, too.

He didn't speed off or nothing."

The kid had an eye for detail. Wilson wrote it down. "And the second guy?"

"I saw him put something in the back seat of a black and white coupe. He had a dark shirt with long sleeves and dark pants. But I didn't see his face. I got spooked when he looked at me. I ran back into the house and shut the door."

Wilson stopped writing. Bob Carter owned a black-over-white Impala. "Sounds like you know a lot about cars."

"My dad's a mechanic. I think it was an Impala, but like I said, I got spooked. I didn't even see which direction it headed in."

Wilson played a hunch. "Ever see these men or their cars before?"

"I don't think so, but I might recognize them if I saw them again."

A uniform called out to Wilson. "Lieutenant Revill wants to see you in the front yard, detective."

Wilson handed Kirk his official business card. "Do me a favor. Tell this officer everything you told me. Don't leave anything out."

The kid looked at the card like he'd been deputized. *At least I made one person happy today.*

* * *

Wilson joined Cunningham and Revill in the front yard. The general still entertained questions from some reporters.

Revill offered a cigarette to Cunningham. "What's your verdict, Mo? What does your gut say?"

Cunningham took the cigarette and lit it. "I haven't seen a staged production like that since my kid's Christmas pageant. I don't think Walker was even in the room when it happened."

Revill said, "Tell me why."

Cunningham did. "The line of fire from the yard to the wall was pretty straight. The window sash didn't alter the bullet's path by much, if at all. It still should've hit him right in the forehead. He wasn't even grazed. And who only fires a single shot at a stationary target? It smells wrong."

Wilson was glad to pile on. "A neighbor's kid told me there were two shooters in two separate vehicles. He got a good look at the cars. One was a black-over-white Chevy. Bob Carter drives a black-over-white Chevy."

Cunningham got cautious. "Walker's got a lot of friends in this city. He's close to the mayor. If I write this up as I see it, I'll be lucky to keep my badge. You CID boys know all the angles. Tell me how I can write this up without losing my job."

Revill had an idea. "Dig that bullet out of the wall. Wait to see what Carl Day's crime scene boys tell you. Write up a preliminary report and send it to me. I'll tell Chief Curry that CID is taking over the case. We've been monitoring Walker for a while now. That should get you off the hook."

Cunningham thanked Revill. He went back into the house.

Wilson and Revill walked back to the car. They ignored questions from reporters.

Wilson got behind the wheel. He started up the engine.

Revill rode shotgun. "How'd you know Bob Carter drives a black-over-white Chevy?"

Wilson thought fast. He'd just made his first mistake. He'd allowed the dirt pile to spill into official business. Revill never missed anything. "It came up during the Walker announcement. Guess it just stuck in my head."

Revill lit a cigarette. "Funny how that happens, isn't it?"

Wilson put it in gear and backed down the street. There was nothing funny about it.

Chapter Twenty-Five

Tippit drove along Stemmons Freeway. Rain steady on the windshield. The wipers moved in time with "Surfin' USA" on the radio.

Ruby dozed in the back seat. He had a big night ahead. The Bon Vivant Lounge beckoned.

Driving for Jack was a gas. He liked the low-lifes and highlights of the Dallas nightlife. *Ruby, Ruby, burning bright. See the fat man dance beneath the neon lights.*

He made the rounds. The Carousel Club. The Vegas Club. Other dives he controlled around town.

He swept in. He swooned over oil men. He glad-handed politicians. He charmed executives. He flattered their girlfriends and mistresses. He spread good cheer and moved on to the next hellhole. Like a cut-rate Santa Claus.

Tippit didn't mind. He had it made. He rode Ruby's coattails. He drank for free. He met beautiful girls. He got paid by Ruby. He got paid by the Feds. He had immunity from prosecution. He told Wilson all.

About Ruby's weekly pilgrimages to The Egyptian Lounge to give Joe Campisi his cut. About Ruby's late-night phone calls to Carlos Marcello. Calls made from phone booths at gas stations and drug stores and diners all over town, none of them controlled by The Boys. Ruby was careful.

The Bon Vivant Lounge at the Cabana Motel was different. It was schmooze central. The Carousel and Vegas clubs catered to swells on the slum. The Bon Vivant was swank on parade.

Thursday night was Cop Night at the BV. Dallas PD brass arrived in packs.

Captains and chiefs. Eastbrook was a regular. He and Ruby talked shop. They shared laughs. They swapped secrets. They colluded and didn't care who heard it. Sometimes they got sloppy. Tippit had to pour Gus Rhodes and Jerry Sill into a cab last week. Eastbrook's favorite detectives had too many Mai Tais.

But tonight was Friday night. Friday night was Rich Kid Night at the BV. It was for Big D's bigwigs. Where oil barons and compadres sipped champagne to celebrate their growing empires.

Ruby played it smart. He didn't drink. He mingled with movers and shakers. He liked being seen with influential people. Influential people liked being seen with dangerous men.

Ruby shared stories. He laughed at bad jokes. He listened to rich man troubles. He heard past grievances. He soaked up current gossip. He played *macher* to the swells. He vowed assistance whenever they needed it.

Ruby got sloppy in other ways. He ran his mouth on the ride home. He shared secrets.

Tippit listened. Tippit told Wilson everything he saw and heard.

Tippit should've felt guilty. Ruby had been good to him. Tippit didn't feel guilty. He needed the money.

They were a few blocks away from the Bon Vivant when Ruby woke up. "Turn that shit off. I hate The Beach Boys."

Tippit complied. Jack was post-snooze cranky.

Ruby stretched and yawned in the back seat. "I've been meaning to ask you something. It's been eating at me for a while now."

Tippit stayed calm. His .38 was on his hip. He'd kept it in reach since the Crawford incident. *Had Wilson screwed up? Had Dallas PD brass learned about the feds?*

Ruby stopped yawning. "You ever notice that 'burlesque' and 'barbeque' are almost the same word, but pronounced different? That's strange, ain't it?"

Tippit breathed again. *The way his mind works.* "You're asking the wrong guy. I've got enough trouble with English."

"I've noticed," Ruby said. "You've been awful quiet lately. And not in a good way. Things still bad on the home front?"

"Slowly getting better." Marie had let him back in the house. He only had couch privileges. He got home late most nights anyway. It was good to see the kids and have a decent meal. It was better than a cot at the precinct. "She's still frosty, but thawing."

"How's your buddy Wilson? You don't talk about him much anymore. We had a deal, you and me."

Wilson had given him a script. "I ran into him at headquarters today. He said Walker's been burning up the phone lines to Chief Curry and Mayor Cabell. He thinks Dallas PD is dogging that Schneider thing and the shooting at his house."

"Schneider the Swish." Ruby laughed. "There's been some whispers about the general along those lines. Not that you can hold it against him." He sighed and looked out the window. "The heart wants what it wants, I guess."

Tippit glanced at him in the rearview. "You gonna sing a Doris Day song or do you want to hear what else Wilson told me?"

"Don't be a smart ass. I'm all ears."

Tippit stuck to Wilson's script. "Wilson thinks the Walker shooting is a setup. A gimmick to keep his name in the papers. That one of his guys did it. They said Walker wasn't even in the room when it happened."

"That's so?" Ruby sat back like he'd just finished a big meal. "That's good. I'll have to tell him when I see him later tonight."

Tippit caught that. "He's going to be at the lounge?"

"He's too respectable for that. You and me'll swing by his place in Turtle Creek later.

"Hubba, hubba, hubba." Tippit made the next left. "You're coming up in the world, Jack."

Ruby watched raindrops streak down the window. The rain had let up some.

His silence said a lot.

Tippit pulled off Stemmons Freeway. He cruised into The Cabana Motel parking lot. He stopped in front of the lounge entrance.

Ruby danced out of the car. "Go grab something to eat. Be back here in half an hour."

Tippit shook his pack of Chesterfields. "Thanks, but I brought my dinner."

Ruby shot his cuffs and straightened his tie. The doorman tipped his hat. Ruby gave him a five-spot for opening the door.

Tippit circled the lot. He pulled into a spot next to a red Corvair. He got out and lit a Chesterfield. He leaned on the roof of the Olds. *Just another driver stretching his legs.*

Carl Ford was hunkered down in the back seat of the Corvair. His camera aimed at the front of the lounge.

Tippit didn't turn around. "Hope you got my good side."

"I would if you had one." Carl advanced the roll in his camera. "I took lots of interesting pictures tonight. Wilson's gonna be happy."

"Wilson wouldn't be Wilson if he was happy." Dan had been different since the Schneider thing. Terse. Edgy.

Schneider wasn't Wilson's first kill, but his first murder. He'd get over it in time. He had nothing to worry about. Tippit had scattered Schneider's .45 in storm drains all over town. "I thought you'd be debriefing Oswald tonight."

"Wilson wanted me here instead." Carl took pictures of an approaching Chevy. "Good thing he did. Lots of new faces tonight."

Tippit watched the lot. He took a drag. "Anyone I'd know?"

"Never seen them before. But then again, you all look the same to me."

Tippit grinned. *Score one for civil rights.* "Get to a phone. Tell Wilson that Ruby's going to a meeting at General Walker's place after this. I don't know who'll be there, but I'd slap a fresh roll of film in that thing. You might need it."

"Good thing I brought extra."

Tippit watched as a breeze carried his smoke across the lot. "You know the address, so don't follow us too close. Jack's been twitchy all day. He might spot you."

Carl began climbing to the front seat. "I'll call Wilson now and get up there early. Find a spot on the street."

"Wait." Tippit watched a Cadillac glide in front of the club and stop. "Take their picture."

He watched the driver get out. He watched him open the back door.

Carl took pictures through the back windshield.

A squat old man toddled out of the backseat. White crewcut and horn-rimmed glasses. His blazer was wrinkled. The second button was missing. Tippit saw dandruff flakes on his shoulders.

Two men in blue suits stepped out.

Tippit tossed his cigarette aside. *Holy shit.*

Carl worked the lens. He snapped pictures. "More new faces. Been like this all night."

Tippit recognized the second suit. It was Niles Lundt. HB Lundt's son. The Lundts were big oil. They were one of the wealthiest families in the world.

That explained Ruby's good mood. He was making some new friends.

* * *

Oswald had been different since the Walker shooting. He'd stopped checking in. He didn't return Wilson's calls.

Wilson caught him at home. Wilson threatened to drag him outside.

Wilson parked in a narrow alley. It was too narrow for Oswald to run.

Wilson killed the lights. He had some tough questions for the kid. The best confessions happened in the dark. "Talk."

Oswald fidgeted.

Wilson said, "I don't have time for this shit. Were you involved in the Walker thing?"

Oswald looked at the brick wall. "No, but..."

Wilson couldn't let him retreat now. "Start at the beginning."

Oswald inhaled. He took a running start at it. "Mr. Blaine and his wife came to my house on Sunday afternoon. They never visit. They came in separate cars."

"Why didn't you call me?"

"I didn't have time," Oswald said. "Then Ruth took Marina and the baby to the park. Mr. Blaine drove me to a friend's house."

The old tactic. *Isolate the subject.* "Where? What friend?

"He said his name was Juan, but I didn't believe that. It was near South Dallas. Near Carl's church."

Wilson would press for more on 'Juan' later. "What happened then?"

"Juan and Mr. Blaine were happy. They said the general's tour went better than anyone expected. Then things got weird."

"How weird?"

"Mike brought out a rifle. He was acting proud of it. Put gloves on, like it was an antique. But it wasn't. It was just a cheap foreign hunk of junk he'd gotten in the mail."

Wilson needed specifics. "What make and model?"

"Nothing special. Just a carbine with a scope. Mr. Blaine kept trying to hand it to me, but I wouldn't touch it. It didn't feel right. Why was he wearing gloves? Then he tossed it to me. Guess he figured I'd catch it, but I didn't. It hit the floor and screwed up the scope. I thought Mr. Blaine was gonna slug me for a minute, but Juan calmed him down."

Wilson encouraged him. "You were smart, Lee. What happened then?"

"They started badgering me about helping the cause. They wanted me to shoot through General Walker's window. They swore the general wouldn't be home. That it would help the cause. It would look like some Communist had tried to kill him. But I wouldn't go. They yelled at me for hours, but I wouldn't budge."

Wilson remembered the teenager's description. Skinny. Long nose. Bushy hair.

His description matched Blaine.

Wilson tried to keep him calm. "What did Juan look like?"

"Not like any Juan I've ever met," Oswald said. "He was pale, on the thin side. Maybe around my age, too. He didn't have an accent or anything."

That didn't help. He'd just described most men in Dallas.

Oswald's voice caught. "I told you something like this would happen."

Wilson steadied him. "What about New Orleans? Is that still on?"

"Yeah," Oswald said. "They've got a job lined up for me, but Mr. Blaine said Marina and the baby will stay with them. They said my family can't come until I'm settled."

Wilson didn't buy it. They were isolating him again. Making him comply. Marina's family was KGB. She'd see what the Blaines were up to. She was probably working with them now.

Wilson couldn't tell Oswald that. He'd never believe it.

Wilson started up the Galaxie. "I can help you while you're in New Orleans if you let me."

"No, you can't," Oswald pouted. "You can't help me from five hundred miles away."

Wilson drove out of the alley. "You're not the only one in this car with secrets."

* * *

Denton watched the street. He watched every car that pulled into Walker's driveway. Comrades paying tribute to the returning hero. The Midnight Ride tour had been a success. The attempt on his life had failed.

Denton knew better. He knew the truth.

He watched Walker's men flit around the guests like flies around meat.

Walker's men talked tougher than they were. Schneider's death had rattled them. The Swish Street locale threw them. They wanted Eastbrook to avenge him. They wanted Swish Street to run red with blood.

Eastbrook forbade it. Swish Street was sacred ground. Too many respectable people frequented the area. Secrets might come to light. Schneider wasn't worth the risk.

Walker's men weren't cops. Cops would've gotten revenge anyway. Walker's men followed orders. They stood down.

Denton followed orders, too. Eastbrook had given him one. To work with Mike Blaine on the Walker shooting. The general's men wouldn't do the deed. They knew suspicion might fall on them. They had alibis. Eastbrook told Denton to make sure it went as planned. That no innocents got hurt.

It was amateur hour from the start. Blaine was no de Mohrenschildt. He was dumber than he thought. His plan was shit. It was too complicated.

Blaine had Denton help browbeat one of his saps into doing the deed. He even gave Denton a code name. Juan.

Blaine miscalculated. The sap was smarter than he looked. The sap refused.

Denton did the deed. Blaine's mail order rifle was shit. It jammed after one shot.

Eastbrook ordered Denton to keep the gun. They'd pin the shooting on a Commie later. Maybe they'd pick a winner at tonight's shindig.

Denton watched a Cadillac glide to the curb. He watched as Bob Carter jogged down the driveway to meet it.

He watched an old man with a white buzz cut toddle out of the back seat. His blazer was shiny from too many ironings. His shirt collar was frayed. He didn't match Walker's tony crowd.

Carter greeted him like a long-lost uncle. "Mr. Milteer. How good of you to come."

Carter practically bowed at the ankles. He apologized for the full driveway. He escorted the old geezer up to the house.

The Cadillac pulled away. Jack Ruby's Oldsmobile took its place. Tippit at the wheel.

Jack rolled out of the back. He shot his cuffs and straightened his tie. Denton watched him swagger up to Walker's house. *See that fat man go.* Sweat stains broke out on his back halfway up the driveway. He raked a comb across the three strands on his head. Jack was still vain.

Denton caught movement in his sideview mirror. A red Corvair parked across the street, several cars back. Someone was moving inside. It had been empty when Denton got there.

Tippit bumped the mirror as he leaned inside. "License and registration, please."

Denton wasn't amused. "Look who's here. Jack's new errand boy."

"Don't knock it." Tippit dug out a smoke. He didn't offer Denton one. "Comes with some nice perks. Look at the high-class crowd I get to hang around with. Present company excluded, of course."

Denton still wasn't amused. "You're out here cooling your heels just like me, asshole."

Tippit lit up. "Yeah, but I'm getting paid more than you."

Eastbrook had warned him to avoid Tippit. He didn't want a scene. Denton adjusted his rearview. *Where's that Corvair?*

Tippit blew smoke into the car. The smoke hit his eyes. It hit his lungs mid-breath. He coughed and gasped. "What the hell is the matter with you?"

Tippit feigned an apology. He fanned the smoke away from him. "Sorry, Harry. The wind took it."

Denton kept coughing. "What are you doing out here anyway? I thought Wilson would've brought you on his task force by now. Guess that business with Molly queered that."

Tippit stopped fanning the smoke. "Good old Harry. Always pushing too far."

"Ain't you heard? This is what's called 'camaraderie'. The captain says a little hazing among fellow officers is good for morale."

Tippit pushed off the car. He walked back to Ruby's heap. "You ought to learn to laugh a little. You'll live longer."

Denton stirred his lungs. He spat in Tippit's direction. It landed behind him. It made him feel better anyway.

He adjusted his sideview. He looked behind him. The red Corvair was gone.

Tippit and his big mouth.

Chapter Twenty-Six

Monday, April 15, 1963

Zeke had called a meeting. Nine-thirty AM in the study room of the Oak Cliff Library.

Fritz and Wilson arrived in separate cars. They browsed the shelves. They drifted into the study room separately. Wilson was the last one in.

Zeke shut the door. The lock was busted. He slid a chair under the knob.

Zeke had been in Dallas for eighteen months. His devolution from FBI field agent to strip joint bartender was complete. Cigarettes and late nights had yellowed his skin. His cheeks were hollow. His thin mustache was peppered with gray. The bags under his eyes were heavy and dark. *The street always takes its toll.*

Zeke said, "Washington is capping The Pipeline investigation as of today."

Wilson's gut dropped.

Fritz steadied himself on the back of a chair. "They have enough to go to court?"

"No. It's over, captain. The wires at the diner have gone dry. Washington thinks we've gotten everything we can in Dallas." Zeke looked at Wilson. "I passed along your suggestion about bugging other locations. They aren't interested. Manpower and budget concerns."

Wilson kicked the chair in front of him. No Pipeline meant no peripheral access to the FBI. No getting out of Dallas.

Zeke continued. "I think the Walker shooting had something to do with their decision. They think Dallas is too wild and beyond saving. The administration knows it won't win any moral victories here. The good citizens of Dallas don't seem to mind a bit of corruption."

Fritz stood up slow. "Not all of us think that way."

"Washington doesn't care. But don't look too broken up about it. You two are getting what you wanted. Your precious department is safe from the clutches of the big, bad bureau."

Wilson didn't care about Dallas PD. His only connection to the FBI was in peril. A post in Washington got further away by the second. "What about all the hours we put in? All the work?"

Zeke said, "James Bookhout, my colleague at the bureau, is reviewing it. So is the U.S. Attorney's office. But it's not big enough to move on either Eastbrook or Ruby. They'll probably just sit on it. Maybe add it to bigger charges somewhere down the line if needed."

Wilson felt the room shift. The Pipeline fed his dirt pile. He didn't have enough for leverage yet. Revill was shutting down his task force. He needed more time. More proof.

Without The Pipeline, Wilson was just another local cop peddling a pet theory. He'd lose credibility. He'd become a joke. Again.

Wilson got desperate. "I have something that'll keep them interested."

Fritz glared. *Don't.*

Zeke pitied him with a smile. "You've got nothing they want. Dallas is dead to them. A picture of Earle Cabell kissing Khruschev wouldn't be enough to change their minds."

"I'm talking about something federal. I'm talking about the interstate trafficking of guns and ammunition."

Fritz sat down. His face was scarlet.

Zeke folded his arms. "You're talking about Ruby?"

Wilson said, "I recently uncovered it through my task force. Ruby's been shipping truckloads of guns to New Orleans. The last shipment was about a month ago."

Zeke shrugged. "The US Attorney might be interested. Keep him apprised."

Fritz pulled out a handkerchief. He patted his brow. *That was close.*

Wilson wasn't done. "My task force also has evidence that Walker is tied to hate groups beyond Dallas. All over the country."

Fritz almost punched the chair. *Danny!*

Zeke feigned a yawn. "Tell me something we don't already know. His Midnight Ride tour more than proved that. You're swinging at pitches in the dirt, Danny. Spare your pride and head back to the dugout. Desperation is a bad look."

Wilson had no choice. He bet it all. "I have photographic evidence of Joseph Milteer meeting with Niles Lundt and General Walker last night."

Zeke grew still. "Bullshit."

Lucky number seven. Wilson grinned. "Would I lie to you? After all we've meant to each other."

Fritz stopped dabbing sweat. "Who's Milteer?"

Wilson repeated facts from his dirt pile. "An ex-Klansman out of Georgia with no love for our beloved president and his brother. He's been involved with pro-segregation and anti-Commie groups for years. His old man croaked last year. Left him a quarter of a million bucks. He's started throwing cash around to causes he deems worthy. Causes like Walker and Hargis's Midnight Ride tour. I think the tour's success has encouraged him. I think he's ramping up for something bigger." *Think, but can't prove.*

Fritz looked lost. "Why haven't you mentioned him in any Pipeline reports?"

"Because I didn't know until this morning. He didn't come up before because he's not based out of Dallas. But I have pictures of him at a meeting at Walker's house last night. I've got photos of him and Niles Lundt at the Bon Vivant Lounge, too."

Zeke squinted. He focused on details. "How long have you've been watching Walker?"

"Long enough."

Zeke grew suspicious. "Prove you saw Milteer. What does he look like?"

"Sixty. Short. Round. Horn-rimmed glasses. Silver crewcut. Looks like a harmless old man, but the meanest ones always do."

Zeke blinked. He licked his lips. "I want those pictures. Where are they?"

Carl had gotten Oswald out of bed last night. He'd made him develop them. "Quid pro quo."

Zeke grew wary. "Careful, Dan. You're flying pretty high. You might get a nosebleed. Your wings might melt."

"Wouldn't be the first time."

Zeke folded his arms again. He'd come to deliver bad news. He was used to being in charge. This wasn't part of his plan. "Produce those photos immediately or I'll arrest you for withholding evidence and obstructing a federal investigation."

"Desperation's a bad look for you, too." Wilson leaned forward. "You want to cap The Pipeline and head back north? Fine. But if you want Milteer, I want in."

Zeke snapped. "You shit-kicking son of a bitch. I don't need your goddamned pictures. I'll put Smith and Marsh on Walker and the Lundt family. I'll put men on Milteer, too, wherever he is."

Wilson said, "Go ahead. The Lundts have more money than God. They've got ex-FBI men working security for them. Washington wouldn't approve any action against Lundt. "The bureau's got men on Milteer in other states, but not all the time. And they sure as hell didn't have anyone watching Walker's house last night. I did. I've got proof linking him directly to Walker and Lundt. Give me time and I'll prove more. I'll salvage your career while I'm at it, but I get something, too. Call it a going away present from you to me."

Zeke sneered. "How about a junior G-man badge and a certificate from Hoover?"

"How about making me the Dallas PD's liaison to the FBI?"

Fritz lowered his head. *The boy's gone and done it now.*

Zeke stopped sneering.

Wilson pushed his luck. "The Walker riot bought me good will. The chief and Revill like me. So does the mayor. Make the request and they'll grant it. Once it's official, you get your pictures of Milteer and Lundt and Walker.

I'll even throw in a list of everyone who attended. It makes for interesting reading. Agree to my terms and we all leave with bright futures. Tell me you'll think about it and the price goes way up."

Zeke bristled. "Don't get greedy."

"Don't get stupid and I won't have to."

Fritz folded his handkerchief. "Dan worked day and night for months. He deserves this. Give it to him."

Zeke shook his head. "You good ol' boys sure stick together, don't you? Deserving doesn't count."

Wilson said, "But leverage does. You taught me that."

Zeke's eyes darted. He looked at the scarred wooden table. At initials carved in pen. At the crooked chairs. Their seats smoothed from use. At forgotten books on bowed shelves.

Zeke said, "I'll make the call, but I can't guarantee it'll do any good."

"Yes you can."

Zeke went to the door. He tossed aside the chair under the knob. "You'll have your goddamned appointment by lunch. I want those pictures an hour later. All of them. The list and the negatives, too."

Zeke stormed out. He left the door open.

Fritz pulled himself out of his chair. "Boy, you've got no idea how close you came to killing your career just now. You're on the verge of becoming a goddamned menace."

Wilson didn't need Fritz's cautious wisdom anymore. He'd gotten what he wanted. "Only to the wrong people."

Chapter Twenty-Seven

Saturday, August 2, 1963

W ilson worked the grill. Connie played hostess.

Not even a scorching Dallas summer afternoon could wilt such a red-letter day. Officer Carl Ford had been promoted to detective.

Carl looked sharp in his dress blues. He couldn't stop smiling. Neither could Wilson. He was part of something good for a change.

Chief Curry had kept the promotion quiet. Few of the rank and file were happy that a black man had made detective before them. That he'd passed the same tests they'd failed.

The ceremony at headquarters had been small and quiet. Carl's brother, the reverend, had led the invocation. Carl's mother and sisters had brought pies to the cookout. His mother had learned to walk well with a cane. Carl's nieces and nephews played with the Tippit and Wilson kids.

Missy watched it all from beneath the back deck. She wasn't a kitten anymore, but still small.

Wilson saw Ed Mannes peering over the shrubs between their properties. A bald, beady-eyed varmint married to the neighborhood flirt. Ed stayed home and read. No one blamed her for stepping out.

Wilson tended to the hot dogs and burgers sizzling on the grill. "Afternoon, Ed. Hungry? There's plenty to go around."

Ed scowled at the squealing kids, at Carl's family helping Connie set up

211

the table. "You brought their kind here? To Highland Park?"

Wilson flipped a burger. "A cop's family is always welcome here."

Ed squinted at Carl talking to the Tippits. Carl's sister brought out plates and silverware. "It ain't right. Makes the whole neighborhood look bad."

Wilson flipped another burger. "That's the beautiful thing about those shrubs, Ed. They keep you from seeing what's happening next door. Run along before I run you in on a peeper charge."

The shrubs rustled. Mannes retreated.

Connie was all smiles as she brought over a serving plate. She couldn't have looked prettier if she'd tried. She was immune to the harsh Dallas summers. "What did that weasel want?"

"No idea. He just stood there and went away. You know how he is."

"I know how you are. You probably said something vulgar."

Wilson flipped another burger. "Not exactly vulgar."

Connie didn't scold him. "I never could stand that creepy old bastard anyway."

He smiled. She never ceased to surprise him. "They teach you to talk like that in Junior League?"

"They also taught us it's rude to keep guests waiting for their food. How long?"

He grabbed the tongs. He plucked hot dogs and put them on Connie's plate. "Come back for the burgers. They'll be done in a minute."

"These'll do for now. I want the kids to get something in their bellies before they get overheated."

Connie held the plate high as the children crowded around her. Missy darted out from under the deck. She dove under the serving table. Whatever hit the grass belonged to her.

Wilson caught Tippit's eye. He waved for Carl and him to join him at the grill.

He and Carl could talk shop in front of Tippit. He'd proven his loyalty. His intel on Ruby and his friends had helped the dirt pile grow.

Tippit took a Miller from the ice bucket by the grill. He opened it and handed it to Wilson. "You look like you could use this."

Wilson took it. "More than you know." He flipped another burger.

Carl's dress blues were still crisp despite the heat. "I can't thank you enough for this, Dan. All of it. It means a lot to me and my family." He looked down at the new shield on his uniform. "Never thought I'd get one of these."

"You earned it." Wilson had folded the Extremist Task Force into his FBI liaison assignment. He'd kept Carl on as his investigator. He worked files. Compiled reports. Ran leads. He learned to think like a detective. He flourished.

Carl's commitment had earned Wilson's trust. He gave Carl access to his safe deposit boxes. He worked the dirt pile. He investigated the Bannister - Walker - Milteer triumvirate. He got to know the files better than Wilson. And he still debriefed Oswald twice a week via long distance.

Wilson flipped another burger. He asked Carl, "How's our friend in New Orleans?"

"Not good." Carl tapped his temple. "Up here. New Orleans is a bad place for him."

"Don't blame the town." Tippit sipped some beer. "That kid was never wrapped too tight."

"He's even worse now," Carl said. "He got fired from that job in the coffee company that Bannister got him. Now Bannister's got him playing the pro-Castro radical full-time. Writing to leftist groups back east. Subscribing to leftist newsletters. Joining pro-Castro groups all over town. He's got Lee making a damned spectacle of himself."

Wilson had read Carl's debriefing reports. He surmised Bannister's intent. "He's building up Lee's Commie bona fides. Don't ask me why."

Tippit said, "If the kid is so miserable, why doesn't he just leave?"

"Because he's stuck," Carl said. "Bannister barely pays him enough to make ends meet. And Marina's pregnant. The Blaines want her to come back to Dallas to have the baby."

Wilson recognized the pattern. They were isolating Oswald again. "They've got Lee coming and going. If he leaves, it's without his family. If he stays, he's stuck doing Bannister's handiwork. And it's about to get a whole lot tougher on him."

The charcoals hissed as the meat dripped on them. He told Carl, "That's why I need you in New Orleans by tomorrow night. Official business. Revill and the feds have already signed off on it."

Carl didn't hesitate. "I'll head out at first light. What do you need me to do?"

Tippit didn't know much about Wilson's duties as FBI liaison. He clued him in. "I compile the Dallas portion of the FBI's weekly intelligence briefings. I also get to read the finished product for the entire southern region."

Tippit sipped beer. "Hubba, hubba, hubba."

Wilson continued. "I read how the feds were tracking large numbers of Cubans flocking to New Orleans for the past month. They hit town and vanish. The bureau couldn't explain it."

Carl caught on fast. "But you could. Thanks to the dirt pile."

"I told them about Bannister's camp in Lake Pontchartrain."

Tippit sipped more beer. "Hope you didn't tell them how you came by that information. For my sake."

"Relax. I said it was an old tip from a confidential informant from my task force days. I kept Bannister's name out of it, too. I knew his name would jump off the page. Hoover might quash it. I just lit the fuse and watched the flame take." Wilson had saved the best for last. "Bobby Kennedy saw the smoke. He's ordered the feds to raid the Lake Pontchartrain camp."

"You clever bastard." Tippit laughed. "Good old Danny Boy."

Carl asked, "You think Bannister's making some kind of move?"

"He's up to something. Maybe another invasion. Maybe something closer to home."

The reason didn't matter. The raid did. The raid had raised his profile with the bureau. Forget Hoover. Wilson had impressed Hoover's boss.

Tippit drained his beer and got another. "When's the raid?"

Wilson only trusted him so far. Tippit had proven his loyalty, but still worked for Ruby. "I'm guessing it'll happen sometime soon." He looked at Carl. "That's why I want you in New Orleans. To keep an eye on Lee until after the raid. Bannister and his friends will get swept up in this. Lee might get swept up, too. He has to know he's still got friends. If I ask the feds to do it, they might get suspicious about Lee."

Carl asked, "If he doesn't get arrested, you want me to bring him back?"

"Maybe." Wilson flipped another burger. "For now, just shadow him and tell me what's happening."

Tippit opened his beer. "I heard something when I was with Ruby last night. He said Kennedy's coming to Dallas."

Juice from the burger hit the coals. Flames shot up. "Jack's dreaming."

"Don't be so sure," Tippit said. "He spends lots of time with Walker and his friends these days. Jack said the date's being worked out, but it looks like November. Johnson's pushing for it. Ruby's excited. He wants a picture with Jack and Jackie."

"Never gonna happen." Carl tossed his empty bottle in the trash bag by the grill. "That'd be like me going to a Klan rally."

Tippit said, "They'd welcome you before Kennedy."

Wilson started piling the burgers on the plate. Carl nudged his arm. "We've got company."

Wilson saw Harry Denton walking around from the front of the house.

Wilson handed the tray of burgers to Tippit. "Give these to Connie. See if she needs help with anything. I'll find out what this asshole wants."

Wilson took off his cook's apron. He tossed it on the ground. He regretted leaving his Magnum upstairs.

Denton watched him approach. He worked a toothpick in the corner of his mouth. "You should've kept the apron. It suits you."

"Want a plate?"

"No thanks." He looked at the Fords. "Fried chicken and chitlins ain't my thing."

"That's the first time you've ever refused a handout. What do you want?"

Denton thumbed over his shoulder. "The captain wants to see you. Out front."

Wilson waited for Denton to go first. He wouldn't let Denton behind him. Eastbrook was sitting in the back of his unmarked Galaxie, the window open. He fanned himself with his Stetson.

Eastbrook watched Wilson approach the car. "You're a better man than I am, Danny. Having a cookout on a hot day like this. I know Ford's your pet coon, but this is a bit much."

Wilson stood back from the car. He kept Denton and Eastbrook in view. "I get paid to hear your bullshit during the week. This is my day off. State your business or leave."

Eastbrook feigned insult. "Someone's gotten uppity since his promotion. A promotion I approved, by the way."

"Because Chief Curry told you to. Last chance. What do you want?"

Eastbrook looked back at Denton. "We stop by to pass along some friendly advice, and this is the thanks we get." He sighed dramatically. He looked at Wilson. "You've disappointed a lot of people."

"Story of my life."

"Being friendly with a colored officer is one thing," Eastbrook said. "Working with one is something else. But promoting one? Having them at your home like this? Well, that crosses more lines than I can count. And I can count pretty high."

"Especially when you're counting something in an envelope."

Denton moved.

A gesture from Eastbrook stopped him. "I thought we had an understanding after that Farley business. About getting along and going along."

Wilson said, "I saw Carl's promotion certificate. Saw your signature at the bottom."

Eastbrook smiled. "Well, like you said, Chief Curry forced my hand. The men don't resent me for it. But you? Well, that's a horse of a different color. The wrong horse. Wrong color, too. They don't like you helping that boy jump the line. Ruffled a lot of feathers. Figured you ought to expect the cold shoulder from a lot of them come Monday." His smile broadened. "One white man to another."

"I'll get over it."

"But they won't," Eastbrook said. "They'll remember this for a long time. You've come a long way in the department since the Farley incident. Not

216

even I can take that away from you. Believe me, I tried. But everyone needs friends in our line of work. And you're on the wrong side of a lot of important people." He stopped fanning himself. "Lucky for you, I've come here with a solution."

"A solution to a problem I don't have."

Eastbrook put his Stetson on. "Curry and Revill can only protect you so much. If I start shining a light on you, cracks are bound to show. Cracks we've talked about before. Cracks that just might get wide enough to bring your whole career crashing down."

Wilson looked at the sky. He prayed for strength. Eastbrook didn't know how close he'd come to prison. He'd probably never know. "Let me guess. You just happen to have some plaster in your trunk."

"I might. If you're ready to be reasonable."

Wilson played along. *More dirt for my pile.* "How reasonable?"

"Sharing some of that FBI information you get could show you're still on the right side. Could make folks realize you're still a good and true white man. A reasonable man who understands the natural order of things."

Eastbrook nodded toward the backyard. "This disgusting display of affection could be written off as you just trying to further your career. Assuming the right people posed it that way, of course."

Wilson might've admired Eastbrook's style if he didn't know him so well. "And if I tell you to kiss my ass?"

Denton moved. Eastbrook opened the door.

Wilson belted Denton with a left hook. Denton fell against the back wheel.

Wilson kicked Eastbrook's door shut. "I'm not Ruby."

Eastbrook gripped the door. "You hear a lot, don't you, boy?"

Show him how much. "They miss you at the Eat Well Diner. You and Helen Markham have a fight?"

Eastbrook's eyes went wide.

Denton's heels scraped the pavement. He was trying to get up.

Wilson kicked him back down. Wilson stuck his finger in Eastbrook's face. "You dig into me? I take a jackhammer to you. Let's see how fast your friends run when your name shows up in the morning edition."

Denton was getting to his feet. He reached under his coat. "You son of a bitch."

A beer bottle shattered on the sidewalk in front of Denton.

"Careful, Harry." Tippit was at the end of the driveway. His .38 at his side. Carl was behind him. "Do something stupid. I'm begging you."

Eastbrook burned hate. At Wilson. At Tippit. At Carl.

Wilson smiled. "See that? Looks like I've got all the friends I need."

Eastbrook barked at Denton. "Get me the hell out of here."

Denton scrambled around to the driver's side. He got behind the wheel. He turned the key.

Eastbrook glared at Wilson. "I thought you were smarter than this."

"I'm as smart as I need to be."

Denton put the Galaxie in gear. He peeled away from the curb.

Tippit tucked his piece back under his camp shirt. "Just when it was starting to get interesting."

Wilson watched Eastbrook speed away. He'd lost nothing. Eastbrook had always hated him anyway. Now it was in the open. Now they'd come for him head-on.

Wilson herded Carl and Tippit back up the driveway. "We've got a party to get back to. Let's enjoy it. That's an order."

Chapter Twenty-Eight

W   ilson walked through New Orleans International Airport. His
          back was already drenched in sweat. It wasn't just from the
          humidity.

A bad moon had risen over The Crescent City. The newspapers covered
Bobby Kennedy's camp raid. The FBI had gone in heavy. They snagged a
haul. Two tons of dynamite. Ammunition galore. AK-47s. Heavy machine
guns. Pistols. And a handful of Cuban trainees. The rest scattered in the
bayou *muy rapido*.

Bannister and Ferrie weren't at the camp. The camp's intent went
unspoken in the press. Bobby's office said the camp was illegal. Rumors
of a second Cuban invasion went unconfirmed. So did rumors of CIA
involvement. *Score one for the Kennedys. Score one for Oswald. Score one for
me.*

Wilson read the FBI's after-action debrief. Captured trainees had kept
their mouths shut. They wouldn't even speak to their court-appointed
lawyers. They awaited approval from above. Probably from Bannister.

Latin tempers flared in New Orleans post-raid. Anti-Castro Cubans
attacked pro-Castro Cubans. Street brawls ensued. Arrests were made. The
Big Easy became The Big Mess.

The FBI credited Wilson. Hoover was said to be impressed. Bobby was
said to be impressed, too. The raid exceeded Wilson's wildest expectations.

His star went supernova. Success bred possibility. Wilson capitalized. He chose a side.

He pitched Revill and the Dallas FBI: NOPD is uncooperative. The FBI field office is sluggish. Washington blamed it on the heat. Wilson blamed it on their closeness to Bannister's operation. No one wanted The Big Mess to spill over to The Big D. *Let me go to New Orleans. See what I can learn and report back.*

They booked him on the next thing flying.

But only one arrest mattered to Wilson. Lee Oswald had gotten pinched. He'd been handing out pro-Castro leaflets on Canal Street during the unrest. He was rotting in a jail cell. Carl said he was going stir crazy.

Wilson walked outside. Into the late summer Louisiana heat. Carl's red Corvair idled curbside. Wilson climbed in. He didn't have to tell Carl to step on it.

Carl's tires screeched as he pulled away. He steered around a slowing station wagon. Airport traffic was the worst.

Wilson undid his collar. He pulled down his tie. He was dying for a cigarette, but it was too hot to smoke. "How's Lee?"

"Losing his shit from what I heard." NOPD was lily white. Black guards worked the jails. They talked to Carl. Being a black detective from Dallas scored him points. They told him about Oswald's condition. "He can't make bail, and he hasn't talked to a lawyer yet."

Wilson counted his few blessings. "What the hell was he doing out there anyway?"

"Bannister had him fanning the flames," Carl said. "I saw Lee passing out pro-Castro flyers. A couple of Bannister's Alpha 66 boys saw him. They took to fighting. Made it look pretty good."

Wilson knew Alpha 66. They were part of Bannister's operation. The scuffle was a con. It further solidified Oswald's Commie bona fides. *I bled for the cause. Check my record.*

"Lee get hurt?"

A pedestrian wandered in front of the Corvair. Carl hit the horn. The pedestrian jumped back. "Everyone pulled their punches, but Lee got the worst of it."

Carl took a folded piece of paper from his shirt pocket. He handed it to Wilson. "I snagged this from the street after Lee got busted."

Wilson had seen it before. "More of that 'Fair Play for Cuba' stuff he sent us. So what?"

"Check the stamp on the bottom."

Bannister had Oswald print them a few weeks before. Oswald had mailed a copy to Wilson for his records.

Hands off Cuba!

Join the Fair Play for Cuba Committee

New Orleans Charter Member Branch

Free Literature, Lectures

It was bogus. The Fair Play for Cuba folks in New York had shunned Oswald. Bannister had him print the flyers anyway. More bad press for a Commie group. Reds had infiltrated the Sacred South. An old-fashioned psych warfare op. *Just like back in Korea.*

He saw the stamp at the bottom. Carl was right. The stamp was new. **544 Camp Street**.

Wilson channeled Tippit. "Hubba, hubba, hubba."

Guy Bannister's office was on 531 Lafayette Street. Camp and Lafayette were separate entrances to the same building. Oswald had gotten brazen.

Wilson refolded the pamphlet. He pocketed it. "Bannister must be pissed."

Carl took it further. "Might be why he sent those Alpha 66 boys to rough him up."

Carl had certainly earned his detective shield. "Who'd he send?"

"Carlos Bringuier and a couple of his boys. Like you said, Bannister kept it in the family."

Wilson had a file on Bringuier. He was one of Bannister's boys. The Cuban exile version of Oswald. He worked the anti-Castro side of the street. Oswald handled the pro-Castro side. Never the twain shall meet except at Camp/Lafayette Street. Bannister had both sides of the same coin. Heads he won. Tails he won.

The Corvair hit the highway. Carl picked up speed.

Wilson hoped for cooler air. Hot air just came in faster. "I got the bureau to send me an old timer to meet us at the jail. He'll grease the skids. A federal badge should keep my name off the visitor logs. I don't want Bannister to see it when he checks them later."

Traffic into the city thickened. Carl slowed down. "Jailbirds talk, and so do guards. Bannister will find out Lee had two visitors. And the old timer will tell the bureau that Oswald's your informant."

James Hosty at Dallas FBI had assured discretion. It didn't matter. Wilson had already decided. He was pulling Oswald out of New Orleans. "I'll get him sprung and put him on the next bus back to Dallas. His family, too. Bannister will think he got spooked after the arrest. We'll consider next steps when he's back home."

Carl inched along with traffic. "I don't think he'll go. Lee's changed since he's been here. Bannister's got his hook in him deeper than ever. He's committed to the cause. Even more than he was back home."

Wilson looked out at the sagging city. Carl was right about Lee. New Orleans had changed him. Dallas was Twilight Town, but New Orleans was a different world. Like Korea. A state of mind. Outside and inside melded. Humidity warped men and buildings to its will. It drove men mad.

A high water table required above-ground crypts. The living mingled with the dead. Past and present intertwined. Heat humbled all. It made bad men worse.

Oswald had saved Wilson's career. The kid needed direction. He was no good to anyone in jail or dead. Wilson owed him a chance at a life.

"After you drop me off at the jail, head over to their apartment. Tell Marina to start packing. You'll drive back to Dallas tomorrow. We're done here."

"Can't say I'm sorry to go. This place gives me the creeps."

They inched past a cemetery. Green streaks rose from the bottom of the stones. The swamp sought to reclaim the land. To reclaim all. *It won't get Lee. It won't get me.*

* * *

Oswald eyed Agent John Quigley. The bureau man took notes.

Oswald said, "I won't talk in front of him. I don't know him, and I don't trust him."

Wilson eyed Quigley, too. He didn't look like a bureau lifer. Like he was marking days to his pension. He looked barely forty. His blonde hair was cropped short. He was lean. He had an alert, squared-away bearing.

He'd also served his purpose. He'd gotten the jailer to ignore Wilson's fudged signature in the visitor log.

Wilson kept Oswald focused. "Don't worry about him. Worry about yourself."

"What do you think I've been doing?" New Orleans had been good for Oswald's appearance. He'd filled out. Had some color. He looked fresher. Not as feral as Dallas. Having a purpose agreed with him. "It's too dangerous to trust anyone but you. Tell him to leave."

Wilson couldn't do that. The guards would notice. They'd remember.

Wilson said, "The same people who got you locked up have left you here. I'm the only one who came to see you, and I'm the only one who'll get you out. I'm getting you released and bringing you back to Dallas."

Quigley didn't look up from his notebook. "No. I'm afraid that's out of the question."

Wilson hadn't expected Quigley to speak. "You're here to observe, not participate. This is my interrogation."

"Is that what you think?" Quigley set down his pen. He reached into his pocket. He produced a key. He tossed it on the table.

Wilson froze. He recognized the key.

"It's time for some clarification," Quigley said. "You see, I'm not here to take part. I'm here to take over." He closed his notebook. He sat back in the metal chair. "You came to New Orleans to save Mr. Oswald. I've been sent here to save you from yourself." He held up a hand. "And before you waste time arguing, this comes directly from Attorney General Kennedy himself."

Oswald pushed away from the table. He shouted at the door. "Guard! I want to go back to my cell!"

A slot in the door slid open. A guard peered inside.

Quigley shook his head.

The guard shut the slot.

Quigley told Oswald, "Sit down and keep quiet or I'll arrest you on federal gun trafficking violations right here and now."

Oswald looked at Wilson. Oswald whimpered. "Danny?"

Wilson couldn't speak. He couldn't look away from the key on the table. A safe deposit box key. *His* safe deposit box key. *Impossible.* His own key was still in his pocket. *Was this a copy?* A darker idea hollowed him. *Had Carl given it to them?*

Implications swarmed. *They found my boxes. They have my files. They have my dirt pile. They have everything.*

His future imploded. The dust from it washed over him. Choked him. Blinded him.

Quigley continued. "You've impressed a great many people in a short amount of time, Detective Wilson. The Attorney General is particularly impressed by your promotion of Detective Ford. That's why we've given you the courtesy of having this conversation now."

The room tilted. His mouth went dry. *How did they know?*

Quigley said, "Agent Kowalski was wrong about you. I believe you knew him as Zeke. His field reports portrayed you as a desperate rube. A poser with visions of grandeur." He tapped the safe deposit key. "He had you all wrong. Bullying yourself into becoming the Dallas PD's bureau liaison was ham-handed, true, but your files prove you're a capable investigator. Cunning and resourceful. My boss admires such qualities."

Wilson sagged. He was worse off than Oswald. He'd lost his leverage. He'd lost everything.

Oswald croaked, "Danny?"

Quigley smiled. "Your information on Bannister's camp was nothing short of a bombshell. Pun intended. But it made us curious. How could a Dallas cop know so much? We put you under a microscope. You'd be amazed what one can see wriggling under such a lens. My compliments to Connie, by the way. She keeps a lovely home."

Oswald whimpered, "Danny?" A prayer to a god he no longer believed in.

Wilson dropped his head in his hands. *They were in my house. Of course they were. They're the FB-fucking-I.*

Quigley continued. "We didn't find anything in your den, of course, but we did find the receipt for new safe deposit boxes from the bank. Pandora's Box would be more appropriate. You amassed quite a treasure trove for yourself. The Attorney General was quite pleased."

Wilson felt some of the dust settle. He saw light. "The AG. Not the director."

"No. Hoover plays his games. We play ours. We've decided to keep him out of this for now. After all, he allowed Bannister to have his camp. Their friendship is a bit too close for our liking."

Quigley moved on to the next point. "Still, the raid you orchestrated was a wild success. We not only have all their armaments, but four witnesses who'll testify to anything we want. The threat of extradition back to Cuba is a powerful motivator."

Wilson shut his eyes. Everything he'd done. Everything he'd learned and studied. All of it plucked away. He felt worse than useless. He felt like the rube Zeke said he was.

Quigley soothed. "Relax, gentlemen. There's no reason to worry. Nothing's going to change. In fact, the Attorney General insists on it. That's the other purpose of this meeting. To make sure we all continue rowing in the same direction. Only now, it'll continue with a bit more oversight."

Quigley looked at Oswald. "Your aunt is already trying to secure bail for you. I imagine you'll be released sometime tomorrow. You'll remain here in New Orleans and continue following Bannister's orders. Detectives Wilson and Ford will continue to be your contact. Continue as you have been, and the rewards will be substantial. If you lie, the consequences will be unthinkable. The wrath you'll face will be mine, not theirs."

Oswald's voice cracked. "You. Bannister. Wilson. What's the difference?"

"Pray you never have to find out."

Quigley called for the guard. The door opened. The guard came in. He took Oswald away.

Oswald glanced over his shoulder at Wilson. His eyes were dull. Resigned to his fate. Wilson couldn't help him anymore. They both knew it.

The first door closed. The one behind them opened. A guard waited to escort them outside.

Quigley pocketed his notebook and stood. He gestured at the key in front of Wilson. "You can take that. We have copies."

Wilson picked it up.

Neither man spoke until they were outside. Heat radiated off the pavement. Wilson's stomach turned.

Quigley put on sunglasses. "You handled that better than I expected. I thought you might take a swing at me."

Wilson fished out a cigarette and lit it. *Fuck the heat.* "Would it have done any good?"

"No. I'm tougher than I look. And don't sulk. Bobby hates sulkers."

Wilson drew the smoke in deep. He let it out slow. *Bobby.* "Sounds like you two are close."

"Close enough. But cheer up. This isn't the end of the world. Far from it, in fact. You'd hoped your information would get you noticed in Washington. It has. Just not in the way you expected. You played a game you didn't understand against people you didn't know. But if it's any consolation, you put together much more than you should have. Keep doing what you're doing, and we'll see about finding you that spot in Washington you've been dreaming about. The Kennedys have their faults, but they reward loyalty."

"That how you got a job?"

Quigley smiled. "You have no idea." He moved off. "Keep up the good work. We'll be in touch."

Wilson's temper spiked. He grabbed Quigley's arm. "Did Carl give you that key?"

Quigley looked down at his arm. Wilson let him go.

Quigley said, "No. He's too loyal to you. Approaching him was never a consideration." He straightened his sleeve. "I've been on your side of this conversation a time or two. I've lost track of how many cases I've had quashed with a phone call. But your hands aren't entirely clean in this."

Wilson looked away. "Here it comes. The threat."

Quigley said, "A few slight changes in details could paint quite a different picture. Like you've been working to protect Ruby this whole time. And there's the Schneider killing to consider. Lots of loose ends on that case."

Wilson took a drag. "I had nothing to do with that."

"Of course not." Quigley patted his arm. "Oh, and don't waste any time trying to dig up dirt on John Quigley. He's a good man. Out fishing with his son as we speak. Have a safe flight back to Dallas. I'll be in touch."

Wilson stopped him before he left. "What do I call you?"

"Nothing. I call you."

Quigley disappeared among the tourists. No one paid him any mind. Wilson wouldn't soon forget him. Or the damage he'd left behind.

Wilson finished his smoke. He ground it under his boot. He walked in the opposite direction of Quigley. He needed a drink. The heat was overwhelming.

I'm no different than Oswald now.

Chapter Twenty-Nine

Saturday, September 28, 1963

Denton was in the prone position. The stock of the Enfield flush with his shoulder. His sights were on a steel human outline five hundred yards away.

Behind him, Captain Eastbrook and Bob Carter looked on through binoculars.

Denton accounted for wind. Distance. He rested his finger on the trigger. He exhaled. He squeezed.

The Enfield bucked. The round struck the ten ring. Dead center.

The *plink* of lead hitting steel thrilled him. The sharp smell of cordite focused him. He worked the bolt. He ejected the spent round. He fired again. He repeated the action until the magazine was empty.

Each shot left a new scorch mark in the middle of the target. His last shot had been a lark. A headshot.

Carter lowered his binoculars. "Do that again."

Denton didn't like Carter. He was an arrogant bastard.

Denton ejected the last of his spent brass. "I just did it ten times."

Carter tossed him a fresh magazine. "Do it again. Head shots only. Show us how many times you can make one. Fire as fast as you can manage."

"Go on," Eastbrook encouraged. "Show him how good you are."

Denton resented being ordered around on Denton land. This had been a sprawling ranch until Dallas encroached northward. The Denton name didn't mean as much these days.

He slapped the fresh magazine into the Enfield. He loaded the chamber. He aimed at the head of the target. He exhaled and fired. He hit the center of the head. He worked the bolt. He repeated the action until the magazine was empty again.

Carter lowered his binoculars. He whistled.

Eastbrook lowered his binoculars. He was smiling.

Denton had hit ten out of ten times. The steel head was bent backward.

"That's some fancy shooting," Carter said. "General Walker could've used a man like you in Germany. He might have use for you now."

The compliment meant nothing. Denton got to a knee. He started picking up brass. His father had taught him good habits. "What's that supposed to mean?"

"Inside." Eastbrook beckoned Denton toward the shack. "Voices carry on the wind."

The shack was corrugated steel scraps Denton had pieced together. A place to get out of the wind and rain. Away from Kay and other things, too.

Eastbrook had brought a six-pack of Lone Star. He handed one to Denton. It was hot, but Denton was too thirsty to care. He opened the can and drank.

Eastbrook fanned himself with his Stetson. There was nowhere to sit. "You remember what I told you a few months ago, Harry? About being ready for a fight?"

Denton nodded. *Get to it already.*

Carter said, "That fight's coming to our doorstep right here in Dallas. We'll need every God-fearing American man we can find to man the ramparts if we hope to win this battle. Men like the captain here say you are."

Eastbrook had put Denton on Walker's men for months. Denton heard Carter and his men talk big. About ending Communism. About preserving the purity of white blood. About the supremacy of the white man.

But Denton respected action, not words.

Eastbrook pulled the tab off a beer can. "Harry's a deliberate man, Bob. Give it to him plain, and he'll give you a plain answer. I trust him, and so can you."

Carter said, "You know Kennedy's up for re-election next year."

The condescending bastard. "Think I read that somewhere."

"Then you may have read that folks aren't taking as kindly to him as they did last time. The Bay of Pigs and the missile crisis have taken a toll. This fall, he'll be travelling to different cities to solidify support early. One of those cities will be Dallas."

"Sounds like I'll be working overtime."

Carter said, "We'd like to work for our cause. To help us end Kennedy's reign of tyranny once and for all."

Denton finished his beer. He chucked the can outside. He knew they hadn't watched him shoot for fun.

They'd just asked him to kill the President of the United States of America. But Denton didn't think about that. They needed him to do a job. He'd do it. "Where and when?"

Carter smiled. He looked at Eastbrook. "You were right about him, Billy. He didn't even bat an eye."

Eastbrook beamed. "I told you he's the best man I've got."

Carter looked at Denton. "You understand what we're talking about here. What we're asking you to do."

"You didn't stutter, and my hearing's pretty good. I asked you where and when."

Carter said, "The exact dates are still being worked out. So are locations. It's best if we keep contact and discussion about this to a minimum."

Walker's guys loved chains of command. They loved playing spy. "How much of a minimum?"

"The bare minimum. Compartmentalization is our key to success. The date of the Dallas trip will be announced soon. Captain Eastbrook will tell you where and when you should be in position. You'll bring your rifle to that place at that time and do your duty."

Carter took his hand from his pocket. He pointed at the ground to stress his point. "You're not to speak about this to anyone after today. I can't stress that enough. Not even to each other. Not even when you think it's just the two of you. Our enemies are capable and cunning. Any discussion could risk the entire operation."

Denton said he got it. So did Eastbrook.

Carter checked his watch. He said he was late for another meeting. He shook their hands. He got in his black-over-white Impala. The same car he'd given Denton to use the night of the Walker shooting. A strange car in the lot might've raised suspicion. A familiar car was easy for neighbors to forget.

Eastbrook put his Stetson on. "You did me proud, son. Real proud. You handled yourself like a champ."

They watched the Impala kick up dust as Carter drove away. Dust from land his family had worked for generations. Land that wasn't worth much to anyone except him. Land worth defending from the likes of Kennedy and his kind.

Carter had told them not to talk about it. But Carter was a Yankee. His orders didn't mean shit in Texas. "I don't trust him, Captain. His kind talk big but never do anything."

"This is bigger than them. Bigger than all of us." Eastbrook nudged Denton's shoulder. "But not bigger than you."

The compliment felt good. The captain needed him.

But Denton needed something from the captain. "Who else is involved in this? I ain't talking about the shooting part. I'm talking about the planning part. Walker's boys are a bunch of tin soldiers."

Eastbrook batted some dust off his shirt. "You've seen who attends the meetings at Walker's house. You tell me."

Denton had a candidate. "They rely on Ruby too much. They'll bring him into this."

Eastbrook scratched at his nose. "You might be right about that."

Denton pushed his luck. "Might be good to have another set of eyes on him again. Give you a fuller picture of what they're fixing to do. Things Carter might not tell you. Maybe head off trouble before the big day. Or after."

Eastbrook winced. "That's a taller order than you think. Jack's grown mighty fond of JD. He's come to rely on him."

Denton spelled it out for him. "This ain't about what Ruby wants. It's about what you need. Tippit's a Wilson man. I'm not. Get Ruby to bounce Tippit and you'll be one step ahead of Carter." He saved the best for last. "Unless you don't mind Wilson being this close to this operation."

Eastbrook chewed it over. He didn't chew long. He spat in the dirt. His mind was made up. "Get yourself together and lock this place up. We'll drive over to Jack's place. Him and me need to have ourselves a conversation."

* * *

After lunch, traffic crawled. Wilson drove to Love Field. Tippit rode shotgun. Carl sat in the back.

Carl said, "How come I've always got to sit back here when I ride with you two?"

"We don't want to be noticed," Wilson said. "A black man and a white man driving through Dallas together would get noticed. No offense."

Carl sat back. "None taken."

Tippit glanced back at Carl. "Maybe I can snag you one of those fancy chauffeur hats like Lundt's drivers wear. Some white gloves, too. Me and Dan can sit in the back. Ride in style."

Carl threw up two middle fingers.

Tippit laughed. He pulled out a Chesterfield and lit it.

Wilson got down to business. The reason for the drive. He took a Telex from his jacket. He handed it back to Carl. "Read that. Tell me what you see."

Carl read the title. He read the directions. He traced the diagram below it. "This what I think it is?"

Wilson slowed with the flow of traffic. "The president's motorcade route. He's coming to Dallas in November."

Tippit blew smoke rings. "I told you."

Wilson said, "Revill put me on the task force preparing for the visit."

Tippit said, "You and your goddamned task forces."

Wilson ignored him. "And since I'm handling the intel, I wanted us to drive the route. Point out problem areas." He looked at Tippit. "Obviously, none of this gets back to Ruby."

Tippit blew the smoke rings apart. "Nothing to worry about there, Kemosabe. Ruby sent me packing last night."

Wilson hadn't expected that. "Why?"

Tippit shrugged. "Said it was time for a change. He let me keep my gig at The Vegas Club as a consolation prize."

Carl asked, "Denton back driving for him again?"

"Give that man a cigar."

Wilson didn't like the timing. Kennedy's trip had just hit the wires. Ruby was cozy with Walker. Ruby made a sudden change in personnel.

Ruby hates change. He thrives on routine. Tippit's out. Denton's back in. Other changes could be telling. "Eastbrook must've ordered it."

"That's my guess." Tippit blew the smoke out the window. "Ruby didn't tell me that much. Just asked for the keys to the Oldsmobile after I drove him home. He practically ran up to his apartment. I think the fat prick was crying."

Carl held up the motorcade Telex. "Sounds like a coincidence."

Wilson pulled off. He parked on an airport side road. The sounds of plane engines approaching and taking off droned loud. The droning helped him think.

He remembered details Tippit had told him. "Eastbrook's had Denton sniffing around Walker's men for months. He's pulled Denton off Walker and put him back on Ruby. Eastbrook's got a reason. A reason that involves Ruby."

"No shit." Tippit flicked the cigarette butt out the window. "Eastbrook's always got something cooking."

Wilson wasn't done. He made links. His dirt pile on Bannister and Milteer was FBI compromised. But its contents remained valid.

Wilson made connections. The meeting at Walker's house a few months prior. The pictures Carl had taken of attendees. The New Orleans camp ramp-up. The resulting raid.

Wilson gave voice to thought. He put it in street terms. "Eastbrook and

Ruby are part of Walker's crew. Walker's part of Milteer's crew. Walker's Midnight Ride tour made money. The New Orleans camp expanded soon after. The FBI raid killed their plans. Kennedy's tour is announced. He's coming to Dallas."

Carl sat back. He knew the files better than Wilson. He pondered the same connections.

Tippit yawned. "That big brain of yours is working too hard. Ruby runs guns and dope. Planning something while Kennedy's in town doesn't fit. Jack's the last one they'd tell. The prick blabs anything he hears."

Tippit had a thought. "You should run this by Oswald. See if he's heard anything."

Wilson wished he could. "We don't know where he is."

Tippit looked out the window. "Shit."

Carl said, "Ruth Blaine brought Marina back here a few days ago. Lee was on some anti-Commie junket for Bannister in Baton Rouge. He hasn't checked in with us in days. Even Dan's feds can't find him. He could be anywhere."

Wilson fought down concern. Quigley's power play had backfired. Oswald had changed since his stint in jail. He'd grown more independent. Vague. And now, elusive. 'Quigley' couldn't make him pay if he couldn't find him.

Wilson had faith in the kid. "He's got a reason. He'll turn up. He's still on our side."

"He's on his own side," Tippit said. "We all are."

Wilson couldn't argue.

Chapter Thirty

Saturday, October 5, 1963

Carl watched the street from the church door.

Tippit stood beside the pulpit.

Wilson grilled Oswald in the front pew. "You've been out of touch for a long time. Where have you been?"

Oswald looked at his shoes. But not like before. He was more annoyed than timid.

Carl had been watching Ruth Blaine's house. He'd nabbed Oswald leaving that afternoon. He'd brought him to the church and called Wilson.

Wilson had brought Tippit along. A fresh face to pull Oswald in line. To see what Wilson and Carl couldn't.

Wilson pushed for an answer. "When did you get back?"

A shrug. "A couple of weeks, I guess." He'd grown a spine in Louisiana.

Wilson said, "You didn't call. We were concerned."

"I told Carl I was working."

"For Bannister?" Wilson asked.

Oswald's eyes flashed. "That bust on Canal Street did me some good. Helped me infiltrate Red groups around the state. Got my name on a lot of membership lists. Enough to make a difference when the time comes."

Carl asked, "Bannister tell you that?"

Oswald raised his chin. His back was straighter. He had swagger, even sitting down. "He was happy with what I did. He gave me some time off.

235

He let me come back here to see my second baby be born."

"That was nice of him. You must be grateful."

"I earned it."

Oswald's eyes told the story. Wilson had seen that look in other men. In Korea. Eyes vacant of fear and dread. Flat, lifeless eyes. Resigned to whatever fate threw at him.

Wilson lobbed a curveball. He'd gleaned some intel from the FBI reports. "I hear you were in Mexico."

Oswald remained flat. "Not yet. Mr. Bannister wants me at one of the Mexico camps in January. Says I'll be part of the final prep before the Cuban invasion."

Tippit laughed.

Oswald's head snapped up. "Don't laugh. Mr. De Mohrenschildt's gonna bring me to Haiti. He said I can help the effort from there. They're doing it right this time."

Wilson was worried. This was crazy talk. "There's not going to be an invasion, Lee. The camp in Lake Pontchartrain was raided, remember?"

Oswald's eyes narrowed. "You still don't get it. Even after all this time. Everything I told you would happen *has* happened. I was right about everything. The camps. The guns. All of it was true. You don't believe me? Wait til you see what happens next."

Tippit kicked the pew.

Oswald flinched.

Tippit played bad cop. "Watch your tone."

Wilson played good cop. He switched topics. "Carl found you leaving Ruth's house. She letting you stay with Marina?"

Oswald settled down. "No, but that's for their own good. She's helping me get a job."

They've still got him on a leash. They're not done with him yet. "Where?"

"A clerk in a warehouse somewhere. I'm supposed to meet the fella next week. It's just to get me some spending money. Until I ship out to the Mexico camp in January."

Tippit laughed again. "For D-Day, Part Two."

Wilson ignored him. "Where downtown?"

Oswald shrugged. "I don't remember the address."

Wilson said, "You've got to tell me where it is and who you'll be working for. You can't trust them. You can't—"

Oswald stood up. "You're wrong. You've been wrong this whole time. They've been taking care of my girls. They've got plans for me. I've seen them with my own two eyes. Mr. De Mohrenschildt, Mr. Blaine. They've all promised."

Tippit shoved him back down. "They're holding your family hostage, you stupid bastard. They're telling you what you want to hear."

Oswald dug in. "Then why let me come back to Dallas to be with my family? Why didn't Mr. Bannister keep me in Louisiana?"

Wilson kept playing good cop. "Why bring your family here at all? Why not let them stay in New Orleans with you?"

Oswald had an answer. "Because Mr. Bannister had me busy. I was all over the state. I couldn't take care of her like I wanted. But I'm back now. And after the baby's born, I'll be back working for the cause."

Wilson grabbed Oswald's shirt. He almost pulled him off the pew. "You're here because they want you here. The president's coming here next month. They'll make trouble, and they'll pin it on you. Just like they tried pinning the Walker shooting on you."

Oswald smiled.

Wilson recoiled. Oswald never smiled.

Oswald laughed. "Is that what you boys think?" He looked at Tippit. At Carl. He looked at Wilson.

He laughed again. Not the shy titter from De Mohrenschildt's backyard. Or their meeting at the park. A genuine belly laugh. "The president's visiting Dallas, but it won't be Kennedy."

Wilson almost pitied him. The poor bastard's gone.

Oswald said, "Kennedy will be long dead by then. That Dallas visit will be Johnson's homecoming."

Tippit grabbed Oswald's neck. He pinned him face down in the pew. "Explain."

Oswald squirmed. He talked fast. "Bannister got drunk after the raid. He said it's been planned for weeks. They've got some boys from the other camps to handle it."

Tippit pushed down on his throat. "Where?"

"I don't know," Oswald gasped. "Bannister might not even know. He doesn't talk about things too far in advance. Not even when he's drunk. Says it's bad luck."

Wilson signaled Tippit to let him up. "When?"

"Soon." Oswald rubbed his neck. "He said the Dallas trip would be Johnson's first official visit as president."

Wilson got up. He paced the sanctuary. Facts gelled.

Bannister's network hated Kennedy. Their tracts openly called for his death. Bobby's too.

The New Orleans camp raid had been a Kennedy operation. It ruined their plans. It broke the camel's back. They got desperate.

JFK out. LBJ in.

Wilson had it all wrong. Everything would be over before Dallas. It was planned here. It would be done elsewhere. Far from suspicion. *The eyes of Texas are upon you, Mr. President.*

Wilson looked down at Oswald. At the man he'd protected. At the man he'd killed for.

He couldn't trust him anymore. But he was still valuable.

Oswald rubbed his neck. He avoided Tippit's glare. He looked back at Carl for sympathy. Carl kept watching the street.

Tippit loomed. Ready to hit him again.

Wilson crowded Oswald. "You want to act like a skel? I'll treat you like a skel." He pointed at Tippit. "From now on, he's your guardian angel. You won't always see him, but assume he's always there."

"I want Carl."

Tippit kicked the pew. Oswald jumped.

Wilson closed in. "You're back to checking in with me twice a day. Same as before. You miss a call, I feed you to the feds. You lie? I feed you to the feds. I'll have you thrown in general population. I'll tell Ruby you tipped us off about the camp. You'll have a shiv in your belly that night."

Oswald's arrogance evaporated. "I won't hear anything. I'm not working for them now. Mr. Bannister gave me time off, remember?"

"You're still working for Blaine, whether you know it or not. They'll get you a job with someone they know. Someone they control. That's why you'll tell me everything Blaine says. Everything he has you do. You'll dig for information about where they're planning to hit the president. You'll get me specifics within a week."

Oswald pounded his legs. "I can't promise that. I can't just call up Bannister and ask him."

Wilson was done coddling him. "Figure it out. Call your old buddies from the camps. See who's doing what. You come up empty? You're useless to me. And I feed you to the feds."

Oswald dry heaved. He raked his hair. "I can't. These guys move around a lot. I don't know who to call."

From the back of the church, Carl said, "You've got David Ferrie."

Oswald's eyes welled up.

Carl said, "You and Ferrie are pals from way back. Call him. Get him to talk. It's your ass if you don't."

Oswald ran his hands over his face. "I'll try."

Tippit closed in. "Trying's not good enough, asshole. Information or hard time. Your choice."

Wilson watched Oswald crumple. His friends were no longer friends. Their soft touch had turned hard. This wasn't New Orleans. He was trapped. Stuck. He'd gotten too cocky. He'd said too much. He hadn't told them everything. And they knew it.

Wilson told Tippit, "Take him back home. Get yourselves acquainted."

Tippit pulled Oswald off the pew. He steered him out the back door. Oswald didn't resist.

Wilson joined Carl at the front door. They watched the street. They saw Tippit's car pass by. They saw Oswald slumped in the front seat.

Carl said, "I knew New Orleans would ruin that boy. We can't trust him anymore."

Wilson needed a cigarette. "Let's hope proves us wrong."

* * *

Harry Denton leaned against Ruby's Oldsmobile. He smoked. He waited for Ruby to come downstairs.

The fat bastard was still up in his apartment. He was primping for his big night. Dinner at the Lundt mansion on White Rock Lake. He swore he'd be fifteen minutes. That had been an hour ago.

Denton stewed. The Jew bastard had gotten too big for his britches. He overestimated his value. Time to show him his place in this new order of things.

To show him that Harry Denton wasn't a flunky anymore. He'd been chosen. Anointed by purpose. He would save his country.

Even Eastbrook had treated Denton better since the Carter meeting. Like he was someone important. Not an equal, but close.

Even Carter had changed his tune. He spoke to Denton like he was a human being. His men did likewise. Burying ten out of ten rounds in the head of a steel target had left an impression. It proved Denton's value. To Eastbrook. To the general. To the greater cause of freedom and liberty.

Denton liked being an important man. A man whose hand would shape America's bright future.

He wouldn't be at the table at White Rock Lake. He'd be there in spirit. His skill had made that possible. He'd given important men options. Options that keep their beloved country from falling into the hands of the Reds and the mongrel hordes that threatened it.

November was fast approaching. November would change everything. Denton smiled. I *will change everything.*

The front door of Ruby's apartment building flew open. Jack pranced down the stairs. He was pink as a piglet. He smelled of Old Spice and hair tonic. He sported a new blue suit. His shirt was white, his collar starched. A white pocket square added flair.

"Sorry for the wait, kid. Took some extra time to look good for my big night. Can't show up looking like a schlub. The general and his pals admire a snappy dresser. Know what I mean?"

Denton buried a left hook in his gut. He followed it with a hard right uppercut. He grabbed Ruby by the collar. He pushed him through the open car window. He held him there.

"Here's the story, you Jew bastard. From now on, you don't keep me waiting. Not five minutes. Not fifteen minutes and certainly not more than a whole fucking hour."

Ruby broke wind. He gagged.

Denton shook him. "You want to stay in good with Eastbrook and the general? Start treating me with respect. I'm not one of your fag flunkies. The next time you treat me like that asshole Crawford, you'll be sorry. I'm more important than you."

Denton pulled Ruby out of the car. He grabbed his tie. He jerked his head up and squeezed. "Know what I mean?"

Ruby was red. He gasped. "Sure, kid. Sure. I get it. You're a big man now. Everybody knows that. You oughta hear how they talk about you. How we'll all be working for you someday."

Ruby fired an elbow into Denton's throat.

Denton reeled. He bounced off the car. Ruby kicked him in the balls.

Denton hit the sidewalk. He landed on his back.

He drew his .38. He aimed at Ruby's gut.

Ruby was in a boxer's crouch. "Go ahead. Shoot. Kill me. Explain that to your boss."

Denton thumbed back the hammer. "No one would care."

"Keep telling yourself that." Ruby winced. He rubbed his sore belly. "We're all expendable. Haven't you figured that out yet?"

Denton lowered his pistol.

Ruby mocked him. "Yeah. Now it dawns on you. You fucking *shvantz*." He checked his reflection in the sideview mirror. He pulled out a comb. He raked at the three hairs on his head. "Get up and dust yourself off. We don't want to be late."

Denton holstered his weapon. He got up. Ruby went to get in the back.

Denton blocked the door. "Tonight, you drive."

Ruby smirked. He got behind the wheel. "Put a beggar on horseback and he'll ride to Hell."

Denton climbed in the back. He could get used to this view.

Chapter Thirty-One

W ilson was panting. He'd run the entire way from headquarters. Hosty's call had said it was urgent.

He took the elevator up to the fifth floor. He ran when the doors opened. He bolted past the desk guard. He hadn't shown ID.

The guard yelled for him to stop. Wilson didn't stop. He feared the worst. *Oswald's intel had been right. Milteer and Bannister got Kennedy in Miami.*

The guard chased him. The guard threatened to shoot.

Hosty wasn't in his office. Wilson ran down a narrow hall. He searched for Hosty. He looked in offices on both sides. Agents reading files at their desks. *Why aren't they doing something?*

Wilson ran past a small conference room. He saw Hosty rearranging file boxes.

Wilson slid on the marble floor. He doubled back. "Is he dead?"

Hosty said, "He's fine. Miami went fine."

The guard caught up. He grabbed Wilson. "I'm sorry about this, Jim. This guy just ran by me without..."

Hosty said, "Let him go. He's with me."

The guard shoved Wilson into the room. He went back up front.

"The president's safe." Hosty gestured at a newly cleared chair. "He left Florida twenty minutes ago without a single protest or arrest. I asked you here for something else. Something that couldn't wait."

Wilson sat. He tried to catch his breath. The cramped room reeked of moldy paper and roach powder. Warped file boxes filled with old crimes crammed every available space.

"I thought something happened in Miami. I thought he'd been shot."

Hosty sat. "The Secret Service cancelled the motorcade thanks to you." 'Quigley' had told him to work with Hosty. The agent looked like a bank manager, not an FBI man. His black eyebrows framed deep-set eyes. Black hair was swept back from an impressive forehead. His shirt collar was too tight. Deskwork killed his waistline.

Hosty continued. "You've had one hell of a month, Dan. First, the New Orleans camp raid. Then the Chicago plot. Now Miami. Hoover and Kennedy think you're worth your weight in gold. And those two never agree on anything."

Wilson said, "I've got good sources."

Oswald's conversion in the church had held. He'd called David Ferrie. He'd told him he was homesick for New Orleans. Wilson had put an illegal bug on Oswald's rooming house phone. It verified Oswald's loyalty.

Ferrie had liked bragging to his old friend. He'd boasted Kennedy wouldn't make it out of Chicago alive. That four Cuban shooters along the motorcade route ensured success. A *gringo* named Vallee would deliver the kill shot. He'd take the fall if necessary.

Wilson hadn't heard from 'Quigley' since New Orleans. Wilson passed the info on to Hosty. Hosty passed it on to the Secret Service. The service shrugged. They filed it with all the other threats they received daily.

Wilson took it a step further. He contacted Abraham Golden. Abe was an old friend. He'd been the first black Secret Service agent to work a protection detail. He'd once guarded Kennedy. He'd transferred to the service's Chicago field office to be closer to his family.

Golden owed Kennedy. He investigated. He'd busted two Cubans in a rooming house along the motorcade route. He'd busted Vallee with a trunk full of ammo on his way to the motorcade route.

Officially, the feds had denied evidence of a plot. Wilson didn't care. They knew he and Oswald had saved Kennedy.

Wilson had made Oswald stay on Ferrie. More phone calls ensued. Ferrie bemoaned Chicago. He said they'd clip Kennedy in Miami. Cuban exiles still resented The Bay of Pigs. They resented the missile crisis capitulation. They resented losing the New Orleans training camp. Their indignity burned *mucho calor.*

Wilson passed the new plot on to Hosty. Officially, the feds shrugged. Privately, they acted. They'd called off the Miami motorcade.

Bannister's bunch was zero-for-three. Wilson and Oswald were three-for-three.

Wilson's FBI stock soared. He'd built up significant goodwill. He spent some of it. He offered an unsolicited opinion in writing. He strongly urged the feds to call off Dallas.

Hosty said, "I asked you here because I spoke to the White House this afternoon. Unfortunately, the president is still coming to Dallas."

Wilson couldn't have heard that right. "You've got to be shitting me."

"I wish I was," Hosty commiserated. "The White House knows we've stopped two previous attempts. They're confident we can protect the president in Dallas." Hosty held up his hands. "For what it's worth, I agree with you. But my agreement doesn't count."

"After all we've given them? The camp? Chicago? Miami?" He used information from his dirt pile. "Walker and Bannister's network coordinated those attacks. Milteer was part of it. Dallas is worse. All the players live here."

Hosty ticked off facts. "You haven't uncovered any evidence that directly implicates Bannister, Walker, or Milteer. The Cubans we arrested in Chicago didn't confess. On paper, Miami was far more dangerous than either Chicago or Dallas. Nothing happened there. Even your confidential informant doubts anything is planned for Dallas. That's their justification for the trip remaining as scheduled."

Wilson slammed his fist on the table. He ticked off some facts of his own. "Jack Ruby's been meeting with out-of-town hoods for weeks. Walker lives here. Kennedy's motorcade is practically driving past his house in Turtle Creek. And the motorcade route is identical to the Chicago route. Long stretches of tall buildings where any crackpot can hit him. Kennedy will be a sitting duck in the plaza if he makes it that far."

Hosty hesitated. "I probably shouldn't tell you this, but the Attorney General has read your reports. He agrees with you. But the White House knows the president needs Dallas to win re-election next year. The campaign didn't get images of adoring crowds along parade routes in Chicago or Miami. They want the president to be seen in public. They think coming to Walker's backyard will make a statement."

"Ask them what kind of statement a dead president will make?"

Hosty waved him down. "Their mind is made up. If you want to change their mind, you'll need solid evidence you simply don't have right now."

Wilson didn't have it. But he had a compromise. "Have them change the motorcade route. Bring him straight to the Trade Mart from Love Field."

"And miss filming the president driving past an adoring public?" Hosty shook his head. "The campaign's got a lot of people coming out. All of them want to see what Jackie is wearing."

Hosty leaned forward in his chair. "I'm not telling you to stop, Dan. I'm telling you to keep pushing and push hard. Beat the streets. Wring Oswald for every ounce of information he can find. If you find anything that's even the slightest bit actionable, I'll bring it to the Director and the Attorney General. But anything short of something conclusive?" He sat back. "Well, there's nothing either of us can do."

"Actionable," Wilson repeated. "Is that a real word?"

"If not, it is now. Add it to your collection of phrases. Bring me something I can use, and I'll use it. There's still time."

"And if I don't find anything?"

Hosty said, "Then maybe nothing's going on."

Wilson knew better. This was Dallas. There was always something going on.

* * *

Tippit got to the railyard later than intended. It was already past sunset. His shift had run long. Traffic had been heavier than normal. He didn't know why Wilson wanted to meet out here. The church was more convenient.

Wilson had changed since New Orleans. Even Carl had noticed.

Wilson was quiet. More guarded. Less confident. In another man, Tippit might've mistaken it for fear. That was impossible. Dan Wilson was too smart to fear anything. Too prepared.

Tippit blamed the Kennedy visit. The whole city was off kilter. He hadn't felt so much tension since the Bulge. The excited dread was palpable.

Tippit parked between Wilson's black Galaxie and Carl's red Corvair. He found the two detectives standing at the edge of the railroad tracks. The Dallas skyline loomed in the background. Civilization clashed with desolation. The sky took on a late fall glow.

A train horn sounded in the train yard.

Wilson smoked a Lucky.

Carl smoked a Kool. He turned as Tippit approached. "Hail, hail. The gang's all here."

Tippit opened a fresh pack of Chesterfields. It promised to be a long night. "Mighty romantic spot you picked out, Dan. You thinking of proposing?"

Wilson eyed the skyline. "I've got something to tell you boys. I didn't want anyone around when I did. And it's not the kind of conversation for a church."

"Hubba, hubba, hubba." Tippit lit his cigarette. "Let me guess. You're working for the feds."

Wilson ignored the humor. "I killed Tommy Schneider in cold blood."

Carl looked at him. He didn't say anything.

Tippit pocketed his Zippo. "I already knew that."

Carl shifted his weight. He hadn't known.

Wilson flicked his ash. "I wanted both of you to know the kind of man I am before the ball goes up. It might be important later."

Tippit toed the gravel. "You picked a hell of a time to grow a conscience."

Wilson said, "I killed Schneider because I caught him watching my house. He'd followed me home from the church. He saw the three of us meeting with Oswald."

247

Carl hung his head. "Shit."

"He knew about Oswald. He threatened Connie and the kids. He threatened all of us. He told me Walker wouldn't stop until I played ball. I made him drive to Swish Street. I shot him and made it look like some hustler mugged him."

Carl held his gut. He bent over. "Jesus." Carl looked at Tippit. "You knew this?"

Tippit took a drag. "I suspected. I got rid of the gun anyway."

Carl cursed. He dropped his cigarette. Wilson's confession hit him in waves.

Wilson kept talking. "I told myself I'd killed him because he'd been following me. That I was protecting Oswald. Our families. Us. But that's not the whole reason. I'd decided to kill him when I saw him at my house. I did it because it had to be done. To send a message to Walker that a line had been crossed. I killed him because he needed killing."

Tippit watched Carl's hand start to shake. He fumbled for his Kools. He needed menthol magic to ward off what he'd heard. To hide being an accessory after the fact. "And you didn't tell me?"

"Was no reason to tell you until now," Wilson said. "Tippit knew. My father knows, and now so do you. It's the only secret I've ever held back. But things being as they are, I figure we're beyond that now."

It took Carl three tries to light his cigarette. "What's that supposed to mean?"

Wilson explained. "I told you this because the next few days will be rough for all of us. I've tried everything I can to get the president's trip postponed. I failed. He'll be here on Friday unless we find a reason to stop him. Not just any reason. Not a rumor. I need rock-solid evidence strong enough to convince Washington to call it off."

Wilson took a final drag. He dropped his cigarette and ground it beneath his boot. "I'm not holding out on either of you, so if you've been holding back something, now's the time to come clean. I don't care what you did. I don't care why you did it. I'm sure you had your reasons. But I need to know anything that could call this trip off."

Tippit knew that was directed at him. Wilson always feared that Tippit had held out on him. He'd feared Ruby's money had influenced him. But Tippit hadn't held back.

"You know everything I do," Tippit said. "Chicago and Miami weren't enough to change their minds?"

"No., Wilson said to Carl. "You're closer to Oswald than me. Does he have anything new?"

"Everything's in my reports." Carl gave a rundown for Tippit's benefit. "Lee checks in with you twice a day. Goes to work at the warehouse and comes back home. Gets a ride with a buddy to Fort Worth every Friday. Spends the weekend with his family at Ruth Blaine's house. Michael Blaine has brought him to some political meetings around town, but that's it."

Tippit thought of something. "What about that Mexico bullshit?"

Carl said, "Oswald still thinks Bannister is sending him there in a couple of weeks. That de Mohrenschildt is bringing him to Haiti before the invasion next year."

Wilson lit another cigarette. "Did you tell him nothing happened in Miami?"

Carl nodded. "He just shrugged. He helped save the president's life, but doesn't seem to give a damn. It's like he can see himself storming the beaches of Cuba."

Wilson took a drag. "Walker's got to be planning something. They've got him isolated. They've limited his options. They've kept him from his family. They're stringing him along until he's useful to them."

Tippit didn't have Wilson's big brain. He didn't have Carl's determination. But Wilson had explained it well. He followed his logic. It made sense.

Wilson asked Tippit. "What about Ruby?"

Tippit toed more gravel. "Haven't seen much of him since he replaced me with Denton. When I've seen him at The Vegas Club, he hasn't been himself. His schtick feels forced, like he's trying to act like everything's fine. He had a couple of bigwigs with him and another guy at the club last night. I recognized the car from the Bon Vivant Lounge. Benson Lundt's Cadillac."

Carl perked up. He'd taken pictures of the car and its passengers at the

Cabana Motel. "You see who was inside?"

"Some old guy with Coke-bottle glasses and Benson were in the back seat. Ruby got out with another guy he kept calling 'Mr. Brading.' But it sounded like he was ribbing him about it. I saw them huddled together at a back table. They booked a loud band last night. I could hear what they said."

Wilson told Carl, "Brading's in our files."

Carl said, "He's not muscle, but he's been busted more than thirty times. Embezzlement mostly. Runs one of Marcello's oil companies now. Moves money around for The Boys. Makes it look legit. Works with another con man named Brown."

"Oil," Wilson concluded. "That explains the Lundt connection. And Ruby means The Boys are involved. Maybe they're moving money around to finance something." He asked Tippit, "Harry Denton still working for Ruby?"

"Sticks to him like glue these days," Tippit said. "But even he's been acting different. Hasn't even bothered to insult me in weeks." He kicked a pebble. It skittered toward the tracks. "Guess the fun's gone out of ribbing me since he won."

Wilson closed his eyes. He let smoke slowly drift from his nose. "Something's boiling. I know where to look, but all I see is steam. Crooks meeting crooks won't get the trip cancelled. I've got circumstantial evidence, but nothing solid."

Tippit and Carl were quiet. Neither had anything to add.

Tippit said, "Tell us what you want us to do."

Carl added, "Even if it isn't strictly legal."

Wilson kept his eyes shut. "Oswald's still our best witness. He links Walker, Ruby, Eastbrook. All of it. We have to protect him on Friday."

"How?" Carl asked. "The three of us are working the president's visit."

Wilson slowly opened his eyes. "JD won't be."

Tippit smiled. "That's news to me."

Wilson said, "I've seen Personnel's assignment roster for the motorcade. Eastbrook has you on regular patrol duty in Oak Cliff."

Tippit was disappointed. "And Marie wanted me to tell her what Jackie looked like in person. Fucking Eastbrook."

Wilson's brain started working. "Carl, tell Oswald that if something pops on Friday, he should head straight home. Tell him to stay there until JD comes to get him."

Tippit didn't like it. "Traffic will be a mess. I might get reassigned at the last minute."

Wilson wasn't done. "Tell him to get to a public place and call us from wherever he winds up. One of us will get him and bring him to the church. We'll keep him safe until we can bring him in."

"I'll tell him tonight," Carl said. "Where will I be working on Friday?"

"With me in the plaza. Oswald's warehouse is right there. If something pops, we'll grab him and get him to the church. Chief Curry and Revill want a strong undercover presence in the plaza. To stop any protests that might pop up at the end of the route."

"Protests," Tippit laughed. "We'll be lucky if that's all it is."

Wilson said, "Oswald stays our main concern, not Kennedy. The president's got a small army to protect him. Oswald just has us. We can't use our department radios. We'll use my answering service to get messages back and forth to each other."

Tippit finished his cigarette. He ground it under his boot. "Kennedy's got protection. Oswald's got protection. Who's protecting us?"

"Us," Wilson said. "Just like always."

Chapter Thirty-Two

Thursday, November 21, 1963

Harry Denton paced beneath the neon glow of The Cabana Motel sign. The boozy laughter from the Bon Vivant Lounge was an insult. Like visiting a whorehouse on Christmas Eve.

Denton hadn't eaten a decent meal in days. Tomorrow was the big day. The day he'd strike a blow for the cause. His place in history was at hand.

But greatness was several long hours away. Tonight, Eastbrook had him playing wet nurse to Ruby. He was stuck driving the fat bastard as he squired Brading and Brown around Dallas. A couple of jumped-up wise guys from out of town.

It had been an eventful day. They'd dropped in on Benson Lundt at his office. Denton didn't know or care what they'd discussed. Ruby and his friends were giddy afterward.

Later, they'd celebrated with a bottle of guinea red at the Egyptian with Campisi. Now, it was time for drinks and debauchery at the Bon Vivant.

Ruby and Brading's conduct turned his stomach. Even that arrogant old prick Milteer had the good sense to call it an early night.

Celebrating now was absurd. It tempted fate. There'd be no reason to celebrate tomorrow, either. Denton took the long view. Kennedy's death wasn't even half the job. There was still a country to repair and save.

There'd be a world of trouble after the deed was done. Questions asked. Suspicions cast. Endless investigations made.

Someone was bound to crack. Weak links would snap in the weeks to come. Walker's men were prime candidates. Paper tough guys always folded at the first sign of trouble.

The plan's perfection was its size. Old Man Milteer had kept a tight grip on details. No one knew everything. Not Eastbrook. Not Walker. Not Ruby. Especially not him. He'd just helped move money around.

Denton didn't know how many shooters there'd be. Or where they'd be. Each part was independent of the other. Ignorance was the best protection.

Dallas would be different after tomorrow. The rank and file—his fellow Minutemen and Birchers—would keep their mouths shut. But people would speculate. They'd brag. They'd want a piece of the glory only a few had a right to claim, but never could.

Not until the job was done. Not until all of Kennedy's wrongs had been righted. Until his ilk were behind bars or dead. Until the white man had retaken his rightful place in this country. Until America stood atop the smoldering ashes of Communism. Then Denton, and thousands of patriots like him, would rise up and take control.

Only then would Ruby and his kind know what they had wrought. They'd realize too late that they had no place in these new United States of America. A country where Denton would be seen as a hero. Another Washington.

Then, Denton would turn his attention to those who had sneered at him for so long. The Tippits and Wilsons of the world would pay for their scorn. He'd make them grovel.

Denton's hands began to shake with prideful anticipation. He balled them into fists. Steady hands would save the country. His hands. *My time is almost here.*

Eastbrook's unmarked Galaxie entered the parking lot. Kenny Croy was at the wheel. He waved to Denton as he drove by. He parked in a spot by the door.

Eastbrook got out. He'd left his Stetson in the car. He strode toward Denton, buttoning his suit jacket. He was dressed to impress whoever he was meeting inside.

The captain stopped next to him. "Did you remember to bring it?"

Denton said, "Got it in a blanket in my trunk."

Eastbrook said, "Give it to Croy. I'll give it to Sill tomorrow. As for you, be ready at eight in the morning. You'll get a call telling you where and when. Wear your uniform and bring the Enfield." He continued to the lounge. "Happy hunting."

A surge of pride coursed through Denton. Pride that men like Walker and Eastbrook trusted him with such an important task.

Denton opened the Oldsmobile's trunk.

Kenny Croy ambled over. "Big day tomorrow."

Denton took the blanket containing Michael Blaine's rifle from the trunk. He handed it to Croy. "Keep it in the trunk until the captain says otherwise."

Croy did what he was told. "The boss has me driving for him all day. What about you? They put you somewhere good?"

"Me?" Denton watched Croy put the rifle in Eastbrook's trunk. "Don't worry about me. I'll be around."

* * *

Connie had just come downstairs from tucking in the kids when Wilson got home.

"You're early." She embraced him and kissed his cheek. "With the president coming tomorrow, I didn't expect you for hours yet."

Wilson tossed his keys on the hall table. "Tomorrow will be a long day. I was hoping to see the kids before bedtime."

"It's not too late." She took his hand and pulled him toward the stairs. "You know them. They'll be chattering at each other for another few minutes yet."

Wilson eased her back toward him. "Later."

He felt something brush against his leg. Missy always got between them when they embraced.

Connie said, "I swear that cat is jealous of me."

"That's her problem." Wilson held her close. She was his anchor. He needed her softness and warmth. He needed to be reminded of love among the hatred swirling around him. Her perfume killed the stench of corruption in the world.

She embraced him, too. "They tell you where you'll be working tomorrow?"

Wilson rested his chin on top of her head. "Dealey Plaza. Jack and Jackie will drive right past me." *If they're still alive.*

Connie sighed. "Some men have all the luck." She loved Jackie's style. "I was thinking about getting some of the girls together and heading down to Main Street. I want to see if Jackie's as…"

Wilson took her by the shoulders. He held her away from him. "I don't want you anywhere near that motorcade. I don't want you anywhere near downtown. Is that clear?"

"Okay, Dan. Okay." Connie winced.

Wilson realized he was gripping her too hard. He stopped.

She gently took his face in her tender hands. "What is it, honey? What's wrong? I've never seen you this worried."

He watched her search his eyes. He feared what she'd find there.

He pulled her back to him. His files were no longer a secret. His leverage was gone. He'd come far, but not far enough. Not as far as he'd hoped. Not as far as he should.

Connie and the kids were all he had left. The bright future he'd planned was now a scorched sliver of a dream. All his scheming and plotting were supposed to give them a better life. But he was still at the mercy of the bureau.

He'd been just clever enough to be stupid. The bureau liked him now. New Orleans and Chicago and Miami had won them over. But after tomorrow, he'd be blamed for what he hadn't done. For what he hadn't stopped.

Wilson flinched when he heard loud rapping at the back door.

He pushed Connie to the staircase. "Go upstairs. Grab the shotgun. Lock yourself in the kids' room. Now!"

He waited until he heard the bedroom door click. He pulled his Magnum. He moved into the kitchen. He shouldered the swinging door open. He aimed at the back door. The goddamned lace curtain Connie had made him hang blocked his view outside.

He dropped to a knee. He kept the pistol trained on the door. "Who is it?"

"It's Carl. It's important."

Wilson went to the door. He parted the curtain with the barrel of the Magnum. It was Carl. He was alone.

Wilson holstered his weapon and let Carl in. Wilson locked the door behind him.

Carl didn't hold back. "Tippit had to work a double, so I followed Lee after work. He didn't go home. He's up at the Blaines' house with Marina and the kids."

That wasn't good. "It's Thursday. He only goes there on Fridays."

"Doesn't feel right, tomorrow being what it is."

They knew Oswald lived by routine. Visiting his family a day early wasn't routine. *Had Michael Blaine wanted to give him one last word before tomorrow?*

Carl said, "Maybe we ought to pay him a visit. Talk to him together."

Wilson knew Walker or Ruby might have someone watching the house. "I'll take a run by there early tomorrow morning. See where he goes."

Connie called out to him from the hall. "Dan? Everything okay in there?"

He'd forgotten to tell her the coast was clear. "It's fine, honey. It's just Carl."

"And me without a stitch of makeup on!" She was still arranging her hair as she hipped the swinging door open. Wilson saw the twelve-gauge against the wall in the hall. She'd come down ready to shoot. *God, I love this woman.*

Connie kissed Carl on the cheek on her way to the stove. "I've got dinner already waiting. We weren't expecting company, so you'll have to make do. You boys sit while I plate everything. Get yourselves something to drink."

Wilson opened the fridge. He handed Carl a can of Lone Star.

Carl pulled off the tab. "A mighty nice last supper if that's what this is."

"A last supper for some." Wilson pulled off the tab. "Not for us."

* * *

Tippit sat alone on his couch. He'd grown to find comfort in the dark, in solitude and among the night sounds of his house. Marie's snoring serenaded him from the bedroom. The kids had been in bed for hours.

His half-drunk bottle of Lone Star had grown warm in his hand. The last cinder of his Chesterfield had burned out an hour ago in its ashtray. He hadn't thought about lighting another.

Regret was a cruel enemy who often visited at night. When the distractions of the day retreated, the mind had time to turn on itself. To turn on him.

His relationship with Molly Farley and her boys loomed large. How he'd asked Wilson to help him steal another man's family. How he'd allowed himself to dream of making Molly and the boys his own.

Things were supposed to be different. Tippit and Molly's respective divorces would've been finalized by now. They should've been spending tonight and the rest of their new lives together.

Instead, Tippit was spending another lonely Thursday night on his couch. Hal Farley was rotting in the ground. Molly and the kids had disappeared to parts unknown.

Tippit was stuck in a nightmare. Marie barely tolerated him, but gladly accepted every cent he forked over each week. His children looked at him with pity no child so young should have for their father. He wondered if Harry Denton hadn't done Farley a favor.

Tippit's job was at a standstill. Any juice he'd had with Ruby was gone. Eastbrook now despised him for taking Wilson's side.

And Wilson? A thoroughbred stumbling toward a finish line that might not be there. The steadiest man he'd ever known was close to cracking. He'd gotten ambitious. He'd played all the right odds. He'd lost anyway. The cold water of corruption had gotten into his bones. It froze him. He couldn't live with having killed a man.

That was Dallas. Once you thought you had the town figured out, it knocked you out. And by the time you woke up, everything was different.

At least Carl had kept his perspective. That was something.

Tippit wasn't a smart man, but he tried peering into the future. Everything would be different after tomorrow. Events were rushing in that direction. If something happened to Kennedy, there'd be a reckoning. Local politicians would avenge their national embarrassment. They'd turn the city upside down. They'd hold someone responsible.

There was a possible upside. Walker and his friends would become Public Enemy Number One. Minutemen and Birchers and Klan would get the fight they'd been itching for. They wouldn't just lie down. People would die.

Dallas PD would tear itself apart. Wilson would be in his glory. He'd have been proven right. *That could be good for me.*

But if nothing happened, Wilson would lose his mind. He'd be proven wrong. Wilson couldn't take that. Trust was hard to regain, especially from yourself. *That could be bad for me. I'll be a man without a country.*

Tippit wished he could help Wilson. He wished he could help himself. But momentum dictated the future. All he could do was ride the wave. See where he landed. To follow Wilson's orders. To help Oswald if it came to that.

By this time tomorrow night, all would be known, but nothing would be settled.

He swirled the warm beer at the bottom of the bottle. There was just enough left for one last swig. He set it on the coffee table. *Best leave it for the morning. I'll need a good belt to brace myself for the day ahead.*

Chapter Thirty-Three

Friday, November 22, 1963

Morning

Wilson waited outside the Blaine house in Irving. Their light green Rambler station wagon was in the driveway.

Wilson tapped the horn twice, then rolled past the house. The same signal Carl used to call Oswald at his rooming house over on Beckley.

Wilson parked out of view of the house. He checked his mirrors and waited.

Lee came out wearing a gray flannel jacket. He had a paper sack tucked under his arm. It was bigger than his normal lunch bag.

Oswald checked both ends of the street before ducking into the back seat.

Wilson eyed Oswald's parcel. "What's that?"

"Cheese sandwich." Oswald opened the bag and showed him. "Ruth didn't have a smaller bag."

Wilson looked inside. A wrapped sandwich, a container of milk, and an apple. "Why aren't you home?"

Oswald refolded the bag. He placed it on his lap. "I got a line on an apartment downtown that's close to my job. Since I'm making regular money now, I wanted to ask Marina if she'd take a look at it with me this weekend." A shrug. "She doesn't want to move. She likes it here with Ruth.

Likes having help with the kids." Another shrug. "I didn't like that. I told her we're through." He held up his left hand. No ring. "I really mean it this time."

The Oswalds split up once a month. They always got back together. "You picked a hell of a day to become domestic."

"Why?"

Wilson glared at him. "Don't be stupid."

Oswald grinned. "You're still worried about Kennedy. I heard the police chief on the radio. He's deputizing citizens and everything."

Part of that plan had been Wilson's idea. He wanted people to overreact. To disrupt anything unusual. To screw up any plans. "The chief understands what we're up against. So should you."

Oswald waved him off. "I told Carl not to sweat it. Nothing's going to happen. Walker isn't even in town. Ferrie said he'll be in Louisiana at some meetings."

Wilson didn't like Oswald's cavalier attitude. "That doesn't mean anything."

Oswald said, "They're running scared after Chicago and Miami fell apart. Ferrie said Bannister doesn't think they can get Kennedy now. The feds are on to them. Some hotheads might try something, but not Walker's bunch."

"Michael Blaine tell you that?"

A third shrug.

Wilson said, "You're not worried they'll figure out you told us about Chicago and Miami?"

"Nah." Oswald squinted out the window. "They'd never think a fella like me could ruin their plans. Want to know why you didn't find any shooters in Miami? They were told to clear out long before the feds started looking for them. They've got someone helping them on the inside."

Wilson hadn't considered that. "Bannister?"

"Who knows? Who cares? That's your problem now. Come December, I'll be in Mexico helping Mr. de Mohrenschildt with the second invasion of Cuba. I'll have all the money I need to get Marina and the kids into a place of our own. I'll get her back. You'll see."

The kid was getting cocky at the worst time. "Let's get through today before you become the Napoleon of the Caribbean. If something happens today…"

"It won't."

Wilson snatched Oswald's flannel jacket. He pulled him off the back seat. "Stop arguing and listen. If something happens today, go to a public place. A library or a department store. Blend in and call my answering service. Give them your location, and one of us will come get you. Got it?"

Oswald pulled back. "I got it. Let go of me."

Wilson released him.

Oswald straightened himself out. "You're getting all fired up over nothing. If they were fixing to do something today, I'd know."

Wilson spared him the news about Ruby meeting with strangers all week. His fear that Walker and his men being out of town was a convenient alibi. "You don't know everything. None of us do."

Oswald grabbed up his lunch bag. "Yeah. That's what you keep telling me." He began opening the back door.

Wilson said, "Where are you going? I'm driving you to work."

Oswald got out. "No thanks. I've got more friends besides you." He slammed the door. He walked down the street to his co-worker's house. "I'll talk to you later."

Wilson watched him walk away. He thought about catching up to him. About cutting him off. Of putting him in the car and driving him to work like he'd planned.

But he'd already put the kid in enough danger. The Blaines could be watching. It was best to let him get on with his routine. Oswald thrived on routine.

Wilson put the Galaxie in drive. He drove past Lee as he walked to his friend's car.

I sure hope you know what you're doing.

* * *

261

Kay was still asleep as Denton gave himself a final look in the mirror. He straightened his gear belt. Made sure his .38 was easy to draw. He pulled his cap forward to shield his eyes. The badge pinned to his shirt shone. Not just from the buffing he'd given it that morning. It gleamed with pride and purpose.

He looked like any other cop who'd be working the motorcade route. No one would notice him. Not even his fellow officers. All eyes would be on the president's limousine. On Jack and Jackie. On American royalty about to be deposed.

He checked his watch. It was almost eight o'clock. He stood by the phone on the bedside table. He waited for it to ring. Kay had danced the late shift at The Carousel Club. She was a sound sleeper. Let her sleep through history. She wouldn't appreciate it anyway.

The phone rang. Denton answered on the first ring.

A southern accent said, "Stockade fence near the underpass. Noon sharp. See the yellow curb lines as reference."

The line went dead.

Denton hung up. He had his orders. His date with destiny was set.

He went to the closet. His Enfield was already in its canvas gun case. A man walking the plaza with a rifle would cause a scene. A uniformed officer carrying a gun case would not.

Denton went into the hall. He locked the door behind him. He didn't want to wake Kay. He didn't want her remembering when he'd left or what he'd been wearing. The less she knew, the better for him.

All would be known soon enough.

* * *

Tippit pulled into the Rebel Diner at 11:30 AM sharp. The note in his locker had told him to be on time. It didn't say who he was meeting, but he had an idea.

It was dead time at the Rebel Diner. It was after breakfast and before lunch. The lot was empty except for a lone Dallas PD patrol car. Reserve

Officer Kenny Croy was behind the wheel. Croy meant Eastbrook.

Tippit backed his unit into the space beside it. He spoke out the window to Croy. "You leave that note in my locker?"

"I did," Croy said, "but the man who wrote it is inside."

"Hubba, hubba, hubba. Sounds official."

Croy played it cool. "I wouldn't know. I just drive him. But you'd best get in there. He's been waiting on you."

Tippit went into the diner. A bell above the door tinkled as he opened it. A waitress had propped herself in the far corner of the counter. She'd nodded off on her feet.

Captain Bill Eastbrook had the back booth. It was away from the windows. He sipped a cup of coffee. He pulled apart a buttered roll. A copy of the Dallas Morning News was folded at his elbow.

Tippit didn't wait for an invitation. He slid in across from him. "Morning, captain."

Eastbrook rubbed crumbs off his fingers. "You want coffee?" He tried to get the waitress's attention.

"Let her sleep." Tippit fished out his Chesterfields from his shirt pocket. "Condemned men still get a final smoke?"

Eastbrook grinned. "This ain't that kind of a conversation." He wiped his hands on a paper napkin. "Busy day, ain't it?"

"Not for me." Tippit tapped out a cigarette and lit it. "I thought you'd be with the motorcade."

"I've got more important things to do." Eastbrook balled up the napkin. He dropped it on the half-eaten roll. "Like talking to you." He unfolded the newspaper. He turned it so Tippit could read it. "You see this?"

It looked like an advertisement. Tippit read the headline of the black bordered page. "'Welcome Mr. Kennedy to Dallas.' It's better than those 'Wanted for Treason' posters I've seen all over town. Maybe the president's got a few admirers in town after all."

"It's not a fan letter." Eastbrook refolded the paper and set it aside. "It's a declaration of war. A resounding indictment of Kennedy's failures and all his Commie claptrap. General Walker had one of his men write it and run it. What do you think about that?"

"I don't think about it at all," Tippit said. "I've never been much for politics."

"But you're a patriot. Served your country. Got medals."

"Served my city, too. Got wounded twice. Got medals here, too. Look at where it got me."

Eastbrook ignored the sarcasm. "Would you say you're a good white man, JD?"

"I'm white. I'm a man." He let smoke trail from the side of his mouth. "As for good? That depends on who you ask."

"What if I asked Dan Wilson?"

"He can speak for himself."

Eastbrook's grin widened. "That's the trouble with you. No one's got a fix on the kind of man you really are. Your fellow officers either don't know you or don't have an opinion of you. It's held you back some as far as advancement is concerned, but I'm not telling you something you don't already know."

Tippit flicked his ash into the ashtray. "I asked you for help once. Put my hand out. All I got was the back of yours."

Eastbrook's eyebrows rose. "You think Ruby took you on because he likes you?"

Tippit shrugged. "I was useful. He knew I was close to Wilson. He wanted to know what he knew."

"And you told him."

"What I could," Tippit said. "Dan's not much of a talker. I might've told you, too, if you'd asked. But you never took my calls."

"You've got me there." Eastbrook scratched under his chin. "I guess I'd always figured you for a Wilson man." He wavered. "Maybe I was wrong about that."

Tippit played along. "I'm my own man. Always have been. Dan and I are ex-partners who became friends." Wilson would want him to throw Eastbrook a bone. "But I'm always open to having more. You want to be my friend, cap?"

Eastbrook moved his coffee closer. He turned the mug slowly. "That business outside Wilson's place this summer still stings. I don't like how you backed his play against me and Harry."

"Harry's a moron," Tippit said. "He went for his gun, and I stopped him. That boy's gonna land you in some mighty hot water one day if you let him."

"He has his uses," Eastbrook said. "As could you."

He's as slick as I've heard. "I'm listening."

Eastbrook sipped his coffee. "A man never can tell when opportunity's going to walk right up and present itself. Comes in all sorts of ways, like offering to buy him coffee."

Tippit took a drag. "Sounds like today might be my lucky day."

Eastbrook looked down at his coffee. "Kennedy's visit has this whole town jumpy. Folks do all sorts of crazy things when a president comes in. They cheer and scream their heads off. They forget themselves. Get caught up in the moment."

Eastbrook looked up from his coffee. He looked at Tippit. "But we're a different sort, you and me. We're professionals. We keep our heads while others lose theirs. You catch my meaning, son?"

"Went right over my head."

"Then I'll lob the next one nice and slow. Because after today, there'll be two types of people in Dallas. Friends of mine and enemies. It's time for you to decide which one you want to be."

Tippit smoked. "And if I want to be your friend?"

"Ruby tells me you're a man who knows how to find things. I might need you to find something for me today." He opened his hands. "And the best part? You don't even have to go out of your way to look for it. Should the need arise, that is."

Tippit squinted through the cigarette smoke. "You gonna tell me what I'm supposed to look for, or do I have to guess?"

Eastbrook set his coffee mug aside. He pushed a napkin toward Tippit. He kept his hand on it as he stood. "I already went to the trouble of writing it down for you. When the time comes, you'll know what to do. Find it and we'll be friends." He clapped Tippit on the shoulder. "You've seen how I reward my boys. You don't want to see what I do to my enemies."

Eastbrook strode out. The bell at the door tinkled as he went outside.

Tippit waited until Croy and Eastbrook drove away. He didn't want them to see his reaction.

He turned the napkin over. He saw what Eastbrook wanted him to do. An address: 1026 North Beckley Avenue.

He knew the area. It was a three-minute drive from Molly's old place on Patton. A four-minute drive from Jack Ruby's apartment.

1026 North Beckley Avenue was where Lee Oswald rented a room.

Eastbrook wanted more than a favor. He wanted Oswald.

Reality hit hard. Eastbrook knew about Oswald.

Tippit ran to the payphone in the men's room. He sank a coin in the slot. He called Wilson's office. He checked his watch as the phone rang. It was almost noon. Kennedy was due at the Trade Mart at any time now. Wilson would already be in the plaza.

Tippit hung up. He retrieved his coin. He called Wilson's answering service. The operator answered. Tippit talked over her. "Tell Wilson JD called. Tell him Eastbrook knows everything. Have him reach me through dispatch as soon as possible. It's an emergency."

Tippit hung up. He ran out of the diner. He jumped into his patrol car. He started up the engine. He got on the radio as he peeled out of the lot. "Dispatch, Car Seventy-Eight back in service."

He didn't hit the lights. He weaved through cars on his way south. There were too many players on the loose. He needed to know where they were.

Eastbrook had planned his approach well. Tippit was running out of time. So was Oswald.

Chapter Thirty-Four

November 22, 1963

Dealey Plaza—Noon

K ennedy was late. He should've been in the plaza by now.

Wilson prowled Houston and Main on foot. Between the County Records Building and the County Criminal Court Building. In front of the DalTex building and Oswald's schoolbook warehouse. The slowest part of the route.

The Kennedy campaign had bussed in supporters from neighboring counties. Main Street was packed. Dallas PD reported twenty people deep in some places. No visible protesters or trouble.

Wilson didn't trust it. Kennedy hatred in Dallas was radiant. Someone should be making noise somewhere.

Some of the crowd had begun spilling into the plaza. Every parking lot was reported full. Spectators mingled with office workers on their lunch break. People staked out spots along the curb. They wanted to see Jack and Jackie. To see American royalty with their own two eyes.

Mayor Cabell called the concrete colonnades of Dealey Plaza 'the front door of Dallas'. Today, it was the end of Kennedy's motorcade route. Where the convoy of limousines and reporters would take Stemmons Freeway to the luncheon at the Trade Mart.

Wilson heard an announcement on his field radio. "All units be advised.

Motorcade departing Love Field. President is en route to downtown."

The dispatcher repeated the message. Wilson watched cops—in uniform and in plain clothes –milling around the thickening crowd. They were getting into position. They'd keep civilians from knotting up at key areas on the sidewalk. They'd watch for troublemakers.

A crumpled 'Welcome Mr. Kennedy to Dallas' handbill was in the gutter. 'Wanted for Treason' handbills, too. Tumbleweeds of hate.

Wilson had worked countless parades and marches and protests. He'd seen crowds take on lives of their own. Someone tripping or brushing a spectator could turn a crowd violent in a flash.

Wilson checked his watch. It was high noon. He'd driven the motorcade route several times since the route was confirmed. He'd driven it with department brass. With members of the Secret Service advance team. Love Field was ten miles away. A fifteen-minute drive.

But the motorcade was meant for attention, not speed. Kennedy's men wanted pictures of their boss waving to throngs of adoring supporters. The American flags. The pro-Kennedy signs. Dissidents be damned.

Wilson spotted Carl smoking a cigarette against a concrete colonnade across the street. The president would turn off Main onto Houston. Then from Houston onto Elm. The pace would be achingly slow. *Just like Chicago.*

Wilson had extra men assigned to the plaza. He wanted maximum protection while the president was most vulnerable.

Wilson jogged across the street. He joined Carl at the colonnade. They didn't face each other. Wilson made like he was checking the plaza. "What do you think?"

Carl smoked. "It's worse than I thought." He looked up Main Street. "Tall buildings. All those folks on rooftops and hanging out of windows. Thousands of civilians within spitting distance of the president. Nothing holding them back except cops who hate his guts."

Carl turned his head and spat. "It'll be a miracle if he makes it this far."

"They're running late," Wilson said. "They just left Love Field."

"Around thirty minutes, I'd say."

Wilson figured that was about right. He looked up at the book warehouse on the corner of Houston and Elm. Oswald's building. "Any sign of our friend?"

"Nope. You tell him we'd be here?"

"No, but I told him the plan. He'll call us to come get him if he needs us." He hoped he wouldn't have to.

Carl crushed his cigarette against the concrete colonnade. "You want me here for the duration?"

"Yeah. Give a holler if you see anything. I'll be across the street."

Carl put his hands in his pockets. "Wanna put ten bucks on him making it here without any bother?"

Wilson started walking toward the book warehouse. He hoped for a glimpse of Oswald inside. "No, I wouldn't."

* * *

The parking lot between the railroad tracks and the fence was a sea of Detroit steel. Cars and trucks parked bumper to bumper. Everyone wanted to see the show.

Harry Denton intended on giving them one.

He'd parked next to the exit. It would be easier to get away after.

Denton took his gun case from the back seat. He squeezed between the cars toward his assigned place at the picket fence.

The jammed lot was a mixed blessing. He wouldn't be easily spotted. But it would be tough to get back to his car afterwards. Being in uniform would help him blend in.

Denton got to the fence. He looked over. A young man with thick glasses milled around the slope. He had a camera. Denton told him to clear out. The man didn't like it, but saw his police cap and obeyed.

Denton looked through the trees. The overpass to his right was a problem. Railroad men had begun to gather. They ate their lunch. They had a bird's-eye view of the president. Someone should've cleared them off there. At least the trees and the fence line concealed his position.

He checked his watch. A few minutes after noon. Probably twenty minutes until Kennedy got there. *Plenty of time.*

Denton pulled the Enfield from the case. He brought the stock to his shoulder. He worked the scope. He peered through the lens.

He saw Dan Wilson standing between two concrete pillars across the plaza. He was squinting as he looked over the sunlit plaza.

Denton placed the crosshairs on Wilson's chest. Smugness wafted off him like heat. He admired the bastard. He looked like he belonged in the movies.

Denton had resented Wilson long before the Farley killing. His swaggering superiority had always irked him. He had a famous daddy. A college degree. A couple of medals from Korea. He acted entitled. Above it all. Like nothing could ever touch him.

Denton let his finger hover around the trigger. He enjoyed the power he held over Wilson. The son of a bitch had mocked him for months. One squeeze would put him in his place.

But Wilson wasn't Denton's mission. Kennedy was. *Kennedy is my destiny.*

Denton took the crosshairs off Wilson. He saw the two yellow marks on the curb on Elm. Just as the caller had said. When the car reached that spot, Denton would do his duty.

He rested the Enfield against the fence. He checked his watch again. Ten past noon. His moment was almost here.

He heard horns blaring from the roadway. He peered over the fence. A green Ford pickup truck had stopped on Elm. Traffic backed up. The words 'Air Conditioning' had been stenciled in black letters on the side. The letters looked fresh. The truck looked ancient.

A passenger got out. He moved to the back. He wore a thin gray jacket, plaid shirt, and woolen cap with a tassel on it. An odd outfit for a warm afternoon.

Denton watched the man lift a satchel from the flatbed. He watched him trudge up the hill.

As he got closer, Denton saw it wasn't a satchel. It was a gun case similar to his. He was about to tell the man to stop. The shoulder strap snagged on the grass. The man paused to yank it clear.

Denton recognized him. Larry Crawford from The Carousel Club.

Denton grabbed Crawford when he came around to his side of the fence. "What are you doing here?"

Crawford shrugged. "Jack told me to bring this, so I brought it. What's it to you?"

Denton threw him against the fence. "Clear out of here before I break your jaw."

A man called out to them from behind. "Knock it off. You'll draw attention."

Denton pegged the man at about six feet tall. He wore a dark suit and sported a dark fedora. He had a lantern jaw and a flat nose. Both had been broken more than once.

Denton forgot about Crawford. He felt destiny slipping through his hands. "Who the hell are you?"

The man laughed. "Secret Service." He patted his breast pocket. "Says so on the badge I got this morning. Don't worry your pretty little head about me, Opie. I'm not cutting in. There's still plenty of room on the dancefloor."

The man looked at Crawford's gun case. "Give it over."

Denton watched Crawford give it to him. The stranger set it on the hood of a car. He opened it. He took out a scoped bolt-action rifle. Denton thought it was a Mauser, but the dimensions were off.

The man tossed the empty case to Crawford. "Take that and stand over there. Watch the road. Tell us if anyone starts poking around."

The stranger took an ammo magazine from his pocket. He slapped it into the rifle. He worked the bolt. He winked at Denton. "Listen to that action. Music to my ears. Can't beat craftsmanship from the old country. They sure know how to make 'em over there. Know what I mean?"

Denton sagged. He recognized the accent. He was from Chicago. Just like Jack Ruby.

Denton's legs went numb. He propped himself up against a car. "This is my spot."

"It still is," the stranger said. "You'll do your thing and I'll do mine. Guess someone figured two guns are better than one."

271

The man brought his rifle to his shoulder. He sighted the scope. "There they are. Right on the curb like they're supposed to be. When's the mark getting here?"

The mark? Is that all this is to him? Another hit? This wasn't some bookie who'd missed a payment. This was history.

The stranger glanced at Denton. "Snap out of it, Opie. When's he getting here?"

"I don't know. I don't have a radio. Soon, I think. He's already late."

The stranger went back to adjusting his scope. "That'll give you enough time to powder your face. Your mascara's running." The man chuckled. "And here I was, thinking all you Texans were supposed to be tough guys."

Denton wondered how much this man knew. About the target. About him. *Will he get rid of me after I kill Kennedy?*

The stranger lowered his rifle. He placed it on the hood of a parked car. "We're all set. Waiting's the hard part. Smoke 'em if you got 'em."

The man pulled a cigarette from his pack and lit it. He began pacing.

Denton looked up at the overpass. A railroad man looked in their direction. He brought up his hand to shield his eyes.

Denton half-hoped they got caught. He asked the stranger, "Who sent you?"

The man snatched Denton's face. His stubby fingers locked Denton's jaw open. The lit cigarette dangled close to Denton's eye.

"Quit pouting like some goddamned schoolgirl. This is a job. You're getting paid, and so am I. It'll be over in a few minutes. Be a man, shut your mouth, and do the job." He felt a pistol jammed hard against his belly. "One more sound out of you, I'll do this thing on my own."

The man pushed him away. He tucked his gun in his pants. He resumed pacing. "You goddamned zealots ruin everything. I swear to Christ."

Denton didn't argue. He'd let his Enfield do the talking. *Let this hood take his shot. I'll put one in Kennedy's eye.*

Chapter Thirty-Five

Friday, November 22, 1963

12:25 PM

The crowd on Houston and Main grew thick. Word of the president's approach had spread. The motorcade was close.

Wilson saw Chief Curry's lead car out front on Main. A pair of motorcycle cops cruised behind.

The president's limousine was several car lengths back. Nothing was between them.

Blood roared in Wilson's ears. The sounds of the cheering crowd and the radio chatter died away.

Kennedy's limo should've been in the middle of the procession, not the front.

Secret Service agents should've been on the running boards. They weren't.

Two motorcycles rode in front. Two were slightly behind it. Several more clustered further back. They were supposed to flank the limo, not follow it.

The plastic bubble should've been on the car. It wasn't.

The president was exposed to the slow right turn onto Houston.

Wilson had an unobstructed view. Kennedy smiled as he waved to the adoring crowd. A woman in a pink suit and white gloves waved from his left. *Christ, that's Jackie.* They're so close. Too close.

Wilson broke into a jog. He matched the limo's speed as it turned onto

Houston. He searched the crowd. He looked for sudden movements. Something raised. Any movement forward.

Civilians aimed cameras. They screamed as history rolled by. The plaza blurred. Wilson's world shrank to several feet of concrete and asphalt.

The limo crawled left onto Elm.

Wilson pushed through the dense crowd. He tracked the limo. It went down the slight hill toward the highway. It passed the shadows of tall buildings. It coasted into sunshine.

The limo took the center lane down Elm. Two motorcycle cops in front. Two hung back.

Wilson kept pushing through the crowd. He looked across the street.

That's when he spotted him. Standing in front of Oswald's building.

A short man. Gray buzzcut. Thick black glasses.

Walker's ally Joseph Milteer.

He'd always been scowling in Carl's photographs. But he was smiling now.

Wilson broke through the crowd. He ran toward Milteer.

One of the motorcycles backfired.

* * *

Denton watched the motorcycle cops turn onto Elm. He saw Curry's lead car speed toward the freeway.

He heard the crowd cheer. He kept his scope on the two yellow marks on the curb. He waited for the limo to enter the kill zone.

A shot rang out from his left. *Hold.*

A puff of dirt rose up from the lawn across the lane. No one reacted.

A civilian down front raised an open umbrella.

The front of the president's limo passed the first yellow mark on the curb. Hood flags fluttered.

The blurry image of the president's head in his scope. The limo slowed.

Denton fired. His bullet pierced the windshield. Kennedy clutched his throat.

The stranger fired.

Denton worked the bolt. He cleared the spent round. The chrome around the limo's windshield was dented.

The stranger cursed. He ejected the spent round.

Kennedy was still clutching his throat. His right shoulder flinched forward. Another shot grazed him.

Denton took aim.

Another shot from elsewhere. Governor Connally slumped to the left.

Kennedy's head filled Denton's scope. His head rocked forward.

Denton fired. So did the stranger.

Kennedy's head exploded. A pink cloud. Kennedy rocked back and to the left.

A piece of skull flew. It hit the trunk. Jackie lunged for it. A Secret Service agent caught up to the limo. He tackled her back into the car.

People on the grass hit the deck. Cops and civilians scrambled. Some run up the hill. They were coming their way.

The stranger tossed his rifle to Crawford. He pulled out his credentials.

The stranger told Denton, "Pick up the brass, then beat it. I'll keep them off you until then."

Denton focused. He started looking for shells.

People got closer. Women screamed. The stranger held up his Secret Service credentials. He told people to clear the area. He told them they'd get shot if they didn't.

Denton found his two shells. He pocketed them. He felt around for the stranger's two. He couldn't find them. They'd probably rolled under a car.

More people shouted. Their shouts grew louder. Denton heard more people rushing the hill. More screams echoed from the plaza.

"Leave it," the stranger shouted. "Get out of here. We're about to have a lot of company."

Denton grabbed his gun case. He squeezed between cars. He looked up at the overpass. Railroad men were running toward him.

Civilians flooded the area. The stranger yelled for them to stay back. The stranger held up his credentials. He waved his gun around.

Denton ran to his car. He dumped the Enfield and his case in the backseat. Eastbrook's Galaxie pulled in. Croy was driving.

Eastbrook got out. His gun drawn.

Denton froze. *I'm a dead man.*

Eastbrook shouted, "You get everything?"

Denton blinked. "I missed two shells."

Eastbrook beckoned Crawford. He ordered Croy out of the car. "Take mine. Wait for me at the safe house."

Eastbrook moved into the lot. "We'll find the brass later."

Denton grabbed his Enfield and gun case. He got behind the wheel. Crawford climbed in.

Denton floored it and peeled out.

He'd just made history, but didn't have time to appreciate it.

* * *

The motorcycle backfire had made the crowd jump. The crowd recoiled.

Wilson stumbled. His field radio skidded into the street.

Wilson picked up his radio. He stood up.

A shot cracked through the plaza.

Several shots echoed.

Wilson dropped his radio. He pulled his Magnum.

Spectators screamed. Spectators ran. They scattered. They ducked low and flooded into the street.

Wilson waded into the herd of humanity. He tried to hold his ground. He kept his pistol high. He struggled to see Kennedy's limo between the heads of panicked civilians. The car was gone. The last of the motorcade raced to catch up.

Wilson dropped a shoulder. He knocked people aside. He tried to cross Houston. He had to get into the plaza. He had to get to Oswald.

People lay flat on the lawn across Elm. He couldn't tell if they'd been hit.

The crowd fled in mass. They ran blind. They held their hands over their heads.

They carried him backward. He fought to keep his footing. He pushed against them. He shouted he was a cop. They didn't care. They kept coming anyway.

He got across Houston. A crowd of uniforms piled into the book warehouse. Oswald's building. A police motorcycle was dumped at the curb.

Wilson tried to get into the warehouse. The entrance was packed with blue.

He heard another round of screams. He saw people running up the embankment by the underpass. People pointed and shouted in that direction.

Wilson saw Carl across Elm. His badge was out, on his belt. He was tending to a woman.

Wilson called out to him. Wilson pointed at the warehouse. "Get in there and find Lee."

Wilson ran. He saw the breadth of the sweeping plaza as it sloped downhill. People on the lawn helped others get to their feet. Some remained flat in the short grass. Parents had thrown themselves on top of their children. *Korea all over again.*

He dodged civilians. He followed the crowd up the steps to the stockade fence atop the hill.

A crowd had formed. It blocked the narrow space into the parking area.

Wilson kept his Magnum high. He grabbed men with his left. He shoved them aside. He pushed through until he broke through.

Eastbrook was by one of the cars. An overcoat over his right hand. A pistol concealed beneath it.

The pistol was aimed at Wilson's belly.

Wilson aimed his Magnum at Eastbrook.

They locked eyes.

Both wondered if the other would shoot.

Both wondered if he should.

Eastbrook lowered his pistol first. "Keep that crowd back. This is a crime scene."

Wilson holstered his Magnum. "What happened?"

"Someone shot at the president," Eastbrook said. "We're checking for brass now."

Eastbrook stalked away. Wilson spotted two uniforms walking through the back of the lot. Their guns drawn.

He beckoned them over. "Keep this area sealed off. Captain Eastbrook's orders."

Wilson left the cops behind. He had to get Oswald. He jogged down the side road behind the plaza. Elm was too crowded. He'd reach the book warehouse from the back.

He looked through the slats in the curved concrete colonnade overlooking Elm. People on the lawn had begun to get to their feet. Women held their heads and wiped away tears. Men did likewise.

He rounded the curve of the structure. Horns blared from Elm. He watched a man in a thin gray jacket run toward a Rambler station wagon. He climbed in. The Rambler drove away toward the freeway.

Wilson recognized the Rambler. From Austin's Barbecue. From that morning in Fort Worth. It was Michael Blaine's Rambler.

Wilson kept running toward the back of the book warehouse. Workers huddled on the loading dock. They traded stories. They acted out what they'd seen.

Wilson climbed onto the loading dock. Men moved to stop him. They saw the badge on his belt and stopped.

Wilson asked one of the women, "Anyone leave this way?"

She shook her head. So did her co-workers.

"Where's Lee Oswald?"

"Dunno," one of the men said. "Haven't seen him."

One of the women said, "He was in the lunchroom upstairs when I got back."

Wilson went inside. Officers crammed the first floor.

He saw Carl outside the front door. He waved Wilson over. Two uniforms blocked his way.

Wilson pushed between them. He asked Carl, "Did you find him?"

Carl lifted his lanyard. "These bastards won't let me in."

Wilson brought him inside. He found the staircase. They took the stairs two at a time up. He saw a lunchroom through a door with a narrow window. Tables and chairs beyond.

Wilson shouldered the door open. He looked around. No Oswald.

He told Carl, "Go upstairs. See if you can find him. I'll look downstairs."

They split up. Carl took the staircase. Wilson hit the hall. It led to an open space. A secretary was at one of the desks.

Her eyes were already swollen from crying. She looked startled when she saw Wilson.

Wilson opened his coat, revealing his badge. "Have you seen Lee?"

"Lee?" she repeated. "You just missed him. He passed through here a minute ago."

Wilson ran in the direction she'd pointed. He rounded a long counter into another hall. Cops were running up the stairs. Wilson went down the same staircase.

The staircase led to the front entrance.

Wilson punched the wall. He couldn't have missed Oswald by much.

Wilson hoped the kid was doing what he'd told him to do.

Wilson heard shouting from upstairs. Another uniform came down. Wilson stopped him. "What's going on?"

"They found something on the roof. They want us to keep people out of the building."

Wilson had to get word to Tippit. He had to know Oswald was coming his way.

Wilson prowled the first floor. He looked for an office. He found a reporter using one. A secretary at the desk. Her hand shook as she tried to smoke.

Wilson pushed the reporter aside. He ended the call and dialed his answering service.

"Hey," the reporter protested. "I was using that."

Wilson ignored him. He waited for the operator to answer.

It was ten rings before she did. *They must be getting calls from everyone.*

"Any messages from a 'JD' or a 'Tippit'?"

"There's one. He called an hour ago. Says 'Lee's in trouble'. Says here that he'll call back when he can."

Wilson wished he'd had time to check earlier. "Give him a message if he calls back."

"I can't promise that, sir. We're overwhelmed at the moment. They're saying the president's been shot."

Wilson gripped the receiver. He prayed she was wrong. Wild rumors always flew after something like this. "Write it down anyway. Tell him Lee's heading his way, and so am I. Tell him I'll call when I can."

Wilson hung up. The secretary's eyes overflowed with tears.

"Did I hear her right? Are they saying the president is dead?"

Wilson ran outside. He ran back to where he'd parked his car at headquarters. Carl would have to fend for himself.

They all would until he got to Oak Cliff.

Chapter Thirty-Six

Tippit had cuffed the shoplifter in Hodges Supermarket. He brought her outside. The kid was dope skinny. She looked like she hadn't eaten in a month. She smelled like she hadn't bathed for even longer.

He was about to put her in the back seat. The call came over the radio.

"Attention, all units. Attention, all units. All available officers are to report to Houston and Elm immediately to help secure the area. Stage One in progress."

The dispatcher repeated the message. Stage One meant dangerous public unrest. A riot or similar violent event.

Damn. Wilson had been right.

The shoplifter wriggled in her cuffs. "What's going on? What does that mean?"

Tippit didn't have time for a petit larceny beef. He found his keys. He unlocked the girl's cuffs and turned her loose. "It means today's your lucky day, honey. Go home and stay away from that store. You go in there again and I'll lock you up for a month."

Tippit got behind the wheel. He started the engine. Eastbrook's orders be damned. Wilson's too. Something big had just happened downtown. Wilson needed him. So did Oswald.

He snagged the mic and called in. "Car Seventy-Eight. I copy. I'm en route to Houston and Elm from Bonnie View Road. Over."

He hit the lights and siren. He was about to put it into drive.

The dispatcher responded. "Seventy-Eight, that's negative on Houston and Elm. Hold your position in Oak Cliff as ordered. I repeat. Hold your position in Oak Cliff as ordered. Resume regular patrol. Do you copy?"

Tippit punched the steering wheel. The action was downtown, not way out here. Eastbrook wanted Oswald bad. As bad as Wilson wanted Oswald safe.

Tippit killed the lights and siren. He grabbed the mic again. "Car Seventy-Eight. I copy. Remaining in Oak Cliff."

Tippit popped the mic back on the hook. He watched traffic on Fordham Road. He was stuck in Oak Cliff. Oswald was his priority.

Tippit threw it in gear. His tires kicked up dust. He sped out of the parking lot. He went north on Bonnie View Road. He hoped he wasn't already too late. He hoped Oswald was a good marine who obeyed orders.

Tippit parked at The Gloco Gas Station on North Zang Boulevard. He watched traffic coming off the Houston Street Viaduct from downtown Dallas. Oswald always took the bus home. His bus should be coming any time now.

The gas station was on a slight rise. He could look into passing vehicles and buses. The station owner liked having cops on his property.

If he saw Lee's bus, he'd follow it. He'd grab Lee before he got home. He'd get him to the church until Wilson or Carl got there.

Tippit waited. No buses. The radio traffic made him anxious. Dispatch had lost radio discipline. The crosstalk was confusing. Reports contradicted.

Cops reported three shots. Cops reported five shots. The shooter was cornered in the book warehouse. The shooter was cornered between Elm and the railroad tracks. Three men were seen fleeing in separate cars. Five civilians had been shot. No civilians had been shot. A Secret Service man had been killed. No Secret Service men had been shot.

Only one consistent fact: President Kennedy was at Parkland, and it didn't look good.

The dispatcher cut in, saying, "All units. All units. In relation to earlier downtown incident. Be on the lookout for a white male, early thirties, five-feet-ten-inches tall and weighing one-hundred-and-sixty-five pounds."

The dispatcher repeated the description. It was worthless. It described Oswald and half the men in Dallas.

Tippit fought the urge to get to the payphone. He wanted to call Wilson's service. To see if Wilson had gotten the message about Oswald. To see if Wilson had left a message for Tippit.

He couldn't risk being out of the car. He couldn't risk missing Oswald's bus. The kid was too important. He was their only link to everything now.

Tippit watched civilians gather in front of the diner across the street. The owner consoled his wife. Her shoulders shook. She doubled over in tears. A waitress plopped on the steps and sobbed.

Word was spreading fast. Scenes just like this were playing out all over the city. Maybe all over the world. President Kennedy had been shot.

The owner held his wife. He spotted Tippit's patrol car parked across the street. He gave a half-hearted wave. Tippit waved back. There wasn't much either of them could do.

Tippit watched traffic crawl off the viaduct. No bus in sight. He checked his watch. Ten-to-one.

He backtracked in his mind. The distress call from dispatch had come over the radio after twelve-thirty. Kennedy had been shot before then. If Oswald had caught a bus right after the shooting, he might've made it out of downtown. He might already be home.

Tippit threw it in drive. He headed south on Zang. He drove to Oswald's rooming house on North Beckley.

He slowed. He paid attention to the cars parked on the street. He looked for anyone watching the place. The street was clear. No one was even walking a dog.

Tippit slowed in front of Oswald's rooming house. He used Carl's signal. Two quick beeps on the horn.

Tippit rolled past the house. He pulled in at the curb. Curtains stirred in the front room. No Oswald.

Tippit's mind revved. Supposition spawned supposition. *Maybe his bus is stuck in traffic? What if he caught an earlier bus and someone grabbed him?*

They'd take him somewhere close. Somewhere safe. Jack Ruby's apartment was over on Ewing. A good place to start.

He was about to pull away from the curb. A black car slowed past him on the right. It sped up. He couldn't make out the passenger. But he'd seen Harry Denton behind the wheel.

Tippit hit the gas. His prowler lurched. The engine revved. It slowly kicked into gear.

Denton's car was more than a block away. Tippit watched the black Galaxie bob and weave between cars. He watched it change lanes without horn or brakes. It slid into the northbound lane to pass cars. It ducked back in, barely missing oncoming traffic.

Tires screeched. Trucks slid. Sedans stopped short to avoid the maniac behind the wheel.

Tippit kept up.

Denton ran red lights. It blew stop signs at will.

Horns blared. Tires squealed. Drivers cursed.

Tippit closed in. Less than half a block between them now.

Denton cut left. He narrowly missed a delivery truck. The driver slammed on the brakes. The truck fishtailed over the double yellow line. It blocked the northbound lane.

Drivers cut their wheels to avoid the truck. The sound of horns and the stench of burnt rubber filled the air.

Tippit floored it. He shot between the blocked northbound lane and cars stopped in the southbound lane. He skidded through a narrow gap between the truck and car fenders.

He cleared the knot in time to see Denton turn onto West Tenth Street.

Tippit threaded his way through traffic. He smelled burned oil. His fancy driving must've knocked something loose. He hoped the engine didn't seize before he caught Denton and whoever was with him.

Tippit turned onto West Tenth. Denton's black car was half a block ahead. It had slowed way down.

Tippit gunned it. He rode the space between lanes on the quiet residential street. He caught up fast. He cut off Denton before he reached Bishop Avenue.

He put his hand on his gun as he got out of the car. He kept it holstered. He didn't want to give Denton an excuse.

He peered into the car. The passenger seat was empty. The driver wasn't Denton. The driver was wide-eyed and terrified. He gripped the wheel and didn't move a muscle.

Tippit realized this was a Chevy. Denton was driving a Ford Galaxie.

Tippit cursed. He'd lost Denton. He could be anywhere by now.

Tippit ran back to his car. He had to find a phone. He had to tell Wilson that Oswald might be lost.

He turned onto Bishop and drove south to Jefferson. He parked at the corner and jogged across the street. The owner of Top Ten Records liked cops. He let him use the phone.

The tiny record was crowded. People clamored in doorways and windows. They hoped to hear news about the president's condition. The reporter was relaying unverified reports about Kennedy's condition. People gasped. Men choked back tears.

Tippit excused himself through the crowd. They saw his uniform and gave way.

He picked up the receiver at the counter. He dialed Wilson's answering service. After ten rings, the operator didn't pick up. *Shit.*

He hung up and ran back to his prowler. Every operator in the city must be swamped with calls. It wasn't every day the president got shot.

He got behind the wheel. He slowed things down. He thought back to where he'd lost Denton.

What if that turn on West Tenth hadn't been random? He'd thought Denton would keep going west. Going toward Jefferson would've been the smart thing to do. They could've easily disappeared into traffic.

But what if Denton went north? To a part of town no one would think to look for him.

No one except Tippit.

He knew Ruby kept a string of apartments on Patton. He'd helped Molly get a mortgage on her house there. Denton and Kay used to live next door. A couple of Ruby's dancers lived there now.

Tippit put it in gear. He did a U-turn on Bishop. He took a right on Sunset and floored it.

Denton wasn't running. He was going home.

* * *

"What the hell was that?" Crawford shrieked. "You almost got us killed back there!"

Denton ignored Crawford's cowardice. He'd just saved a nation. He'd just outrun Tippit. It had been quite a day so far. And it wasn't over yet.

"Quit screeching, you damned ninny. We lost him, didn't we?"

Crawford looked out the back window. "Just because he ain't there anymore don't mean we got away. We're dead if he recognized us."

"No," Denton corrected him. "*He's* dead if he saw us. That's a promise."

He drove along Ninth. He checked his mirrors. Running into Tippit in front of Oswald's house was bad luck. Bad timing. But it had been worth the risk. Grabbing Oswald would've pleased Eastbrook to no end.

Denton hadn't expected Tippit to be there.

Denton had been against Eastbrook approaching Tippit. He was too close to Wilson. Maybe it was the captain's way of keeping Tippit busy. Of keeping him away from Wilson. To keep Wilson off balance. Denton couldn't begin to understand all of Eastbrook's machinations.

That was the genius of Eastbrook's plans. No one knew everything except him. He was probably planting evidence to implicate Oswald right now.

Denton checked his rearview again. He had to get Crawford to Ruby's crash pad on Tenth and Patton. They had the rifles that had hit Kennedy. They had to keep a low profile until Eastbrook told them what to do.

Crawford's nervous blinking kicked into high gear. "Why are you driving so damned slow? We've got to get inside."

Denton wished he'd shut up. "Because people remember fast cars. We don't want to be remembered now."

Denton hoped Ruby's dump had a television. He hoped the cheap bastard had paid the electricity bill. He'd like to watch what he'd wrought in peace.

286

He wanted to bask in the glow of his glory alone. He'd just liberated a nation.

Denton rolled on Ninth. He pulled into the alley between two houses off Patton. Between 404 and 410 East Tenth Street. He put it in park but kept the engine running. He pulled his .38 and told Crawford, "Check the house. Make sure it's open. I don't want to get stuck here."

Crawford pulled his own .38. He got out. He tried the side door of 404. It was locked. He checked 410.

It was open. Crawford went inside.

Denton kept an eye on his rearview. He watched Tenth. He willed Crawford to hurry. The car was a coffin. He wanted inside fast. Eastbrook was supposed to send someone to get the car later. Every car in the department would need to be accounted for during the investigation.

In his rearview, a patrol car passed on Ninth. *Shit.* Tippit had remembered.

Denton forgot about Tippit and Molly. That Molly had lived down the street. That Tippit knew Ruby let girls stay in the area. *Double shit.*

Denton almost hit the horn. He had to get Crawford back in the car. If he left the mongoloid there, Jack would be furious. So would Eastbrook. He rolled down the window. He called into the house, "We've got to go. Tippit found us."

Denton heard a crash before Crawford came outside. The stupid bastard was still holding his .38.

"Put that away and get in. We've gotta move."

He saw Crawford freeze up. Denton followed his gaze.

Tippit's car slowly rolled by the house. It stopped. It blocked the driveway. Denton threw it in reverse. "Get in, goddamn it."

"No." Crawford slid the pistol into his jacket pocket. "He'll just find us again."

Denton called out to Crawford. But Crawford walked out toward Tippit's car. Both hands in his jacket pockets.

Tippit remained in the car. "Fancy meeting you here. You out for a stroll?"

Crawford kept his hands in his pockets. "Just cleaning up the place for Jack. He's got a new girl coming in next week. All the way from Atlanta, I hear."

Denton knew Tippit wouldn't buy it. "You hear what happened?"

Crawford kept his hands in his jacket pockets. "Can't say that I have." He bent and looked inside Tippit's car. "I've been here all morning cleaning up. What happened?"

Tippit tilted his head forward. He looked past Crawford.

He looked directly at Denton.

Denton gripped the pistol tight.

Tippit smiled. *Gotcha.*

"You just wait there a second." Tippit opened his door. He stepped outside.

Crawford pulled his .38. He shot Tippit three times in the chest.

Tippit dropped.

Denton grabbed the wheel. *NO!*

Crawford ran around the front of Tippit's car. He shot him a fourth time. He bolted west toward Jefferson.

Denton hit the gas. His Galaxie backed down the alley onto Ninth. He turned west and took a left on Storey Street. He sped south.

He found Crawford crossing the street. He cut him off.

Crawford bounced off the hood. He'd ditched his jacket. His .38 was tucked in his belt.

Crawford scrambled into the back seat.

Denton took Jefferson and went east. Time for Plan B. Back to The Carousel Club.

The Galaxie veered. Denton reached back. He grabbed Crawford by the hair. He yanked him up to the front. "What's the matter with you? You didn't have to kill him! In broad fucking daylight!"

"He saw us," Crawford screamed as he tried to pry his hair free. "He saw this car. Saw you driving it. Saw me in it. He saw where we'd parked. He would've told Wilson. You think Jack or Bill would want that?"

Denton snatched the .38 from Crawford's belt. He tossed it in the back. He didn't want the crazy bastard shooting him, too.

"You know I'm right," Crawford said. "It's better this way now. Cleaner, too."

"You didn't make anything cleaner. You just made everything worse."

He told Crawford to give him the field radio Eastbrook had left in the car. It was different from the radio Dallas PD used. He'd told Denton to only use it in an emergency. This qualified.

He remembered radio protocol. "Alpha One, this is Alpha Two. Copy?"

Eastbrook's reply was immediate. "Channel Twelve."

The radio didn't have twelve channels. It was code for switching to channel two. Denton did it. "We have a situation on Tenth and Patton."

"We just got the call. We're close. Was it you?"

"It was Alpha Three. I caught up to him on Storey. I have him now. Heading to second location." The Tenth Street houses had been the first location. The Carousel Club was the second.

"Copy that," Eastbrook said. "All is in hand. Standby for more later. Over and out."

Denton dumped the handset on the seat. Eastbrook had plenty of work to do. He wouldn't be in touch for hours. In the meantime, Denton and Crawford would have to kill time at The Carousel Club. At least the TV worked.

Crawford rubbed his scalp. "See? I told you he wouldn't be mad."

Denton clipped him in the back of the head. "That's an open channel, shithead. Anyone could be listening. We won't know the damage you've done until later. You'd better pray he's not furious."

"I ain't worried," Crawford stuck his elbow out the window. "Ruby will keep him in line. Things are different now. Ruby won't let no one yell at me. Not after what I done today."

Denton laughed. Presidents and cops were expendable, but a toothless go-fer and a two-bit strip club owner were untouchable? Crawford might be the dumbest white man alive.

Eastbrook would tie up loose ends. Crawford and Ruby would be in a ditch with matching holes in their heads.

Eastbrook might consider Denton a loose end, too.

But Eastbrook had taught him a lot. He'd taken steps. If he went down, Eastbrook would come tumbling after him.

Denton drove the speed limit along Jackson. He regretted the Tippit thing. Not that he was dead. That cocky prick deserved a bullet. He only wished it had been him who'd pulled the trigger.

Tippit's death would cause trouble for Eastbrook. It would damage the greater good. Denton may have won the battle. It would be up to men like Walker to win the war.

Denton turned on the police radio. The dispatcher said, "…hospital. I repeat. President John F. Kennedy has just been pronounced dead at Parkland Memorial Hospital. All units are to remain in position until further instructions."

Denton smirked. "Tell me something I don't already know."

Chapter Thirty-Seven

The drive to Oak Cliff was a blur. Ninth and Patton was full of ghosts.

His patrol days. The Farley house. The dead drops for Zeke at the library. It all led him back to Oak Cliff.

His arrogance had gotten Hal Farley killed. He hoped his arrogance hadn't killed his friend. His only true friend.

The dispatcher said an officer was down at Tenth and Patton in Oak Cliff. Every available unit converged. Kennedy paled to a cop in trouble. They hated the Yankee bastard anyway.

Wilson turned onto Tenth off Patton. A cluster of patrol and unmarked cars blocked the street. A patrolman waved him through. Another patrolman signaled for him to park up on a field at Ninth and Patton. But it wasn't a field. It was the old Farley house.

The property was overgrown. The house looked withered and forgotten. The windows had been busted out and boarded up. Gray paint cracked. Rust stains streaked down from the clogged gutters.

Wilson parked. He walked back to Tenth and Patton. He dreaded what he would see there.

Tippit's Number Ten car was further up the street than he'd thought. Mid-block between Patton and Denver. It blocked a driveway. A loose ring of uniforms kept curious pedestrians and reporters back. A TV camera crew filmed everything.

Eastbrook was front and center. He hovered around the front of Tippit's car. He directed uniforms and detectives.

A uniform on crowd control recognized Wilson. He let him pass.

Wilson approached Tippit's patrol car. Tippit wasn't there.

Wilson's cop training kicked in. He read the scene. Streaks of thickening blood pooled on the asphalt. The blood pattern told the tale. Chest and head shots. At least one round had struck an artery. No one could lose that much blood and live.

No.

The ambulance boys must've known Tippit was dead. They'd rushed him to the hospital anyway.

Why not keep him here? Preserve the scene. Examine the body in situ.

But he knew why they'd taken him away. Just like he knew who they'd blame for his death. He knew who'd do the blaming.

Wilson sank to his knees. He knelt beside where his friend had fallen. Where he'd taken his last breath. *He died working for me.*

Wilson closed his eyes. He prayed. *This is my fault. My scheming caused this. My calculations and actions. My dream of a federal badge.*

He'd built his dirt pile. He'd sought leverage for a promotion. He hadn't expected it might bury a president and a friend.

Wilson squeezed his eyes shut. He begged Tippit to help him one last time. To show him what he had seen before he'd died. *Show me who did it, JD. Let me avenge you.*

Wilson sensed someone standing beside him. He didn't care. He pleaded with JD for help.

He began to shake. He summoned gods and angels and demons and anything that might help him see. Help him avenge his friend. *Let me see!*

But Tippit was silent. He didn't reveal a thing. And neither did anyone else from the great beyond.

Instead, he heard another voice. "Time to leave, Wilson. Captain's orders. Let's go."

Wilson lowered his head. He squeezed his eyes shut tighter. *Please JD. Show me!*

One of the other men said, "Leave him alone, Croy. Tippit was his partner for Christ's sake."

"You're in enough trouble for letting him through," Croy said. "The captain wants him gone, so he's gone."

Wilson was beyond imploring. Beyond desperation. He needed something. Not much, just a flash. A quick image. *Give me that much, JD. I'll do the rest. I promise.*

In his mind, Wilson saw JD standing beside the patrol car. His uniform clean. His hat straight. No blood. A Chesterfield dangled from his mouth while he played with his trusty Zippo.

That crooked smile he always got when he was about to tell you something good.

He cocked his head to the houses.

Hurry, JD! Show me now!

A hand gripped his right shoulder. "Last warning," Croy said. "Get up."

Wilson opened his eyes. Tippit was gone.

Croy had scared him away.

Wilson twisted Croy's right wrist as he stood. He wrapped his forearm around Croy's neck.

Croy screamed. Wilson wrenched his right arm backward and up. Cartilage popped.

Civilians looked away and cringed.

Eastbrook didn't look away. For the second time that day, each man regretted not killing the other.

Eastbrook's men closed in.

Wilson twisted Croy's arm. He kept Croy close. He kept looking at Eastbrook. "One more step and I break it."

The captain held up a hand. His men stayed put. Those who weren't Eastbrook men knew the score. They held their ground and kept the civilians back.

Wilson saw Eastbrook had something in his hand. A wallet.

Eastbrook said, "Let him go. What are you trying to prove?"

Wilson booted Croy in the ass. He fell into one of the uniforms.

Wilson kept his fists at his sides. "I've got all the proof I need."

Eastbrook raised the wallet. "What a coincidence? Looks like I've got some proof right here. Found it under a car. In the pocket of a jacket, the suspect tossed as he was running away. Guess he was trying to change his appearance some."

Wilson watched Eastbrook open the wallet. He made like he read it. He turned to a man standing next to him. "Bob, you're an FBI man. You ever work with my friend Dan Wilson over there?"

"Can't say as I have," Bob said. "Don't think I'd want to, either."

Eastbrook showed him the wallet. "You boys know all the crooks in town. You ever heard of a Lee Harvey Oswald?"

Wilson lunged.

Four officers grabbed him. They pushed him back toward his car.

One of them stepped up to Wilson, "That's enough, Dan. Get out of here before you get hurt."

The uniforms released him. Wilson staggered back to his car. He felt the civilians watching him as Eastbrook said, "What about this name? Alec Hiddell?"

"No," the FBI man said. "Can't say as I have."

But Wilson knew the name. An alias from Oswald's file. He didn't know how Eastbrook had come by it. Oswald wouldn't have fled. He wouldn't have left his jacket behind. He wouldn't have shot Tippit. He knew Tippit would protect him.

Civilians watched Wilson stagger away. No one helped. He didn't blame them. He had the air of death about him.

The deaths of Farley and Schneider and Kennedy and Tippit.

He walked back to his car. Behind him, cops shouted. Sirens wailed. Tires screeched as cops sped away. They had a name. They had someone to hunt.

Wilson made it back to his car. He collapsed against the hood.

He heard the dispatcher on the radio.

"Attention, all units. Suspect in officer shooting has been seen entering the Texas Theater on Jefferson. Do not respond. I repeat, do not respond. Officers already responding."

Wilson hung his head. The Texas Theater. A nice public place. A place where a man could blend in. Where he could hide out for a while if he had to.

Oswald had followed orders after all. *I let him down, too.*

A roundish woman in glasses and a housecoat stopped on the sidewalk. She listened to the dispatcher repeat the message.

"They get him?" she asked. "They get the man who killed that officer?"

Wilson raised his head. "No."

Wilson climbed behind the wheel. He started up the engine. They'd bring Oswald to headquarters. He had to be there when they brought him in.

They hadn't caught the man who'd killed Tippit. But Wilson would.

A Note from the Author

This novel was inspired by actual events. It highlights some details and people who were only uncovered in depth by researchers in the past few years.

While I have been inspired by a tremendous amount of factual, historical material, my DALLAS '63 novels are works of fiction. Many true events and people have been changed for dramatic effect.

It is my hope that what you read here will inspire you to research this subject and arrive at your own conclusions.

About the Author

Terrence McCauley is an award-winning, bestselling author of thrillers, crime fiction and westerns. A resident of Dutchess County, NY, he is currently working on his next novel. Please visit his website at www.terren cemccauley.com

AUTHOR WEBSITE:
   https://www.terrencemccauley.com/

SOCIAL MEDIA HANDLES:
   Facebook: https://www.facebook.com/terrence.mccauley
   Twitter/X: https://x.com/tmccauley_nyc
   Instagram: https://www.instagram.com/terrencepmccauley/
   Threads: @terrencepmccauley

Also by Terrence McCauley

The University Series (Four Books):
Sympathy For the Devil
A Murder of Crows
A Conspiracy of Ravens
The Moscow Protocol

The Charlie Doherty Mysteries (Five Books):
Doherty's War/Against The Ropes
The Wandering Man
Prohibition
Slow Burn
The Fairfax Incident

The Aaron Mackey/Billy Sunday Westerns (Four Books):
Where The Bullets Fly
Dark Territory
Get Out of Town
The Dark Sunrise

The Jeremiah Halstead Westerns (Four Books):
Blood On the Trail
Disturbing the Peace
The Revengers
Born to Hang

The Ralph Compton Series (Three Books):
The Kelly Trail
Ride the Hammer Down
Stagecoach to Hell

Several unattributed ghostwritten novels

www.ingramcontent.com/pod-product-compliance
Lightning Source LLC
Chambersburg PA
CBHW020353110726
47899CB00006B/1703